Brain Warp

BRAIN WARP

A Medical Thriller

Gil Snider

iUniverse Star

New York Lincoln Shanghai

Brain Warp
A Medical Thriller

Copyright © 2003, 2007 by Gilbert M. Snider

iUniverse Star
an iUniverse, Inc. imprint

iUniverse books may be ordered through booksellers or by contacting:

iUniverse
2021 Pine Lake Road, Suite 100
Lincoln, NE 68512
www.iuniverse.com
1-800-Authors (1-800-288-4677)

Because of the dynamic nature of the Internet, any Web addresses or links contained in this book may have changed since publication and may no longer be valid.

ISBN: 978-1-58348-472-2 (pbk)
ISBN: 978-0-595-88074-4 (cloth)
ISBN: 978-0-595-87993-9 (ebk)

Printed in the United States of America

This is a work of fiction. All of the characters, names, incidents, organizations, and dialogue in this novel are either the products of the author's imagination or are used fictitiously.

To the loving memory of my father, Abraham Snider, whose warmth and humor I hope to pass on to my sons—

And to all other fathers. For better or for worse, you are more important than you will ever know.

The choice is yours.

Acknowledgments

I wish to thank Dr. Charles Ashby and my late father-in-law, Dr. Michael C. Kozonis, for their advice on how to run a code; Dr. Monica Deitell, for her psychiatric insights; Dr. Ihor Kulczycky, for our entertaining conversations and his firsthand insights into the politics and history of Eastern Europe and Ukraine, the country of my father's birth; Peter Stillman, Susan Crawford, and John Talbot, for their valued literary criticism and editorial advice; Mike Altman at iUniverse for his guidance; and Dr. Lindsay Gibson, for her assistance.

Special thanks to my family and relatives in Boston and Michigan for their support.

And most of all, thanks to my wife, Judy, and my sons, Jonathan and Nicholas, who provided me with the inspiration and support to fulfill a lifelong dream.

PROLOGUE

▼

It was dark in the niche between the packing crates. Dark and almost intolerably cramped, but safe.

Alex Rinsky knew this was the best place in the factory to hole up for an ambush. From his vantage point, he had a perfect view of the entire factory floor below, and he controlled stairway and elevator access to the walkway he was on. All he had to do was sit and wait.

Whoever had called him with a transparent pretense for this meeting must have thought he was an idiot, but you don't survive in his business by being gullible. He went nowhere and did nothing without obsessively factoring in his safety. Stoolies were a despised class, anathema in any society, and his benefactors as well as his victims distrusted him. Since his last tip had resulted in the imprisonment of two high-ranking Mafia *pakhans* and the death of a bodyguard, he took it as a given that he was being hunted.

His caller's big mistake was in letting him decide on the meeting place. Ever since he was a boy, he and his friends had used this factory as their clubhouse and hiding place. He knew all of its secret places, vantage points, and escape routes as if it were his own home. He was well prepared for company and, when they showed up, all it would take was a few bursts of semiautomatic fire and he could close up shop, take his stash, and retire to the anonymity of a small town in the mountains. He just wished someone would show his face so he could get the damn thing over with.

Rinsky was stretching his legs when he heard a dull thud behind him, where the crates were pushed together and didn't allow a gun sight. His breath quickened as he gripped his semiautomatic and listened intently, his ears searching the silence. It hadn't been a metallic sound, like a weapon or a grenade; it sounded as if someone had lost his balance, and stepped down too hard in order to catch himself. Rinsky's leg muscles tensed. The crates behind him were just over waist high, and he could jump up, twist around, and fire off a blind burst before his stalker knew what had hit him. Even if he missed with his first shots, there was no cover in that corner of the walkway. His assailant would be a sitting duck.

Another thud, this one a little closer to his hideout. Rinsky jumped up, screaming invectives, and sprayed the walkway behind him with a wide arc of semiautomatic fire. As the last echoes of gunfire died in the cavernous factory, he was surprised to find that there had been nothing behind him but a blank wall, now newly perforated with a straight line of waist-high bullet holes. What looked like two knotted socks weighted down with sand were lying on the otherwise barren floor.

His consternation distracted him momentarily, just long enough to miss the flash of movement from the rafters above him and to his right, and Rinsky was caught off guard as a knife pierced his right wrist and paralyzed his hand.

He screamed, dropped the rifle and struggled to withdraw the knife, a good three inches of the blade protruding from the inside of his wrist, but a leather-clad figure descended, jumped on top of him, and knocked him to the floor. With a quick, practiced motion, a gloved hand grabbed the knife handle and buried the tip of the blade deep into the floor. Pinned facedown by his flaccid right wrist like a bug in a display, Rinsky was helpless as a heavily booted foot crushed his other wrist to the floor.

"Alex, Alex," a voice above him clucked condescendingly, "why do you make me do this? You know the Corporation can't tolerate ratting." His attacker grabbed Rinsky's hair and pulled his face up from the floor. "We would lose respect, and that's bad for business."

"I ... I ... didn't mean to ..." Rinsky whimpered.

"Shut up," Leather Man's voice boomed in the empty factory, and he pulled harder on Rinsky's hair, arching his neck backward. "What you meant to do is irrelevant to me. It's what you did that matters. My superiors have already tried you. My job is to carry out the sentence. Good-bye, Alex."

Leather Man pulled another knife out of a holder strapped to his ankle, sliced across Rinsky's throat in a single, smooth motion, and then jammed the knife through Rinsky's left hand into the floorboards.

Propping his back comfortably on a crate as he witnessed Rinsky's diminishing death throes, Leather Man lit a cigar and puffed slowly, watching the smoke rise in lazy curls and eddies up into the unlit recesses of the factory's ceiling, occasionally blowing smoke rings in Rinsky's direction. After a few minutes, the thrashing stopped. Leather Man leaned over and slowly ground his cigar out on Rinsky's cheek, pulled the knives out of the floor, and carefully wiped them clean on Rinsky's clothes before walking down the stairs and out the back door of the factory.

CHAPTER 1

▼

Damn, late already.

Dr. Peter Branstead glanced at his watch, furiously pedaling his bike in and out of eastbound traffic on West Fourteenth Street, avoiding the plumes of smoky exhaust from the buses and trucks that crept slowly toward Union Square. Tall and slender, Peter maintained his athletic build by an almost religious adherence to a daily cycling regimen he had developed during his medical school days, having sworn not to succumb to the propensity of physicians to expand their waistlines as they expanded their practice.

As the neurology service's attending physician at St. Mark's Hospital for the month of June, Peter thought that he had allotted adequate time to cover his clinical responsibilities as well as the tutelage of the house staff and medical students. But the first day of the month on a new service was always overloaded. He had to make rounds on a score of new patients that neither he nor the residents knew at all, learning about them through thumbnail sketches provided by the medical students, the only medical caregivers who didn't switch service on the first day of the month. And Peter had not been prepared for the complexity of his new service.

AIDS was St. Mark's specialty. Over a hundred years ago, it had positioned itself geographically between the wealthy West Village and the earthier East Village. By the 1970s, these two neighborhoods experienced a tremendous influx of gays and drug addicts respectively, two high-risk groups for HIV infection. Each AIDS patient on Peter's service suffered from some bizarre form of meningitis that had previously been rarely seen by medical science until the human immunodeficiency virus stormed its way out of central Africa to single-handedly rewrite the world's infectious disease textbooks.

His service also had a few cocaine addicts whose last high had been cut short by massive intracerebral hemorrhages that had left them so disabled that they couldn't handle a fork, let alone a syringe.

Two patients were the survivors of cardiac arrests, doomed to live out the rest of their lives in the twilight of a vegetative state, neither dead nor fully alive. Their families maintained perpetual bedside vigils, hoping that someday their loved one would open his eyes and, as if awakening from a long nap, take a nice, long stretch and ask what was for dinner.

Next were the less critically ill patients, alert enough to greet their physicians and families, but still incapacitated by their disease. Some were recovering from strokes and brain tumors, some learning again to walk, to care for themselves, and even to speak. There were young women with multiple sclerosis, victims of a guerrilla war fought within their own nervous systems, with undetectable terrorists hidden deep within their body's immunologic jungles waiting silently to choose the time and place for their next attack.

A blast from a car horn and a screech of brakes interrupted Peter's thoughts.

"Hey, moron. If you're gonna ride your fuckin' bike in the city, why doncha watch where the hell you're goin'?"

Nothing like a vehicular encounter with a Manhattan cab driver to bring you back to reality.

Peter wheeled his bicycle into the lobby of his office on University Place and chained it to a pipe under the stairwell. Once he walked through the door, there would be no time for thoughtful reflection, and today he had to be out of the office on time. He and Megan Hutchins, the girlfriend with whom he had been sharing a loft in SoHo for the last year and a half, were having the Falconers over for dinner tonight, and Megan would never forgive him if he was late.

After only two years, Peter's practice was thriving. His casual style and tendency to run late did not sit well with the aristocrats from the Fifth Avenue high-rises and West Village townhouses, to whom time was money, and sharing a waiting room with plebeians was distasteful. But his style was appreciated by the everyday people who constituted the bulk of his practice: elderly grandmothers from Little Italy, aspiring gay actors from Christopher Street, African Americans from Stuyvesant Village, and young Puerto Rican mothers from the East Village.

Alone with his patients in the consultation room, Peter treated each one as if he or she was the only patient that day, always inquiring about the family, particularly of the European and Asian immigrants, to whom family ties remained of critical importance. He would frequently jot notes in the margins: "son, Tony, enrolled at Cornell," "mother admitted last week, heart failure," "son-in-law picked up—DUI." These notes frequently gave him insights as to why Mr. Rinatelli might be asking to change his seizure medicine to a cheaper one, for example, what stress might have provoked Latecia Hobson to have another attack of multiple sclerosis, or why Maria Rodriguez's migraines were getting worse.

The first patient, Cyrus Roberts, was a stocky, powerfully built, middle-aged black man with two months of gradually progressive slurred speech and right hand clumsiness, noted when he was using his computer at work. His primary physician had ordered a CT scan of the brain and found evidence of some minor strokes, which he told the patient were due to hypertension and heavy cigarette smoking. But because of continued progression, he sent the patient on to Peter for a second opinion.

Roberts's conversation was sprinkled with small verbal slips; he reported his job as a "survivor" rather than a "supervisor," and he turned "keyboard" into "kerber" and finally "cardboard" before he got the word out correctly. Peter also noted Roberts's clumsiness with a pen and the droop of his right shoulder as he walked to the exam room.

Peter threw the CT scan up on the view box and focused on the left temporal lobe. It was there, all right—a faint blurring of the cerebral cortex that suggested swelling in the area. Unaware of the details of Roberts's neurological problem, the radiologist had glossed over the subtle, but crucial, abnormality. Peter walked over to the exam room and tapped on the door.

"All set in there?"

"Come on in, Doc. Hey, next time you order gowns, get a man's size, okay?" Cyrus Roberts's ample frame had caused wide splits in the paper gown.

The examination proceeded quickly. Peter tapped a reflex in Roberts's arm, with little response.

"I've found your problem, Mr. Roberts. I think you're dead," Peter quipped, and drew a smile from the patient.

"Come on, Doc, I got too many unpaid burls to be dead right now." Another verbal slip.

Peter glanced up at Roberts, whose smile was just slightly crooked.

He had seen and heard enough. He'd bet his bicycle there was a tumor in the left temporal lobe, and with the rapid onset and history of cigarette smoking, metastatic lung cancer was the most likely candidate.

"What's going on, Doc?" Roberts asked as they sat in the consultation room.

"For one thing, I don't think your problem is a stroke."

"Then level with me, Doc. What's wrong?" Roberts stared him straight in the eyes.

Peter knew this man didn't accept bullshit from his staff, and he wouldn't accept bullshit from his doctor, either.

"Is your wife with you?"

"Nope, she's at work. Lay it on me, Doc. I can handle it."

"I think the greatest likelihood is that you have a brain tumor right here," and Peter pointed to the blurred area in the CT scan. "I may be wrong, but that's my best guess."

Cyrus Roberts sank back into his chair, rubbing his hand over his short, curly hair, and sighed deeply. "I knew it wasn't a stroke. Black men don't get to be my age and not have a whole pile of friends and relatives with strokes, and I've never seen one of them get slowly worse over a monk. Damn, I mean a month. How bad is it? How long have I got?"

"Good questions, but I can't answer them right now. I'd like you to get a chest X-ray and an MRI and have you come back in a week with your wife. We'll set up some extra time to talk."

"MRI? No thanks, Doc. Not with my claustrophobia. No way you're going to get me into that coffin."

Peter's thoughts shot back to his residency when his chairman, Dr. Lawrence Wheatley, had insisted that each resident undergo an MRI scan "for the experience."

Peter had never thought of himself as being claustrophobic, but he hadn't been prepared for the feeling of being slowly drawn, head first, into a narrow tunnel about the length, width, and height of the inside of a casket.

"You okay, Dr. Branstead?"

"Sure," Peter had lied, the beads of perspiration gathering on his forehead and chest. His breath had seemed to fill the chamber, displacing the oxygen.

"There'll be a noise starting now." A pulsating machinery sound began, reverberating through the chamber. His heartbeat quickened, almost synchronizing with the pulsations of the machine, and his breath came faster and deeper.

"Ten minutes more, Dr. Branstead."

Eyes closed, Peter tried to envision sweeping Rocky Mountain vistas or sunsets over broad Pacific beaches, but the incessant throbbing machinery noise blocked his imagery. He opened his eyes to see the cylinder wall just inches from his face, so close that he couldn't even focus on it. He spread his arms outward and his hands immediately touched the sides of the cylinder almost as soon as he moved them. He felt a smothering closeness.

"Five minutes more, Dr. Branstead. Doing okay?"

"Yeah, sure," he lied again, licking his dry lips with an even drier tongue. He wiped his sweating palms on his trousers, and tried to swallow the little saliva left in his mouth past a lump in his throat the size of a lemon.

"Try not to move, Dr. Branstead, or we'll have to shoot this run over. Just a few minutes to go."

Peter swallowed harder. He began to feel the cylinder closing in on him, imagining the full weight of the two-ton machine pressing down on his chest. His heart pounded, and the lump in his throat seemed to grow to the size of an orange.

"Okay, test is over, Dr. Branstead. We'll pull you out now. You did real well."

The inside of the cylinder moved past him, and then the blessed ceiling fluorescents shone in his eyes as his head emerged from the machine. He stumbled off the table with the technician's help, his heart rate and breathing finally slowing down. Dr. Wheatley was standing by the MRI console.

"Care to try it again with contrast enhancement, Dr. Branstead?"

"No, thanks. I'll pass for now."

"Very well. Just remember that your patients may not have that choice. Have a good day, Dr. Branstead."

"Honest, Doc, ever since I was a kid I've been afraid of close spaces."

Peter's thoughts snapped back to the present. "Don't worry, Mr. Roberts, you'll be well sedated. You won't feel like doing much for the rest of the day, but I promise you'll make it through the MRI just fine."

He shook Roberts's hand and led him to the receptionist.

Whereas the thrill of crisis attracted some physicians to their specialty, Peter enjoyed neurology for being reflective, not reflexive. Neurology had its own emergencies, but Peter enjoyed the intellectuality of neurology grand rounds and the opportunity to really *think* about the patient's problem.

"There's a Dr. Gregory Johnson at St. Mark's Hospital on the phone," his nurse interrupted. "Shall I tell him you'll speak with him, Dr. Branstead?"

"Be right there."

Greg Johnson was the senior resident on ward service this month, which delighted Peter. Greg was a superb clinician and a hard worker, and Peter felt very comfortable having him in control of the ward service so that he could oversee, rather than micromanage.

"What's up, Greg?"

"We got a few new hits through the ER today, Dr. Branstead, and I'd like to staff one with you this evening rather than wait until morning rounds."

"Any problems?"

Greg's voice sounded distinctly uneasy. "I don't know. Just a feeling I have about one of the patients, and I can't explain it over the phone. Can I meet you at the nursing station up on 6B, around five o'clock?"

"I'll be there."

By the time Peter got to the neurology ward, the medical students had already gone home to study, and the junior resident and intern had been excused to finish their ward work. The usual change-of-shift chaos had subsided, but the nursing station was still busy as the evening shift rounded on their patients and frantically paged house staff before they left the hospital for last-minute problems discovered at shift change.

It was right in the midst of this frenetic thronging of nursing staff that Peter greeted Greg Johnson. Greg was African American, and at six feet was almost as tall as Peter. It was both his height and his demeanor that commanded respect from nursing staff. He was self-assured without being imperious, and he always managed to successfully balance his remarkable intelligence and clinical acumen with a disarmingly friendly smile and natural warmth. Peter had considered inviting Greg to join him in his practice, but Greg was bound for academia and had just accepted a neuroimmunology fellowship at the National Institute of Health. Peter hoped that, with Greg's outstanding interpersonal skills, he wouldn't shut himself up in a lab with plates of T cell cultures but would devote some time to patient care.

Retreating from the nursing station, Peter and Greg sat down at a table in the doctors' lounge and closed the door. Peter turned down the offer of a cup of coffee, but listened while Greg fixed his own at the coffee urn.

"Here's the story, Dr. Branstead. John Doe is a sixtyish derelict found wandering around the East Village, completely demented. Couldn't find his ass with both hands in broad daylight if his life depended on it. No ID, no known family, no available past history ... your standard Bowery drunk, maybe not quite as dirty and unshaven as we usually see. Physical exam and neurological exam were pretty unremarkable other than his confusion, which is pretty bad. Can't give us any history at all. Hallucinating, rambling speech, the works. All the metabolic stuff, and cultures are negative. CT scan from the ER is normal. EEG shows mild generalized slowing, nothing unexpected for a demented old man. Spinal tap was clear—zero cells, normal protein and glucose. So, we admit the guy, start him on IM thiamine and IV fluids. But all day, he keeps getting more and more confused."

"Greg, this is an alcoholic going into DTs. We see dozens of these guys a month. What's the big deal?"

Greg shrugged. "Sure, that's what I've been thinking. So we transfer John Doe to the ICU and load him up with lorazepam. His heart is racing away at a mile a minute, but all of his other vital signs are normal, kind of unusual for DTs. Well, one of the ICU nurses recognizes him from a previous admission. Turns out his name's James Wolmuth, so we pulled his records. He drank more than just a bit, but, aside from some minor orthopedic procedures, there was no other medical history of note and no record of ever having DTs."

"Greg, the first rule of medicine is that common disorders occur commonly. When you hear hoofbeats, you look for horses, not zebras. These guys *always* lie about their drinking. Sorry, Greg. It's hard for me to get real worked up about this."

"I know, I know, but here's the thing. Surrendra Patel was the chief ward resident last month, and, in that month, they had three cases just like Wolmuth. And all three went into prolonged convulsions complicated by cardiac arrest and died in spite of full resuscitative measures."

Peter's interest was piqued. Alcohol withdrawal seizures were generally brief, and death was unusual. Three deaths in a row were downright spooky.

"I notice you haven't told me anything about the drug screen."

Greg smiled. "You're one step ahead of me. Something just came back this morning."

"Don't tell me. Cocaine?"

"Wrong. It's positive for an SSRI, one of the new generation of antidepressants. Have you ever seen anything like this from antidepressants?"

"They can cause confusion, seizures, and cardiac arrhythmias, but you'd have to take a whopping dose. Was it ID'd?"

"Not yet. It's a 'send out' and has to go to a lab in Indiana. But listen to this. The three guys who died last month all had positive urine screens for SSRIs and had blood sent out for a GC/mass spec. The lab in Indiana says they can't identify it on any sample. Apparently, it's not in use in the United States. But unless it's super potent, it's not very likely to be the cause of death. Levels were very low in all three men."

Peter's brow furrowed. Gas chromatography/mass spectrometry was the most sensitive drug analysis they had available. "That is odd. But let's keep that in the back of our minds for now. What's your differential diagnosis?"

"What about herpes encephalitis?"

"With a normal EEG, normal spinal fluid, and no fever, herpes encephalitis is pretty much out of the running. What about Creutzfeldt-Jakob disease?" This was a "mad cow" look-alike caused by newly described microorganisms called prions that caused rapidly progressive mental deterioration and seizures.

"No muscle twitches and a minimally abnormal EEG," Greg replied. "The textbooks say you can't diagnose C-J on that basis."

"Did they post the other three guys?"

"Yep. Pathology was negative for C-J. They did immunohistochemistry for prion protein on two of them, and nothing showed."

"Doesn't sound like there'd be much sense to biopsy Wolmuth," Peter said. "Anything cardiac?"

"Minimal atherosclerotic coronary artery disease. No evidence for MI, no pulmonary emboli. It seems that all three men just ... sort of ... died. No good reason."

"You can see sudden unexpected death in epileptics, especially if they're poorly controlled or not taking their medication. That's uncommon, though. And three in a row?"

"Exactly," Greg agreed. "Besides, there was no prior history of epilepsy. Frankly, nothing fits very well."

Peter drummed his fingers on the table when an insistent vibration from his pager interrupted his thoughts.

"It's the ICU."

"Damn, it's Wolmuth."

As they entered the ICU, James Wolmuth was in the midst of a seizure, and the room was already beginning to fill with medical personnel. Two nurses were bedside opening the crash cart, and the respiratory therapist was bagging the patient.

"What's the scoop?" Greg asked.

"Mr. Wolmuth here was getting pretty agitated," the head nurse reported. "We had him sedated and restrained, but the sedation obviously wasn't cutting it. A few minutes ago, he began hallucinating and struggling at his restraints, and out of the blue, he started convulsing. The odd thing was that just before the seizure, his pulse shot up to one-fifty, but it looked like supraventricular tachycardia, so no one got worried."

Peter took charge. "Draw up fifteen hundred milligrams of fosphenytoin and drip it in over ten minutes. Get anesthesia up here and have him intubated, call surgery for a central line, and slip a foley into his bladder. He's going to be bed bound for a while."

Another nurse broke in, "Dr. Branstead, his seizure is quieting down, but he's no longer in SVT. He's in ventricular tachycardia now."

"This is the exact scenario Surrendra told me about. Better call a code," Greg inserted.

This is getting serious, Peter thought. Supraventricular tachycardia was a basically harmless rapid heartbeat that wouldn't cause any danger unless it persisted for a very long time. However, ventricular tachycardia was different. It could quickly deteriorate into ventricular fibrillation, a deadly and frequently irreversible loss of the heart's ability to pump blood. It had to be stopped, and fast.

Within thirty seconds, physicians, nurses, and technicians swarmed James Wolmuth's bedside. Dr. Bruce Rathburn, the cardiology fellow, appeared at the bedside, panting from the exertion of pushing his ponderous bulk up five flights of stairs, two steps at a time, to get up to the ICU.

"Somebody want to fill me in on what's going on around here?" Rathburn gasped.

Greg looked up at Rathburn from his chest compressions. "Sixty-five-year-old white male, no significant known medical problems other than drinking. Admitted yesterday in a confusional state with a negative workup. No history of heart disease, but he developed supraventricular tachycardia, probably from his agitation, went into a generalized tonic-clonic seizure, then V tach before he could even get an anticonvulsant."

"Any pulse?"

"I've got one in the neck, but I can't get a femoral pulse," a nurse called out.

"Okay, we're in business. Epinephrine one milligram, IV push, and magnesium sulfate two grams IV. And get an amp of lidocaine ready."

"V tach at two hundred," the nurse called out. "Complexes are becoming irregular. Dr. Rathburn, the heart rhythm looks like ventricular fibrillation. BP zero. I've lost the carotid pulse."

"Shit. Hand me the paddles. Defibrillation set at two hundred joules. Everyone clear?"

He placed the defibrillator paddles to Wolmuth's chest and looked around quickly while everyone drew back from the bedside. For a few seconds, the only sound in the room was the frantic beeping of the cardiac monitor.

Wolmuth's body lurched as Rathburn depressed the button on the paddle and the shock hit the chest wall, triggering a simultaneous contraction of every muscle in his upper torso.

There was a momentary pause while the capacitors in the defibrillating unit discharged before a tracing was visible.

"Nothing, Dr. Rathburn. Still in V fib. I can't feel a pulse anywhere."

"Another milligram of epi and seventy-five milligrams of lidocaine. Crank up the juice to three hundred joules. Everyone clear the bed."

There was a bigger jump, this time shaking the entire bed.

Another brief pause. The EKG tracing was looking much worse.

"No change, Dr. Rathburn."

Although he was struggling to pull James Wolmuth back from the brink, Rathburn remained calm and unhurried. Mentally, he was not dealing with a flesh-and-blood human being. He was dealing with a heart—a mass of muscle fiber and nerve cells, of shifts in sodium, potassium, and calcium ion fluxes that hopefully would cause the muscle to contract and the heart to beat. To think in any other way at a time like this would have driven him crazy years ago.

"Okay, give one more milligram of epinephrine and turn up the defibrillator to three-sixty."

Peter tapped Greg on the shoulder and motioned for him to join him in the doctor's lounge. This was not behaving like a horse. This was a real zebra, and a deadly zebra at that. They faded back from the bedside, James Wolmuth no longer needing their care. Rathburn would fruitlessly keep the code going for another twenty minutes or so on his own.

"Greg, something is definitely wrong here."

"A self-styled angel of mercy on the staff? That's what I'm thinking."

"Maybe. Get the names of the other John Does from Patel, and I'll pull their charts and try to find a common denominator. For now, let's keep this under wraps."

CHAPTER 2

▼

Megan Hutchins strode down West Eleventh Street to get to her office. She snuck a peek at her reflection in a store window, frowned, and drew in her belly. She was attractive enough to have worked her way through college in Illinois by doing some local modeling, primarily for shoes and skirts because of her slender, well-toned legs, and she retained a model's self-consciousness about her appearance. She had managed to keep in shape in college with a regular jogging regimen, but after a few weeks in New York City, the wolf whistles, catcalls, and outright rudeness convinced her to give up jogging. She promptly gained ten pounds, no thanks to Peter's taste for high-calorie foods.

The two had met while Megan was finishing her master's in clinical psychology, during her clinical rotation on the psych wards at New York University Hospital where Peter was doing two months of psychiatry. Initially attracted by Peter's wavy, light brown hair and boyish good looks, after a few dates she found him refreshingly different. With her brilliant, hazel eyes and a face framed by long, brunette hair, men were quickly attracted to her. But the physicians she met were too full of themselves, and she took quickly to Peter's warmth and self-effacing sense of humor. Peter was emotionally honest and didn't play typical psychiatry mind games with her. Both she and Peter had lost parents at an early age, and there existed an unspoken understanding about certain things that helped establish an easy relationship. Although they had been going together for almost three years and had been living together for well over a year, discussion of marriage had been taboo by mutual consent.

Megan checked her watch just before she entered the office of West Village Counselors. Nine-o-four. Drat.

"Running a bit late, Miss Hutchins." Amanda Ivy peered at Megan from over her reading glasses as she sat at the receptionist's desk.

"I'm afraid so, Mrs. Ivy," Megan sighed as she walked to her office.

Mrs. Ivy was both business manager and receptionist for the practice, and she ran it just like her father, one of the first African American master sergeants in the newly integrated U.S. Army of the 1940s, had run his own household. Rigidly formal and obsessively neat and punctual, she kept the practice's disparate psychologists in line, the finances in order, and the schedules running on time.

As Megan reviewed the day's cases in her office, Mrs. Ivy buzzed on the intercom.

"Harriet Halleck called this morning. Mr. Halleck has been acting peculiarly over the past three or four weeks and appears to be getting worse. Your first slot was a cancellation, so I squeezed him in. They're here now. Shall I let them in?"

"Tell them I'll be out in a minute, Mrs. Ivy."

Megan pulled Frank Halleck's file from her drawer and sat down with it to refresh her memory before going into the waiting room. Frank was a remarkably intelligent fifty-two-year-old man with a round, friendly face and graying, wavy hair who worked as a laboratory assistant. Although at one time Megan had wondered if he might benefit from an antidepressant, Frank had declined psychiatric consultation, and Megan had signed off on his case several months ago after his mild depression lifted spontaneously. To hear of a sudden behavioral change was unanticipated.

Megan was not at all prepared for what she saw when she got to the waiting room. With a distinctly compulsive component to his personality, Frank Halleck had never shown up for an appointment without a jacket and tie. Today, Frank was in his shirtsleeves, and it was a food-stained shirt at that. Unshaven, disheveled, and gaunt, he looked like he had just gotten out of bed. But Megan was most disturbed by his eyes. Even in the worst depths of his depression, Frank's eyes had been clear and energetic. Now, he had a vacuous, distant stare, and he didn't acknowledge Megan's entrance into the room.

Harriet Halleck appeared marginally better off than her husband did. Harriet was a female carbon copy of Frank, round-faced, with short, thick legs and graying hair. The two had been married for almost thirty years and had seen two children grow up and marry. They had developed an exceedingly close, loving relationship, although Harriet had always been the more emotional of the two. But now she looked like she hadn't slept in weeks, her eyes underlaid by dark circles and age lines showing around them for the first time since Megan had known her. Nonetheless, Harriet managed a weary smile.

"Thank you for seeing Frank on such short notice. I wouldn't impose myself on you like this, but I'm at my wit's end. I just don't know what to do." Tears began to well up in her eyes.

"Harriet, please. You're not imposing."

"Come with us, Frankie." Harriet helped him up out of the chair, and he tottered into Megan's office like an old man.

In the privacy of Megan's office, Harriet broke down.

"The last month has been a nightmare," she sobbed. "That's when Frank began forgetting things. They were little things, so I really didn't think much of it until he began getting irritable and started yelling at me for no reason at all. I thought it was stress at work. But things have just gotten worse every day."

Megan listened while Harriet proceeded to detail a long list of behavioral changes: worsening confusion, nighttime wanderings, deteriorating personal hygiene, even turning on the garbage disposal at three in the morning and leaving it on because he thought it was the dishwasher. Through it all, Frank sat immobile and impassive.

"The final straw came last night. I had just come back from the grocery when Frank started screaming at me for sneaking out to have affairs with other men. We've been married for thirty years. Frank just kept going on and on about this, and there was nothing I could say that would change his mind."

"Frank, what do you have to say about all of this?" Megan asked.

"All of what?" Frank asked in return.

"Frank, your wife has just emptied her heart out about your behavior. Don't you have anything to say?"

"Who the hell are you and why should I be talking to you about anything? Harriet, let's go home. I'm tired."

Megan was stunned. Frank Halleck had changed dramatically in less than a month.

"Harriet, Frank has to see a doctor as soon as possible. My boyfriend's a neurologist. Sign a release for Dr. Peter Branstead, and I'll talk to him tonight. I'm sure he'll fit Frank in sometime in the next day or two."

As the Hallecks turned to leave, Megan attempted to lighten the mood. "By the way, Frank, tell that adorable cat of yours that Charlie sends his regards."

Harriet wheeled around and shook her head frantically. Frank also turned. He stared wide-eyed at Megan.

"Cat," he shouted angrily. Then, "cat, cat, Cat, Cat, CAT, CAT. That's it. CAT, CAT. That's what did it. CAT, CAT, CAT, CAT."

He kept chanting on and on, louder and louder, while Megan watched in stupefied silence, and Harriet rubbed Frank's arm and reassured him that everything was going to be all right. After several minutes Frank finally calmed down, his eyes resuming their original vacant stare.

"I didn't mention it because I didn't want to get him started, but he's been obsessing on you-know-what for a week, and this is how agitated he gets when I even mention the subject. I've actually had to give poor little Goldie away."

Harriet turned, dried her eyes with a handkerchief, and held her husband by the arm. "Come, Frankie. Let's go home."

It had been a long, exhausting day. Megan had had to struggle to concentrate on her remaining clients that afternoon. Her meeting with the Hallecks had devastated her emotionally in a way that she hadn't felt since she was five years old and her mother had died, her car hit head-on by a drunk driver. Megan often thought that her interest in psychology was a quest to find solace in helping others work through the pain of desertion that she still felt.

Never one for being loving and affectionate with his only child, Megan's father had enmeshed himself in his sales work, and he'd spent the better part of his time on the road. Megan had been left with an assortment of relatives until her father had remarried three years after his wife's death. His new wife was a closet alcoholic who had physically and verbally abused Megan and cheated on Megan's father throughout their marriage. Megan's younger stepbrother was her sole comfort in those years, and the two had frequently huddled together in bed while her stepmother stormed around the house in drunken rages or shacked up vociferously in the next bedroom with that evening's paramour.

Eventually, her stepmother's affairs had become too blatant to be hidden even from a traveling businessman. Megan's parents had divorced, and her stepmother and stepbrother had moved away. Over the years, Megan had written and sent pictures in an attempt at reconciliation, but she had never received a reply.

Megan leaned back in her armchair and stared at the ceiling. "I'm sorry, your hour is up. We'll get back to this at our next session, shall we?" she said aloud to the empty room. With a deep sigh, she got up from the chair and packed her briefcase.

Megan left her office building and walked down West Eleventh Street toward Greenwich Avenue. Megan loved walking through the West Village, with its stately townhouses flanked by majestic white elms, sycamores, and gingkoes bursting out of the narrow sidewalks. The side streets of the West Village had a small-town ambiance, all the more unique for being nestled between some of the busiest streets in Manhattan. To walk down Bank and Charles Streets had a therapeutic effect on Megan, calming her down after a day of listening to other people's traumas.

But this evening something caught Megan's attention, and she slowed her pace cautiously. Perched incongruously on the steps of a townhouse, his arms resting casually on his knees, was a grotesquely unkempt derelict. He was wearing a pair of baggy, dirt-stained slacks; a grimy tee shirt; and, in spite of the warmth of the evening, a full-length army surplus overcoat, obviously well slept in by its appearance, with gaping tears at the shoulder seams. His shoulder length hair was matted with the filth of the streets and an angry, jagged scar stretched across his left cheek. The derelict eyed her intently as she approached, but not in the leering way some men did. He stared directly and unwaveringly into her eyes.

The intensity of his stare made her distinctly uncomfortable, and she looked straight ahead and picked up her pace as she approached him. But out of the corner of her eye she could see his head turn to follow her as she passed him and continued on toward SoHo.

CHAPTER 3

▼

Set apart from Greenwich Village by Houston Street as it slashes across lower Manhattan, SoHo is a mélange of colors, sounds, and textures. Its graceful multi-colored ironwork buildings, constructed at the turn of the century to meet the mercantile needs of the growing capitalist class, now housed professionals, artists, and midlevel corporate managers. Attracted by the central location and floor-to-ceiling windows that allowed as much haze-filtered sunlight as possible into the newly renovated loft spaces, they came in droves. In turn, their presence spawned the development of antique shops, art galleries, nouvelle cuisine cafes, and clothing salons that filled the spaces where, a half century earlier, throngs of immigrants toiled in crowded sweatshops.

Traversing the fractured sidewalk of Mercer Street, Megan bounded up the graffiti-sprayed stoop and rode the ancient freight elevator up to the second floor.

"Charlie, sweetie." Megan bent down and scratched the head of their black and white spotted cat, who greeted her noisily as she walked through the door.

"About time," Peter called from the kitchen. "Can't make veal a la Branstead without the veal."

"Sorry. Got held up at the office." She dropped the veal off on the kitchen counter and rushed to the bedroom.

Of necessity, dinner preparation at their apartment had become an effort of teamwork and compromise. It had to be. Peter loved heavy cream sauces. Megan's tastes, on the other hand, were less elegant and more healthful, her pref-erence running to simpler vegetarian dishes. "Lips that touch tofu shall never touch mine" Peter had threatened, but eventually they compromised by switch-ing off on the main course, and tonight was Peter's turn.

Megan quickly changed into a sleeveless, short, cotton dress for comfort, her legs bare in the warmth of the June evening. Peter was already sautéing the veal when she returned. Preparing the salad, her mind was occupied by Frank Halleck's horrible descent into madness and Harriet's anguished helplessness.

"You know, the weirdest thing happened today in the hospital," Peter suddenly remarked. "We've had a rash of unexplained deaths on the neurology service. The victims are all unidentified derelicts admitted in a confusional state and, after a day or so, they suddenly convulse, go into cardiac arrest, and die. Just had one today. Greg Johnson … you know Greg—the tall black guy at the departmental Christmas party—was right on it, but the only finding was a minute quantity of an unknown SSRI in the blood."

"Why did you call them 'victims'?"

"All I've got are suspicions, but these might be intentional poisonings, perhaps by someone on staff."

Megan was stunned by the implications. "Are you going to report this?"

"It could all be alcohol withdrawal. I'd look like a jerk if I went to the medical staff board without clear evidence. I'm going to cancel my office for the next few days to do some in-house investigating of my own."

"Don't close the office, Peter. I've got an emergency that came up." She then went on to recount her experience with the Hallecks, including Frank's obsession with cats.

Peter cocked an eyebrow as he listened. "He's got a rapidly progressive dementia. But what's this 'cat' business about?"

"He's a research assistant. Used cats as lab animals. I think Frank's work with cats made him obsess about some imagined power his own cat had developed over him." Megan bent over, and petted Charlie. "No, no, no. Don't worry, Cutie. Nobody's going to dice up *your* brain for science."

Peter shook his head. "Doesn't make sense. Tell Frank's wife to bring him to the ER sometime tomorrow. This has been coming on too fast for an outpatient workup."

Megan considered telling him about her encounter *en passant* with the young vagrant but changed her mind.

"The next time Daniel and Rachel come over, why don't I cook the entree?"

Peter looked at her and grinned. "You are kidding, aren't you? Put a slice of your vegetarian meat loaf in front of Rachel, and it would end up in Charlie's bowl. She's never met a cholesterol molecule she didn't like."

Megan patted Peter's abdomen affectionately. "Pot calling the kettle black?"

"Rachel and I are pretty compatible in that way," Peter mused. "And I always did have a weakness for blondes."

Megan smiled wickedly and brandished a ten-inch French chef's knife.

"Listen, Buster, you do anything to come between me and my best friend and I'll have just three words of warning for you: John ... Wayne ... Bobbitt."

"M-e-e-g-a-a-n!" The door flew open, and Rachel Falconer breezed in, greeting Megan with a hug and a kiss on the cheek. Daniel Falconer, following behind her, smiled and shook Peter's hand.

"How's it going, Pete?" Daniel's standard greeting, short and succinct.

The Falconers were a study in contrasts. Rachel's personality instilled either affection or annoyance in people. Raised in central Ohio, she was brassy and loud and stood out from her more restrained classmates and friends. As a literature major at Wellesley College she had found her social niche in the school's New York City contingent and had sworn an oath to someday live in Manhattan.

Rachel's physical appearance was equally striking. Five feet seven inches tall, with shoulder-length naturally blonde hair and finely chiseled features, she had come to New York with a slender athletic build, which was beginning to show the effects of the Greenwich Village culinary experience. However, she maintained a rigorous physical training regimen, and the added pounds only served to subtly feminize her underlying muscle tone.

When they'd first met, Daniel was studying for his doctoral degree in international relations at Harvard's Ukrainian Research Institute. His family had been living in the Back Bay area of Boston for many generations, and he had absorbed his constrained emotionalism from the environment. Rachel had viewed it as her God-given responsibility to propel Daniel out of the libraries and lecture halls and into real life.

Their friendship had developed rapidly into a deeply loving relationship, and Rachel had ended up accompanying Daniel to Washington when he was awarded a position as visiting faculty at Georgetown University. After marrying a few years later, they'd transitioned their jobs into their marriage. Rachel's happiness had become complete when Daniel had accepted a tenured position at New York University and they'd moved to Greenwich Village.

Since the breakup of the Soviet Union, Daniel's research had become a hot ticket item in academic circles, and he was constantly traveling to what was now the Commonwealth of Independent States for conferences and lecturing. For her part, Rachel had managed to parlay her literary background into a freelance job writing travelogues of Eastern Europe and Russia, enabling her to accompany Daniel on most of his trips.

"Peter, it's so good to *see* you again."

Peter endured her hug. Megan looked on and sighed. Peter always kept an emotional distance from others, even in their relationship. Another issue for another time.

"What travelogue are you working on now, Rachel? I'd love to read it." Megan asked over the clinking of wine glasses.

Daniel smiled and answered for Rachel, whose mouth was stuffed with veal. "Rachel is very self-conscious about her writing. She doesn't even let me read it. She writes for journals of very narrow interest that don't have much public circulation. I think she'd freak out if she ever saw one of her articles on a newsstand, wouldn't you, Rache? Right now she's working on a travelogue for Western Ukraine and the Carpathian Mountains."

"We just got back from there," Rachel interrupted, spearing an artichoke heart with her fork. "You wouldn't believe how indescribably beautiful they are at this time of year."

Megan reached out and held Peter's hand. "Why can't we go on a romantic trip sometime?"

"Reality check. Remember our student loans?"

"If the university weren't paying our way, we wouldn't be able to travel much, either," Rachel added between mouthfuls. "But I'll let you in on a little secret. Daniel made some overseas connections and might finagle some money to get us all over as a foursome later this year."

"Sounds good to me," Peter said, and was barely able to get the words out before Megan kissed him full on the lips.

After waving good-bye from the window as Dan and Rachel strolled together down the street, Megan walked to the kitchen and sighed as she stared at the pile of dishes in the sink. Unfortunately, French cooking still required American cleaning. She began scrubbing the dishes as Peter straightened up the loft and turned off the lights.

"Wouldn't a trip overseas be so romantic?" Megan's reverie was interrupted by the gentle sensation of Peter's insistent lips softly kissing the back of her neck, causing a brief shiver to run down her spine. "Peter, please. If I don't finish washing these dishes, we'll have an army of cockroaches by morning," she protested unconvincingly.

"I love you," Peter murmured as he drew her skirt slowly up above her hips. Megan set her hands on the edge of the sink to steady herself as her head swam and her heart pounded under Peter's caressing hand. As her passion rose, the rhythm of her breathing matched that of Peter's.

"Screw the dishes," Peter whispered. He turned her around and kissed her deeply as his free hand switched off the light.

CHAPTER 4

Peter held on tightly to his mother's hand as they rushed down the long hospital corridor to his father's room. He stared up at the nurses and doctors as they passed by, some smiling back at him but most simply hurrying by, ignoring the mother and her little boy, their minds focused on other things. To Peter, the corridor stretched on for miles and miles as his little legs began aching from the strain of keeping up with his mother. He looked up at her to see if she would slow down just a bit, but her eyes were fixed straight ahead, staring down the hallway to his father's room at the end.

Outside the room, Peter's mother began putting a white hospital gown over her clothing.

"Do I have to put one on, too?"

"Yes, dear, even the nurses and doctors have to put on gowns, masks, and gloves before they go into Daddy's room. The sign on the door says so."

"All," "mask," and "room." At not quite four years of age, those were the only words he could read on the sign. He didn't want to wear a mask. It might frighten Daddy. He turned to his mother to ask if he really had to, but she was talking to Daddy's doctor and didn't pay attention to him.

Peter quietly opened the door. It had been two weeks since Daddy had had to come into the hospital, but it felt like forever, and until now he hadn't been able to see him at all. Mommy said that he was very sick, and the doctors had to give him very strong medicines, so strong that he had to stay in the hospital to get them because if he even caught a cold while he was on these medicines, he could die. But Peter didn't have a cold. He didn't even feel sick, so he really didn't need all that stuff on him.

Peter stepped into the room, the door closing behind him. His father was lying in his bed, asleep. He had never seen him look like this. Daddy had always been so big *and strong that he could lift Peter up from the ground, throw him in the air, and catch him again, all with one hand. He had been the biggest Daddy on his block, maybe even at his school, but now he was so skinny and pale that Peter almost didn't recognize him. As Peter tiptoed toward the bed, his father opened his eyes and smiled. With great effort, he slowly raised himself up so he was resting on his elbow, so weak he could barely support himself.*

"Hey, Sport, good to see you. I missed you."

Peter ran the few steps to the bed and threw his arms around his father's neck while his father held him tightly in his skinny, wasted arms and cried.

His mother screamed as she burst through the doorway to grab Peter and pull him back outside.

"Peter, get away from Daddy! You'll kill him!"

You'll kill him ... kill him ... kill him ...

Peter was sitting bolt upright in bed when he awoke, his heart pounding furiously. His face was clammy with sweat, and his breath came in hard gasps. It took him several minutes to calm himself enough to lie back down next to the slumbering Megan.

His father had died just a few weeks after that visit, his acute myelogenous leukemia deteriorating into blast crisis that failed to respond to even the experimental chemotherapy protocols he had been on. The dream had started a few months later, and it still wouldn't leave him.

Peter turned off his alarm clock, set to ring in only fifteen minutes, slipped silently out of bed as not to wake Megan, and got ready for work.

By the time Peter got to the neurology ward, Greg Johnson was already waiting with the full contingent of medical students and house staff. Casual talk about final exams and the Mets' grim outlook for the pennant race broke up on Peter's arrival.

"Good morning, Dr. Branstead. The medical students have a fine selection of clinical material to present to you this morning. I hope you're not too pressed for time."

"I've canceled my office, so take your time."

But there was barely enough time to finish rounding on the first patient before Greg's beeper interrupted them.

"ICU. Here we go again," Greg muttered.

"Not another one? You didn't tell me we had another one."

"Sorry, Dr. Branstead. He was next on the list. He came in late last night, confused and hallucinating just like the others, but he seemed medically stable. I put him in the ICU mainly for observation. I also took the precaution of loading him up with fosphenytoin for seizure prophylaxis, but it doesn't sound like my idea worked."

By the time they arrived in the ICU, John Doe was in a full-blown convulsion, and Bruce Rathburn was already at the bedside.

"What are you doing here?" Greg asked.

"Preemptive strike. I heard you admitted another John Doe last night, and I thought I'd check things out from the very beginning. Saves me a vertical fifty-yard dash from the doctor's lounge." Rathburn turned to a nurse. "John Doe's looking a bit shaky, if you'll pardon the pun. Why don't we have anesthesia mosey on up here, just in case? Someone tell me what he's doing."

"I can't tell if the heartbeat is wide complex supraventricular tach or accelerated junctional tach, Dr. Rathburn," one of the nurses called out.

"No big deal. What's his rate?"

"Two-fifty, BP stable."

"Good. His seizure is subsiding. Maybe he's over the hump. Let's give him six milligrams of adenosine for starters."

"Just a second. I think he's in ventricular tachycardia now. Could you check the monitor, Dr. Rathburn? I'm not sure what his heart's doing."

"Oh boy, we've got trouble. Lidocaine seventy-five milligrams, IV push. Run the IV with lactated Ringer's wide open, and give a gram of mag sulfate over fifteen minutes."

"It looks like he's in V tach, rate two-seventy-five, BP ninety over fifty. No spontaneous respirations."

"Anesthesia, can we get him intubated? One milligram of epinephrine IV."

"V fib, Dr. Rathburn. I can't get a pulse. Shall we call a code?"

"In case you haven't noticed, this already is a code. He's in pulseless V tach now. Give another milligram of epi, fast, and lidocaine seventy-five milligrams, IV push."

"No pulse, no BP, Dr. Rathburn."

"Damn it, damn it, damn it. Give me a break. Okay, set the defibrillator at two hundred joules." Rathburn was starting to sweat. Nothing was making sense.

Greg and Peter retreated again from the bedside, taking the ward staff with them, and left Rathburn to his misery.

"Greg, you'll have to finish rounds without me," Peter said. "Make sure the lab has the blood samples that were drawn in the ER. I've got a neurotoxicologist friend uptown. I'm going to run this by him and send him samples of blood and spinal fluid from every John Doe that's died in this hospital in the past month. Apologize to the med students for me. We'll have to do rounds on the run this afternoon."

"Okay, Dr. Branstead. What do I tell Bruce?"

They both looked over in the direction of the code. Interspersed between futile attempts at cardiac defibrillation, Rathburn's chest compressions were punctuated by the sound of cracking ribs. It took only four minutes of oxygen deprivation before brain cells began dying.

"Tell him I'm a No Code," and he left the ICU to go down to medical records.

Megan rode up in the elevator to her office, brushing stray cat hairs from her skirt. She would have to call Harriet Halleck and tell her to bring Frank to the St. Mark's Emergency Room, and Peter would examine him there. She only hoped that there was something that Peter could do for him.

"Good morning, Mrs. Ivy."

"Good morning, Miss Hutchins. Mrs. Halleck called earlier this morning, almost as soon as the office opened. She wants you to call her. It's urgent."

Megan walked into her office, closed the door, and called Harriet Halleck. The phone was picked up after one ring.

"Hello, Harriet, this is Megan Hutchins. I spoke to Peter last night and he said he'd be glad to see Frank if you bring him to the emergency room anytime ..."

"Megan, that's why I called. Dr. Albright admitted Frank to East Side Psychiatric Center last night."

Megan knew of Dr. William Albright. He was Frank's employer and a well-published research psychiatrist at New York University. He was very demanding, and the workload that Frank suffered under was a frequent topic of conversation during Frank's therapy for depression.

"How did that happen?"

"I took Frank to the lab yesterday afternoon to pick up some of his things, and Dr. Albright was there. He was concerned about Frank's behavior at work."

"Did you tell him that he was going to see Peter?"

"Yes, but he insisted that Frank was having a psychotic break, that it wasn't neurological at all, and that he needed admission immediately."

"Did you ask him to call me first?"

"He got very huffy and said that he knew what he was doing, and there wasn't time."

No time for a phone call? Megan thought. *Give me a break.*

"I told him I would agree to a psychiatric hospitalization if Dr. Branstead was allowed to see him at East Side Psychiatric Center during his admission. He didn't like the idea, but he said that would be acceptable."

Megan thought the whole scenario was a bit odd, but before she called Dr. Albright, she had to know how to proceed. "Harriet, did you tell Dr. Albright about my relationship with Dr. Branstead?"

"No, I didn't think that was any of his business."

"Good. I'll call Dr. Albright today, and I think it best he not be aware that I know Peter. Frankly, Harriet, I don't think it's ethical for him to admit his own employee to a psychiatric hospital under his own care. Let me look into this."

"Thank you so much." Harriet's voice sounded tired and frightened.

"Dr. Albright speaking."

"Dr. Albright, my name is Megan Hutchins. I'm Frank Halleck's therapist."

"How do you do, Miss Hutchins? Mrs. Halleck told me about you. I thought you might call." Albright's voice was self-assured, bordering on arrogant.

"I could have Mrs. Halleck deliver a written release in a few minutes if you wish, Dr. Albright."

"That won't be necessary, Miss Hutchins. I believe it is Miss Hutchins, isn't it? I detest this contemporary habit of addressing women as 'Ms.'" He pronounced it "mizzz," with obvious sarcasm.

"Miss will be just fine, Dr. Albright." His pomposity was getting abrasive. "To get back to Frank, I've been his therapist for quite some time, and I had the opportunity of seeing Frank and Mrs. Halleck in my office yesterday. His behavior was very disturbing."

"I agree, Miss Hutchins. Frank's been under a great deal of stress recently. I'm at a crucial point in my research, and we're compiling data preparing a paper for publication. I'm afraid Frank took too much upon himself and has had a bit of a breakdown."

"Any insight about his perseveration about cats?"

"Much of our studies are done with cats as test animals, and among Frank's responsibilities was sacrificing the laboratory animals. I suspect his guilt and the stress probably precipitated a psychotic break."

"What about a neurological consultation?"

"Mrs. Halleck told me you recommended a neurological opinion, but I really feel that immediate psychiatric intervention is necessary until we can get Frank stabilized. I assure you this really shouldn't take more than a few days."

"Well, I'm not sure if Mrs. Halleck told you, but some of Frank's behaviors have really been more compatible with a dementia than a psychosis."

"Such as?" There was a tinge of frostiness in his voice.

"His memory is terrible. He's been wandering about at night, disoriented in his own home. He's ceased to care at all about his personal grooming. And he's had severe personality changes, going from extreme passivity one moment to intense paranoia and agitation the next. At the very least, I think you should entertain the possibility that this represents an organic psychosis and have Frank admitted to a hospital for medical clearance before you begin treating him psychiatrically."

"Miss Hutchins," Dr. Albright began, the touch of frostiness now distinctly glacial, "I do not believe your training as a therapist qualifies you to make medical diagnoses. As for myself, I have spent a great number of years researching the clinical aspects of dementia and psychosis, and I believe that my medical background as well as my laboratory and clinical research give me ample justification for admitting Frank to East Side Psychiatric Center. In addition, an internationally known colleague of mine is coming to visit in a few days, and I intend to present Frank's case to him for a second opinion. I don't mind if Mrs. Halleck's neurologist pays Frank a visit, although I will not allow Frank to be removed from the premises while he is my medical responsibility. Now, Miss Hutchins, will that be all?"

Megan was incensed. She wished she could reach her hand through the phone and grab Albright by his self-important neck, but it was not in Frank's interest for her to get into a shouting match with Dr. Albright, who obviously knew he held all the cards.

With one exception.

"I also wanted to tell you," Megan began, "that as a therapist I find it highly unethical for an employer to have his employee admitted to a psychiatric facility on his own service." Megan's voice picked up slowly as she went along. "I'm sure you can appreciate that as Frank's employer you already hold a position of power over him. I feel that, to avoid adding the power you would get by gaining access to his most private and intimate thoughts, you really should excuse yourself from a position as Frank's psychiatrist and hand that responsibility to someone without a vested interest. In fact, I would consider it my responsibility as Frank's therapist to bring this issue up with the Ethics Board of the Psychiatry Department at New York University if you don't."

There was a momentary silence before Albright spoke.

"Now you be quiet and listen to me, young lady," Albright began in slow, measured tones. "I have spent years establishing an academic and clinical reputation in my field, and I don't intend to let some Mizz-Know-It-All with a few paltry years of clinical experience tarnish it, least of all over an issue that she knows nothing about. I have very powerful friends, both in the academic and the business and political communities and if you dare to try and lock horns with me, I will make certain that you will be finished professionally in this city and that you'll consider yourself lucky to find a practice any closer than Bridgeport. So don't let me ever hear you trying to make threats to me again. Have I made myself abundantly clear, Miss Hutchins? Have I?"

Megan clenched her hand so furiously that her nails dug into her palm, but she realized that she had played all her cards, and he had called her bluff.

"I believe so."

"Good. Then I feel that I have adequately fulfilled my obligations to my patient by communicating my plans to you, and I believe further contact between us will be neither necessary nor in Mr. Halleck's best interest. Have a good day, Miss Hutchins."

"Good day, Dr. Albright," Megan said to empty air. She set the phone down on its cradle and took several long, deep breaths to calm down.

It was late afternoon before Peter finished going through the charts of all John Does who had died of cardiac arrest following a seizure in the past month. In addition to the five on the neurology service, he'd found two more who had been admitted to medicine service and one to the psychiatry service locked ward. All were virtually identical situations: men in their fifties or sixties found wandering and disoriented on the street with no ID and no known family. Extensive workup was all either completely normal or showed minor abnormalities clearly unrelated to the patients' present condition. All had alcohol levels of zero, which in itself was a remarkable finding in this patient population. Almost all had had lumbar punctures and CT scans of the brain, with undistinguished results.

Nursing staff had identified a few from previous admissions, and Peter had dug up their old charts. Some, but not all, had a history of episodic alcohol abuse but appeared to have recently been doing well—no evidence of malnutrition, vitamin deficiency, or liver abnormalities that would indicate recent alcoholic binges. In fact, by their lab work they appeared healthier now than during prior admissions.

Most disturbing was their hospital course following admission. Over twenty-four to forty-eight hours, their dementias invariably progressed. They began hallucinating, became increasingly agitated in spite of heroic doses of sedatives, and progressed into a single, prolonged convulsion culminating in cardiac arrest and death, in spite of full resuscitative efforts.

He started with the hypothesis that the men had been poisoned on the street. In all probability, the dementia, seizures, and cardiac arrest were part of the same pathologic process. A batch of hootch could easily be spiked without the victim's awareness. On the Bowery, wine selection criteria were necessarily broad. But the contaminated moonshine theory wouldn't explain why they all had alcohol levels of zero on admission and continued their clinical deterioration in the hospital.

What about an in-house killer? Almost all of the victims had had IV lines at one time or another, making their veins readily accessible for injection with some undiscovered toxin or drug. However, they had been admitted to different units: three had been on the neurology ward; two were admitted to medicine, but had been on different inpatient units. Two were admitted directly to the intensive care unit, where they were under constant surveillance; and one had been admitted to the psych locked ward, where anyone having contact with the patient was thoroughly screened. Although they had all come in through the emergency room, this happened on different shifts, and some hadn't gotten peripheral lines put in until they got to the floor. The one admitted to psychiatry hadn't gotten an IV until he actually started going into convulsions. It remained possible that someone, perhaps even nonmedical staff such as a transporter or housecleaning personnel, could have been wandering about the hospital surreptitiously poisoning these poor men, although they wouldn't have had ready access to those admitted to the ICU or the psych service. There certainly would have been easier victims on almost any ward service in the hospital. Besides, it would take a highly sophisticated mind, extremely knowledgeable in medicine, to choose a drug that would escape detection for this long.

There was only one inescapable conclusion: someone on the medical staff was selecting itinerant vagrants as guinea pigs and killing them right in front of the unsuspecting hospital staff.

A deep sickness roiled in the pit of his stomach. This couldn't be happening in St. Mark's Hospital, but it was, and before he could present his findings to the medical staff board, he needed to call Steve Bergstraum.

Dr. Steven Bergstraum was an old friend of Peter's from their residency days when he had been Peter's senior resident. A brilliant neurologist, Steve had used his remarkable intelligence to become one of the world's experts in neurotoxicology and had secured a tenured position on staff at the Neurologic Institute on the Upper West Side at the remarkably young age of thirty-five. Peter had relied on Steve's expertise in the past on cases of industrial chemical exposure, but now he really needed some advice.

"Pete, long time no hear. You and Megan tied the knot yet?"

"Not yet, but I think were getting close," Peter lied.

"Yeah, yeah! I hear you. I've been there, too. But don't let her get away. She's a real catch."

"Send me the bill for the couple counseling, but I need your professional expertise in a more neurological vein."

Peter then recounted the story of the demented vagrants, including his detective work in the medical records department. Steve periodically interjected questions about clinical and laboratory specifics.

"What I need to know is whether you've ever heard of a toxin that can cause a rapidly progressive dementia and fatal seizures. If so, I've got to investigate the possibility that someone is poisoning these guys."

There was a long silence. Peter let him think.

"You got me on this one," Steve said. "But don't go to the authorities yet. Why don't you do this: send me samples of blood and, if you've got 'em, spinal fluid from as many of the victims as you can. I don't need much. I've got nuclear magnetic spectroscopy, gas chromatography, the works. All I need is one cc of blood, but the more the merrier. If you can, send me some blood drawn in the ER, and I might be able to tell you whether it was administered in the hospital or out on the street. It will take me a couple of days, though, and you'll have to promise me one thing."

"What?"

"Coauthorship of any publications."

Good God. Just like Steve.

"I'll be more than happy to give you top billing. Call me as soon as you figure something out."

"Regards to Megan. Talk to you later."

Megan finished the notes on her last patient. Two emotionally exhausting days in a row had wiped her out. The debacle with Albright was her own fault. He was obviously a master at control and manipulation, and he had caught her off guard. There was nothing she could do but shrug it all off and explain things to Harriet.

Megan packed up her papers into her briefcase and left the office. It was late, and even Mrs. Ivy was gone. As she rode the elevator down, she tried to go over in her own mind how to tell Peter what had transpired between her and Dr. Albright. Peter was much more politic than she was. Perhaps he'd have better luck.

It was dusk by the time Megan left the building. She turned and started walking down West Eleventh Street, then stopped abruptly. There was a man, dressed in the same clothes that the scar-faced man had been dressed in the day before, standing by the same stairway, looking in her direction. In the dim light, his face was too indistinct to see clearly, but she was certain it was he. Chilled by a transitory flash of fear, she hesitated in her tracks, unsure of what to do. Lower Manhattan was full of equally disreputable-appearing men, and she walked by at least a half-dozen of them on a daily basis. But it was her uneasy recollection of his stare that finally convinced her to turn around and walk the other way. He seemed to know her, and it was obvious that she was being stalked. Was he some psychotic that she had examined during her training, finally discharged from a state hospital and free to pursue his obsessions? Frightened, she picked up her pace to a rapid stride, hurrying down the street as quickly as she could without running, and struggled to recall his face among those of the myriad that she had interviewed.

As she turned onto Hudson Street, she glanced back quickly. She was being pursued, all right. The man had left the stairway and was more than matching her pace, closing the distance between them. Racing down Hudson Street, she searched anxiously for a cab. Her pursuer had already turned the corner. No more than a hundred feet separated them. She dashed directly into the middle of the street, waving her arm wildly. A taxi, its Off Duty light on, screeched to a halt a few yards in front of her.

"Whaddayoufuckinuts?" was all that Megan heard from the driver, but she ran to the side and jumped in before the cabbie could finish the sentence.

"Drive. Now! That man's stalking me."

The cabbie recognized the look in her eyes as one that he had seen in many women over the years. He turned around and the cab lurched forward into traffic.

Megan turned around and looked out the back window of the cab. Her pursuer was standing on the exact spot where she had jumped into the cab, staring at her as it sped away. In the harsh light of the street lamp, she could barely make out the long scar angling across his left cheek before he turned around and faded away into the darkness.

CHAPTER 5

▼

As the ministerial Chaika limousine made its way swiftly down the streets of Kiev, its riders safely shielded from view behind a thick layer of dark bulletproof glass, Prime Minister Valentyn Boshevsky mused about his rise to power.

Physically and psychologically, he was a brutish man. His arms were disproportionately large, the arms of a bear affixed to a man's torso. His dark, deep-set eyes, overshadowed by thick black eyebrows that almost met at the bridge of his nose, gave him a Neanderthal appearance. A street fighter since childhood, he had honed his fighting ability during army service and had developed a reputation for cunning and savagery in the ring.

Brutal political maneuvering that outflanked anyone who stood in his way accelerated his advance up the ranks of the Communist Party. When Ukraine declared its independence from the floundering Soviet Union in 1991, Boshevsky saw no ethical contradiction in switching his allegiance to the newly formed ultra-rightist Radical Nationalist Party. Ukrainian sovereignty had been his lifelong dream, and pursuit of this dream required a flexible political morality, as well as a life free from emotional entanglements.

Boshevsky turned back to the window to casually eye pretty young girls in their short, summer skirts as the limousine passed them by. On days when he wasn't quite so busy, he would stop the limousine when a particularly attractive young woman caught his eye and have one of his bodyguards procure her for him. It was easy to find young women, single or even married, who would freely consent to sex in hope that a political connection could be used to their advantage, perhaps to secure a state job.

Today, however, the pleasures of the flesh had to be put aside. He had a highly important meeting to attend to this morning critical to the success of his plan. The Verkhovna Rada, the chief legislative body of Ukraine, was torn apart by factionalism, incapable of making the decisions necessary at this critical juncture of Ukrainian history. With over thirty political parties represented, legislative sessions resembled a pack of wolves fighting over a carcass more than a deliberative organization of elected officials. But as his father had always taught him, a team of wolves can be made to pull together strongly if only they have a master who is bold, resourceful, and powerful enough to harness them together. And now that he had spent nearly three decades manipulating, bullying, and clawing his way to the top of the political heap, Valentyn Boshevsky would be that master. The only obstacle was President Anatoly Labrinska, an obstacle that would soon be removed.

Boshevsky turned toward his bodyguard, sitting in the seat across from the prime minister and also gazing out the car window. Ivan Turgenev was a highly ambitious, handsome young man, personally chosen for the position from the ranks of other National Security Service agents by Boshevsky himself. Although his skills with weaponry and martial arts made him a superlative bodyguard, it was his overwhelming ambition that was most important to Boshevsky. Working with ambitious men could be dangerous; given the proper inducement, there was always the risk that they could turn on you. However, no one understood their mentalities better than he did. If you could harness their ambition, they could be indefatigable workers, as Ivan had proven himself to be, and manipulating such men was a skill on which Boshevsky prided himself.

"Have you ever been inside St. Sophia's?" Boshevsky asked.

Turgenev turned and shook his head. "No, I haven't, Your Excellency. I've never even been on the cathedral grounds. I hear it's beautiful."

Boshevsky nodded. "Magnificent building. Someday I'll have to give you a day off so you can spend an afternoon there with your wife."

"That would be most kind, Your Excellency. By the way, I must tell you that Katerina and I were most honored when you visited our apartment last week. She was so excited about your visit that it was all she could talk about for days."

Boshevsky lit up in one of his rare, truly heartfelt smiles. "It was my pleasure. I'm an old friend of her father's, and I haven't seen Katerina since she was little. It was quite a surprise to see her all grown up. You're a fortunate young man, Ivan."

"I didn't know that you were a friend of Mr. Efrenov. He never mentioned that to me."

Boshevsky smiled again. "Vasha and I go back a long way, although we've drifted apart as the years have gone by. I helped him make some of the connections that set him up in business when I was just starting in politics. I am glad to see that he has done quite nicely for himself. You chose your in-laws very well, Ivan."

Turgenev flushed crimson. "Your Excellency, I assure you that I had no idea that Katerina's father was so wealthy. We met at school, and I had never been to her house or even met her parents until we had been engaged for several months. I assure you, Excellency, that my motives were pure and driven solely by my love for Katerina."

"Oh-ho-ho. Don't be so touchy, my dear Ivan. I meant no harm." Boshevsky laughed and threw his arms up in a mock defensive posture. "I only meant to say that your father-in-law is very well connected and a good man to know. It was partly on his recommendation that I gave you this job."

"Really? I had no idea ..."

"Don't be so naïve, boy. Our society works on personal connections. That is the grease that oils the machinery of government and commerce in Ukraine. But don't worry, I wouldn't entrust my life to an incompetent, no matter how well connected. I would watch out for Vasha, though. Not all of his connections are, shall we say, on the up and up."

Ivan flushed again, this time more in embarrassment than anger. "I am aware that Mr. Efrenov occasionally has some unsavory visitors to his home. But I assure you that I keep myself clear of them. I have no respect for criminals, and I regret that my father-in-law has managed to get himself involved with such an element."

"Very commendable, my boy. But don't be too hard on your father-in-law. These are difficult times, and sometimes the solutions to problems can't be as direct and open as we would like them to be. I assure you that Vasha has the best interests of you and his daughter in mind. Perhaps that is a lesson in practicality that you have learned. Listen closely, Ivan, and I will give you another important lesson."

Boshevsky motioned to Ivan to bend over closer to him, even though they were the only two in a soundproof limousine.

Conspiratorially, Boshevsky whispered softly into Turgenev's ear. "Knowledge is power."

Turgenev laughed. "So that is your secret of life, Excellency? No disrespect, sir, but my grammar school teacher beat you to it by about twenty years."

"Ah, my dear Turgenev, you hear but you don't really understand. When President Labrinska and I have our little meetings, do you know what we discuss? We trade information, but we are like two card players. We save our best cards and jealously guard them close to our chests. When a particular piece of information is no longer useful to us, or when it gives us the opportunity to mislead the other or to use it to gain an advantage, we give out just enough information to suit our own purposes. Words must be carefully chosen, secrets meticulously guarded. Ideally, if you can find out someone else's secrets without having to give him anything in return, you can gain a tremendous advantage. But you have to play the game very, very carefully."

Turgenev shrugged. "Very interesting, Your Excellency, but why are you telling me all this?"

"Because I like you, my boy, and I think you have great potential. Besides, there is another reason that I'll tell you in a few minutes." Boshevsky leaned forward and opened a panel to the driver's compartment. "Stop here. I have something I want to show Ivan."

Boshevsky stepped out of the limousine, and Turgenev followed. They were in a park just a few kilometers from the Cathedral of St. Sophia, and the limousine was parked by a low rise in the center of the park. Boshevsky motioned to Turgenev, and the two walked up a path to the top of the rise.

At the top was a larger, grassy clearing, circled by a pedestrian walkway and lined by benches. During busier times of the day, young mothers would sit and watch their children run and play games on the grass. Elderly pensioners tended to congregate here as well, enjoying the warmth of the sun while they took in a game of chess with their friends.

The clearing was roughly circular and unadorned by shrubbery. Standing in the middle of it, Boshevsky and Turgenev had an almost unobstructed view of the Dnieper River and the Old Town of Kiev to the east. To the south, they could see the monumental statue of the poet and nationalist, Taras Shevchenko, with its deep-set eyes framed by thick, bushy eyebrows and peering over a shaggy walrus mustache. The statue seemed to be gazing down the walkway to the clearing in which they stood.

"It's very beautiful, Your Excellency. How come you brought me here?"

"This spot is dear to me, Ivan. When I was a boy, my father would take me here. With Shevchenko's statue looking right at us, he would put his hands on my shoulders, recite his poetry to me—it was considered subversive by the Stalinists in those days—and make me pledge my loyalty and honor to my fatherland."

Boshevsky sighed and looked east to the river. "Ivan, someday this is where I will have my monument."

Turgenev's eyes grew wide, but he said nothing.

"Now that we're alone together, there is another example I want to give you knowledge being power."

"What is that, Your Excellency?"

"I happen to have known of your dalliances with your mistress on Khoryva Street for quite some time now ..."

"But ... but ... how did you ...?" Turgenev stammered, the sweat suddenly beading up on his forehead.

Boshevsky watched Turgenev's face closely as the blood quickly drained out of it. "I have my sources, Ivan. You don't get to the top of the heap without keeping your ear very carefully to the ground. But don't worry, my boy. I have absolutely no intention of telling anyone about it. As long as I'm alive, your secret is quite safe with me. But should I die or experience any, shall we say, unexpected accidents, my lawyer has a rather large file of photographs and some of the most intriguing video tapes I've seen in a long time, to be delivered to your father-in-law with my posthumous regards."

Turgenev rubbed his sweating palms on his slacks. "What do you want from me?"

"Absolutely nothing but your one hundred percent effort to keep me alive. Ivan, I simply can't afford to put my life so completely in someone's hands and then risk his selling out to the highest bidder to have me done away with at an opportune moment. That may not be at all on your mind now, but I'm certain that someday you will be tempted, and I want you to think more than twice about betraying me. I know that Vasha may not give a damn about his own fidelity in marriage, but when it comes to his daughter, I promise you that he is from the old school. And I don't have to remind you that some of his business acquaintances would have no hesitation in helping Vasha settle any matter of family honor, for the right price. So, Ivan, do you understand now what I mean by 'knowledge is power'?"

Turgenev nodded numbly.

"Good. Then today you have learned a very valuable lesson," Boshevsky remarked, patting Turgenev on the cheek. "Now, excuse me. I must make my way to St. Sophia's alone on foot. That's part of the preconditions for the meeting. Just tell the driver to wait here for me. I'll only be a few minutes.

"And by the way, tell him to keep the motor running and the air conditioner on. You look a bit pale."

With that, the prime minister took off at a fast walk toward the cathedral.

Striding through the entranceway to the cathedral grounds, Boshevsky skirted the crowds of tourists congregating in the churchyard, entered the church, and sat down in a pew far back in the shadows.

Boshevsky wasn't happy with this choice of meeting place. He felt unclean meeting here with Marko Cherkasy, the *pakhan* of the entire Ukrainian Mafia. This was the most revered church in the entire Ukraine, and, as he looked above him at the mosaics of the saints and angels lining the domed ceiling, their round orb-like eyes stared back at him disapprovingly. He shifted uneasily in his seat and glanced at his watch, impatient to get this meeting over with.

"Good morning, Your Excellency. Deep in prayer?"

Boshevsky recognized the sarcastic voice of Marko Cherkasy, who had sat down a meter or two to his right.

Cherkasy was a thin, wiry man with angular facial features and an upper lip that was deeply deformed by a large scar incurred in a knife fight in prison many years before. He habitually wore sunglasses, even in the dimly lit church, making him appear to be a cheap Mafia cliché. But after a few meetings, Boshevsky had realized that by hiding his eyes Cherkasy also hid his emotions and intentions. If a man was to live his life playing poker with the world, it was best to hide his bluffs.

Cherkasy's sartorial tastes were flashy and expensive and ran to imported silk suits. The Italian cut of the one he was wearing stood apart from the formless Ukrainian-made woolen suit that Boshevsky wore. In addition, his fingers always sported a varied collection of large, gold rings, which tended to draw attention to a couple of large tattoos on the backs of his hands—two grinning pirates' skulls, cuirasses firmly clenched between their teeth. The ostentation surprised Boshevsky, who had thought that a man in his position would have preferred to keep tattoos as inconspicuous as possible.

"You're late," Boshevsky growled. "I don't like to be kept waiting."

Cherkasy ignored Boshevsky's remark and stared up at the mosaics on the ceiling. "I don't think I ever been in this church. What's it called? Saint Sophia's, right? Very nice, Valentyn. Ve-ry nice."

"Why do we have to meet here, of all places?"

Cherkasy continued staring upward. "You know our agreement. Neutral territory. No bodyguards or guns, and no bugs or taps, right? So, here we are. Besides," and at this point Cherkasy almost sounded nostalgic, "I don't get to church a whole lot nowadays. I just thought I'd relax a bit and enjoy the scenery.

It's a funny thing," Cherkasy went on, gazing about at the frescoes on the walls. "My mother used to tell me about this church all the time when I was a kid. Took me all these years and a half-dozen prison sentences before I get to visit. Ironic, don't you think, Excellency?"

"Let's get on with business," Boshevsky grumbled. "I've got a busy day ahead."

"Okay, okay. Give me an update."

"Several months ago we had some mishaps at our Ukrainian research facility and had to move the research to the United States. I've been told that the technical problems are pretty well taken care of now, other than some fine tuning of the dosages, which should be completed in the next few days. Dr. Zabrovych is President Labrinska's psychiatrist, and he has been administering UR-416 to the president for several weeks now and tells me that it is having the desired effect on him. That is why the president has canceled all public appearances recently."

Cherkasy nodded slowly, his face expressionless, eyes hidden behind the sunglasses. "The Brotherhood is impatient for results, Excellency. President Labrinska's aides have introduced legislation privatizing an additional fifty percent of the industries in the eastern *oblasts*, and they plan to do more before the president's annual address to the Rada. When it comes to a vote, the legislation has to be turned our way."

"Don't worry, Marko. Scorpion tells me we are on schedule and should have the necessary results before the address. You can tell the Brotherhood that their investment will be paying off very soon."

Marko Cherkasy got up to leave and looked around. The tourists continued to stream through the cathedral, and the pews were virtually empty, except for a smattering of elderly parishioners just finishing their morning prayers. They had not been observed.

"Perhaps I'll call Scorpion myself. For confirmation."

"Be my guest," Boshevsky sneered. "Just remember the arrangement. To keep things secret, I would be his sole contact in Ukraine, and only my encrypted diplomatic phones would be used. Scorpion does not appreciate interference with his work, so try not to make him angry."

Cherkasy shuddered. Standing in a church seven thousand miles from New York City, the *pakhan* of the entire Ukrainian Mafia crossed himself three times at the thought.

"Never mind. I'll take your word for it."

Boshevsky smiled. "I thought you'd see things my way. Good day, Marko. If you'll excuse me, I have to pay a call on an ailing friend."

Without further conversation, they both turned and left the cathedral by different exits.

A few minutes later, Boshevsky found himself in the waiting room of the presidential mansion, awaiting entrance to the living quarters. The buildings in this part of Kiev had originally belonged to the aristocracy and wealthy bourgeoisie, but when the elite of the Communist Party took power in the 1920s, they had expropriated these beautiful old mansions and spent vast sums of government money lavishly renovating them under the pretense of making them into museums to capitalist decadence. Even in the anteroom, the walls were of richly hand-carved mahogany paneling. Niches in the walls were repositories for elegant statuary of French and Italian origin, most likely stolen from captured Nazi art warehouses during the Great Patriotic War, and a lavish crystal chandelier hung from the vaulted domed ceiling with its hand-painted, mock-Baroque frescoes.

The heavy wooden doors opened slowly, and the servant beckoned the prime minister into an even more lavishly decorated reception room. Seated in a large fin de siècle–style chair in the center of the room was Iryna Labrinska, wife of the president.

Boshevsky walked briskly over to the seated woman. In many ways, Iryna Labrinska was the power behind the throne. Although the president was the consummate politico and ruled the nation, Iryna ruled the presidential mansion, including the president's personal staff, with an iron hand and had absolute control over who could meet with the president. Boshevsky knew better than to try and lock horns with her and had generally been as deferential as his personality would allow him to be. But Iryna had been privy to the extent of the behind-the-scenes political intrigues and the magnitude of the stakes that were involved, and she distrusted him intensely.

"Madame Labrinska, it has been too long since we have chatted. It is good to see you looking so well."

In truth, she looked exhausted. Although officially her husband was incapacitated by a bad case of pneumonia, the reality of his illness as Boshevsky knew it had taken its toll on her. Iryna Labrinska had been forced by circumstances to grasp the reins of power from her ailing husband. For all practical purposes, she ran the government, although this was kept a carefully guarded secret. Only Boshevsky and his compatriots knew this, and there was no value in exposing the sham as yet. The drama would play itself out in good time.

"Thank you for your kind words, Mr. Prime Minister, but I'm afraid my husband's illness has left me quite debilitated."

"Madame Iryna, you really are taking too much upon yourself. At your husband's age, pneumonia can be a very serious condition. Don't you think it would be better for the president to be in the hospital, where he can get the care of the best physicians and medical facilities that Ukraine has to offer?"

Iryna Labrinska straightened up in her chair with a renewed vigor. She recognized the wolf circling around her.

"Mr. Prime Minister," she began in the firm, authoritative voice that Boshevsky had become accustomed to, "I assure you that my husband is getting the best medical care possible in this very house. He is still quite capable of handling affairs of state from his bedside, although he remains too weak to meet with any dignitaries for the time being. Believe me, Your Excellency, I would be the first to notify the Rada if my husband was too incapacitated to perform the duties of his office. He just needs a bit more time to recuperate."

"Please, Madame Labrinska, I am only thinking about your dear husband's health. He has his annual address to the Rada coming up, and I know it must be exhausting for him to work on his speech in his current state. Perhaps it would be better if I ask the Rada to delay the speech for a few weeks to allow him more time to recover?"

She rose out of her chair for the first time. "My husband happens to be working on that speech as we talk. He will be perfectly capable of giving his speech to the Rada at its appropriate time, and we do not need to ask for any continuances. Now, if you will excuse me, the president needs my assistance with his speech. Good day, Your Excellency."

Iryna Labrinska turned and swept out of the room, the servant quickly running to open the door to the president's private chambers and closing it behind her.

"Never mind, I'll let myself out," Boshevsky said to the embarrassed servant.

As he left the reception room and strode through the anteroom on his way to the door, Boshevsky chuckled to himself. *Go dig yourself a big hole, you obstinate bitch,* he thought. *Dig it deep enough to fit in not only yourself and your husband, but also the rest of your damned Liberal Party.*

As he walked down the steps to the limousine, he turned and gave a last admiring look at the presidential mansion.

It's a beautiful place, he thought, *but I really will have to replace those prissy Italian statues.*

Back in the residential suite, Iryna Labrinska sat on the bed where her husband lay and sobbed. Anatoly Labrinska's eyes opened, and he looked up at her.

"Mama, don't cry. Papa will be home from the war soon, and we'll all be a family again."

"Toly, I'm not your mama. I'm Iryna, your wife, and the war was over sixty ago. Please, Toly, I can't cover up for you anymore. I'm so tired. I can't write any more of your speech. You have to do it yourself."

"See. Papa's back home already." He pointed to a corner of the room where a large oil portrait of a saint hung on the wall. "Tell him I'm tired, but I'll clean out the barn when I'm finished with my nap." And the President of Ukraine fell back to sleep.

Iryna dried her eyes and quietly slipped out of the bedroom, closing the door behind her. Waiting just outside the door was a well-dressed, middle-aged man, his thinning hair slicked back impeccably. He was almost two meters tall, and dwarfed the president's wife.

"Dr. Zabrovych, Toly is getting worse by the day. I'm at my wit's end. He absolutely must appear in public in just a few days, but he's in no shape to deliver a speech in front of the Rada."

"Don't worry, Madame Labrinska," Dr. Iosyp Zabrovych said in the calming tones that a psychiatrist used when dealing with a distraught patient, "the president will be just fine. I have seen his depression get quite bad in the past, and after his medication has been adjusted, he snaps right out of it. You just have to be a little patient and wait for it to start working."

"Are you sure this is just a depression, Dr. Zabrovych? I've never seen Anatoly like this. His mind has been deteriorating before my eyes for weeks now, and he keeps getting worse." The de facto ruler of Ukraine dissolved into tears as Dr. Zabrovych, President Labrinska's long-time psychiatrist and confidant, put a supportive arm around her and patted her gently on the shoulder.

"I'm quite sure, Madame Labrinska. Tonight, I must leave for a conference in the United States, and I'll inquire among some experts I know whether there is anything else that can be done. When I come back in a few days, if he is not better, I promise I'll make arrangements to have the president admitted to an excellent neurologist at the Kiev Neurologic Institute, and we'll leave no stone unturned to find out if anything else is wrong."

"Must you leave right now, Dr. Zabrovych? Anatoly and I need you here so much right now."

"I'm terribly sorry, Madame Labrinska. I made this commitment many months ago, and I can't break it now. But I'll only be gone a few days. In my absence, Dr. Sergei Nikitin will be monitoring the president and adjusting his medication. I will be leaving you in very capable hands." Again, Dr. Zabrovych patted her on the shoulder, and then he turned to leave.

"One more thing, Dr. Zabrovych," Iryna called to him before he left the room. "Nobody, absolutely nobody, must know what has happened to the president."

"Don't worry, Madame Labrinska, my lips are sealed. No one will know."

"Do I have your promise?"

"You have my promise," and he smiled gently. "Trust me."

Dr. Zabrovych left the room and softly closed the door behind him.

Nightfall cast its embrace over the sleeping city of Kiev. Floodlights, giving the sacred buildings a mystical, ghostly appearance, had replaced the sunlight that had been reflecting off of the golden domes of the myriad of churches and cathedrals populating the city.

Within the corridors of the Ukrainian National Psychiatric Institute, a solitary figure slipped silently down the darkened hallway of the Department of Psychopharmacology. He had no concern for the night watchman; he was quite drunk and would not be making his rounds for the remainder of the night. However, he didn't want to encounter any researchers or technicians who might be working late in their laboratories. Playing his flashlight across the translucent glass windows of the staff offices as he made his way down the hallway, he halted in front of one lettered

Dr. Iosyp Zabrovych
and
Dr. Sergei Nikitin
Directors, Dementia Research Facility

After quickly glancing up and down the hallway one last time to make sure he hadn't been seen, he opened the door with a passkey, entered the laboratory, and silently closed the door behind him.

The National Security Service had been keeping its eye on this laboratory for some time. Although a great deal of research had been carried out here recently, no grant applications had been filed, and only a few meager publications had made their way to the journals. In response to persistent inquiries from the Ministry of Health, after a great deal of procrastination, a few preliminary studies were trotted out to assure them that the faculty was doing their job, but the studies were rudimentary for men at the apex of their academic careers.

Finally, there were the deaths at the National Psychiatric Institute. A certain number of deaths would be expected in any medical facility, but psychiatric hospitals weren't supposed to admit seriously ill patients without medical clearance, and several patients had died without adequate medical explanation earlier that year. Inexplicably, the bodies were hurriedly cremated without going through an autopsy as required by law. The cause of death was always listed as cardiac arrest, but medical documentation was sketchy, leaving no indication as to exactly what had happened. It was all suspicious, but not enough to warrant a full-scale investigation.

To that end, agent Vassily Kurilev had been assigned to ferret out specifics of the lab experimentation. A quick search of the office disclosed no evidence of patients' charts, but each desk had a high-grade imported computer, technologically superior to any that was routinely supplied to research laboratories in Ukraine. He quickly found a locked drawer, which, on opening it with his passkey, he found to be full of computer diskettes. It would probably take a month to go through all of the information on the diskettes, but he had an idea. Pulling the drawer out as far as it would go, he lay down on the floor and shone the flashlight upward. Taped to the bottom of the drawer was a single diskette, which he quickly inserted into a computer.

Kurilev's eyes lit up as his fingers danced across the keyboard. On the screen, neatly tabulated, were the computerized hospital charts of the six dead patients, each one listed by first name and last initial, with a file number next to the name. He picked out the first patient's record and browsed through it. Much of the documentation was surprisingly meticulous for a Ukrainian psychiatric hospital, even for the National Psychiatric Institute. Vital signs had been carefully charted at frequent intervals, blood testing was abundant, and expensive procedures such as electroencephalograms and even CT scans had been done regularly. This required a great deal of money, more than Zabrovych and Nikitin could possibly account for from government grants.

The doctors' progress notes caught his eyes. For each day, painstakingly detailed descriptions of the patient's behavior and activities were recorded, much more detailed than the usually sketchy doctor's notes. Aberrant behavior was described minutely, even to faulty personal hygiene. This man must have been observed almost constantly.

As he scrolled through the notes, he came to the last day's entry. It began just as carefully detailed as the other day's notes had, but toward the middle of the page was a terse comment:

Tachycardia-Generalized Convulsion-Cardiac Arrest-Death
Time of Death—9:43 a.m.

Considering the detail in which the remainder of the notes had been written, this showed an almost shocking disinterest, with no documentation of any efforts toward resuscitation or attempts at management of the seizure or cardiac arrhythmia.

Even more curious was a brief notation at the beginning of that day's note:

10 mg—serum level 57.4

There was a similar notation each day, giving what he presumed was that day's dosage of some unnamed medication and the blood level for that day. Although dosages varied, the level inexorably rose.

Kurilev skimmed through the other charts. Each appeared identical to the first, each page with the same notation of milligrams and blood levels. Most patients were hospitalized for only a few days. All died when the serum level had risen above 50.

It was time to call home. He switched the computer to e-mail and waited for his boss, Mikhail Pritsak, to come on line.

"Anything?" Pritsak was a man of few words, at least when he was sober.

"Found detailed hospital records on deceased patients. Interesting," Kurilev typed in response.

"Send them."

Kurilev e-mailed the information on the diskette. He waited while the antiquated Ukrainian Internet service established a comlink and the contents were reviewed. It was already 2:00 a.m., and he had only a few more hours before dawn. He wished Pritsak would hurry up. The last thing he wanted was to have someone from housecleaning come and find him snooping around in the office. After what seemed like an interminable delay, Pritsak's reply flashed on the screen.

"Very interesting. Any idea what this all means?"

"Not yet. This was all I could find."

"What are their plans? Who's financing this?"

"Don't know yet. Will have to look further."

"Find it! Critical! The whole operation is very suspicious. I'll e-mail info to Lone Eagle."

Kurilev was stunned. Why send this off to the Americans? This was a local situation, and he felt very uncomfortable sharing internal information with foreign governments.

"Why Lone Eagle?" he typed.

"Suspect Scorpion may be involved. Will need American's help. Keep this absolutely, repeat ABSOLUTELY, Eyes Only."

Scorpion! Kurilev shuddered. He hadn't realized the seriousness of what was going on. He suddenly felt very vulnerable, sitting alone in the darkened office and looked about nervously, almost expecting someone to be in the room watching him.

"Will do. Anything else?"

"Find info on drug and, if possible, funding of research and then get the hell out of there! Over."

Great! Less than four hours before the building would open up, and he had to find a needle in a haystack.

Over an hour passed. Intent as he was on searching through the diskettes in the drawer, Kurilev let his guard down. He suspected nothing until the rope was thrown around his throat and tightened.

Kurilev reflexively tried to jump out of his chair and spin around to face his assailant, but his move was anticipated. Staying behind him, his attacker pulled his thrashing body close to his own. His flailing arms finding nothing to grab onto and his consciousness beginning to fade, Kurilev lifted his leg in a frantic effort to kick back against his attacker and throw him off balance. But his attacker was prepared for that maneuver as well and kicked his supporting leg out from under him, throwing him down to the ground and forcing his neck into full flexion with the force of his knee against the back of his head. Helpless to resist, his airway and cerebral circulation completely cut off, Kurilev sank into unconsciousness. Even so, his attacker continued tightening the rope until he was absolutely certain he was dead.

Walking to the computer, the black-garbed assailant re-accessed the prior e-mail dialogue and swore. He picked up a phone and dialed. In spite of the hour, it was picked up after only two rings.

"Turgenev here, Your Excellency. I'm afraid my suspicions were correct. One of Pritsak's men broke in here and found the diskette detailing the clinical records. He's been terminated, but the data's been sent."

"It's Nikitin, that idiot. Zabrovych keeps all his information locked up safely in his home, but Nikitin must have kept one of his disks in the lab. Hopefully,

Pritsak won't put two and two together until our plans are complete. Then, we can easily dispose of him. But it looks like the cat is out of the bag."

"I'm afraid so, Your Excellency. And Pritsak was going to e-mail the information to some American operative named Lone Eagle."

Boshevsky swore. "I'll call Scorpion and tell him what happened. If the cat's out of the bag, the best thing to do is to kill the cat. Right?"

"Yes, Your Excellency."

"You did a good job, Ivan. We'll trace the e-mail later. I'll call Cherkasy and have his men dispose of the body. Good night."

"Good night, Excellency." Turgenev hung up the phone and went to work. He had a lot to do before the sun came up.

There was a tentative knock on the ornate mahogany door leading to his office, but Boshevsky waited until he had finished the page he was reading before responding. Although a good minute elapsed, the visitor didn't dare knock again. The lack of response indicated that Boshevsky was busy, and no one dared interrupt the prime minister if he was busy.

"What are you waiting for? Come in, already," he hollered impatiently, setting his reading glasses on the desk.

The door opened cautiously, and the diminutive figure of Dr. Sergei Nikitin stood in the doorway, not daring to enter the room until bidden.

"Nikitin, it's good to see you. Come in, come in. Have a seat." Boshevsky wrapped his arm around Nikitin's shoulder, half escorting and half pushing him into the office. Although offered a chair, Nikitin chose to remain standing.

There was a marked contrast between the two men. Whereas Valentyn Boshevsky had great personal power and strength, Sergei Nikitin was balding, pudgy, and weak-willed, a jellyfish of a man who had made his career by attaching himself to men of power. As a psychiatrist and researcher, his skills were mundane and limited, but he excelled as a sycophant, and, by positioning himself as a research associate to Dr. Iosyp Zabrovych, Chief of Psychiatry at the prestigious Ukrainian National Psychiatric Institute, he had maneuvered himself into the highest echelons of his specialty. He hadn't anticipated that this would lead to a close association with the prime minister. Initially a dream come true, he hadn't been prepared for the nightmare it had become.

The prime minister closed and locked the door behind them and walked around his desk to stand in front of the immense window overlooking the Dnieper River.

"And how is our research going, Sergei?" Boshevsky asked.

"Very well, Your Excellency. Our researcher in America has informed me that the final phases of the dosing regimen for UR-416 have almost been completely worked out. Your plan is nearing completion." Nikitin smiled. It was always better to give Boshevsky good news than bad about the research. Much better.

Boshevsky turned and scowled at Nikitin. "It's too bad we couldn't have pursued the last stages here. It would have made things a lot easier."

Nikitin swallowed hard. Boshevsky was dredging up his early failures. After several of his subjects had died, further research had to be moved to the United States to avoid investigation by government agencies that weren't under Boshevsky's control.

"I regret the difficulties we had with our early subjects. The combination of permixitine and UR-416 is very difficult to work with. I'm sure Dr. Zabrovych told you of the complicated pharmacokinetics between ..."

"The pharmacokinetics is not what I'm worried about right now," Boshevsky thundered. He strode around the table, grabbed Nikitin's lab coat by the lapels, and pushed his face within a few inches of Nikitin's. "What I'm worried about is the data files that you kept in your office for one of Pritsak's spies to find last night."

Beads of perspiration sprang up on Nikitin's forehead. "How could he find them? They were well hidden."

"Obviously, not well enough. Nikitin, you buffoon, if your bumbling ruins my plans, I will find the deepest spot in the Dnieper River and make certain that your feet remain eternally planted in it. Have I made myself clear?"

"Yes, Excellency, quite clear," he stammered, still pinned in Boshevsky's grasp.

"Good." Boshevsky released Nikitin's lapels and turned back to look out the window, dismissing the psychiatrist with a wave of his hand.

After Nikitin closed the door behind him, he leaned on it for support. His shirt was drenched in sweat, and his heart pounded savagely in his chest. In spite of his erratic nature, there was one thing about Boshevsky that could be counted upon. The prime minister always made good on his threats.

CHAPTER 6

▼

"Dr. Branstead, are you all right?"

Startled from sleep, Peter jerked his head up from the table in the hospital medical library where he had dozed off, his head resting on an open neurotoxicology textbook. Greg Johnson stood over him, shaking his shoulder.

"Yeah, I'm all right. Thanks, I just needed to rest my eyes." Peter squeezed his eyes shut, rubbed them with his thumb and index finger, and then shook his head.

He'd been up most of the night questioning the evening and midnight shifts of the nursing staff on the wards where the men had died. He had also gone through pharmacy records for possible drug interactions or unaccounted for drugs. He had managed to make it home just long enough to get an hour or two of sleep before waking up to shower, shave, and get dressed to go back to the hospital.

He had spent most of the morning rereading the medical records and lab work, all to no avail. There was no pattern that he could discern, no witnesses to any peculiar behavior, no common thread to implicate any particular staff member or physician. Finally, Peter had gone to the library to rummage through all the toxicology books he could find and even tried a MEDLINE search on the library computer, all leaving him just as baffled as before, and he had dozed off from exhaustion.

"Goddamn it, Greg, this business has got me stumped. I've looked at all the data until my eyes are crossed, and I still don't have any idea as to who could be responsible."

Greg sat down in the chair across the table from Peter, leaned back, and clasped his hands behind his head. "Are you sure this is something inside the hospital? I don't think we've excluded toxic exposure out on the street."

Peter stood up and paced the floor, too exhausted to sit. "You're right, we haven't. That's the next step. But I haven't been able to find anything in the books about a neurotoxin that acts like this. And the pathologist hasn't been much help, either. I went over the micro with Dave Stein slide by slide. Even the electron microscopy didn't show much—no evidence for an underlying dementing illness. Just nice, healthy, alcohol-pickled brains." Peter stopped pacing and looked at Greg. "I hate to say it, but I think it's time I called the cops, or I may be guilty of obstructing justice."

Greg stood up and patted Peter on the shoulder. "Seeing as how I've been working on this little project along with you for the last few days, I think that would be an excellent idea. Prison neurology was never a particular academic interest of mine."

Peter smiled wanly. "Don't worry; you're off the hook. But I think the sooner I get the police involved, the better. Why don't you go ahead and start rounds without me. I'll catch up later."

Leaving Greg in the library, Peter went into the neurology department office, shut the door, and spent the next ten minutes staring at the phone. Once the police were involved, he would be smack-dab at the center of an enormous public scandal, the last place he wanted to be. Finally, he took a deep breath, picked up the phone, and dialed.

The actual phone call was anticlimactic. Before he got to homicide, he had been shunted to five different departmental secretaries, each of whom put him on eternal hold. Even after getting the homicide department, he had to work his way through four levels of police bureaucracy, spelling his name out to so many functionaries that after forty-five minutes on the phone, he still hadn't spoken to a detective. He was ready to give the whole thing up.

"Meinerhoff, homicide," said a tired voice at the other end of the line.

Peter was so surprised to have reached someone in authority he almost dropped the phone. His palms moistened with the anxiety of what he was about to do.

"Yes, Officer Meinerhoff, my name is ..."

"That's Detective Meinerhoff, sir." The voice sounded as tired as Peter felt.

"Er, sorry. My name is Dr. Peter Branstead, Detective, and I ..."

"Could you spell that, sir?"

Peter rubbed his hand across his forehead. He was getting a headache.

"Branstead. B-r-a-n-s-t-e-a-d."

"Go ahead, Mr. Branstead."

"That's Dr. Branstead." Two could play this game.

"Go ahead, *Doctor* Branstead." Meinerhoff's voice was colored with more than just a subtle touch of sarcasm.

Peter summarized the deaths of the eight derelicts as succinctly as possible, leaving out much of the medical trivia that he was certain Meinerhoff wouldn't be interested in. He added his own investigations but left out his calls to Steve Bergstraum. No need to get him involved at this stage. Periodically, Meinerhoff would ask him to back up and clarify a detail or spell out a medical term, but Peter didn't mind. At least it gave him the feeling that the detective was listening.

After Peter stopped, there was a long moment of silence.

"Detective, are you still there?"

"Yeah, yeah. Don't worry, Doc, I'm reviewing my notes. So let me get this straight. You've got eight Bowery bums that wander into your hospital ..."

"They didn't wander in. They were brought in by ambulance, severely disoriented."

"Excuse me, were brought in." Meinerhoff used the same tone that he had used when he had emphasized Peter's title of "Doctor." "They were brought in confused, just like they would be with the DTs; they all had abnormal vital signs, just like they would have had with the DTs; then they each had a convulsion, just like they would have with the DTs; and then ... poof ... they died. Am I correct?"

"Correct," Peter echoed.

"Now, from what you tell me, all the tests are normal, all the lab work is normal, even the autopsy is normal. No evidence of foul play. Am I following you correctly so far, Doctor?"

"Well, yes, you are," Peter said, uneasily. He didn't like where this was leading.

"Now, with your own little ... investigation, shall we call it ... you have uncovered no murder weapon, no motive, and no suspects. Is that right, Doctor?"

"Yes, that's right, Detective, but you've missed the point. These men ..."

"Hear me out, please, for just another minute. Okay, Doctor?"

"Okay, Detective." Peter felt his jaws clench. He recognized the feeling; it was like being back in medical school and being grilled by a sadistic attending on ward rounds. And he didn't like it one bit.

"There have been no complaints from family, right? In fact, as I recall, there is no family—for any of these guys. None. Zip. Zero. Am I correct?"

"Yes, that's correct."

"So basically, Doctor Branstead, if we cut out all the medical bullshit and your paranoia, what we're really talking about here is a bunch of dead bums. Dead bums, Doctor Branstead, and nothing else. Now, if I had a buck for every time a bum died in New York City, I wouldn't have to spend this beautiful June day cooped up in a stinking office talking on the phone to some fucking smartass doctor. I'd have my ass parked on a nice, warm beach somewhere in the Caribbean with an ice-cold Margarita in one hand and a big, fat Havana cigar in the other, ogling a bunch of half naked coeds."

"Now just a God damn minute, Detective," Peter interrupted, "let me make something perfectly clear. I may not be the world's most brilliant neurologist, but I'm not some stupid schmuck, like you seem to think I am. And believe me, I'm busy enough right now that I wouldn't waste my time being given the runaround by a half dozen apathetic civil servants if I didn't think it was pretty damn important. To you, these guys might be just a bunch of dead bums, but to me they were my patients. I was entrusted with the legal and ethical responsibility for their health and well-being, and something went terribly wrong. I'm worried that somewhere, either in my hospital or out on the street, there's some psychopath on the loose who's got a hobby of murdering helpless old men, and I can't stand idly by and let that happen."

For the second time, there was a long pause at the other end of the line. This time, Peter was too preoccupied trying to control his anger to talk. When Meinerhoff did speak, his voice was surprisingly subdued.

"Listen, Doc, why don't we both start all over again. I've had a bad day, obviously you've had a bad day, and I think we're both getting pissed off at the wrong people."

Peter took a deep breath and calmed himself down as best as he could. "All right, Detective. Shall we call a truce?"

"Truce. Look, maybe I was a little abrupt, Dr. Branstead, but all I was trying to say is that I'm really short-staffed here. Everybody and their uncle likes to beat the anticrime drum, but after election day when budget time comes around, all of a sudden City Hall starts crying poverty. I've got a bunch of damn good cops here who are out on the street busting their balls all day, working double shifts for diddlysquat pay and dealing with the worst kind of scum you can imagine. I just don't have the manpower to chase down every death that someone thinks is suspicious unless I have concrete evidence that it really was a murder. I mean, what if this is some weird medical disease that hasn't been written about yet? Hey, maybe you just discovered Branstead's Disease."

"Meinerhoff, I had pretty much the same reaction when my resident pointed out the peculiarity of these deaths, so maybe I should get off my high horse. But these deaths don't fit the clinical pattern of any disease process that I'm aware of, and I'm getting worried because I don't know where this is going to stop."

Meinerhoff let out a long sigh.

"How about this? You bring me one bit of hard evidence—a murder weapon, a motive, a solid suspect, anything—and I'll look into the murder angle personally. Otherwise, my department's going to look like a bunch of idiots running all over Manhattan chasing their tails, and I'll get reamed out but good by accounting for wasting departmental man-hours. Do we have a deal?"

Peter was frustrated at having gotten nowhere, but grudgingly he could see Meinerhoff's point. "All right, it's a deal."

"Fine. And since I'm such a nice guy, I'll give you my direct number, so the next time it'll only take you fifteen minutes to get through to me. But don't spread it around. You're the only guy other than my bookie that I've given this to. Keep in touch, Doc."

So much for his concerns about obstructing justice. Peter hung up the phone not a moment too soon as he was paged stat to the emergency room. *Oh, no*, he groaned as he dialed the ER, *not another one*.

"Dr. Branstead, this is Greg Johnson."

"Please, Greg, tell me this is just an old-fashioned stroke patient."

"No way. Another bum bound for glory. But this one was found convulsing out in the field. By the time the ambulance got there, he had already arrested. He's DOA."

Christ, Peter thought, *the problem isn't in the hospital after all. This is looking bad. Very, very bad.*

Megan wrapped up her meeting with her last client and shut the door to her office. Sitting down behind her desk, she rested her head in her hands and rubbed her face to drive away the fatigue. She had wanted to talk to Peter about Frank Halleck, but he had gotten in so late last night and raced off so quickly in the morning that she hadn't had time, and it was obvious that he was too busy to visit Frank today anyhow.

She had also wanted to talk to Peter about her altercation with Dr. Albright and ask him what she should do about it, but that would have to wait for later this evening, if he got home at all tonight. Something really bad must be going on to get him this preoccupied. Peter might have been diligent, but he was not a workaholic, and he enjoyed his time off. It was strange to not see him for two days, and it made her feel anxious.

From there, her thoughts wandered to the scar-faced man. The events of the previous evening had terrified her. If the off-duty cab hadn't stopped for her, there was no telling what would have happened. But who was he, and why was he obsessed with her? He didn't look familiar to her. She never would have forgotten those eyes or the disfiguring scar. Had he been a client of hers in the past? Or had he simply seen her walking home from work one day and become smitten? She had worked with enough psychotics to have had this happen already, but never to the point of being chased down the street. She shuddered as she thought about it and continued with her paperwork.

After a few minutes, Mrs. Ivy poked her head through the door. "Everybody's gone now, and I've got to leave, Miss Hutchins. I'll lock up after myself if you wish."

"Go ahead, Mrs. Ivy. I'm going to be stuck here for a few more hours. I've managed to get myself buried alive in paperwork, and Peter's going to be home late tonight, anyhow."

"You're sure you'll be all right, Miss Hutchins? I could stay another few minutes if you wish."

"I'll be fine." Megan smiled and went back to her work.

"Oh, just a few things, Miss Hutchins. We had a lovely chocolate cake delivered for you this evening. Would you like a piece?"

Megan laughed and glanced down at her midriff. "No. Once I got started, that cake would be doomed. I'm afraid chocolate cake isn't what I really need right now. Just cut me a piece and leave it in the refrigerator, and take the rest home for you and Mr. Ivy."

"Mr. Ivy's diabetes makes chocolate cake strictly off limits for him, but I do have a special affinity for it myself. Thank you, Miss Hutchins."

"By the way, who sent it?"

"I imagine it was Mrs. Halleck, Miss Hutchins. There was a lovely card that came with it, signed 'For all you've done, H. H.'"

Megan sighed. "Harriet knows my passion for chocolate. I'll have to thank her. Anything else?"

"Oh, yes. Mrs. Halleck also called earlier this afternoon and left a message. She said her husband is getting worse and requests that you ask Dr. Branstead to see him as soon as possible. Have a good evening, Miss Hutchins."

"Good evening to you, Mrs. Ivy."

After Mrs. Ivy locked the door, Megan turned to look out the window at the darkening sky. Better call Peter and let him know she was coming home late.

After four rings the answering machine came on. Peter was obviously going to have another late night, too.

"Hi, Peter. This is Megan. I'm not going to get home until after nine o'clock tonight, so go ahead and cook dinner for yourself. I also have to ask you something about Frank Halleck when I get home. See you later. Love you."

About an hour later, Megan had just about had it. Paperwork had never been her forte, and with the advent of managed care, it had taken on a life of its own. It had become a voracious, self-perpetuating organism that devoured her time and energy and then procreated in the "In" box on her desk when she wasn't looking. It was definitely time for a break.

Megan stood up, stretched, and looked out the window. It was already dark outside, and the sodium vapor street lamps cast their amber light over West Eleventh Street, giving the buildings, cars, and trees an ethereal, unworldly quality. The bustle of rush hour had died down, the crowds and traffic were gone, and the street was totally deserted.

Except for one person.

With a shock, she saw him. Standing in an alleyway directly across the street from her office was the scar-faced man, his face shadowed by a clump of matted hair, wearing the identical tattered coat as the other two times she had seen him. As she watched, he looked straight up at her window; his jagged scar was now clearly visible in the orange-hued light of the streetlamp as his hair fell away from his face. Even from that distance she could feel, as much as see, those piercing eyes. She watched, aghast, as he raised his hand and waved.

Megan recoiled from the window and retreated to the far side of the office and anxiously paced back and forth. How long had he been there? Good God, could he have been watching her sitting at the desk working all this time?

Crouching low so she couldn't be seen from the street, she sat on the floor next to the desk and called home again. The answering machine responded once more.

"Peter, this is Megan. If you're home and can hear me, please pick up the phone. Peter, please pick up the phone. Pick up the phone, for God's sake!"

Megan pressed her fingers to her temples. This was no time to panic. She had to calm down and leave Peter a message.

"Peter, there's a strange man outside my building that I think may be stalking me. I'm afraid to leave. It's 8:45. If you come home soon, call me at the office. I need you to pick me up. Please hurry."

Megan hung up the phone and immediately dialed again.

"St. Mark's Hospital. May I help you?"

"Yes. This is Megan Hutchins. Could you please page Dr. Branstead?"

With the hospital's Muzak droning interminably in her ear, Megan bit her nails nervously and offered a silent prayer that Peter would answer his page.

"I'm sorry, Dr. Branstead isn't picking up. He must have left the hospital and turned off his beeper, because he's not answering that, either. Dr. Greg Johnson is covering the ward service. Would you like me to page him instead?"

"No, thanks." Megan hung up the phone, her spirits sinking. She had no way of contacting Peter. Knowing Peter, he had probably taken himself out to dinner or a movie after getting her first message.

Megan turned off all the lights in the office. At least she wouldn't be seen from outside the office. She slowly crept up to the window on her hands and knees and peeked over the windowsill. The alleyway across the street was empty. She cautiously looked down the street in both directions. Nobody. Opening the window, she stuck her head out just far enough to look downward to the entranceway to her office building. Nobody.

Megan could hear her pulse throbbing audibly in her ears in the silence of the office. He might be waiting for her in an alleyway, but she would have to take that chance. She couldn't imagine the terror of spending the night alone in her office, alone in the entire building with that man outside. Besides, if she could run to the end of the block, she'd be on Bleecker Street, safe in the presence of throngs of shoppers, even at this hour.

Megan gently opened the office door. She stuck her head out, looked both ways down the hallway, and breathed a sigh of relief. She was alone. She slipped out the door and raced to the elevator. As she approached it, she realized that the elevator motor had been running and was slowing noisily to a halt.

Megan looked around wildly, unsure of what to do or where to go. As she was about to run to the stairway at the end of the hallway, the elevator door slowly opened. Megan stood rooted to the spot as its occupant smiled at her, his mouth twisted by the jagged scar running along his left cheek.

"Hello, Megan. I've finally caught up with you."

Megan turned to run, but her heel caught on the carpet, and she lost her balance. Before she had time to put her arms out, her head smashed into the wall, and she fell to the floor, the darkness closing in around her.

CHAPTER 7

▼

The shower was as hot as Peter could stand it. It had been an exhausting day, and he hadn't recovered from the previous night's lack of sleep. He was reminded of how he felt after a weekend on call during his residency. Too busy to eat or sleep for two nights in a row, he would stagger back to his apartment too exhausted to figure out which he wanted to do most, eat or sleep, so he'd always showered first to clear his mind.

He let the water wash over his face and aching body for over twenty minutes, feeling his taut muscles slowly relax and his mind unwind. By the time he stepped out of the shower, the bathroom was as steamed up as a sauna. Too bad the rest of the apartment building would be washing their dinner dishes with cold water.

He had decided to surprise Megan by cooking the entire dinner and having it ready for her when she got home, driven less by love than guilt at having rushed out of the apartment that morning after Megan's altercation with Albright. As a physician, he was accustomed to dealing with some of the more pompous, self-impressed assholes of the medical profession on a more-or-less equal basis. When dealing with those in a lower position in the medical hierarchy, such as nurses or technicians, doctors like Albright could be incredibly overbearing. After her experience, Peter was certain that Megan could use a little indulging tonight.

He walked into the bedroom to get dressed and checked the flashing answering machine for the first time since arriving home, pushing the Play button as he sat down on the bed to put on his socks.

"Hi, Peter. This is Megan. I'm not going to get home until after nine o'clock tonight, so go ahead and cook dinner for yourself. I also have to ask you something about Frank Halleck when I get home. See you later. Love you."

So much for good intentions. If Megan wasn't going to be home for dinner, he might as well go to a restaurant. He was too tired to spend a lot of time cooking for himself, and when Megan worked late, she usually picked up something for herself at Balducci's anyway.

But after Peter left the apartment and locked the door behind him, he had a brainstorm. Why not surprise Megan and stop by her office with some takeout food, and perhaps some down-and-dirty sex on the waiting room couches? *Wonder what Freud would have thought about that,* Peter mused to himself as the elevator door closed loudly behind him and the antiquated freight elevator, loudly complaining all the way down with every turn of its ancient pulleys, made its way slowly to the lobby floor.

A few minutes later, Peter stepped out of a cab in front of Megan's office building. Fortunately, he had checked his watch after leaving the apartment and realized that it was practically nine o'clock already. He could think of nothing worse than arriving at the office at 9:30 with an armful of goodies to find that Megan had already left for home. Better to surprise her early, and they could go out to a restaurant together instead. And there were still those waiting room couches …

Peter bounded up the stairs to Megan's floor, taking two steps at a time. Stepping out of the stairwell, he was at first puzzled and then shocked by what he saw.

Megan was lying limply on the floor. Hunched over her, facing in Peter's direction but oblivious to his presence, was the most slovenly street person he had ever seen. His long, tangled hair obscured his face, and his grimy, oversized coat sported several gaping rips along the seams exposing long stretches of ragged lining. Shocked momentarily into paralysis, he saw that the derelict had removed Megan's jacket and was in the process of unbuttoning the top buttons of her blouse.

"Get your filthy hands off her, you son of a bitch."

Surprised by the intrusion, the derelict looked up incredulously at the onrushing figure of Peter, throwing his arms up defensively just as Peter launched himself over the prostrate body of Megan. The full momentum of his body struck the derelict at shoulder level and threw him backward as the bodies of the two men tumbled together down the hallway.

Peter was the first one up, and he grabbed the derelict by his coat lapels and pulled him up to his feet. He pummeled the man's face and chest with his fists until, somehow, the man found the energy to throw a hard right uppercut directly into Peter's stomach, just below the sternum. Peter doubled over help-lessly, the breath knocked out of him.

The derelict struggled to catch his breath. When he finally spoke, it was in a voice harsh and raspy with the effects of a three-pack-a-day cigarette habit.

"Jesus Christ, Peter, I wasn't hurting her. She knocked her head against the wall. I was only loosening her clothes to get her some air. You didn't have to try to beat the shit out of me."

Peter looked up, still gasping for breath and too bewildered to throw any more punches. "How do you know my name? And who the hell are you?"

With the edge of a grimy coat sleeve, the man wiped a thin trickle of blood from his mouth where Peter had split his lip open.

"I recognized you from pictures of you and Megan. And to answer your sec-ond question, I'm Alan Lamplin, Megan's stepbrother."

Megan had the sensation of being suspended in the middle of a thick, dark fog. She could see nothing, hear nothing, and her body didn't even feel like it was part of her. Slowly, bit by bit, the fog lifted, and the darkness of the night seemed to lighten as the haziness of her mind gradually cleared. For a moment, she thought she could hear Peter's voice calling her. What on earth was he doing out on a night like this? But the voice was getting louder and more insistent. She wished Peter would just leave her alone for a minute and let her sleep just a bit more. Instead, she felt her shoulders being shaken gently, and Peter calling her again, telling her to wake up.

Megan opened her eyes to the glare of the fluorescent lights of her office. She blinked her eyes several times before they adjusted to the flood of light, and then she saw Peter's face directly over her. Disoriented for a second or two, she strug-gled to figure out how Peter had gotten into her office and why she was lying on a couch in the waiting room, when suddenly the memories of her last few seconds of consciousness flooded back to her.

"Oh, my God, Peter. You're here! I can't believe it!" and she threw her arms around Peter, burying her face in his chest.

"Everything's all right. Just lie down and rest for …"

"It was horrible. There was a man outside the building, a man who's been stalking me. You didn't answer the phone, so I tried to leave, but then he came at me from the elevator. It was like a nightmare!" She held him close and rested her head on his shoulder; her eyes squeezed shut to blot out the memory.

"Megan, there's something I have to tell you right now."

Megan opened her eyes and looked over his shoulder, saw the scar-faced man standing on the other side of the waiting room, and screamed.

"He's in here, Peter. Right behind you."

"He's not going to hurt you. That's Alan Lamplin. That's your stepbrother, Alan."

Megan looked once more at the scar-faced man. She began feeling dizzy.

"Watch it, Pete. She's going out again."

Peter lowered Megan down to the couch and motioned to Alan to get a glass of water from the kitchenette.

"I've been talking to Alan while you've been out of it. He came to New York a few days ago looking for you. Since our home phone number isn't listed, he looked up your office address, but he wasn't sure that it was really you until he looked in your face the other day. He's been trying to talk to you, but you keep running away."

Megan slowly sipped the water Alan gave her, and looked again into his eyes. They remained intense and piercing but were softer now.

Alan gave a twisted half smile. "Hi, Meggie. Long time no see."

"Alan, why didn't you just call me at the office and tell me you were in town?" Megan asked as the three of them turned down Greenwich Avenue on their way to SoHo, Megan positioning herself between the two men.

Alan puffed nervously on the generic cigarette he held between two nicotine-stained fingers.

"I did. Several times. But your damn receptionist wouldn't interrupt while you were with a client and wouldn't take a message unless I left a phone number. I mean, look at me, Meggie. I'm a bum living out on the street. What was I supposed to say? 'If she can't reach me on my cell phone, have her leave a message on my voicemail?' Give me a break."

"Don't be ridiculous. You could have left your name, and I would have told Mrs. Ivy to patch you through the next time you called."

Alan's face turned serious. He took another puff on his cigarette and stared down at the ground as they walked. "I was afraid to leave a message. After all those years without contact, I assumed that you didn't want to have anything to do with me."

"The worst I could have said was 'Alan, why didn't you call me sooner?'"

"No. The worst you could have said was 'Why the hell are you bothering me, now that I've finally put my past behind me?' I had to speak to you face to face, so you could see me for who I am and who I've become. There was no other way."

Megan put her arm around him. "Alan, I've missed you terribly all these years. I must have written to your mother a dozen times asking how you were, where you were, but she never answered. And you know Dad. He wasn't any help at all. But how did you ever find me? And what's happened to you?"

"I hope it's a long walk to your apartment, because this is going to be a long, long story."

They were just passing by St. Mark's Hospital. "Go ahead," Peter interjected, "we've got lots of time."

Struggling with painful memories, Alan took a long, deep drag on the cigarette and exhaled slowly before he began his story.

"As Megan can tell you, without any offense taken by me, my mother was, to put it mildly, a deeply disturbed individual. After Megan's dad divorced Mom, she cut off all communication between him and Megan and me. Frankly, if it hadn't been for the alimony checks, she probably would have left without a forwarding address. She got married twice more, each time to an asshole that would routinely beat the shit out of both of us whenever he got drunk, which was usually pretty often. After Asshole Number Two, she finally learned her lesson and didn't remarry, but by that time I was already in my late teens and living away from home most of the time. When I did come home, she would get drunk herself and try to beat me up anyway, but by that time I could hold my own, so she generally left me alone.

"After a few years of living out on the streets, I became a drifter and a fighter, as you can tell from these souvenirs," and he pointed to his disjointed nose and the long jagged scar across his left cheek. "I'd get into a fight, go to jail, move to the next town, get into another fight, and the whole scenario would be repeated over and over.

"After a while, my rap sheet got pretty long, and one judge decided that I needed to spend some time in a psych hospital. That marked a turning point of sorts in my life. Although at first it really pissed me off to be in there, eventually I realized it was a lot better than jail. At least on the psycho wards, the really crazy guys are usually locked away instead of running the place, and nobody's trying to sneak up behind you to cornhole you in the shower."

Megan reddened, but Alan missed this in the dim lighting of Washington Square Park. He lit another cigarette with the dying ember of his first and continued.

"It was like being R. P. McMurphy, only I knew better than to rock the boat. Nobody bothered you as long as you behaved yourself. Once in a while, the shrinks would see you for a few minutes for a med check, sometimes not even that long if they had a private practice to run off to. As far as I was concerned, the big problem was the pills. The fun stuff—y'know, Valium, Ativan, Ritalin—that was okay. And even some of the not-so-fun stuff, like Elavil and Prozac, wasn't so bad. But, man, the tranquilizers were murder. Made you feel like a walking pile of shit all the time, stumbling around like a zombie. After a while, I learned the trick of tucking the pills in the back of my mouth until after the nurses checked me out. When they left, I could spit 'em out and decide which I wanted. I got pretty good at identifying them, even the generics."

"Didn't anyone suspect that you were just there for a free ride?" Megan asked.

"Sure. The first few hospitals only kept me for a week or so ..."

"The first few?"

"Well, at first the shrinks would catch on fairly quickly, and they'd give me the boot. But after living around a bunch of loonies for a while, it's not so hard to pick up a few of their habits, speech patterns. You know what I mean."

"You mean you'd fake psychiatric illness just to stay in the hospital?"

"Sure. What would you like me to show you: Mania? Psychosis? Dementia? Pick a diagnosis at random from the DSM-IV. How about something neurological? I can fake a pretty good Parkinson's shuffle. That way, the staff thinks I've been taking my Haldol instead of spitting it into the toilet."

As they crossed Bleecker Street, Alan suddenly slowed his walking down to a deliberate shuffle, hunching his shoulders, and putting on the unblinking, expressionless face and even the classic tremor of Parkinson's disease. *Damn good job*, Peter thought.

After a few seconds, Alan broke into a grin and resumed his pace. "But you couldn't keep that up for very long. Sooner or later someone would catch onto you, wouldn't they?"

Peter was intrigued. He had seen a few cases of Munchausen's Syndrome, a psychiatric disorder where a patient who craved attention would invent a symptom complex to fool the physicians, but he had never seen one who actually bragged about it.

"Yeah, sooner or later one of the more experienced nurses might get suspicious. But if the shrink was right out of his residency training, too busy thinking about the Dow Jones, or thought he knew it all and didn't listen to the nurses, I'd usually get away with it for a while. At least until I could make a recovery and get an honorable discharge. The trick was to get out before the shrink caught on, 'cause if I was ever labeled as a Munchausen's, it'd screw me for any further admissions, at least to that hospital."

Megan laughed, threw her arms around Alan's neck and kissed him on the cheek. "I just wish I could have seen the look on those psychiatrist's faces when they found out they had been duped."

She imagined Dr. Albright's humiliation at being hoodwinked and was savoring the fantasy. Peter looked on with a twinge of jealousy as the three walked down Thompson Street toward Houston Street.

"Wouldn't it have been easier to get a job?" Peter asked.

"I tried. Several times. Sooner or later, the boss would do something to piss me off, and I'd tell him to go fuck himself and get myself fired. I just can't kiss ass, Pete. That's why I'd always end up on the street. Feels like home to me, by now."

Megan interrupted. "You still haven't told me how you hunted me down." She took her arms from around Alan's neck only long enough to link it through his arm and give his biceps a quick squeeze.

"A few months ago, Mom died. I wasn't home at the time, but as near as I could tell from the doctors, she had hopelessly pickled her liver." He waved his hand at the sympathetic looks on Megan and Peter's faces. "Don't worry about it. There was no love lost between Mom and me. I just wish we'd had a chance to patch up some of our differences before she died." His voice trailed off for a moment before he shook his head and continued.

"At any rate, I was going through her stuff and I came across a shoebox full of letters, most of them from Meggie. The old witch had been saving them all those years, but she'd never told me about them. I guess she was afraid I'd up and leave, which I probably would have, not that my filial instincts were all that great anyway.

"I must have read those letters a hundred times each, practically memorized them. She kept all the pictures you sent her, too. That's how I recognized Peter when he slugged me. But she had thrown away all the envelopes, so I didn't know your address. I had to track you down from your business listing in the Yellow Pages and wait outside your office. It took me a while to make sure it was really you, particularly since you kept running away from me."

The "Don't Walk" sign was flashing as they reached Houston Street, and Alan grabbed Megan's hand as the three sprinted across the street.

"So there you have it: 'A Portrait of the Sociopath as a Young Man,'" Alan finished as they caught their breath. "What's happening with you guys?"

Megan gave a brief synopsis of how she and Peter had met, Peter's practice, and their relationship. Then, she described her practice in some detail, ending with yesterday's altercation with Dr. William Albright.

"Alan, have you ever had to deal with a psychiatrist as arrogant as that?"

"I know the type. I've locked horns with a couple of shrinks like that before. Not much you can do about 'em, so I'd just brush 'em off. You know, fuck 'em if they can't take a joke. Pete, what've you been up to lately?"

Peter told Alan about the series of derelicts admitted to his hospital and the mysterious circumstances of their deaths, ending with his discussion with Detective Meinerhoff. Alan listened intently, asking questions about specifics, including details of the vagrants' behavior. He became defensive when Peter warned him that there might be tainted moonshine in the area.

"Nah, you got me all wrong, Pete. I know you won't believe this from looking at me, but I was never much of a drinker, and since Mom died I haven't touched a drop. I'm pretty sure I've seen some of these guys, though. The word on the street is that they checked in to East Side Psychiatric for detox, and somehow, their brains got turned into oatmeal while they were there."

"Albright!" was Peter and Megan's simultaneous reaction.

Alan lit his third cigarette. "Hold your horses, guys. Let's think about this for a minute. What if Peter goes to homicide and tells them that some Bowery bum with a rap sheet a mile long and a psych history of epic proportions told him there was human experimentation going on at a prestigious private psychiatric clinic on the Lower East Side. Do you really think they're going to believe it?"

Megan sighed. "Alan's right. We still don't have a shred of credible evidence."

Peter nodded in agreement, but he finally had a lead. It was imperative that he saw Frank Halleck tomorrow.

By this time, they had finally arrived at their apartment building. They all stood around self-consciously, momentarily silent.

Alan broke the silence. "Well, Meggie, it was great seeing you again after all these years. We'll have to get together again soon ... uh, the three of us, that is," he said with a quick apologetic glance at Peter.

Megan excitedly turned to Peter. "Let's have Alan stay with us. He could sleep on the sofa in the living room." She then turned back to Alan. "It's not the most comfortable couch, but it's sure better than a flophouse." Megan wrinkled her nose. "You could at least come in and clean up. Peter could lend you some of his clothes until we can buy you your own. Isn't that right, Peter?"

Peter hesitated for just a moment. But hesitate he did.

"That would be great. Stay with us, Alan. It wouldn't be any trouble at all."

Alan looked straight into Peter's eyes, with the same look that had been so disconcerting to Megan two nights previously. Peter felt distinctly uncomfortable under the intensity of Alan's gaze.

After several seconds, Alan dropped his cigarette and looked down as he crushed it out. "Thanks, Meggie, but I really have some things I have to do. I've got to spread the word on the street about East Side Psych. And besides," he turned to Peter, "I might be able to get some information that would nail Albright."

Megan was obviously disappointed, but she gave Alan a big hug. "Okay, Little Brother, but take care of yourself. We still have a date to get together and talk."

"Sure thing. Listen, thanks for everything, Pete. Everything but the broken jaw, that is."

Peter smiled apologetically. "Sorry. But stop by again soon. We'd be glad to have you over for dinner. Or a shower. How long are you going to be in town?"

"Don't know, but I'll be in touch in a few days. See ya later, Big Sister," and they hugged again before Alan departed, his hands tucked into the pockets of his ragged overcoat.

"It was so incredible seeing Alan after so many years. I thought I had lost him forever. He's a real survivor."

"I'm just glad he's not a patient of mine," Peter said acidly as he pulled off his socks. "I'll bet he's a real handful if he gets pissed off."

"Well, I'm sure he's become a sociopath after the life he's lived. He even admitted to it. You get trained in dealing with that kind of behavior as a clinical psychologist. All I can say is that he was very nice to us, particularly since you almost punched his lights out."

"I might remind you that I 'almost punched his lights out' because I thought he was about to rape you. And I would think that, as a trained clinical psychologist, you would realize that guy was manipulating the hell out of you." Peter's tone picked up as he threw his shirt down on the bed.

"He's not a 'guy,' he's my brother. And I haven't just met him an hour or two ago; I've known him since I was a child. I haven't seen him for twenty years and, believe it or not, I've missed him a lot during that time. I'm very excited to have him come back into my life. What's wrong with that?"

"I'll tell you what's wrong. I'm not too enthralled about being pushed out of your life while you're welcoming him back in."

Megan flushed brilliantly. "I can't believe it. You're jealous. Of my own brother! Well, let me tell you something, Dr. Branstead. You're absolutely right. I do have a special place in my heart for Alan, because for most my childhood he was all I had when my father would leave us alone with Alan's psychotic mother while he went traipsing all over the East Coast. You have no idea what it's like to be a child with only one person in the whole world you could count on for support, one person who understood what I was going through because he was going through the same hell as I was. I can't count the number of times Alan and I fell asleep together in the same bed because we were too afraid to sleep separately, with his mother staggering through the house on a drunk, screaming at the top of her lungs. Or all the times that she left us completely alone all night while she shacked up with some stranger on the other side of town. Alan and I are veterans of the same war, Peter, but I was lucky. The war ended for me when Alan's mother left. It never ended for him, and he had to learn to deal with it as best as he could."

"Well, the least you could do is try to keep your hands off of him."

"How dare you say something like that! And if I seemed to have my hands on Alan, as you so elegantly put it, it was only because for the first time in three years I could be with a man that let me get emotionally close!"

Megan stopped and threw her hands up to her mouth as if somehow she could stop the words from coming out, but it was too late. The words hit Peter like a slap across the face.

"I'm sorry you feel that way," Peter stammered. "I thought you understood. I thought it didn't make a difference to you, but I guess I was mistaken," and he turned to leave the bedroom.

"Peter, I'm sorry. I didn't mean to ..."

But Peter had already slammed the door behind him.

CHAPTER 8

▼

If nothing in life was certain except for death and taxes, the weekly Branstead-Falconer racquetball game placed a close third. For the past five years, Peter and Daniel had had their weekly slot scheduled at the Village Racquet Club, and they had kept to it as faithfully as humanly possible. Although Daniel's periodic trips abroad necessarily led to occasional postponements, these were usually made up promptly on his return, and Daniel generally timed his briefer trips so that he left the day after and returned a day or two before their appointed game time.

Unfortunately for Peter, in fourth place on the Inevitability Top Ten was the likelihood of Daniel winning. Not that Peter was a poor player—he had been one of the best in both his college and medical school classes. The problem was that for Peter, racquetball was exercise and an opportunity to socialize outside of the hospital. For Daniel, racquetball was a socially acceptable means of sublimating aggression. Daniel's style was hard playing and strategy-driven. Even though the scores were usually close, and occasionally Peter might get away with a two- or three-point win, the series overwhelmingly favored Daniel. Fortunately, Daniel was restrained in his post-game commentary, and the scores of the games were never leaked past the four walls of the racquetball court.

Today, Peter got up early and left the apartment quietly before Megan had awakened. There had been plenty of time for him to think in the middle of the night, when worries and anxieties always pushed their way to the forefront of consciousness, unhindered in the darkness and silence by any of the distractions and preoccupations that diverted the mind during the day. Megan's reactions to Alan had forced Peter to take an analytical look at their relationship for the first time in three years. Even after living together for over a year, the two maintained an impervious emotional wall that neither seemed capable, or at times even desirous, of breaking through. To Peter, the relationship had reached a crossroads, and he had to either fish or cut bait and leave.

Peter changed slowly in the locker room, his thoughts still fixated on Megan. By the time he got to the court, Daniel had already been warming up for several minutes.

"Running a bit late today? I'm already warmed up. Go ahead and take some shots." Daniel casually hit the ball towards Peter.

The ball sped right by him and bounced off the back wall.

"Whoa! Focus, man. Or you're going to be in big trouble."

"Yeah, I know." Peter's voice was flat, reflecting his exhaustion. "Go ahead and start. I don't need to warm up."

"Don't need a warm-up is right. You look like you need a cold shower and a pot of coffee. Are you sure you want to play?"

"Just shut up and serve, okay."

"All right, all right. Jeez, touchy today."

Daniel served, a bit more gently than usual, and the ball dropped into center court, where Peter lined up his shot and slammed it into the left-hand corner. The ball shot down the left-hand wall, where Daniel couldn't turn around fast enough to hit it, and it got by him.

"Don't be condescending. Just play, damn it." Peter picked up the ball to serve.

Daniel opened his mouth to say something but thought better of it and silently took his position in backcourt.

Peter stood on the left-hand side of the service zone and bounced the ball a few times, following it closely with his eyes and trying to concentrate on the game and put the previous night out of his mind. He bounced the ball one more time and slammed it into the right-hand corner.

The ball caromed off the right side wall in what should have been a perfect cross-court serve, but Peter stumbled clumsily in the service zone, directly into the path of the speeding ball.

Daniel served perfectly into backcourt. Peter took it off the back wall with a backhand ceiling shot that forced Daniel to run to the back wall to hit it. In sole possession of center court when the ball came off the front wall, Peter smashed it into the corner in a low kill shot that Daniel couldn't possibly get to in time.

"Good shot. Your …"

But Daniel didn't finish his sentence before Peter hit his own ball before it had time to take a second bounce, slamming it against the front wall so hard that it sped all the way to the back wall.

Pushing Daniel out of his way, Peter raced back and smashed the ball again as it bounced off the back wall. The ball shot by Daniel's head, so close that he had to duck to keep from being hit.

"Hey, I thought you didn't want any practice ..."

Peter ran forward and, with a grunt of effort, hit the ball with a forehand smash into the left-hand corner.

"Pete, if you want a warm-up ..."

Peter wasn't listening. Before the ball had a chance to bounce, he hit it again with a low volley shot from center court, hard enough that it rebounded over his head into backcourt.

Daniel silently backed up against the side wall and watched as Peter continued his solo game, unmindful of his presence. He raced frenetically, from front to back, side to side; sometimes he would plunge directly into the wall as he sped across court to make the shot and then push himself off to sprint back to the other side of the court. Each swing was accompanied by a loud grunt of effort and followed by a sharp intake of air.

This was no longer a game to Peter. He was working out some deep, pent-up rage ... against whom Daniel had no idea, but there was nothing he could do but watch until it finished playing itself out. And at the rate Peter was going, it had to play itself out soon.

With one final swing, Peter slammed the ball low into the front wall, a perfect kill shot. There was no way that he could get to the ball in time from where he stood, but Peter bellowed out a yell and burst forward in a frenzied attempt, regardless. The ball bounced just below Peter's outstretched racquet as his momentum carried him, full force and left shoulder first, directly into the front wall with an echoing boom. When that subsided, the only noise on the court was the light tapping sound of the rubber ball bouncing its way into the back court before bumping into the back wall and rolling to a stop in the back corner.

"What the hell is the matter with you?"

Peter leaned against the front wall of the racquetball court, the back of his head resting on the wall as he strained to catch his breath after his maniacal exertion. He didn't say a word, didn't move for a long moment, and then wiped his forehead with a shirtsleeve already soaked in sweat.

"I've been running on fumes for the last two days. It feels like the entire world's supply of shit has been aimed at my particular fan." Peter slid down the wall until he was sitting on the floor, his head still pressed back against the wall. He closed his eyes and didn't say another word.

Daniel broke the silence. "Screw the game. Let's go out for coffee. We both could use a good dose of caffeine."

An hour later, they were seated around a small, marble-topped pedestal table in the back of the Cafe Reggio on MacDougal Street, Peter cradling his second cup of coffee in his hands. Although the warm June sun beckoned them outside to catch the breezes wafting southward from Washington Square, they sought the privacy of the Reggio's dark, atmospheric interior.

The decor inside the Reggio was one of meticulously designed chaos. The walls were covered with a mélange of etchings, Greek Orthodox icons, imitation Rembrandts and Caravaggios, and cheap plaster busts of writers and composers, all interspersed by exposed water pipes painted the same dull, dingy brown as the walls and the sagging tin ceiling. The seats were either wire-framed chairs, their hard wooden seats padded just enough to make them tolerable, or battered pews salvaged from long-defunct churches and stuck against the wall. Cafe Reggio had managed to survive the intense competition from other Village coffeehouses only by catering to the most undiscriminating of customers.

"Megan's long lost stepbrother showed up last night under rather peculiar circumstances," Peter began.

"I didn't know she had a stepbrother. I've never heard her talk about any family at all except her father, and she doesn't even talk much about him."

"Yeah, well she never told me much about her stepbrother either, so don't feel too bad. At any rate, this guy's been knocking around psychiatric hospitals on the east coast for the last five or ten years pretending to be nuts for room and board and now he …"

"What did you say?"

"He fakes psychiatric illness so he can stay in mental hospitals. He's got Munchausen's Syndrome."

Daniel burst out laughing. "I don't believe it. You're telling me that Megan's stepbrother is a professional psycho?"

"Well, yes. I guess you could say that."

Daniel chuckled and shook his head in disbelief. "Boy, I'd love to be able to put that on my résumé."

"Dan, cut it. I'm trying to be serious."

"Serious about what? How could you possibly be serious about someone who's made a career out of finagling his way into nuthouses! This guy's got a real talent.

The movie industry pays actors a fortune to do what he does every day just to survive. And haven't you ever met some obnoxious prick that you would love to see being made a patsy for once? I work with a whole university full of self-impressed experts on one thing or another, and you get pretty damn sick and tired of seeing them looking down their noses at you. I wish I had someone like this ... this ... what's his name?"

"Alan. Alan Lamplin." Peter's voice was sullen.

"This Alan guy to con these jerks just once. I'd really like to meet him someday."

"Great, just great," Peter exploded. "Whose side are you on, anyway?"

"What the hell are you talking about? Who's taking sides?"

Peter took a long draught from his cup. "Megan's gushing over this guy. She thinks he's the greatest thing to come into her life since ... well, since before I did, at any rate."

"Jesus Christ, this is her brother. She hasn't seen him since she was a kid. How do you expect her to react? For God's sake, don't make this into a battle for Megan's affection. That puts her in a position of having to choose between the two of you. Sibling affection is totally different from amorous love, and the two can coexist quite nicely. You're an only kid, so you don't understand that."

"I don't know. The way she acted with Alan ... it just made me think there were aspects of our relationship that have made Megan very unhappy."

"That's a crock. In all the times I've seen you and Megan together, I've never once seen her unhappy. Did you two have a fight last night?"

"Yeah, a big one, I guess."

Daniel smiled broadly, reached over the table and offered Peter his hand.

"Congratulations, pal, your first lover's spat. And may you have many, many more over the years, because that's what will keep you two together."

"Thanks a lot, Chum," Peter said glumly as he shook Daniel's hand. "We thank you for your support."

"Stop feeling sorry for yourself, Schmuck. Megan's a great gal, and she's crazy about you. Just relax and talk things out. You know what your problem has been? You guys have been too happy."

"What's that supposed to mean?"

"There's nothing that cements a relationship like two people going through a crisis together. You've heard of couples that get divorced after twenty years of marriage, stay apart for five years, and then remarry, haven't you? You think they do that because there's no one else out there? Bullshit! And what about the army vets with their cockamamie reunions. It's all the same thing. When people have been through a war together, their relationship takes on new meaning. Look, when life runs smoothly, it doesn't make a difference who you share your bed with. It's when the going gets tough that you really find out who you can rely on, who's going to be there when the shit starts to fly. That's when commitment becomes important, when emotional bonds are made. I can promise you that from personal experience. And that's why Megan's relationship with Alan is so important to her."

Peter said nothing, but he stared down into his coffee and stirred it aimlessly.

"I tell you what. When I come back from Ukraine, why don't you, Alan, and I go out for beers? Guy's night out!"

"What do you mean, when you get back from Ukraine? I thought you weren't planning on going back there for a while."

"Sorry, I must have forgotten to tell you. Something very important has come up, and I've got to leave for Kiev tomorrow morning, but I probably won't be there more than a few days. Not to worry, I'll be back for our game next week."

This struck Peter as rather odd. Daniel's trips were usually planned weeks or even months in advance. Just three days ago, Daniel mentioned he had no plans to go overseas.

"Must be pretty urgent."

"Yeah. Some foreign policy issues have come up, and I have to go over there in an advisory capacity with the State Department. Some heavy stuff going on, but I can't tell you anything more. Sorry."

Peter shrugged. "No sweat. I've got problems of my own at work." He was happy to shift the conversation away from him and Megan.

"What's up?" Daniel bit into a cannoli and washed it down with a sip of coffee.

"The craziest thing. In the last month or so, there have been a slew of old rummies admitted to St. Mark's, demented as hell, and while they're in the hospital they deteriorate, have convulsions, and die. Makes no sense at all."

"That's odd. Is there some epidemic going around the Bowery?"

Peter summarized his investigations within the hospital, including his conversations with the neurotoxicologist, his run-in with Detective Meinerhoff, and the clues he'd gotten from Alan regarding Dr. Albright and the East Side Psychiatric Center.

"Do you know anything about this Albright character?"

"Only that he had a knock-down drag-out fight with Megan regarding one of her clients, whom he's hospitalized in his clinic under questionable ethics, considering he's the guy's employer. I'm going over to East Side Psych to visit him this afternoon. Hopefully, we can have a civil interaction."

"I'd be very, very careful around this guy. I wouldn't tell him about your investigations, and I certainly wouldn't tell him of your relationship with Megan."

"Come on, Dan. This guy's an academic psychiatrist. The worst he can do is call me a schizoaffective personality disorder with underlying hostile developmental traits and charge me two hundred bucks for the visit. I'm not a moron. I'll be playing my cards close to the vest."

"I'd still be careful. He sounds serious about his threats. Make sure your ducks are all in a row before you go back to the police on this one or you could end up in big, big trouble. Do you have any idea how he's doing this?"

"Not a clue. I'm hoping my neurotoxicologist friend can help. There's going to be a neurology grand rounds at St. Mark's tomorrow on Alzheimer's disease, and I'm going to try to pick up some pointers."

Daniel glanced at his watch as he stood up to leave. "Gotta go. Lots to do before I leave tomorrow. But I'd really like to know what you find out. Just tell Rachel. She'll know how to get in touch with me."

Peter stood up, and the two shook hands.

"Listen, Pete, don't do anything with Megan that you'll regret later. Take some quiet time, sit down, and thrash things out between the two of you. She's worth it. She's worth anything. And don't you ever forget it."

Daniel turned and left, leaving Peter alone to nurse the remains of his coffee.

Megan pushed the elevator button for the third floor and shivered slightly as the door clanged shut and the elevator rose noisily. The elevator ride brought back reminiscences of the previous evening—the initially frightening encounter with Alan, the bittersweet reunion, and the fight with Peter. It had been a terrible night, and several times she had almost awakened Peter to talk, but she'd stopped herself when she'd remembered how exhausted he must be. And when her alarm had gone off that morning, Peter had already left for his racquetball game. She would just have to wait for that evening.

The elevator arrived at the third floor, and Megan walked to her office and grabbed the doorknob. But the door was locked.

A locked office door would generally not be a subject of consternation, but in all the years she had been working at this office, the door had never been locked when she arrived in the mornings, for the simple reason that Master Sergeant Ivy, punctual to a fault, always arrived early to open up the office. Finding the door locked was a singular enough occurrence that Megan checked the front of the door to make certain that she was really at West Village Counselors and then rechecked her wristwatch to make sure she hadn't set her alarm wrong and arrived an hour or two early.

Megan rummaged around in her purse for the office key and unlocked the door. The waiting room still showed the signs of last night's drama; a cushion was still pushed up against an arm of the sofa where Peter had laid Megan down, and the half-empty glass of water remained on the end table.

"Mrs. Ivy, are you here?"

No answer.

She walked cautiously and somewhat nervously through the office, still somewhat unnerved by her experiences the night before, opening up the doors to the individual offices and calling Mrs. Ivy's name into each room.

Still no answer.

"Megan, is that you?" said a woman's voice from the waiting room.

"It's me. I'm in my office," Megan called out. She recognized the voice of Susan Weinberg, one of her coworkers.

"What happened to Mrs. Ivy?" Sue dropped her attaché case on the floor and sat down on the couch.

"Haven't the foggiest. I figured she was doing something in the back somewhere and had locked the front door for security, but she's not anywhere."

"She's not on vacation, is she?" Sue asked.

"Mrs. Ivy? Vacation? Get real! I can't remember the last time she took a vacation. And I can't believe she'd take off sick without telling someone."

At that moment, the phone rang. The call wasn't coming in on the regular line; that was still on answering service. It was the unlisted line. Megan answered the phone.

"West Village Counselors, Miss Hutchins speaking."

"Megan, this is Walter Ivy."

"Walter, good to hear from you. Sue and I just got into the office and were wondering what happened to Mrs. Ivy. Is she all right?"

"Not really. I've been up all night with Amanda, and I'm taking her to the doctor's, so she won't be in today."

"What's wrong, Walter? Why are you taking her to the doctor?" She glanced up at Sue, alarmed.

"Amanda was acting very bizarre last night. Every fifteen minutes she'd get out of bed and wander around the apartment, turning on all the lights, turning on the kitchen stove, letting the water run in the bathtub. When I asked her what she was doing, she would repeat over and over that it was time to go to work, time to go to work. At three o'clock in the morning! I had to follow her around all night. I was afraid she was going to burn the apartment down. And if I didn't show her the way back to the bedroom, she'd walk into the clothes closet instead. She's never acted crazy like this before."

"Walter, listen to me. You don't live too far from St. Mark's Hospital, do you?"

"It's not the closest one, but I could get there pretty quick if I had to."

"Good. Take Amanda in a cab down to St. Mark's, go to the emergency room, and have Peter paged. He'll know what to do with her. I'll give him a heads up that you're coming."

"Thanks, Megan."

Megan hung up the phone and collapsed in her chair. She couldn't handle this any more. She was too stressed out to have to deal with clients today.

"Sue, could you do me a big favor?"

"Sure. What do you need?"

Megan smiled wearily. "What I need is a two-week, all-expense-paid trip to Cozumel, but I'll settle for having you call my clients for today and canceling all my appointments."

"Whatever you say. Taking the day off?"

"Yeah. Things are getting too complicated for me right now. I don't think I can deal with other people's problems. I've got enough of my own."

"Anything you want to talk about?"

Megan shook her head slowly and waved her off. "Sue, you don't even want to go there." Opening her eyes, she laboriously pushed herself up from the chair and trudged into her office, picked up the phone and called St. Mark's.

"Dr. Peter Branstead, please. This is Megan Hutchins."

She drummed her nails nervously on the desktop, the hospital Muzak droning in her ear while she tried to compose a conversation in her mind.

Hi, Peter. I hope you didn't take my comments personally last night.

No way.

Good morning, Peter. Anything you want to talk about?

No damn way.

Hi, honey. I'm sorry about what I said last night, but you were acting like a real asshole.

The latter was succinct and accurate, but not conducive to an ongoing, long-term relationship.

"Dr. Branstead speaking."

Megan snapped out of it, surprised at his officious tone. "Peter, it's me, Megan."

"Sorry, Hon. The operator didn't tell me who was holding the line. What's up?"

"I just wanted to talk a bit about last night. I'm really sorry I said what I did but ..."

"Megan," Peter whispered emphatically, "I can't talk about that right now. I've got all the med students standing around. Can we please talk about it later?"

"Oh, sure." She felt like an idiot. Of course, he'd be on rounds at this time. She blushed, glad that Peter couldn't see her embarrassment over the phone. "But don't hang up. Something terrible has happened. Mrs. Ivy didn't show up for work today, and her husband called just a few minutes ago. She became confused last night, just like Frank Halleck."

"What's her connection to all of this? She doesn't have anything to do with Albright, does she?"

"No. It doesn't make any sense at all. Maybe we're wrong about Albright after all. Maybe this is just some sort of weird disease that's going around, and it has nothing at all to do with him."

There was a long moment of silence at the other end of the line. "I don't know. I can't figure this out right now. What's Walter going to do with Amanda?"

"That's the reason I called. I told him to bring her right over to St. Mark's emergency room. The ER should be paging you when they arrive."

"Thanks. I'll see you tonight, and we can talk things over then, okay?"

"Okay. See you tonight," she said apprehensively.

"One last thing. I love you. Madly."

Megan smiled. "And I love you, too. Later."

Megan sat back in her chair, closed her eyes, and took in a deep breath, then exhaled slowly. The last twelve hours had left her emotionally spent. On an impulse, she got up from the chair, walked to the window, and looked out at the street. She sighed downheartedly. No Alan in sight. She felt guilty about wishing for Alan rather than Peter, but she so needed someone to hug that her heart ached.

Megan shook her head angrily for having allowed herself the luxury of self-pity. She felt she needed comforting right now. But how?

Chocolate cake.

Megan brightened. Chocolate will get you through times of no therapy better than therapy will get you through times of no chocolate. No better time to test the hypothesis than now.

Megan took the remainder of Harriet's chocolate cake from the refrigerator, sat down at a table, and slowly cut off a piece with her fork, watching approvingly as the chocolate icing drooped slightly over the tines. She lightly touched the cake with her fingertip, and it bounced back slowly. Wonderful! She put the fork into her mouth and slowly and deliberately withdrew the fork through tightly sealed lips. Closing her eyes, she rolled the cake gently around in her mouth with her tongue, savoring the texture of the cake and the sweetness of the icing. Definitely homemade. Bless your heart, Harriet Halleck.

Megan was a certified chocoholic. As a child, she would keep jars of chocolate syrup hidden around the house in cupboards, under the sink, and under her bed so that if her stepmother found one jar and threw it away, she would still have her stash of others to rely on. Even as an adult, chocolate had been the one vice that she found impossible to completely give up, so she carefully rationed herself. But if there was ever a time for a splurge, brother, this was it.

Megan cut off another piece with her fork, eyeing it with the same anticipation as she had the first piece, and put it in her mouth. She closed her eyes and leaned back in the chair to savor it better and felt her anxieties melt away like a Dove bar on the steaming asphalt of a hot summer day. Everything was going to work out fine. It had to.

CHAPTER 9

▼

Although the boundary between SoHo and Greenwich Village is as distinct as West Houston Street, the West Village and the East Village blend imperceptibly with one another. However, the two communities retain striking differences. The West Village, historic residence to a myriad of literary, artistic, and intellectual luminaries, maintains a haughty air of lofty superiority to its surrounding neighborhoods, whereas the East Village remains firmly grounded in the gritty, earthy reality of underclass life. Unlike its trendy, upscale neighbor, much of the East Village neighborhoods have been left to the entropy of urban decomposition. Little Ukraine is an exception.

The Ukrainians had settled in this corner of the East Village in the early part of the twentieth century, and they maintained Little Ukraine as a well-kept island of stability even as other ethnic enclaves of Manhattan succumbed to the shifting patterns of postwar immigration. Its shops were cluttered with shelves of Cyrillic books and newspapers; clothes racks of traditional, cross-stitched peasant blouses; and glass cases full of hand-painted, wooden Ukrainian Easter eggs. Distant echoes of the long-defunct Yiddish theater that had once thrived along the adjacent stretch of Second Avenue remained in the small neighborhood restaurants that still served *kasha varnishkes*, potato pancakes, and pirogies. And, just as the ancient cathedrals of Kiev defined and unified the city that surrounded them, the Ukrainian Catholic Church, with mosaics reminiscent of those in the great eastern churches, defined the core of Little Ukraine.

The racket of Second Avenue mercantile traffic faded behind him as Peter walked down East Seventh Street. Devoid of trees to provide respite from the sun's harsh glare or break up the visual monotony of the row of dingy gray, unadorned, four-story apartment buildings, the north side of East Seventh Street was stark and uninviting. However, on the south side, standing out in vivid contrast, stood the East Side Psychiatric Center. Four adjoining brownstones had been gutted and interconnected on the inside. The outside had been refinished in salmon-colored brick, and the concrete window casings had been steam-cleaned of the accumulated grime of a century's exposure to pollution. A long set of bull-nosed concrete steps led up to an elegantly paneled mahogany door, adorned by a gleaming brass plaque announcing simply

East Side Psychiatric Center
Est. 1995

Translucent panes of shatterproof glass threaded with thin and almost invisible safety wires that provided complete privacy from curious onlookers and just as securely restricted egress by the patients had replaced the windows.

Peter walked up the steps and pushed the call button under a security speaker.

"East Side Psychiatric Center. May I help you?" answered a young woman's voice.

"I'm Dr. Peter Branstead. I have an appointment to see Dr. Albright regarding a patient, Mr. Frank Halleck."

After a brief delay, the voice returned. "Come in, Dr. Branstead. Your appointment has been confirmed."

Peter pushed on the heavy, oaken door as a buzzer sounded, making note of its weight and solidity, and stepped into the reception area. The door closed slowly behind him, locking with a loud click.

The reception area astonished Peter. It was surprisingly large, having been formed by connecting the first floors of all four brownstones. The walls were lined with ornate ceiling-length mirrors alternating with richly textured brocade wall dressing. Unexpectedly lofty, the ceiling was graced with a small, central vaulted dome, from the apex of which hung a crystal chandelier that, in company with a series of brass sconces set alongside the mirrors, supplied abundant lighting for the windowless room. The overall effect was of a salon of European aristocracy.

"Good day, Dr. Branstead."

Brought back to contemporary America, Peter first noticed the receptionist seated behind the large desk in front of him. She was a pretty girl in her early twenties, professionally attired in a navy blue suit and a light, cream-colored blouse. Her auburn hair was drawn back tightly into a bun, but the severe effect was softened by midlength bangs set over her forehead.

"Dr. Albright is busy at the moment, Dr. Branstead, but he said he would be down to meet you in a few minutes. Please have a seat and make yourself comfortable. May I get you a cup of coffee or tea?"

Peter declined. He recognized traces of an underlying Slavic accent, presumably Ukrainian. Accustomed to the brusqueness of the typical Manhattan receptionist, he was surprised by her amiability.

Spaced around the room were several antique armchairs with hand-carved mahogany armrests and upholstered with intricately patterned tapestry of late Baroque vintage. Peter looked about expectantly, anticipating a sign admonishing "Please do not sit on the chairs," and remained standing.

The receptionist noted his distress. "Feel free to sit down, Dr. Branstead. This isn't a museum."

"Thank you, Miss ... Rushyk," he said, glancing at the nameplate on her desk. "It's hard to believe that a psychiatrist could make enough money to outfit a clinic like this, particularly in these days of managed care and especially in this neighborhood. These chairs alone must have cost a fortune."

"Dr. Albright is very highly regarded in his field at an international as well as a national level, Dr. Branstead. He attracts a wealthy clientele from around the world, and many of our patients have shown their gratitude by making very substantial financial contributions through our charitable support foundations, particularly the Ukrainian-American Friendship Foundation, which helps fund Dr. Albright's work. Their generosity has also helped establish a clinical unit within the center for indigent patients. I believe Mr. Halleck is on that ward presently."

"Could you tell me how many patients the center houses?"

"Right now the private wards have been closed for renovations for the next few weeks, but we have the capacity for as many as twenty private and ten ward patients."

"What is the nature of Dr. Albright's research?" Peter asked.

The receptionist smiled pleasantly. "I'm sorry, Dr. Branstead, but I'm only the receptionist. You'd have to discuss that directly with Dr. Albright. I believe that's him coming down on the elevator right now."

An elevator door behind the reception desk opened quietly, and out of it strode an aristocratic-looking gentleman who Peter estimated to be in his midfifties. Albright was tall and lean, almost gaunt. He carried himself stiffly, with the demeanor and sense of purpose of someone accustomed to being in a position of authority. His manner of dress was a studied elegance, refined and fashionable but not flashy. His hair was thin and receded at the temples with the onset of middle age and was combed straight back and kept impeccably in place. He had a prominent, beaked nose, and his eyes were steel gray, deeply set, and sharply observant. For some reason, Peter had an eerie sensation of familiarity, as if he had seen him somewhere before.

The gentleman grasped Peter's outstretched hand and shook it firmly.

"Good afternoon, Dr. Branstead. I'm Dr. William Albright." His speech was clipped and curt, a no-nonsense, I-don't-have-time-for-pleasantries tone of voice edged with the affected British accent that Megan had found so obnoxious. But underneath that was the same slight undercurrent of Slavic accent, which Peter assumed was a residual of Albright's childhood.

Dr. Albright turned to the receptionist. "Nadia, have you had the opportunity to familiarize Dr. Branstead with the center?"

"Yes, Dr. Albright, we chatted for a few minutes about ..."

"Good," Albright interrupted, cutting her off abruptly, then turned back to Peter and ushered him toward the elevator. "I understand that you came at the request of Harriet Halleck to oversee her husband's care," he said with a touch of irritation as the two of them entered the elevator. The door closed behind them with a gentle pneumatic shush as Albright inserted a key into a security lock on the button panel.

"*Oversee* is a bit more extreme than I would put it, Dr. Albright. I'm certain you are quite well equipped to care for Mr. Halleck without my interference."

Megan had failed miserably in trying to catch this particular fly with vinegar, and Peter had a feeling that a diplomatic touch of honey would suit Albright's expansive ego a good deal better. "Mrs. Halleck had some questions about what was happening to Frank that she didn't feel had been answered in her conversations with you, and since I know her and Frank, she asked if I could get some further information."

"I didn't realize you were a personal friend of the Hallecks."

"I'm not really a friend. I took care of a relative of Harriet's a while ago," Peter lied.

"Very well. I don't know how much Mrs. Halleck told you, but Frank has been working for me in my neuropharmacology laboratory at NYU for a number of years. He's been an excellent employee, totally beyond reproach. As I am certain Harriet told you, I am not an easy man to work for, Dr. Branstead. I am a perfectionist, very demanding of my employees and, I will admit, overbearing at times. I have a very high employee turnover in my office, of which I am not proud, but I accept it as a fact of life; and for Frank to have stayed with me for all these years is a reflection of his superb abilities and even temperament.

"But our laboratory has been under a great deal of stress recently. Certain experiments have not been going as expected, and the causes have not been readily apparent. As I'm sure you are aware, in academic medicine deadlines have to be met—publication dates being highly inflexible—and I believe Frank has been under too much pressure to get things out on time, and he broke under the strain. I blame myself as much as anybody else for Frank's sudden deterioration and, for that reason, I took it upon myself to assume the financial and medical responsibilities for his care."

The elevator stopped at the top floor. The door gently opened, and Albright briskly strode up to a thick, metal door secured with an electronic lock and pressed a small button under an intercom.

"Secured Ward. May I help you?"

"It's me, Elizabeth. Buzz us in, will you, dear?"

As the buzzer sounded, Albright opened the door, and they stepped into the locked ward.

Although obviously not as well appointed as the reception room, the ward was substantially nicer than most of the psychiatry wards Peter had experienced during his training at NYU. The facility was immaculately clean: no residues of vomit or blood on the carpets, no food stains on the walls, no reek of stale urine emanating from the bathrooms that Peter had been accustomed to during his time on the public hospital wards. The walls were hung with apparently original landscapes that, in conjunction with indirect lighting from wall sconces instead of glaring fluorescents, softened the otherwise stark dormitory appearance of the ward. A few elderly men in clean street clothes walked aimlessly about the corridor and a few more sat in the dining area, slowly shoveling breakfast into their mouths under the watchful eyes of nursing attendants. At the nursing station, the nurses greeted Dr. Albright respectfully as he introduced Peter.

"There are a few things I need to tell you about Frank before you go in to see him. Sadly, he has deteriorated significantly since admission. He was in the midst of a major depressive episode with frankly psychotic features when he first came in. We had actually considered electroconvulsive therapy at first, but his wife was adamantly against it. The only time the staff has seen any animation at all is when he obsesses about cats, on which he perseverates endlessly, and he has been writing the word repeatedly on the wall. He will get quite agitated if you bring up the topic, so we ask that you not do this. He doesn't appear to be a danger to anyone, so we no longer keep the room locked, but we must keep him sedated around the clock because of his agitation. Do you have any further questions, Dr. Branstead?"

"No, not right now. May I talk with him?"

"As you wish," Dr. Albright remarked coolly and turned to the charge nurse. "Elizabeth, kindly show Dr. Branstead to Mr. Halleck's room."

The nurse led Peter to a room all the way at the end of the hall. As they walked, Peter had an irresistible flashback to his recurring nightmare, envisioning himself once again walking down an endless hallway to his father's room to confront his father's death. Peter shuddered, but the déjà vu sensation passed as quickly as it had come. At the end of the hallway, the nurse let Peter into Frank's room and closed the door behind him.

Even after what he had been exposed to in the past few days, Peter was shocked by what he saw. Frank sat silently on the bed, staring blankly into what appeared to be some vast imaginary distance. And scrawled endlessly over the walls was the word "CAT," drawn like some bizarre, obsessional graffiti with variously colored magic markers in a plethora of styles and configurations. But this was not idle doodling that Frank had done to pass the time. Inspecting the walls closely, Peter saw the faint images of pen and pencil writings etched into the wall itself by the force of Frank's writing that had been dutifully scrubbed off by the staff. Layered on top of these were equally spectral writings, this time the words written in food stains by Frank's fingers. He could make out in the faint remnants the reds of spaghetti sauce and ketchup, the orange-yellows of mustard and pureed squash, and the greens of creamed spinach. Looking further, he saw a few versions written in a faded, indistinct umber. With a shiver of trepidation, Peter leaned over to the wall and sniffed.

Underneath the overpowering odor of disinfectant, the writing smelled distinctly of feces.

Presumably, the staff had given up trying to keep the walls clean at this point. In the interests of sanitation, they had provided Frank with washable colored markers, allowing him to festoon the walls with his polychromatic constructions of "CAT" to his heart's content.

Peter looked again at Frank, who had not moved since he walked into the room.

"Frank, I'm Dr. Peter Branstead. Harriet asked me to stop by and see how you were doing."

There was a brief flicker of comprehension in Frank's eyes when Peter mentioned Harriet's name. For the first time since Peter entered the room, Frank's eyes moved jerkily to look at Peter, and his head turned slowly and stiffly, like a tin woodsman made of flesh and blood. A trace of a smile momentarily flitted across Frank's stony visage.

On the pretense of shaking his hand, Peter gently flexed and extended Frank's forearm, feeling the unmistakable rigidity induced by high doses of antipsychotic agents. Frank was being held captive in a neurochemical prison.

Peter shook his head sadly and patted Frank gently on the knee. Of course he was no longer dangerous: he was no longer mobile. There would be no value in examining Frank at this point. The drug-induced state he was in would quash any meaningful cognitive or physical responses.

"Don't worry, Frank. We'll get you out of here."

Frank's eyes glistened wetly, and a tear rolled out of his unblinking eye down his immobile cheek.

Peter slowly got up and left the room. The nurse and Dr. Albright were talking together at the nursing station at the far end of the ward. As Peter turned to close the door, a patient jostled him, hard enough for Peter to lose his balance and stumble. Peter instinctively reached out and grabbed the man by the arm to steady himself and started to apologize when his eyes met the other's gaze.

It was Alan!

Before Peter could cry out in astonishment, Alan started into a fit of coughing. The nurse broke away from her conversation with Dr. Albright and began running down the hall. Before she had taken more than two or three steps, Alan's coughing abruptly stopped but he kept his hands covering his mouth.

"Whatever you do, don't blow my cover. I'll explain later."

"Alan, are you all right?" the nurse gasped, winded from her brief run.

"Yeah, I'm okay. Something must have gone down wrong. Hey, sorry if I scared you, buddy. You look like you've seen a ghost."

"No, I'm fine. I'm just a bit upset right now." Peter struggled to regain his composure and play Polonius to Alan's mad Prince Hamlet.

"Dr. Branstead, this is Alan Lamplin, one of our newer patients. Alan, Dr. Branstead is a neurologist. He's here to visit Mr. Halleck."

"Oh, yeah! Frankie the shit-scribbler; the Michelangelo of manure, the Dali of dung, the Picasso of ..."

The nurse cut him short. "Alan, that's enough. If you can't be appropriate, then go back to your room. We don't need to hear any more of your vulgarity on this ward."

Alan shrugged. "Sorry, Doc. No offense intended." And Alan gave Peter a friendly punch on the arm. "Look, Frankie's an okay guy. Not much of a talker, but a good listener. Know what I mean?"

"Alan, that will be quite enough. It's almost time for your medication. I'll be in your room in just a few minutes."

"Okeydokey. See ya later, Doc. Hope you enjoy the freak show." And Alan sauntered away.

"Dr. Branstead, I'm terribly sorry. Mr. Lamplin is one of our new patients, and he doesn't seem to be adjusting well to ward routines."

"Oh, don't worry. Considering the source, I can't take it too personally. I'm sure nothing was meant maliciously."

Peter admired Alan's performance. And his *cajones*. He only hoped that Alan wasn't getting himself into more than he could handle.

"Well, Dr. Branstead, I see you've met another one of our patients. Mr. Lamplin was just admitted early this morning. Delightful, isn't he!" Albright chimed in as Peter reached the nursing station.

"I've seen worse. But tell me, Dr. Albright, that patient didn't look like he exactly had top of the line medical insurance. Why did you admit him here instead of sending him off to one of the city hospitals?"

"Let me tell you about the East Side Psychiatric Center, Dr. Branstead. This is a one hundred percent privately funded institution. We accept neither insurance nor governmental payments. In that way, I am able to practice psychiatry free of the financial constraints and outside the meddling of managed care, which seems to manage best at insinuating itself into every aspect of patient care. However, our endowment sets aside a percentage of our income to care for, as it is written in our charter, 'the poor, downtrodden, and medically underserved.' Our bene-factors were quite insistent on this.

"As Nadia may have told you downstairs, East Side Psychiatric Center is well-known amongst Eastern Europeans, particularly Ukrainians, throughout the world, and my professional services are actively sought out. As much as I am inclined to disagree with much of psychoanalytic theory, I have been forced to concur, at least in part, with Jung's concept of the collective unconscious. I have come to believe that it is impossible to adequately treat someone with a psychiat-ric illness unless you understand them in their cultural context; you have to know their history, their religion, their geography, and even their mythology. My patients come to me from all over the world because, being of Ukrainian extrac-tion yet having the benefits of a Western education, I can identify with their fears and anxieties and still give them the most up-to-date medical treatment."

Albright had found the perfect niche, Peter thought wistfully. He had an exceedingly lucrative practice, free of outside interference. Nice work if you can get it.

Dr. Albright looked briskly at his watch. "Forgive my haste, Dr. Branstead, but I'm quite busy today, and I'm afraid we must bring your visit to a close shortly. A visiting professor is flying in this evening, and I have to meet him at the airport. I hope to confer with him about poor Frank to see if anything further can be done. Do you understand now why I had him admitted here, Dr. Branstead? This psychotic obsession with cats makes it impossible for Frank to go home or even to be transferred to another facility."

"But is it really necessary to keep him so tranquilized?"

Albright bristled. "Perhaps you would like to scrub Frank's feces off the walls yourself, Dr. Branstead. If you would, I'd be more than happy to cut back on Frank's medication," he said icily. Peter had forgotten that Albright's altercation with Megan had been triggered by a critique of his care and changed the subject quickly.

"One last question before I leave, Dr. Albright. Do you have a minute to tell me about your research?"

Albright looked Peter hard in the eyes before he continued. "As a neurologist, Dr. Branstead, you are certainly aware that the effects of severe depression are sometimes difficult to differentiate clinically from those of dementia. In addition, many patients with Alzheimer's disease may develop a coexisting depression. It is the overlap between these two disorders that fascinates me. My life's goal has been to find a biochemical linkage between these two diseases that might either help to distinguish them or hopefully lead to a specific treatment for Alzheimer's disease."

"Was this the research that Frank was working on when he became psychotic?"

Albright's face darkened. "No. Frank was working on something a bit different. Unfortunately, I'm not free to discuss that research because of the critical phase those experiments are in at this time. I hope you understand."

"Of course," Peter agreed warily. What he understood was that he would get no more information out of Dr. Albright. "I've kept you longer than I should have, Dr. Albright. I can't thank you enough for your time."

Peter offered his hand to Albright, who gave it a single perfunctory shake. As he shook Albright's hand, Peter was surprised to see a large, irregular scar traversing his wrist as it extended beyond the sleeve of his suit jacket.

"A surgical accident in medical school," Albright said casually, obviously having followed the direction of Peter's gaze. "One of the many reasons I chose Psychiatry."

Peter quickly examined Dr. Albright's face. It remained impassive, humorless. Psychoanalytic dispassion carried to the nth degree, thought Peter.

"Good day, Dr. Branstead. I hope you don't mind if I don't show you out."

"Not at all. I'll find my own way, thank you."

The nurse unlocked the door. As Peter exited the ward, he turned around, hoping to get a final look at Alan, but he was nowhere to be seen. Peter took the elevator down to the lobby and stopped by the reception desk.

"I hope you had a pleasant visit, Dr. Branstead."

"'Pleasant' might not be the operative word, but it was certainly illuminating. Perhaps you could help me. I'd like to get some information about this Ukrainian-American Friendship Foundation. Do you have their address?"

"Certainly." She scribbled the address on a slip of paper and handed it to Peter. "They're just a few blocks away on East Ninth Street, not far from Tompkins Square."

The Ukrainian-American Friendship Foundation was located in a four-story converted brownstone just off Tompkins Square, nowhere near as elegant as the East Side Psychiatric Center. Peter rode to the fourth floor in an elevator roughly the size of a toilet stall and about as aesthetic. Walking down the dimly lit hallway, he was surprised at the contrast between the center and its major fundraiser.

But if Peter was surprised at the contrasts outside the office, he was totally taken aback by the contrast inside. The waiting room was an incredibly shoddy affair. There were a half-dozen mismatched dining room chairs, all probably purchased at a flea market, and a single lamp table overlaid with a pile of vintage magazines.

The receptionist's desk was staffed by an attractive, if overly made up, young woman with raven-black hair and a skirt that hugged her body so tightly it might have been painted on. She was embroiled in an animated and obviously personal phone conversation with her boyfriend. After a minute or two she hung up.

"May I help you, sir?" she asked without apology. Her accent was much closer to eastern Jersey than Eastern Europe.

"I'd like to get some information about the Ukrainian-American Friendship Foundation. Is there anyone here that I could speak with?"

"Let me see if Mr. Kalchenko is available. Whom shall I say is calling?"

"My name is Peter Branstead, Dr. Peter Branstead."

Peter sat down and thumbed through a tattered copy of *Field and Stream*, certain that he would be sitting for a while. To his surprise, within a minute or two the secretary directed him to the inner office.

The door was opened by a tall, strikingly handsome man who Peter estimated was in his late thirties with strong, angular facial features accentuated by prominent highly placed cheekbones that hollowed out his cheeks, giving his face a characteristically Slavic appearance. His hair was blond and cropped short in a military crew cut, with eyebrows so fair as to be almost undetectable as they arched over a pair of ice-blue eyes.

"Yuri Kalchenko, Dr. Branstead. I am very pleased to meet you."

Kalchenko smiled broadly and extended a perfectly manicured hand graced by one of the most elegant Rolex watches Peter had ever seen. Peter found his hand encased in a grip that was more than firm, almost uncomfortable, and was relieved when Kalchenko finally released it.

Kalchenko was a powerfully built man, his body perfectly filling out a superbly tailored designer suit, which he kept buttoned up in spite of the midday warmth. Unlike Albright, he was not at all stiff but had a casual amiability belying his formal attire. All in all, he presented a typical picture of a handsome, self-assured young businessman aggressively pushing his way up the corporate ladder.

Except for the tattoos.

In the spaces bordered by the knuckles and web space of each of his fingers were highly detailed monochromatic tattoos of human skulls, some with daggers or bolts of lightning piercing their temples. There were eight skulls in all, those adjacent to his thumbs the largest and most artistically rendered and surrounded by flames. Tattooed on the backs of his fingers were Cyrillic letters.

Peter must have been staring openly at Kalchenko's hands, because he glanced down at them as he sat down in the leather executive's chair behind the desk.

"I was a longshoreman on the docks of Odessa when I was a teenager, Dr. Branstead. We sometimes do very impetuous things when the flames of youth consume our better judgment, don't we. Do you know Ukrainian, Dr. Branstead?"

Peter smiled. "Not a word."

Kalchenko held his fingers outstretched and looked pensively at his knuckles, running his thumbs across the tattooed letters. "When I was just out of my teens, I had these letters tattooed on my fingers. If I would meet a pretty young girl at a bar and the conversation seemed to be proceeding in a promising manner, I would intertwine my fingers like so around my glass," and he demonstrated for Peter by linking his fingers together, "and the letters would spell out 'I Love You.'" He smiled as he separated his hands and leaned back in his chair. "You'd be amazed at how far that little trick would get me sometimes. But I am digressing from the point of your visit. Annette tells me you have some questions about our organization. Are you interested in making a donation?"

"Well, not really, Mr. Kalchenko ..."

"Please, Dr. Branstead, call me Yuri. No need to stand on formality."

He was a welcome contrast to Albright's aloofness.

"Quite honestly, Yuri, I'm primarily interested in the organization itself. I've just come from the East Side Psychiatric Center, where Dr. Albright was kind enough to show me around, and I was surprised to see such opulence in the East Village. He told me your foundation provided most of the funding, and it sparked my curiosity."

Kalchenko rested his elbows on the table and touched his fingertips together. "Ah, so you've met Dr. Albright. I know he comes across as a cold fish, Dr. Branstead, but the man is truly a saint. He is, you know, of Ukrainian descent in spite of his name, and he has dedicated himself and his illustrious reputation to the care of the Ukrainian community, both here and around the world. The Ukrainians have an international diaspora much as the Jews do, and we remain close-knit and proud of our heritage. Dr. Albright's expertise is so world-renowned that the well-to-do of my countrymen would gladly fly to New York to avoid the publicity that might result from a psychiatric admission to a local facility. As a result, we have established the Ukrainian-American Friendship Foundation, which is devoted to fundraising to support the center as well as Dr. Albright's research, which brings honor to our entire nation. As you can see, we ourselves run a shoestring operation, to make sure that the money goes where it does the most good. I myself volunteer for only a dollar a year and make my living solely from family investments."

Peter nodded attentively throughout Kalchenko's exposition. He was an expert pitchman.

"Your contributors are obviously quite wealthy. Are they local?"

Kalchenko smiled politely. "I'm sorry, Dr. Branstead, but our benefactors insist on anonymity. Some of them have loved ones that have been through Dr. Albright's clinic, or they have been through the clinic themselves and have complex business arrangements that might be jeopardized if they were linked even tangentially to a psychiatric facility."

Peter changed the subject. "Does Dr. Albright do any research in the center? He mentioned that he is particularly interested in the clinical overlap between Alzheimer's disease and depression."

"I don't believe so, Dr. Branstead. I've no medical background, but, as I understand it, he is a psychopharmacologist and does most of his work with animals and tissue cultures, primarily at his laboratory at NYU. His work at the center is devoted to treatment rather than research, particularly of indigent patients suffering from severe forms of depression. The Bowery is not too far from the center, and sadly it provides an inexhaustible source of these unfortunates, whom society has chosen to sweep under the rug. As I understand it, Dr. Albright has made a tremendous impact on the lives of some of these men."

I'll say, Peter thought. He wondered how much Kalchenko really knew of Dr. Albright's "research."

"Well, Yuri, you've been of great help to me. Your foundation is a remarkable institution, and I hope it continues to do the great work that it has accomplished so far."

"Thank you so much, Dr. Branstead. Please feel free to call should you have any more questions."

Kalchenko walked Peter to the elevator, then returned to his office, stopping by the receptionist's desk long enough to reach under her chin with a tattooed index finger, lift it up gently, and give her a light kiss on the forehead.

"Thank you so much, Annette. Why don't you take the rest of the afternoon off? Business is slow today."

Annette sighed as she watched Kalchenko head back into his office; then she gathered her belongings and headed out the door. Once he heard the door close, Kalchenko picked up the phone.

"Let me speak to Dr. Albright, please." He drummed his fingers on the table, checking his watch impatiently. When Albright got to the phone, they conversed in Ukrainian.

"I've had a visitor here, a Dr. Peter Branstead. Do you know him?"

"He was just here visiting Halleck. I had to fend off a number of questions, but I don't think he knows anything."

"Well, he was snooping around here, too, asking a lot of questions about the foundation and your research. My instincts tell me this guy is trouble."

"Calm down. The plan is proceeding perfectly, and there's nothing that Branstead can do. Your job is to provide the money, and you can tell our investors that things are going very well. Now leave me alone; I have work to do. Good-bye."

Kalchenko hung up the phone. He didn't care what Albright said. A physician wouldn't waste his time snooping around for no reason, but for now he had other things on his mind. He picked up the phone and stabbed the buttons with his index finger.

Peter finished rounding at St. Mark's late that evening. There was no doubt in his mind that something suspicious was going on, both at the East Side Psychiatric Center and the Ukrainian-American Friendship Foundation. But he still had no proof, no motive, and no evidence. Worse than that, there was no doubt that Frank Halleck needed psychiatric hospitalization in a bad way, and, unless Harriet actively demanded that Frank be transferred, there was nothing that he could do.

And just in case things weren't complicated enough, he now had to explain to Megan that her long-lost stepbrother, who had been the subject of last night's bitter quarrel, had taken it upon himself to jump right into the lion's den. Peter knew that Albright was not running a completely aboveboard operation, and he didn't know what he would do should he suspect that Alan was a fake. His head ached, and his stomach burned with the universally recognized signs of stress. Why the hell hadn't he stopped at a pharmacy for some antacids?

Peter's last stop was at Amanda Ivy's room. Walter Ivy sat by the bedside, gently stroking his wife's hair as she lay in the hospital bed, restrained to keep her from crawling over the guardrails. Exhaustion showed heavily in his eyes. Peter had seen the same look countless times in the faces of spouses of demented patients. There was something about the emotional strain of watching the mental regression of a spouse that no outsider, not even a physician, could fully appreciate.

"Good evening, Walter. How's Amanda doing?" It was a pointless question. Amanda Ivy lay in her bed, her hair disheveled and eyes vacant, diapered and reeking of incontinence. She jabbered almost continuously in meaningless jargon. Other than in his ever-expanding collection of demented vagrants, Peter had never seen such a rapid progression of dementia.

"She's not doing too well, Dr. Branstead. She keeps getting more and more confused. Sometimes, I don't know if she even recognizes me. Any results back yet?"

"Not all of them, but everything looks okay so far. We'll know more in another day or two."

Walter wiped away a tear. "Do what you can. She's all I've got."

Peter walked out of the room to the nursing station, and scoured Amanda Ivy's chart. Nothing. Not a clue as to what was happening to her. He wrote a brief note in the chart and turned to "Physician's Orders." Hesitating for a moment, he wrote "Send 10 cc's of serum in a red top tube to Dr. Steven Bergstraum at Neurologic Institute, re: rapidly progressive dementia," then he closed the chart and made his way out of the hospital.

CHAPTER 10

▼

"Open your mouth, Alan. Good. Now lift up your tongue. Very good. You may go back to your room now." The nurse smiled condescendingly and set down the flashlight.

"Thanks, Nurse. By the way, what are those capsules supposed to do?"

"They're part of your treatment, Alan. Dr. Albright has ordered them for you."

"What kind of medicines are they? I've never seen 'em before."

"I'm sorry, Alan. I'm not allowed to discuss the medications with you. You'll have to ask Dr. Albright about them."

"Fine. Then where the hell *is* Dr. Albright. I haven't talked to him since I was admitted to this dump. Ain't I supposed to be telling him about my potty training or something? Whenever he comes on the ward, he spends maybe five minutes, tops, looking at charts and then splits. What kind of therapy is that?"

The nurse smiled stiffly. "Dr. Albright is very busy right now. A visiting professor of psychiatry is coming from overseas, and Dr. Albright will be meeting with him today and tomorrow, but I'll tell him that you wish to speak to him."

"Thanks for nothing, shithead," Alan muttered and walked back to his room. Once there, he reached his finger into the pocket between his gum and lower cheek and scooped out the two capsules that the nurse had administered. Stashing capsules created a special problem, because saliva dissolved the gelatin fairly quickly, so he had to make certain he carefully wiped his cheek and gums with a washcloth when the nurse called him for medication time. It had been easier in other hospitals. Some of the medications they gave him had the useful side effect of drying out his mouth.

One of the capsules was plain white without any identifiable markings other than a number, which he assumed was a code that had been dutifully recorded in Albright's experimental logbook. The other was light blue and had some unidentifiable brand marking that Alan had never seen before. Although the white one could have been a generic, Alan suspected the capsule had been filled at the center. He carefully wrapped the two capsules up in the same piece of toilet paper that he kept the previously sequestered medications in, pushed them all to the back of his nightstand drawer, and lay down on his bed to think.

It hadn't been difficult at all to get into East Side Psychiatric. Using the direct approach, he had walked up the stairway to the main entrance and requested evaluation for admission. The receptionist directed him to the ward service entrance underneath the stairway, where he was greeted by a disagreeable security guard who in turn directed him to an intake nurse. The bulk of the interview revolved around whether he had a family or job. Alan answered "No" to all the questions, omitting any mention of his stepsister.

After the intake nurse had cleared his admission, he was brought up to the locked ward, by far the youngest one there. Almost all of the patients were in their sixties. Most appeared to be alcoholics who wanted to be detoxed but didn't want to deal with the mice and roaches at the Manhattan Bowery Project a few blocks away. Some were just down-on-their-luck bums who had come in looking for three squares a day and a clean place to spend the night. Admission requirements weren't very strict. As near as Alan could tell, the main criterion was the absence of anyone that would give a shit about you.

Alan had tried to strike up conversations with some of the eight or nine other ward residents, but he quickly realized that they were all in varying stages of dementia. Some simply lost their train of thought, but the ones who had been there longer were clearly confused, and some were even hallucinatory. A few, like Frank Halleck, were kept in their rooms, too far gone for involvement in a social setting. Alan suspected they all met the diagnostic criteria for dementia of the Alzheimer's type. Damn, he thought, if I hadn't been such a screwup as a kid, I could've been a shrink myself.

Although Alan had been admitted to the East Side Psychiatric Center only that morning, he already had developed a sense of foreboding about the place. It seemed logical that, as Peter had thought, human experimentation was being performed right here in downtown Manhattan, and he was one of the guinea pigs. Communication with the outside world was zilch. Other than Peter, there had been no visitors, and the selection process insured that there would probably never be any visitors. There were no payphones on the ward, and the phones at the nursing station had locks on them. The nurses were a bunch of tough old birds, and they all sucked up to Albright, so there was no way he could play them off against him the way he'd manipulated the nursing staff elsewhere.

For the first time since he had started his little act years ago, Alan was scared. He had to get out of here, and Peter was his only hope.

From her seat on the sofa, Megan heard Peter's steps, unusually slow and heavy, trudging up the stairs to their apartment. She was wearing an ankle-length, floral print, cotton shift with a low cut bodice held up by thin straps across her shoulders, and her feet were shod in lightweight sandals. Megan had spent much of the time after she'd gotten home from work looking through her closet for exactly the right thing to wear. They needed to talk about last night, very badly, and she didn't want Peter distracted by anything too sexy or revealing, but she still needed to appear soft and feminine. Dressing too prim might put him on the defensive—make him feel that he was talking to a psychologist rather than his girlfriend.

When she heard Peter fumbling at the lock, Megan pushed the "Play" button on the CD player, and the room was gently flooded by the soft strains of a jazz trio as she sat down on the couch and pretended to be reading a book.

"I didn't get anything for dinner. I thought we'd order out later." Peter crossed the room, ignoring the chairs, and sat down next to her.

"Okay with me," she replied. "I'm not very hungry tonight."

"I want to apologize about last night. You were absolutely right; I was jealous, and I was acting like a jerk. For the past three years, I've felt a wall between us, and I guess that it's one of my own making. There was a closeness between you and Alan that I haven't seen between us in three years. I got scared when I thought that other men could be giving you something that I wasn't."

Megan turned to Peter and laid her hand on his chest. "Don't say 'couldn't' when you mean 'won't.' If I thought you really couldn't, we would have broken up a long time ago. You have a warmth and compassion that few men have. You have to get over this misplaced guilt about your father's death and move on. You didn't kill him, Peter. He died because his time had come, that's all."

Peter stood up and paced in the middle of the living room.

"You don't think I've told myself that a million times? Thinking it doesn't help."

Megan walked over and put her hands on his shoulders. "Sometimes you have to have faith that you can love someone, and your love won't make you lose them. You're not the only one who's been left by loved ones. I have, too. Several times, over and over. And I'm not going to die, and I'm not going to leave you."

She placed her hand tenderly on his cheek.

"Peter, please don't push me away."

She gently drew him toward her and kissed him deeply. In return, Peter clasped her to him and drew her down to the sofa. Their legs intertwined while their hands wandered, searching and hungry, over each other's bodies.

Their love-making over, Peter lay beside Megan, still panting from the passion of their climax, and kissed her tenderly on her neck. He cupped her breast in his hand as they drifted into the peaceful twilight of their intimacy.

Megan purred with pleasure. *A journey of a thousand miles begins with a single step*, she thought as she fell asleep in Peter's arms.

"No, please help me. Help me. No, no, don't. Please."

Alan Lamplin awoke from one of the vivid nightmares that had become commonplace since he had checked himself in to East Side Psychiatric Center. The screams had been incorporated into his dream, but they kept on even though he was awake. It took himself a few seconds to get himself oriented and shake off the effects of the dream. Then he quietly got up, cracked open the door, and peered out into the hallway.

In a room midway between his room and the nursing station a patient was "sundowning," a disorientation that occurred late at night when the diurnal brain rhythms were at their lowest ebb, and the darkness robbed the mind of familiar cues.

The ruckus had not gone unnoticed. Several other patients had been awakened by the noise and had begun their own psychotic chanting. One or two had aimlessly meandered out into the hallway and were walking into other patients' rooms. Alan realized that his lucky break had come. He reached into the back of his nightstand drawer, took his small parcel of slightly soggy capsules, and stuffed it in his bathrobe pocket. *Carpe diem*, he thought and walked out into the hallway.

In all hospitals, the night shift was understaffed, especially in psychiatric hospitals where patients weren't critically ill. Tonight, there was a single nurse to manage the entire ward. Under ordinary circumstances, this would be quite sufficient. But this was not an ordinary circumstance. As the lone nurse attended to the screaming patient, Alan slipped into Frank Halleck's room and turned on the light.

"Holy shit!" Alan looked about the room at Frank's schizoid mural and then at Frank, who lay in bed, staring with vacant eyes at the intruder in his room.

"Frankie, you need a new hobby." But he had no time to lose. He quickly took the bundle of pills and stuck them all the way in the back of Frank's nightstand drawer and shut it in the nick of time.

"Alan, what are you doing in Frank's room?" The nurse entered the room and gently pulled Alan by the arm. Her hair, previously held back by barrettes clasped on either side of her head, was falling across her face in wisps as her hairdo loosened with the exertion of trying to corral the patients. She led Alan out of the room and down the hall toward his room, but Alan wasn't finished yet.

"Isn't this the broom closet? The broom closet should be right near the kitchen," Alan said in the best deadpan voice he could muster. "Mama told me to mop the kitchen floor," and he pulled his arm away from the nurse.

"No, Alan, you're not in your house. You're in East Side Psychiatric Center. You have to go back to your room now and go back to bed."

"Uh-uh. I gotta mop the kitchen, and I gotta do it now. After that, Mama told me I gotta wash the dishes and get it all done by dinner."

"Alan, you're not at home now. You're in a hospital. You don't have any chores to do, and it's only 2:00 a.m. Now please go back to your room." Exasperation showed in her voice. She had an entire hallway of patients to quiet down. She didn't have the time to spend reorienting Alan, and he knew it.

"No. Mama, where's the mop? If I can find the mop, I'll get the floor done. Let's see, the broom closet is somewhere around here," and Alan pulled his arm away from the nurse again and ambled toward the nursing station.

"Oh, all right! Go mop the floor. Just stay out of the other patients' rooms," she said as she ran back into the room of the screamer, who had become agitated again by Alan's ranting.

Alan quickly walked to the nursing station and went to the phone. Damn! The lock was still on it. He unbent a paper clip and picked the lock. He dialed quickly, thankful that at night he didn't have to go through the receptionist.

"C'mon, damn it. Pick up the fuckin' phone already," he swore as the phone rang. Alan glanced nervously down the hall. The nurse was still occupied with the screamer, and some other patients were still wandering around the far end of the hallway.

"Dr. Branstead speaking," the sleepy voice at the other end of the line muttered.

"Peter, this is Alan. Listen, this is important."

"Alan who?"

"Alan Lamplin, damn it. Megan's stepbrother. Now listen ..."

"Alan! What the hell were you doing in East Side Psych today? That place is dangerous."

"I know, I know. Now shut up, Peter, and listen to me ..."

"No, Alan, you listen to me. Albright isn't the kind of guy you can play games with. You've got to get out of there as quickly as ..."

"Peter, will you please shut the fuck up and listen to me!" Alan hissed as loudly as he could yet still whisper.

There was finally silence from the other end of the line.

"Thank you. I know damn well this guy's dangerous. He's doing some sort of experimentation here, with drugs I've never seen before. Everybody here is very hush-hush about what's going on. Security is so tight I had to pick a lock on the phone at the nursing station to call you."

"Alan, how can I get you out of there?"

"Don't worry about me; just listen. I managed to save a few doses of the medication they've been giving us, and I stuck them in the back of the drawer of Frank Halleck's nightstand."

"How the hell did you get into Frank's room?"

"Don't ask. Just shut up and listen. I don't care what bullshit excuse you use, but you have to get back to Frank's room tomorrow as soon as possible and get those pills out of here so they can be analyzed. They're the key to this whole scam. Got that?"

"Yeah, got it."

"Okay. Look, I gotta go. Give my love to Megan, will ya?"

"You can bet on it. Alan ..."

"What?"

"Good luck."

Alan smiled. "Same to you," he replied and hung up the phone.

And not a moment too soon. The night nurse had just come back to the nursing station, her hair in complete disarray, her underarms soaked with perspiration.

"Alan, what are you doing in the nursing station? You're not allowed here."

"Isn't this the broom closet? Somebody must have stolen all the mops. Where are they? I've got to mop the kitchen and wash the dishes."

Again, the nurse held Alan by his arm and led him back to his room. This time, Alan allowed himself to be led without protest. "For the last time, Alan, you're not at home. You're in a psychiatric hospital in New York City. You do not have to mop the floor, you do not have to wash the dishes, your mother isn't here, and it's 2:00 a.m. and time for you to be in bed." By the time she had finished, they were standing in front of Alan's room.

"You promise you'll find me a mop later?"

"Yes, Alan, I promise I'll find you a mop."

"Okay. Then I guess I'll go to bed." Alan smiled coyly, went into his room and shut the door.

The nurse stumbled wearily back to the nursing station and slumped into a chair. God Almighty, what a night this had been. It would take her the rest of the shift just to chart in the nursing notes what had just happened. Thank goodness she had the next day off.

Then, her eyes fell on the phone, with the lock and bent paper clip lying nearby. A scowl darkened her face as she picked up the phone and dialed.

"Dr. Albright, this is Nurse Bancroft on the experimental ward. I'm terribly sorry to wake you up at this hour, but I think we have a problem—a very serious problem."

CHAPTER 11

▼

As dawn broke, the first of a virtual caravan of delivery trucks that would wend its way through SoHo that day rumbled its way over the antiquated cobblestones of Mercer Street. The road had originally been engineered for turn-of-the-century motorcars, but now the worst that twenty-first century vehicular commerce had to offer traversed it daily. As a result, the street resembled a field of rocky moguls that tested the limits of the truck's shock absorbers and suspension as it bounced down the street, the noise of its agitated contents resonating through the canyons of downtown Manhattan.

Peter was roused precipitously by the clamor outside his window, still exhausted by a restless night. Lovemaking had a narcotizing effect on Peter, and he had fallen asleep quickly, his mind eased by the discussion with Megan. However, Alan's early morning phone call had him deeply disturbed, and he found it difficult to get back to sleep in anticipation of how he would break the news to Megan about her stepbrother's little escapade.

Megan stirred and stretched, her arms sleepily reaching out for him. Peter made no effort to withdraw, but allowed the gentle touch of her hand to caress him lightly across his chest, savoring the sensation. Megan opened her eyes and smiled, sighing contentedly as she rested her face against Peter's arm.

Suddenly, Peter looked at the clock and jumped out of bed. "Damn, I've got to get going."

"What's so important that you can't spend a few more minutes in bed?" Megan sat up and wrapped her arms around her legs, resting her chin on her knees as she watched Peter get into a bathrobe.

"Well, for one thing, I've got to find out how Mrs. Ivy is doing."

"Why? What's wrong with her?"

"Megan, she's in the hospital, confused as hell."

Megan had gotten out of bed and straightened the bed. "Oh, really? That's too bad. How long has she been in? I'll have to visit her."

"Wake up! She's been there since yesterday afternoon. You told Walter to bring her in when she started getting confused."

"I guess I did, didn't I."

Peter shook his head. "Why don't you start brewing the coffee while I take a shower, okay, Hon." And he walked into the bathroom.

In the shower, Peter rehearsed what he was going to tell Megan about Alan. He knew she'd be terrified once she heard that Alan was trapped in the experimental ward, but until he found something more concrete than Alan's hearsay evidence, he still had nothing to call Meinerhoff about. He would have to visit Frank that evening and get the capsules to Steve Bergstraum quickly. In addition, there was a grand rounds conference on Alzheimer's disease being given at St. Mark's that afternoon, and hopefully he could get some background information that might help him.

Peter got dressed and walked into the kitchen. Megan was in her robe, rummaging around in the kitchen drawers. To his surprise, Megan had forgotten to put any coffee in the coffeemaker. Worse, instead of putting the coffeepot on the hot plate, Megan had placed a coffee cup on the plate to catch the hot water, which was just about to run over the top of the cup onto the heating unit.

Dashing over to the coffeemaker, Peter pulled the plug from the outlet, stopping the dripping water as the heating unit erupted in a hiss of steam.

"Watch it, Megan. You almost shorted out the coffee maker. Maybe you should go back to bed and get some more sleep."

Megan didn't appear to be paying any attention to his concern about the coffeepot, apparently wrapped up in whatever she was searching for.

"I don't need more sleep. I'm fine, just fine. What I need is to find my wallet." Megan looked up at Peter with a strange, wild-eyed look that he had never seen in her before. "What did you do with my wallet, Peter?"

"I didn't do anything with your wallet. I never touch your wallet." He stormed back into their bedroom, picked up her wallet from her nightstand, and brought it back into the kitchen. "It was on your nightstand where you leave it every night." As he handed it to Megan, she opened it up and started throwing her credit cards and IDs from it and then pulled some bills from the billfold.

"Where's the rest of my money? What did you do with my money? Did you steal that, too?"

"I didn't steal your money. You never carry more than twenty dollars in your wallet. And why would I steal money from you, anyway?" Peter was getting very disturbed. If she was getting this worked up over imagined slights, how was she going to react when he told her about Alan?

"Where's my money? Give it back!" Megan screamed at him, a look of madness in her eyes.

"For crying out loud, calm down. You're being ..." Peter paused in mid-sentence as the realization of what was happening hit him "... totally irrational."

Megan looked at him quizzically, the storm passing as quickly as it came, and she dropped the wallet.

"What did you say, Peter?"

Peter's mouth felt dry. "What's the date today?" he said blandly.

"Why, it's ..." she looked about the room for any clues ... a calendar, a newspaper, anything. But no clues were to be found. "... It's the twenty-eighth, I think."

"No. It's the fifth. What month is it?"

She again looked around, searching for clues. "October, isn't it?"

Peter's gut tightened. "No, it's June. Where are we?"

Megan smiled. "We're home, of course."

"Where is home?"

"We're in Ohio, silly. I've always lived in Ohio. Where do you think we are?"

Peter's stomach clenched tightly, and a wave of nausea hit him.

"Megan, we're not in Ohio. You haven't lived in Ohio for years. We're in Manhattan, in New York City. Don't you remember? For God's sake, don't you remember?"

The smile vanished from Megan's lips, and she stared at him blankly as she tried to sort things out in her disordered mind. Then, for an instant, the mists cleared just long enough for the realization of what was happening to hit her.

"Oh, no. It's not happening to me, too? Is it, Peter?"

Peter took a step toward her, but she backed away, stumbling over a kitchen chair.

"I don't know. But I have to get you to the hospital. Now!"

"No, I won't go. Please, don't make me go." Tears ran down Megan's cheeks as she backed away, clutching her temples and shaking her head.

Peter extended his hand to her and tried to appear calm. "Let's get you dressed so we can go to the hospital."

"No! Leave me alone. Leave me alone," she screamed and raced to the door, opening it and dashing outside into the hallway before slamming it shut behind her.

By the time Peter followed her into the hallway, Megan had already made her way down the steps and out onto the sidewalk, her robe open and her hair streaming.

Peter took the stairs two at a time and sprinted out onto the sidewalk, the bright morning sun temporarily dazzling him. He got his bearings just in time to see Megan run out into the middle of Mercer Street, a delivery truck bearing down on her.

Megan turned toward the truck and threw her arms up as if to stop it with her bare hands. Peter screamed a warning, but it was too late. With a squeal of its brakes, the truck came to a halt, and Peter ran into the street to see the motionless, half-clothed body of Megan lying in the street in front of the truck.

"Oh, dear God!" Peter groaned as he knelt down beside her, opened her mouth and checked her chest. There was no discernible movement, no air passage. He gave three quick, hard breaths into her mouth then placed his fingers over her carotids. Her pulse was thready, but at least she had one. He quickly pulled back her eyelids, and her pupils constricted briskly in the bright sun. But she still wasn't breathing.

Breathe, one-Mississippi, two-Mississippi, three-Mississippi, four-Mississippi, breathe.

Oblivious to anything but the timing of his resuscitations, he didn't hear the driver of the truck come up next to him.

"I'm real sorry, Buddy, but I didn't see her until I was right on top of her. Honest."

Peter waved him off, still counting to himself. "Just get an ambulance, okay?"

By now, the usual crowd of curious New York onlookers had begun gathering around the scene of incipient tragedy, but Peter was oblivious to all of them. After a few more cycles, he was relieved to see Megan start to breathe on her own, at first tentatively, but then with strong, regular breaths. Peter stopped CPR and checked out Megan's condition. There was a small bruise on the back of her head, but otherwise no sign of injury, and her pupillary responses and eye movements remained normal. Then, for the first time, Megan stirred, moving her arms and legs slightly. Peter sat back on the cobblestones, tears streaming down his cheeks, and stroked Megan's hair as he waited for the ambulance to arrive.

As usual, the emergency room at St. Mark's Hospital was filled to capacity. It was one of the busiest ERs in New York City, with a catchment area stretching from the Hudson River to the East Village and from Chinatown to Chelsea. It ran the gamut of economic strata, from the high-rise, high rent apartment buildings lining Fifth Avenue to the flophouses of the Bowery, and it probably saw a more diverse cross section of humanity than any other hospital in the city, and arguably the world.

The emergency room was "the great equalizer." A middle-aged man in a gray suit, waiting to get his coffee burn attended to, shared a room with a psychotic drug addict who had OD'd on Thorazine the night before and had been picked up by the police buck naked on Sullivan Street, holding a Bible and bellowing messages of salvation to the heathens on their way to work. Another room held a butcher from the nearby Manhattan Meat Market, holding his amputated thumb in a cup of ice and trying to make time with a pretty young girl in a short black leather skirt, who was a girl only in the hormonal, but not chromosomal, sense of the word.

Peter made his way through the rush of nurses and residents to the room where his friend and fellow neurologist, Dr. Jay Harden, had just stepped out into the hallway after examining Megan.

"How is she?"

"Medically, she's fine. The truck barely bumped her. No internal injuries, no broken bones, not even any big-time bruises. She probably had a concussion when she hit the cobblestones. CT scan looks good—no contusions, hemorrhages ... nothing."

Peter breathed a deep sigh of relief. "What about her confusion?"

Jay shook his head. "That's another story. She's way out in left field. Really disoriented. Are you sure there are no drugs involved? Maybe a little something on the sly?"

"I doubt it, but go ahead and get a drug screen if you think it's necessary. I'm not going to meddle except for one thing."

"What's that?"

"Could you please have a red top tube of her blood sent stat to Dr. Steven Bergstraum up at the Neurologic Institute?"

"The neurotoxicologist? Sure thing. How come?"

"I can't tell you right now. Just playing a hunch. Can I see her?"

"Go ahead. We had to sedate her, so expect her to be pretty groggy. We'll get her up to the neurology ward in a few minutes. Later." Then, seeing Peter's haggard appearance, Jay smiled and patted him on the shoulder. "Hey, don't worry. I'm sure she'll be all right."

Peter managed a weary smile and walked into the room. "Hi. How are you feeling?"

Megan struggled to open her eyes against the effects of the sedatives. "I'm okay, I guess. Where am I?"

"You're in the St. Mark's ER. You ran into the street and almost got hit by a truck."

Megan tried to look around, but her eyes wouldn't focus.

"When can we go home?"

"Not for a while. You'll be staying in the hospital for a few more days until Jay Harden finishes some tests."

"No more questions. Everybody's asking me too many questions," Megan muttered as her eyes closed languidly and she fell asleep.

Peter held Megan's hand and kissed her fingers tenderly. As he stood up to leave, he paid attention to the cardiac monitor for the first time, beeping at one hundred twenty beats per minute.

"Dr. Branstead, outside call. Dr. Peter Branstead, outside call."

Peter left the room, walked over to the nursing station, and dialed the operator.

"Pete, is that you? This is Steve Bergstraum."

"Am I glad to hear from you. Anything definite yet on the blood samples?"

"You bet. And you're going to love this. Each one of the samples had two unaccounted-for pharmacological agents. I was able to identify one as permixitine. It's a very potent and effective antidepressant in the category of drugs called the selective serotonin reuptake inhibitors, or SSRIs, but it's only in use in Eastern Europe and Russia. The FDA won't approve it because of its unacceptably high rate of seizure induction. Also, how much do you remember about cytochrome P450?"

"We're going back to freshman pharmacology, Steve. Cut me some slack."

"Then let me give you a two-minute refresher course, because this is important. The Cytochrome P450 system is a complex of enzyme systems, each component responsible for detoxifying a different type of chemical substrate. If it weren't for Cytochrome P450, even small quantities of drugs or natural toxins would build up in our bodies until they killed us. Each component has its own set of inducers, drugs that will improve its efficacy, and inhibitors, drugs that basically prevent it from doing its job. It happens that the SSRIs each tend to be excellent inhibitors of various components of Cytochrome P450. Well, permixitine happens to be an extremely potent inhibitor of virtually the entire system."

"Which means?"

"Which means that it would unpredictably boost the blood levels of a wide variety of other drugs that are metabolized by that system. That scared the crap out of the FDA, so they canned it before it even got to Phase I clinical trials."

Peter thought about the seizures in all of his patients. The permixitine certainly made sense, but it still didn't explain why they became confused or why they went into cardiac arrest.

"What about the second drug?"

"Well, that's the hooker. I can't identify that one at all. I searched all of the databases for registered experimental drugs, and it wasn't listed either in the United States or in Europe, so I can't tell you anything about it other than no authorized laboratory in Europe or the United States is working with it. In other words, it's illegal."

"Can't you tell me anything about its pharmacology, its toxicity. Anything at all?"

"Nope. The only thing I can tell you about it so far is that its concentration was higher in the ER samples than in the later samples, so it was probably given outside the hospital. If I had a good-sized amount of the stuff, I could analyze its structure and maybe even tell you a little about its metabolism, but I still couldn't tell you what its mechanism of action was. That would take months or even years of hit-or-miss studies. Sorry I can't help you much on that, Pete. If you could give me any clues on how it works, that would be a big help."

Peter's heart sank when he heard that. He had hoped to draw the noose around Albright's neck, but although he was tantalizingly close, he still had nothing solid to hand Detective Meinerhoff other than his suspicions, backed as they were by a great deal of circumstantial evidence. He needed to get the drug from Frank Halleck's room and hope that Steve's analysis would link Albright to the deaths. The only other person who could give him the answer was hopelessly demented and tranquilized into oblivion.

"Thanks anyway. Would it help if I could get you a sample of the drug?"

"It sure would. And how do you plan doing that?"

Peter dropped his tone down to a whisper. "I think I know who's responsible for all this, and I've got a 'Deep Throat' who may be able to get me some samples."

"Well, bring 'em up here, and I'll run 'em, even if it takes all night. By the way, I analyzed that serum from Amanda Ivy, and it was kind of interesting. I couldn't find any permixitine, but it did have a pretty hefty amount of Drug X. This Ivy lady's not a bum, too, is she?"

Peter's voice suddenly became very serious. "No, Steve. She's Megan's business manager, and she's in the hospital now with acute dementia. Worse than that, I just had Megan admitted today—acute confusional state, just like the rest. I think that they were both poisoned, but I don't know how. I sent you some of Megan's serum. You've got to help me. I think Megan's going to die."

"I'll give it top priority. I promise that if there is absolutely anything I can do ..."

"Thanks, Steve. If you can crack this, I'll owe you. Talk to you later."

Peter hung up the phone and sighed. If he could sneak the drug out of Frank Halleck's room, get Alan out of the clinic, and convince Detective Meinerhoff there was probable cause, he could bust Albright. And hopefully, Albright would spill his guts for a plea bargain and Peter would be able to get the antidote for Megan, Mrs. Ivy, and Frank Halleck. For the first time in days, things seemed to be looking up.

Alan lay on his bed, staring up at the ceiling. What a revolting development this was! This time, he had managed to get himself stuck on the locked ward of a card-carrying member of the International League of Mad Scientists. All around him, his fellow lowlifes were getting brain rot right in front of his eyes, and if Albright found out he was faking, his life wouldn't be worth a rat's ass. He hoped that somehow Peter could get to the authorities and spring him before he ended up at the bottom of the East River wearing Jimmy Hoffa's overshoes.

Suddenly, the door sprang open, and in strode Dr. Albright with another important-looking individual behind him. Two beefy troglodytes in white hospital orderly uniforms flanked them.

"Good morning, Mr. Lamplin. I'd like to introduce you to my research associate, Dr. Iosyp Zabrovych. He's come all the way over from Ukraine to visit our facility, and I've asked him to render a second opinion on your case." Dr. Zabrovych stepped out from behind Dr. Albright, gave a short, curt nod of greeting, his face stern and his brow furrowed. "You should feel quite flattered, Mr. Lamplin," Dr. Albright continued "to have two of the world's greatest experts on the neuropharmacology of dementia both conferring on your very puzzling condition."

Alan stood up and put on the best blank, inexpressive facial appearance he could with his heart beating like a trip-hammer. "You have to leave my room. I have to clean it before Mama comes in. She expects me to have it cleaned up before …"

"Shut up!" Albright bellowed. "Do you think I'm an idiot? We've been checking your blood for drug levels, and it's been absolutely nonexistent. I don't know what your game is, Mr. Lamplin, but I do know that you've been faking, and I must admit you've been doing a good job at it. But enough of this chicanery." He motioned to one of the aides standing next to him, who walked over to Alan and, with a huge ham-like fist, gave him a hard uppercut just below his sternum.

The blow had an instantaneous effect on Alan. Doubled over in pain and unable to breathe, he collapsed to the floor while his awareness faded momentarily and his vision whited out. His mouth gaping open like a fish, it was a full ten seconds before his diaphragm could move again, drawing precious air into his lungs, and his mind pulled away from the brink of unconsciousness. When his vision returned, all he could see were the tips of Dr. Albright's shoes just inches from his face.

"What did you do with the capsules, Mr. Lamplin? I need to know."

"I flushed them down the toilet," Alan gasped when he was finally able to speak. "My mother told me never to take candy from strangers."

One of the orderlies pulled him up by his hair to a standing position and got Alan into a full Nelson, lifting his feet up off the floor. The sudden stretch on his abdominal muscles made Alan gasp with pain. The other orderly stepped in front of Alan and pounded his fist into his palm, preparing for another punch.

"No. I don't want the police finding him bruised. It could lead back to us." He turned to Dr. Zabrovych and the two argued in Ukrainian while the two massive orderlies and Alan remained frozen in position. After several minutes of conversation, Dr. Zabrovych left the room, and Albright barked orders in Ukrainian to the orderlies. They threw Alan face down on the bed, one of them pinning his arms behind his back while the other pulled his pants and shorts down to his knees, then pinned his legs to the bed.

"I thought psychiatrists weren't supposed to enter into sexual relationships with their patients," Alan said nervously, struggling to keep down the panic.

"Fear not, Mr. Lamplin. Sexual violation is not in my repertoire. But we can't afford to have you go to the authorities with whatever information you have about our project."

Dr. Zabrovych came back into the room, followed by a nurse bearing two syringes. She dutifully swabbed off each of Alan's buttocks with alcohol and consecutively plunged one needle into each buttock, emptying its contents forcefully, in spite of Alan's squirming and swearing. As quickly as she'd entered, the nurse left the room, and the orderlies released Alan and followed her out the door.

"It's a pity we won't be able to do pharmacological studies on you, Mr. Lamplin. I would be interested to see how such a large dose of UR-416 is metabolized in the presence of permixitine, but we need to dispose of you quickly to avoid embarrassing questions from the authorities. Good-bye, Mr. Lamplin."

Dr. Albright turned and left the room with Dr. Zabrovych, shutting and locking the door behind him.

He then turned to the nurse who was waiting outside the room. "Watch him for a few hours. He'll quiet down after UR-416 kicks in; then have him disposed of like the others."

Albright and Zabrovych then left the experimental ward, ignoring the din of door pounding and muffled epithets emanating from Alan's room.

Peter glanced quickly at his watch as he picked up the phone. He only had a few minutes before the weekly grand rounds, but there were a few phone calls he had to make. The first was to Walter Ivy.

"Amanda Ivy's room, Walter Ivy speaking."

"Walter, this is Peter Branstead. How's Mrs. Ivy doing?"

"I'm glad you called. She's been a little more confused today. Anything show up on the tests yet?"

"I think I've got some clues. Amanda may have been poisoned."

"You can't be serious. I've been married to this woman for over thirty years. Amanda's very direct and forthright, but she's a wonderful woman. She doesn't have a mean bone in her body. I can't think of her having a single enemy in this world. Who would want to poison her?"

"I don't think the intent was to poison her. I think the intended victim was Megan, and Mrs. Ivy was poisoned unintentionally."

"Megan! Now you're really not making any sense. Megan is the sweetest girl on the face of God's green earth. What do you think is going on?"

"Megan had an acrimonious discussion with someone who I have reason to believe may be mentally unstable. I've met the man, and I wouldn't put it past him to try something like this. I can't tell you anything more about it right now, but I need your help. I need you to think, Walter. Did Mrs. Ivy tell you of anything peculiar that might have gone on in the office that might relate to this?"

"There was the chocolate cake ..."

"What chocolate cake?"

"Two days ago, Amanda brought home a chocolate cake that had been delivered to the office. The card was addressed to Megan, but she gave most of it to Amanda. Something about a diet, I think. Amanda ate pretty much all of it, and I threw out the rest. I can't touch the stuff because of my diabetes."

"Any idea who might have sent the cake, Walter?"

"Amanda never tells me about office patients, but I remember the card was signed 'For all you've done, H. H.,' if that's of any help."

"H. H." might have been Harriet Halleck. On the other hand, it could have been Dr. Albright trying to mislead Megan into thinking it was sent by Harriet.

"Do you know if Megan might have eaten any of the cake?"

"She might have. Amanda said she kept about a quarter of it in the office. Why do you ask? What's happened to Megan?"

Of course she would have eaten it. Megan's resistance to chocolate was zero, particularly when she was under stress. It was all fitting together. Frightfully well.

"I admitted her this morning. All of a sudden, she became confused and ran out in the street in front of a truck."

"Sweet Jesus! Is she all right?"

"Well, physically she's okay. The truck had almost stopped before it hit her. But right now, she's almost as confused as Amanda. I've got to go. I've got some leads, but I need some time to get everything organized. I'll get back to you as soon as I figure out what's going on."

A quick call to Megan's office confirmed that there was no chocolate cake in the office refrigerator and that nobody else in the office had developed any confusion. Next was a call to Harriet Halleck.

"Harriet, this is Dr. Peter Branstead."

"Dr. Branstead, thank goodness you called. Did you get a chance to see Frank yet? I hadn't heard from you or Megan."

"Sorry. I've been very busy since yesterday, and Megan's been ... indisposed. I did get a chance to talk with Dr. Albright and visit Frank on the ward. To be quite honest with you, he's in pretty bad shape, and I'm not sure that Dr. Albright can do anything for him. Have you seen Frank since he was admitted to East Side Psychiatric?"

"No. Every time I go there, they tell me he'd get too upset if I saw him. Dr. Branstead, I'm getting frantic with worry. What's happening with Frank?"

"I'm not sure, but I'm going back to see him again this evening, and I think it would help if you came with me. I'd like to transfer him to my service, and I'll need you there to sign release papers."

"I'll be there, Dr. Branstead. Having Frank locked up in there terrifies me, and I think he's getting worse all the time."

"Fine. I'll pick you up this evening, and we can go there together. By the way, did you send Megan a chocolate cake the other day?"

"Chocolate cake? No, why?"

"Nothing important. Megan got a cake from someone, and it was signed 'For all you've done, H. H.' She thought it might have been you and wanted to thank you for it."

"I'd love to send her a chocolate cake, if I only knew how to bake. Frank always used to make fun of me because I couldn't even follow the directions on a box. I haven't baked anything for years."

"Must have been someone else. See you tonight, Mrs. Halleck."

It was still circumstantial, but he'd found nothing yet to contradict his theory.

As Peter arrived, the auditorium in St. Mark's Hospital was already filling up for the internal medicine grand rounds on "Alzheimer's Disease: An Update on Pathophysiology and Potential Treatment Modalities." The topic was suitably dry for grand rounds but very timely for Peter.

Peter muttered greetings to various doctors and took a seat in the back, not being in a socializing mood. The buzz of conversation in the auditorium fell to a hush as Dr. Laurence Gray was introduced and began his lecture.

"Alzheimer's disease is a degenerative disease of the central nervous system primarily manifested clinically as a progressive, generalized decline in cognitive abilities. First described by Alois Alzheimer in 1907 in a fifty-five-year-old woman ..."

The lecture was following the standard medical review format: a historical review of the literature, a description of the pathological and clinical findings, and finally the differential diagnosis of Alzheimer's disease. Then Dr. Gray would take time to discuss his research and, what Peter wanted to hear most, the possible treatments. The last few nights of limited sleep were taking their toll, and Peter drifted in and out as Dr. Gray droned on.

"... and a substantial number, between forty and seventy percent, will have delusions, frequently revolving around family members either stealing from them or being unfaithful in marriage. Commonly, patients become disoriented and misidentify their location, reporting that they are at home instead of in a hospital ..."

Peter thought ruefully about Megan's paranoid ideas about his stealing her wallet and money, and Frank Halleck's bizarre ideation about his wife's supposed infidelity.

"In addition to hallucinations, other disruptive behavior patterns, such as agitation, overly aggressive behavior, sexual inappropriateness, and wandering make care-giving a difficult, twenty-four-hour-a-day job for family ..."

Poor Mr. Ivy, trailing his wife around the house all night. What if this was permanent? After thirty years of marriage, it would break his heart to put her in a nursing home. He shuddered and focused back on the lecture.

"... The earliest pathological alterations appear in the nucleus basalis of Meynert, the septal nuclei, and the neurons of the diagonal band, shown here in blue, all of which have important and widespread projections to the cortex and limbic system, as outlined by the yellow arrows. Degeneration in these deep forebrain nuclei can be seen microscopically even before clinical ..."

If there was anything certain about this drug, it didn't have any demonstrable micropathology. None of the changes of Alzheimer's disease had been seen in any of the derelicts, even on an ultrastructural basis by electron microscopy.

"... resulting in a buildup of microtubule-binding tau proteins, eventually forming the neurofibrillary tangles pathognomonic of ..."

Peter shook his head in an attempt to wake himself up and hoped his tape recorder was picking all of this up. He swore an oath never again to attend a lecture after a week without sleep.

"The brain has a wide variety of neurotransmitters, chemicals that facilitate communication between nerve cells. In Alzheimer's disease, the chief neurotransmitter affected is acetylcholine. This goes along with clinical observations that drugs that are known to block the effects of acetylcholine, such as scopolamine, may induce amnesia, which fortunately is completely reversible on withdrawal of the drug. And drugs such as physostigmine and donepezil, which increase levels of acetylcholine in the brain by blocking acetylcholinesterase, may improve some of the behavior disorders associated with Alzheimer's disease, albeit temporarily."

At last a possible clue. Peter snapped to attention, wrote "physostigmine" and "scopolamine" on his scratch pad and circled them. Both the lab at St. Mark's and Steve Bergstraum's lab had already checked for scopolamine and other anticholinergics, and none were present. However, a trial of physostigmine or donepezil might be worth a try. At least it would give him the feeling that he was doing something. If you couldn't treat the patient, you could at least treat the doctor.

Dr. Gray flashed an enormously complex slide on the screen, full of chemical equations, some leading in circles, some branching off with arrows going to other portions of the slide. Each category of reactions was color coded, ostensibly for clarity, with perhaps a dozen different colors in all, giving the slide the appearance of a plate of Technicolor spaghetti. At the center of the screen, in bold letters, was the word

ACETYLCHOLINE

There was no way in hell he was going to be able to copy down or even understand this slide. Freshman biochem had been the last time he had paid any attention to those equations, storing them in his short-term memory and promptly forgetting them the moment exams were finished.

Apparently, Peter was not alone in his thoughts. A chorus of groans arose from the assembled audience, followed by laughter as everyone realized they were all in the same boat.

"Ladies and gentlemen, this slide is for effect only. We will only concern ourselves with a small portion of it, particularly since I can't remember most of it myself."

There was a smattering of appreciative chuckles, and one brave soul applauded.

"I would like you to focus your attention near the center of the slide." He aimed his laser pointer at a few strands of red spaghetti. "There is one crucial, rate-limiting enzyme responsible for acetylcholine biosynthesis. If it is impaired or inactivated, the entire system of acetylcholine neurotransmission would grind to a halt. It is also the most severely depleted enzyme in the brains of patients with Alzheimer's disease. It is called choline acetyltransferase, but for the sake of brevity we will henceforth refer to it by its accepted scientific abbreviation …"

And here, Dr. Gray paused to pick up an orange grease pencil and wrote down on the overhead projector the three initials

CAT

Peter's face drained of color, and his face broke into a cold sweat. He did not see the three letters on the screen as a scientific abbreviation. In his mind's eye, he saw them scrawled over the walls of Frank Halleck's room in ketchup, pureed squash, creamed spinach, and his own excrement. He could hear Frank screaming his demented mantra for hours at a time to an unheeding world, while his brain slowed down like an unwound clock, no longer able to create one of its simplest but most crucial chemicals. And with that inability, Frank's brain lost its capacity for reason, for memory, for emotion. It lost its ability to control his basic bodily functions. In essence, his brain functioned at the level of a newborn baby, capable of moving his limbs, of feeling pain, of sensing hunger and thirst, but not much else. And that was where Megan was headed!

Peter jumped out of his chair and excused himself down an entire row of seated physicians. Racing to his office, Peter slammed the door behind him and grabbed the phone.

"Hello, pharmacy? This is Dr. Branstead. How many ampules of physostig-mine do you have? Five? Okay, get them ready. They're for Amanda Ivy and Megan Hutchins. They'll each be getting an ampule intravenously every two hours round the clock until I cancel the order, so order another four dozen ampules. Yes, I said four dozen. If the supplier doesn't have them in stock, then call the company directly and have them overnighted. Just get those ampules, okay? Fine. Thanks. Bye."

Peter hung up and dialed another number. It took about ten rings before Meinerhoff got on the line, during which time Peter wrote CAT over and over on his notepad. Christ, everything was finally fitting together.

"Meinerhoff, homicide," said the familiar tired voice.

"Detective, this is Dr. Peter Branstead. I called you two days ago about the dead bums, as you so elegantly called them."

There was a brief pause. "Oh, yeah. Anything new, Doc?"

"You bet. I've been doing my homework, Detective. First of all, I've got a friend who's a neurotoxicologist at …"

"A neuro what?"

"An expert in nerve poisons."

"Oh, oh. Yeah, right. You guys have a specialist for everything, don't you."

"At any rate, he found an unregistered drug in the blood of every victim, and he thinks it was administered outside the hospital. He also found small quantities of an antidepressant that's only available in Eastern Europe—not licensed for use in the U.S. Finally, I found out there's a psychiatrist with strong connections to Ukraine and a research interest in dementia operating an experimental ward in the East Village, stocked with winos that he recruited off the street, ostensibly for detox. And he happens to have his lab assistant locked in that ward, demented as hell, who I think has also been poisoned."

"All of which means …?"

"All of which means this … I believe this psychiatrist is doing experimental work using human subjects to test out an unregistered, illegal drug. When they get into the terminal phase of toxicity, he boots them out on the street so the clinic won't be implicated, knowing that their deaths will be assumed to be of complications of their presumed alcohol abuse. When his lab assistant figures this out and threatens to turn state's evidence, the psychiatrist poisons *him* to keep him quiet and locks him up in his own ward. In fact, I have reason to believe that this psychiatrist may have also poisoned my girlfriend. She's the lab assistant's therapist, and she had a big fight with the psychiatrist a few days ago and threatened to go to the medical authorities."

"Interesting theory, but it's all circumstantial. Any hard evidence?"

"Tonight I may be able to get an actual sample of the drug and have it analyzed. I'm also trying to get his lab assistant under my care at St. Mark's where I can test him. If he's positive for the drug, the only way he could be getting it is through this psychiatrist."

There was a brief pause as Meinerhoff digested the new information.

"Branstead, you get me something concrete that I can take to the DA, and I'll nail this guy."

"Then you're with me?"

"Yeah, I'm with you. Just get me what I need, and he's as good as busted, okay?"

"Will do. Call you later."

Peter hung up the phone and pumped his fist in the air.

"Yes … yes … yes! You pompous son of a bitch, I've got you right by your balls," he shouted to the empty office.

CHAPTER 12

▼

With rounds over, Peter and Greg Johnson relaxed for a moment in the doctor's lounge, feet propped up on a table, while Peter sipped on one of a series of cups of coffee and recounted the information he had gotten from Steve Bergstraum.

"Let me get this straight. So you think this guy Albright has an experimental ward right here in downtown Manhattan, and he dumps his guinea pigs right back on the street when he's finished with them? Come on, Dr. Branstead, he's not stupid. He's got to realize that you can't do illegal human experimentation in the middle of downtown Manhattan without someone catching on to you sooner or later."

"I've met this guy. He's got an ego that could fill Madison Square Garden. He's so convinced of his invulnerability that he thinks he can get away with anything."

"But I don't get it. What's his percentage? He can't possibly intend to publish it or sell it to a drug company. And if he were just doing it for some sort of bizarre intellectual thrill, why would he risk his academic career and a lifetime prison sentence for something as trivial as that? I don't know. No matter how I look at it, I can't see a motive."

Peter sat down after pouring himself another cup of coffee. "It all has something to do with this Ukrainian-American Friendship Foundation. They certainly have money to burn, and they're funding him for some reason, but I just don't know why."

The insistent buzzing of his beeper interrupted Peter.

Dialing into his voicemail, Peter was surprised at the message.

"Hi, Peter. This is Rachel. I've been waiting for you all afternoon in Megan's room. Please give me a call."

Peter excused himself and immediately rushed off to Megan's room. Sure enough, there was Rachel, sitting in a chair alongside a sleeping Megan.

"Rachel! What are you doing here?"

"Thanks for the warm reception. Whatever happened to 'Rachel, how good to see you'?"

"Sorry, that came out all wrong. I just wasn't expecting you here. I haven't had the time to call anyone yet."

"Megan and I were supposed to meet for lunch. Her office told me she had been admitted to the hospital. What happened?"

Peter shut the door and sat down on Megan's bed.

"She woke up this morning acting very bizarre—really paranoid, confused. She ran outside in her robe into the middle of Mercer Street right in front of a truck. Luckily, the driver saw her and slammed on his brakes, so he only bumped her just hard enough to knock her down."

"Is she all right?"

"Physically she's okay, but she's been so disoriented that we've had to keep her sedated all day."

"This is all very weird. Do you have any idea what's going on?"

Peter paused for a second before answering. "Before he left, did Daniel tell you about the situation I've had with all the deaths on the ward?"

"He mentioned something about it. Why?"

"I think it's connected to what happened to Megan, but I'm not quite sure yet."

Rachel gave Peter a long, curious stare but said nothing further.

"Gosh!" she exclaimed abruptly, looking at her watch, "Gotta go. Listen, I'll be calling Daniel tonight. I'll let him know what's happened to Megan." She stood up and walked around Megan's bed toward the door. Before she left, she stopped and touched Peter on the shoulder. "I'll keep in touch." She closed the door behind her, leaving Peter alone with Megan.

"Megan, are you awake?" he whispered gently in her ear.

Megan stirred and opened her eyes through heavy lids, her eyes out of focus from sedation, and smiled sleepily. "Hi, Peter. I'm glad you're here."

Peter bent over and kissed her on the forehead. "Everything's going to be all right. Don't worry about a thing."

Megan gave a contented sigh and promptly sank back into her medicated sleep. The cardiac monitor registered one-forty. Peter decided that when it hit one-fifty, he would ask Jay to have her transferred to the ICU. Peter kissed her again and left quietly, his heart sinking.

Peter stopped by the nursing station to speak to the charge nurse. "Has the physostigmine been started on Mrs. Ivy and Miss Hutchins yet?"

"Not yet, Dr. Branstead. The bags just arrived here from the pharmacy. We'll be hanging them in a few minutes."

Well, thought Peter, *here goes nothing.*

At that moment, the familiar voice of the paging operator rang out for what must have been the thousandth time that week, this time calling him to the ER.

When he arrived at the emergency room, Greg Johnson was washing his hands just outside of one of the rooms.

"Not another one."

"Dr. Branstead, you must be psychic."

"Yeah, yeah. The Great Swami Branstead knows all, sees all. What's up?'

"Not much to add about this one. Same story as the others. The only difference is that he's quite a bit younger, maybe in his late twenties, so it doesn't exactly fit the MO. In addition, he was found unresponsive in a water-soaked dumpster in an alleyway on the other side of the Village from where the previous John Does were found. And if your theory about East Side Psych and the evil Dr. Albright is correct, it's no wonder they kicked him out. He's a raving lunatic and filthier than a Las Vegas lady mud wrestler. Want to have a look?"

"Yeah, sure. By the way, are you going to leave any water for the rest of Manhattan?" Greg had lathered and rinsed his hands four times during their brief conversation.

Greg grimaced and turned off the water. "Sorry. After examining that guy, I have the feeling that I can't get my hands clean. You might want to put on a pair of gloves."

As the two doctors walked into the emergency ward, Peter saw a gurney with an unkempt, unwashed young man on it. He was rolling side to side, moaning incomprehensibly, with a bag of IV fluid pouring wide open. Peter sighed, the sadness and fatigue getting to him.

"Is this the guy?"

"Nah. That's just a rummy the ER crew is drying out. He'll be out in an hour or two. Our boy is over there."

The two walked over to a remote corner of the ER. The gurney in that corner was hidden from sight by the standard-issue, vertically striped, hospital-green curtain. From the other side of the curtain came the most animalistic howls and screams that Peter had ever heard within the confines of a hospital. If there was any recognizable speech in the howling, it was all in four-letter words.

Greg Johnson grabbed the edge of the curtain and pulled it back with a dramatic flair. "Dr. Branstead, may I have the pleasure of introducing you to John Doe the Ninth."

As inured as he thought he had become in the past week, what Peter saw behind the curtain nauseated him. John Doe was tied down, kicking and thrashing, by four-point leather restraints around his wrists and ankles. He had been stripped naked, and every square inch of his body, including his filth-matted hair and even his teeth, was covered by a thick, greenish-black residue that could only have come from having wallowed in waste liquid that had been allowed to sit and stagnate for months at the bottom of a garbage dumpster. The nurses were laboriously cleaning his body with washcloths, which were then thrown out, irredeemable even by modern sterilization techniques.

Peter shuddered. "What are we going to do with this poor devil?"

Suddenly, John Doe let out a bellow of rage after one of the nurses had bravely decided to attack his face with a washcloth.

"Oh, shut up," she muttered. "They don't pay me enough to do this crap." After she had managed to scrub off most of the residue, she turned to get another washcloth. John Doe strained at his restraints, raising himself up as far as he could, his mouth twisted into a snarl. He turned and glared at Peter who, for the first time, could see the long jagged scar extending down the length of his left cheek.

Peter's face broke out into a sweat, his head swimming. He knew this John Doe very well.

It was Alan.

CHAPTER 13

▼

"East Side Psychiatric Center. May I help you?"

The voice on the intercom surprised Peter. Instead of the delicate lilt of the young receptionist, he heard a coarse, deep baritone with a heavy Slavic accent.

"I'm Dr. Peter Branstead. I'm with Mrs. Harriet Halleck, and we have an appointment with Dr. Albright this evening."

After a pause, the buzzer sounded, and the two entered the reception room.

The reception area was drastically changed. The crystal chandelier, brass sconces, and most of the floor-to-ceiling mirrors had all been removed. Lighting was now provided solely by a series of cheap floor lamps. That and the removal of the mirrors had changed the overall visual effect of the reception room from a luxurious, expansive salon to a dimly lit cave.

"It certainly has changed quite a bit since I was last here," Harriet whispered to Peter, who nodded in stunned acquiescence.

"I apologize for our appearance," called out the man behind the reception desk, his voice echoing against the bare walls. "It's a mess, no?"

"It sure is. What happened here?"

The man sitting at the reception desk was an athletically built man in a security guard uniform with a pugnacious jaw and a nose with a few too many angles to it. Peter glanced down at his hands, which were covered with tattoos of beetles, some partially hidden under his sleeves as if they were trying to escape by crawling up his arms.

"We have to make some renovations in the lobby. Don't worry; everything will be back to normal in a few weeks after construction is complete. Dr. Albright is expecting you. I'll escort you to the secured ward, Dr. Branstead."

"Don't bother, we'll take ourselves."

"I'm sorry, sir. Center regulations. I regret the inconvenience, but it is not allowed to have visitors wandering freely about the premises for the sake of our patients' safety and privacy."

"And who exactly are you?"

The man smiled broadly but eyed them with suspicious caution as he shook Peter's hand. "Gennadi Chursin, Chief of Security for the center. Follow me, please."

The three rode in uncomfortable silence to the top floor of the center, where Chursin unlocked the door to let them in. Dr. Albright was at the nursing station, talking quietly with a tall well-dressed man.

"Good evening, Dr. Branstead, Mrs. Halleck. I was just discussing Frank's case with my associate. Permit me to introduce Dr. Iosyp Zabrovych, Clinical Director and Chief Research Fellow of the Ukrainian National Psychiatric Institute in Kiev. He and I have collaborated on a number of research projects through the years. I was delighted when he told me he would be visiting the United States. I'm hopeful that he will be able to assist me, as Frank presents a unique problem, unprecedented, at least to my knowledge, in the psychiatric literature."

With that, Dr. Albright spoke a few words to Dr. Zabrovych in Ukrainian. Peter could discern his name and that of Harriet Halleck but not much else.

Dr. Zabrovych reached out his hand to shake Peter's. "I em plizz to meet you," he said in a thick Slavic accent.

As Peter reached out to shake Zabrovych's hand, he was surprised to find his wrist crossed by a cleanly cut scar, identical to Albright's.

"You'll have to excuse Dr. Zabrovych's accent," Dr. Albright interjected apologetically. "He is fluent in Ukrainian, Russian, and German, but his knowledge of English is rather cursory. In addition, I must apologize for the sorry state of our reception area, but we are about to undergo a major renovation of the center facilities.

"I promise you, Mrs. Halleck," he said reassuringly to Harriet, "that our construction will not interfere in the least with your husband's care."

Peter steeled himself, and spoke. "That's what we wanted to discuss with you, Dr. Albright. Mrs. Halleck has been very concerned about her husband's deteriorating condition. I have assured her that you were working hard in Frank's best interests, but she would feel more comfortable if Frank was transferred to my care at St. Mark's Hospital as soon as possible."

The look on Albright's face abruptly changed from an overly solicitous concern to a flinty glower. Harriet had her eyes downcast, afraid to look directly at Dr. Albright. She was clearly intimidated by him. Harriet had expressed this to Peter in so many words on the cab ride, and it had taken all of his powers of persuasion to convince Harriet to come with him. He needed her both to sign release papers and to provide a distraction while he went to Frank's room.

"Mrs. Halleck is not a child, Dr. Branstead, and she is perfectly capable of speaking for herself. Aren't you, Harriet?"

Peter saw her nod numbly. *My God, Harriet,* Peter screamed in this thoughts, *this isn't the time to give up. Your husband's life is at stake.*

"I would prefer to hear this directly from Mrs. Halleck. Is this truly your wish, Harriet?" Albright's tone was sharp and condescending. "I know you love Frank dearly, and I can't believe that you would rather entrust your husband's well-being to this ..." he hesitated in an unsuccessful attempt to dredge up an appropriately disparaging term, "... this young doctor who hardly even knows Frank, when my relationship with Frank has gone back so many years. I'm certain you're aware that Frank's illness is precisely in my field of expertise and that I have done everything humanly possible to ferret out the cause of his derangement. With Dr. Zabrovych's help, I feel that we are about to have a breakthrough. This would be precisely the wrong time to give up and try to start from the beginning with another physician of, dare I say, more limited abilities."

Albright then drew himself up fully, putting maximal authority into his final words.

"I feel it is my professional responsibility to inform you, Harriet, that if you insist on removing Frank from my care, I can only predict the direst consequences for him, and you will only have yourself to blame."

Peter's heart sank. Megan was right. Albright was a master of psychological manipulation. He knew Harriet's weak points, and he pulled her strings like a puppet master. If Harriet gave up now, all was lost.

For an agonizingly long moment, Harriet continued to stare at the floor in silence, alone with her thoughts.

"I do love Frank dearly, Dr. Albright. We've been married for almost thirty years; we've seen our children grow up; we've fought; we've seen each other at our worst first thing in the morning; and we've stood by each other through everything that life could throw at us."

Dr. Albright nodded sympathetically and smiled, first at Harriet and then at Peter, although when he turned to Peter the corner of his mouth turned up in a victorious smirk. "I understand, Harriet. We all want what's best for Frank."

"I know, Dr. Albright," she said, now raising her head and looking straight into his eyes, "and that's why I must insist that you release Frank as soon as possible to Dr. Branstead. I'm prepared to sign the papers now."

Albright's face looked as if he had been slapped. In just a fraction of a second, the color drained from it, his smile metamorphosed into a tight-lipped scowl, and his eyes glared furiously. Peter figured this was probably the first time in years that anybody had dared to stand up to him, and his ego wasn't prepared for such a rapid deflation. *Get used to it, buddy, there's going to be a lot more where that came from.*

Dr. Albright collected himself quickly. "Very well, Mrs. Halleck. We will be glad to do as you wish, but I cannot lend my support to this irresponsible course of action. The nurse will give you the appropriate papers to sign." He then turned to Peter. "I'm sure you appreciate the difficulties inherent in transferring a patient of Mr. Halleck's ... demeanor. I hope you will allow us until tomorrow afternoon to make the arrangements."

Peter would have preferred an earlier transfer, but he saw no value in pushing the issue and was afraid that, should he back Albright into a corner, he might come out fighting, which would further traumatize poor Harriet.

"Tomorrow afternoon will be fine, Dr. Albright. Thank you for your cooperation. Now, if you please, I'd like to see Frank for just a few minutes."

"Be my guest," Albright said coldly, resuming his usual icy composure. "I'll be assisting Mrs. Halleck with the transfer papers if you need me." Albright turned to the perplexed Dr. Zabrovych, who had unsuccessfully tried to take in everything that had gone on without understanding a word but clearly had gotten the gist that something bad had just happened. As the two psychiatrists conferred heatedly and Harriet calmed her jangled nerves, Peter took advantage of the circumstances to visit Frank.

Incredibly, nothing had changed in Frank's room. The agitated graffiti, their meaning now comprehended by Peter in all their dark significance, remained splashed over the walls. The bedclothes remained strewn about randomly. Most disturbing, even Frank had not changed. Not a hair. He was still in the same position that Peter had left him in the day before, with the same vacant, unblinking expression staring at the same nothingness as the previous day.

He glanced about the room. There were no observation mirrors or video cameras scrutinizing him. He walked casually toward the nightstand and opened the drawer. Other than a small Bible and a hairbrush, it was empty. Peter bit his lip with disappointment, but as he pulled the drawer out further, there was a small wad of paper wedged into the back corner. It contained a collection of two kinds of capsules, a few partially dissolved by Alan's saliva but most still intact or minimally damaged. Peter quickly stuffed the wad in his jacket pocket, first sprinkling a small amount of powder from both pills onto the bottom of the drawer, a little something for Meinerhoff's forensics team to work on.

Peter leaned over and whispered in Frank's ear. "Don't worry, Frank. We'll get you out of here tomorrow." A single tear slowly coursed its way down Frank's otherwise impassive, expressionless face.

Peter walked down the hallway to the nursing station, his heart beating a heavy cadence against the inside of his chest wall. On his way, he passed by a nurse.

"Excuse me, Miss. When I was here yesterday I met a young man with a large scar across his face. How is he doing?"

"Oh, you must mean Mr. Lamplin. Yes, he's doing much better. We managed to find some family of his that lived in Pennsylvania, and they came by and took him home this morning. I think he's finally going to turn his life around, thanks to Dr. Albright."

"Oh, I'm sure Dr. Albright has made a big impact on his life." Peter tried hard to keep the bitterness out of his voice.

Peter assisted Harriet out of the locked ward. A stony-faced Gennadi Chursin met them at the elevator. The ride down was unpleasantly silent as Chursin glared at them out of the corner of his eye and wordlessly escorted them to the front door.

"I absolutely detest that man. I always have, and I always will," Harriet finally let out after they were safely in the taxi cab on their way uptown to Harriet's apartment. "There was no way that I would let him keep my Frank under his control."

"I'm proud of you, Harriet. That must have been very difficult for you."

"For just a moment, I almost backed down. I felt exactly like when I was a child and my father would yell at me in front of all my friends and humiliate me. I wanted to crawl into a corner and die. But I thought of Frank in that dreadful man's clutches and ... Ooh, I could have strangled him, I was so furious!" She turned to Peter expectantly. "Is there still some hope for Frank?"

"Don't worry, Harriet. I'm sure we're on the road to getting this licked." Another little white lie, but Peter didn't know what else to say.

After dropping Harriet off at her apartment building, Peter took the cab to the Neurological Institute and took the elevator to Bergstraum's lab on the twelfth floor.

"Peter Branstead, Boy Wonder, good to see you again. I would imagine this isn't a social call at 10:00 p.m." Bergstraum pumped Peter's arm vigorously and led him into the lab.

Steve was a roly-poly, ruddy-cheeked, scraggly-bearded character who had long ago decided that patient care wasn't all it was cracked up to be and had thrown his lot in with the academicians, preferring the world of grant applications and publishing deadlines to the daily grind of patient management. Steve was addicted to the adrenaline rush that came when an experiment that had taken weeks or months to set up was in its final phases and the compiled data flowed out of the computer. He loved giving esoteric lectures at international conferences and being on a first-name basis with the most prominent researchers in his field. Steve was an academic elitist, first and foremost.

"I've got a little surprise for you," Peter said as he took the small package of capsules out of his coat pocket.

Bergstraum gave an appreciative "mm-hmm" as he delicately unwrapped the wad of paper and drugs and examined them closely.

"The light blue one is permixitine. I looked it up in an international formulary after I talked to you. The other was encapsulated in a pharmacy. The number is an identification number for an experimental protocol. I can analyze it in a few hours and see if it's the stuff in the blood of those bums. But I still can't tell you what it does."

"I think I already know. What would you say if I told you that this was an inhibitor of choline acetyltransferase?"

Bergstraum drew his hand up to his chin and thoughtfully scratched his beard for a minute. "That makes some sense. But if that were the case, every nerve cell in the body that utilizes acetylcholine as a neurotransmitter would be rendered useless, including the motor neurons that need it for neuromuscular transmission. Whoever took this drug would become totally paralyzed, just as if they had been shot with curare."

"It's the only clue I've got. I need some answers on this, and I need them fast. Not only has Megan been poisoned, but her stepbrother, who was that 'Deep Throat' I told you about, has been poisoned, too. He sneaked his way into this doctor's research ward and managed to save these capsules for me, but it looks like he was caught and must have been given a whopping dose. He looks terrible,

Steve. I'm afraid he and Megan are going to die like the rest of the victims, and there's nothing I can do about it unless you give me some help."

"I'll get the answers for you as quickly as I can. Some people in this building owe me big time, and I've spent the day cashing in my IOUs. It'll be done. Now go home and get some rest. I'll call you the minute I find out something."

Peter left the main entrance of the Neurological Institute and stepped into the warm June night. A light rain had started to fall, the first in several days, but Peter was too exhausted to care whether or not he got wet. He flagged down a cab and collapsed into the back seat. It would be a long ride from 168th Street to SoHo, and, before the cab had even left Harlem, Peter had fallen asleep.

CHAPTER 14

▼

In spite of the overcast and drizzle, Valentyn Boshevsky's mood was buoyant as he bounded up the steps of the Ukrainian Capitol Building. Today was the president's constitutionally mandated annual address to the Rada outlining his proposed legislative agenda for the following year and, for the first time since his decline began, Labrinska was forced to appear in public. When his dementia became readily apparent to the assembled media and legislators, by constitutional law the prime minister would succeed him as soon as the Rada proclaimed the president unfit, which wouldn't take more than twenty-four hours. With Labrinska's party in disarray, he would be perfectly positioned to seize power permanently.

Timing was critical. If UR-416 were dosed too high, Labrinska would die too early, in seclusion. The sympathy vote might sweep another liberal president into power, and Boshevsky would lose. In addition, Labrinska's previous legislative agenda would remain intact, creating unacceptable hurdles to Boshevsky's plans to guide the direction of industrial privatization. On the other hand, if the dose were too low, he would simply appear to be a slightly forgetful old man—insufficient cause for removal from office.

However, today would be the turning point. The expense, the secrecy, the threat of exposure, all would fade into irrelevance when Boshevsky took control of the government. No matter if there had been an information leak. That would be taken care of in good time. There would be no conspiracy investigations when he was in control.

Taking his seat on the dais, Boshevsky looked out at the assembled Rada and guests. President Labrinska's wife, Iryna, was seated in the first row, as was traditional during the annual address to the Rada. Having set herself up as the guardian of all access to her husband when he was elected, Boshevsky had locked horns with the strong-willed woman frequently in the past, particularly in the last month as she zealously guarded her husband from public view as his condition worsened. And no Cerberus in Hades was more resolute or stubborn. Boshevsky allowed himself a fleeting moment of sympathy for this poor woman, forced by circumstances to have a front row seat to the public humiliation of her husband. But sympathy was for the weak.

Serves you right, Bitch, he thought.

A hush fell over the assemblage. With slow, measured steps the sergeant at arms of the Rada strode to the podium and struck his mace three times on the hardwood floor.

"Ladies and gentlemen, the president of the Republic of Ukraine, President Anatoly Labrinska."

The assemblage stood and applauded the entrance of President Labrinska. Rumors of his ill health had spread throughout the Rada, fanned in part by leaks from Boshevsky's office, but nobody really knew the nature or extent of the president's illness. Many had not even expected him to make this speech, and there was some hesitancy in their applause, particularly from Labrinska's own National Democrat Party. This uncertainty audibly increased as President Labrinska was led in.

Labrinska's spryness had been replaced by a slow, shuffling gait. He looked about uncertainly, as an aide, who gently held his arm, escorted him to the podium and at frequent intervals whispered instructions into his ear. Boshevsky stole a glance at Iryna Labrinska. She was not applauding but stood by her seat with her eyes closed, her hands in front of her face, palms pressed together in silent prayer as Labrinska laboriously mounted the podium.

"Ladies and gentlemen of the Verkhovna Rada, assembled dignitaries, friends, and people of Ukraine," the president read from a prepared text, "I come before you today to fulfill my constitutional obligation to inform you of the state of our nation and of the legislative plans of our government for the upcoming year." He read hesitantly, with occasional whispered corrections from his aide.

"We are in the midst of a tumultuous period in the long and colorful history of our great nation, and we face many challenges in the upcoming year. Because of economic constraints and negotiated treaties with our neighbors to the east and west, we will be decreasing the size of the Ukrainian Army to one sufficient to defend our nation without causing impediment to our economic and political goals." His aide had to assist him ever more regularly with pronunciation.

Iryna Labrinska continued silently praying as a tear rolled down her cheek.

"Economically, we are successfully waging a war against an inflation that, up until now, has paralyzed all hopes for economic recovery. In addition, we are in the midst of an ambitious plan to convert previously nationalized industries to the private sector, to improve their efficiency and profitability, and enable us to more successfully compete in the world marketplace."

In the midst of hesitant applause from his own party, Labrinska fumbled with his papers, trying to find his place. A low murmur arose from the communist opposition section, squelched by a few sharp taps from the sergeant at arms' mace.

"Finally, we are fighting an ongoing battle against organized crime and its pervasive effect on the government, the economy, and even the military. I will now address these issues individually and in depth." With that, Labrinska began shuffling papers even more aimlessly. His aide jumped in, trying to set his speech back in order, but suddenly everything unraveled.

"Get your hands off of my speech!" Labrinska shouted to his aide, who whispered urgently for him to calm down. "I'm not crazy, you know," he continued, his voice rising in anger. "I've done this before, and I will not have anybody order me about."

With that, Labrinska pulled the papers from his aide's hands with a violent tug. Some of the papers flew up in the air; some fluttered off the stage and onto the floor; others crumpled in Labrinska's palsied grasp. But instead of trying to resume his speech, Labrinska continued on his tirade while his wife's tears poured from her tightly closed eyes, her body rocking rhythmically as she redoubled her efforts at prayer, and his aide tried even harder to calm him down and reason with him. Even a continuous series of sharp taps from the ceremonial mace could not quiet the rising swell of voices from the floor.

"Get your hands off of me, and let me finish my speech." With that, the aide backed off. The tumult in the Rada quieted down slightly as Labrinska began again.

"Ladies and gentlemen of the Verkhovna Rada, assembled dignitaries, friends, and people of the great nation of Ukraine, I come before you today to fulfill my constitutional obligation to inform you of the state of our nation and of the legislative plans of our government for the upcoming year."

Recognizing that Labrinska was repeating himself without even realizing it, the entire opposition section began booing while the he continued to read his prepared statement, oblivious to the tumult. But Iryna Labrinska had had enough. She swept out of her seat and rushed onstage to the podium. Grabbing her husband by the arm and motioning to his aide to help her, she led him to the back of the dais, passing by Prime Minister Boshevsky, and guided him to the back door of the auditorium.

Hoping to find a clear path out of the building, she rushed to the back door, but the entire press corps cadre, who had been positioned there by Boshevsky's aides, blocked their exit.

Iryna Labrinska forced her way through the crowd of shouting reporters, incited into a journalistic feeding frenzy by the smell of a major political scandal. The president and his wife were pushed into a waiting limousine, which sped away to the presidential mansion.

Boshevsky was not about to let control of events slip through his grasp, even for an instant. A balding, pudgy, heavily perspiring man appeared at the back door of the Rada building in front of the journalists and began to speak in a loud voice.

"Gentlemen, my name is Dr. Sergei Nikitin. I am one of the team of psychiatrists that has been caring for His Excellency, President Labrinska, in his recent illness. For the past few months, President Labrinska has been subject to increasingly severe mental problems, manifest by worsening memory difficulties and confusion. We have been attributing this to stress and overwork, but in the past few days the situation has become increasingly grave, and his progression has become more marked, as can be evidenced by today's events.

"I have just been in touch with my colleague, Dr. Iosyp Zabrovych, who is currently in the United States of America seeking further consultation with experts in the field. He will be returning to Kiev urgently, and he has asked that President Labrinska be admitted to the Kiev Neurological Institute under the personal care of Dr. Alexei Mogilev, the Chairman of the Department of Neurology, for further testing. We will have further press releases as events warrant."

With that, Dr. Nikitin stepped through the back door and wiped his perspiring face with a handkerchief. Walking confidently down the hall towards him was Prime Minister Boshevsky, grinning broadly.

"Congratulations, Nikitin. Your drug works perfectly. You and Zabrovych should be proud of yourselves. Now please get out of my way. I must address the press."

Boshevsky strode out onto the steps. Hands clasped behind his back, he looked about at the thronging crowd of journalists and TV cameras, pleased beyond his wildest dreams at the way things had turned out.

"Gentlemen and ladies of the press, we are all shocked and dismayed at this terrible illness that has befallen our beloved president. Until President Labrinska gets back to full health, the Constitution of Ukraine dictates that I assume his responsibilities as acting president of Ukraine. I will be asking the Rada to confirm this in emergency session this afternoon. We deeply regret that this tragic illness has incapacitated Mr. Labrinska, and our heart and sympathies go out to his courageous wife. Now, if you will excuse me, I must go back and address the Rada."

Boshevsky turned and walked back into the building. Victory was his, and when his power was fully consolidated in a few days, the wolf pack of the Rada would finally be tamed.

Stopping briefly outside the door to the dais he had just left, Boshevsky brushed himself off, straightened his tie, and smiled. If one was going to lead a nation into a new era, one must look his best. He opened the door and strode to meet his destiny.

CHAPTER 15

▼

What had been a light rain the previous evening had continued building through the night, and, by the time Peter got on his bicycle to ride to St. Mark's, the rain was hammering down, and the streets of downtown Manhattan were almost flooded. Avoiding the heavily trafficked Avenue of the Americas, Peter took the small side streets south of Washington Square, pushing himself as fast as possible through Washington Square, down West Eight Street and Greenwich Avenue, and finally pulling up to St. Mark's Hospital. Chaining his bicycle to the railing by the ambulance entrance under the watchful eyes of hospital security, Peter walked in through the emergency entrance and made his way to the neurology ward to grab some towels and dry off before he made early rounds.

His first stop was Alan Lamplin's bed in the ICU. Alan's physical appearance was certainly improved, thanks to the vigorous application of a scrub brush and an electric razor, but he was kept heavily sedated on a lorazepam drip, remained in restraints, and had multiple IV lines and the usual collection of tubes and catheters protruding from his bodily orifices. Peter sighed. Trained as an electrician, all he ever seemed to deal with was plumbing.

He walked over to Alan's bedside and thumbed through the chart. Unfortunately, everything was proceeding exactly the way it had previously with the other victims. His pulse was up around two hundred in spite of the sedation. He had taken the precaution of putting Alan on seizure medications and physostigmine, as he had done with Megan and Mrs. Ivy, but he was not very sanguine about altering the course of events.

Peter rubbed his eyes in exhaustion, more emotional than physical. The horrible ironies were inescapable. Megan was dying, likely from the same thing that was killing her stepbrother, just hours after she promised Peter that she wouldn't die, wouldn't leave him. Even if she pulled through somehow, she would be losing the long-lost brother with whom she had recently been united. And both of their fates were in Peter's hands. There was nobody else, with the exception of Dr. William Albright, who was more knowledgeable about their condition than he was.

Peter turned from Alan's bed, preparing himself to go to Megan's room, when he was paged overhead.

"Dr. Branstead speaking."

"Bergstraum here, Pete." Steve's tone sounded ebullient, almost manic.

"Please tell me you have some good news, or else I'm in real trouble."

"You bet I do. It cost me every last one of my IOUs, and I had half the neuropharmacology department working all night on this drug of yours, but we've gotten most of the basic mechanisms and pharmacokinetics ironed out. And let me tell you, this drug is exciting stuff. You were right in your hunch about choline acetyltransferase. This drug is a reversible CAT inhibitor, which is good news, because if your patients can just survive its initial toxicity, the drug will eventually be cleared from the system, presumably without permanent neurological damage."

"What do you mean 'presumably'?"

"All last night's work was done with lab rats, and I have to generalize my findings to humans without any guarantee of validity. First of all, lab rats are innately pretty stupid, and if you've ever tried to figure out whether a rat is demented or not, you'll understand that it's kind of tough to do. Second, I have to assume that the interaction of this drug with choline acetyltransferase is identical in rats and humans, which may or may not be a valid assumption. Third, the metabolic systems in rats and humans are similar, but not identical. There may be crucial differences in pharmacokinetics that can't be predicted. If you could send some brain specimens from the previous victims, and we could dig up some fresh human liver slices over here, we might be able to replicate our immunofluorescence work and cross-check our pharmacokinetic results, but that would take at least three or four days, maybe more."

Peter rubbed his face and eyes again with his hand, fighting back the headache that was already building. "I'll try and get some of those specimens to you, but I honestly don't have three or four days to wait. Let's go ahead and assume that rats and humans are the same for right now and tell me what you know."

"As I said, it's a reversible inhibitor of CAT. It's metabolized in a multi-step process by the cytochrome P450 system. In the case of Drug X, the first step is demethylation into a physiologically active, 0-desmethyl derivative with an exceedingly long half-life by the 2D6 component, which, as it turns out, is the only subsystem that isn't significantly inhibited by permixitine. Normally, this metabolite would be oxidized and inactivated by another subsystem, but since that subsystem is inhibited by permixitine, the result is a very gradual buildup in biological activity of Drug X, even in the absence of additional drug intake."

"Whoa. Stop right there. Tell me what this all means in plain English, if you please."

"Sorry. These two drugs work together. Drug X induces an Alzheimer's-like disorder while the permixitine permits it to build up over a long period and then triggers the seizures when its own level rises. That makes the combination of these particular two drugs extremely dangerous and difficult to work with, and it explains why your patients progress even while they're in the hospital."

"So Albright's experimentation could have been to determine the specific pharmacokinetics between Drug X and permixitine?"

"Could be, but I'd only be speculating. It would certainly be more than coincidental that every victim has this particularly dangerous combination of drugs in their systems. Every victim except Megan and Amanda Ivy, that is."

"What do you mean?"

"Those two samples had Drug X, but no permixitine. It's the combination of Drug X and permixitine that causes the cardiac instability and cardiac arrest. Whoever tried to poison Megan didn't want to kill her, just get her out of the way for a while. But if I were you, I wouldn't eat any chocolate cake for a while."

Thank God, thought Peter. Megan was safe, as long as he could get her through the acute intoxication phase of the drug. For the first time, he sensed a glimmer of hope.

"But listen," Steve continued. "There's more to this drug, and that's what makes it interesting. What puzzled me from the beginning is how a drug could inhibit CAT and not cause paralysis of every muscle in the body. Acetylcholine is also the neurotransmitter for the nerves that go to muscles. If there's no acetylcholine, there's no muscle contraction. Then your diaphragm is paralyzed so you stop breathing. That's how most nerve poisons work. As it turns out, this drug is selective only for choline acetyltransferase found in the brain itself and in the vagus nerve which, as you know, goes to the heart. This means that there are two forms of CAT, one in the brain and vagus nerve and a different one in the nerves that go to muscles and other organs. Theoretically, a disease process like Alzheimer's disease could affect only the brain form by itself."

There was a brief pause before Bergstraum continued excitedly. "Do you know what this could mean from a research standpoint?"

"No, what?"

"It means that this could be the key we've been looking for in Alzheimer's research for the past thirty years. This drug is the MPTP of Alzheimer's disease. Pete, this could make my academic career!"

Now Peter understood Steve's excitement. MPTP was a chemical byproduct of the synthesis of so-called "designer drugs" that had been made in basement laboratories back in the early 1980s by amateur chemists trying to manufacture street drugs that wouldn't have the chemical formulas specifically outlawed by the Drug Enforcement Agency. MPTP had one very interesting side effect: it rapidly and selectively destroyed the substantia nigra, the minute area of the brain that degenerates in Parkinson's disease. In effect, the addicts that inadvertently injected themselves with MPTP developed acute irreversible Parkinson's disease, sometimes overnight. The neurologist that had discovered this had subsequently made an international reputation for himself, and MPTP itself became the subject for innumerable research papers and conferences, providing invaluable insights into the basis for Parkinson's disease itself. If Bergstraum was right, Drug X could represent a turning point in the understanding of Alzheimer's disease. But that still left Peter in the dark about what to do about Alan and Frank.

"Try to see things from my perspective, Steve. I've got four personal acquaintances on my service, including my girlfriend and her brother, all of whom may up and die on me at any second if I don't find out what the hell to do about this drug. So just tell me how to keep these people from dying, and I'll be happy to cooperate in any research study you want. Okay?"

"Sorry. I was just getting to the good part. Here's my hypothesis. The victims are given the combination of Drug X and permixitine, and Drug X slowly builds up. Now, there are basically two systems controlling heart rate: epinephrine, or adrenaline, which speeds it up, and acetylcholine, which slows it down, primarily through the vagus nerve, which goes directly to the heart. Once Drug X reaches a critical level, it stops production of acetylcholine, and the heart rate gradually speeds up. When permixitine kicks in, it causes seizures, which stimulates the production of more epinephrine from stress. Once the seizure starts, you get into a vicious cycle until the system is overrun with epinephrine and the cardiac rhythm goes out of control. Finally, up steps some well-meaning cardiologist and, naturally, he gives more epinephrine to treat what he thinks is a heart attack. The heart is totally flooded with epinephrine with no counteracting acetylcholine to slow it down and suddenly, to everyone's surprise, it's time to transfer the patient to the Eternal Care Unit. The cardiologist walks away from the code convinced that he did everything possible to save the poor guy when he basically hammered the nails into his coffin. It's ingenious."

Peter had to think this one out carefully. "So the easy thing would be to replace the acetylcholine."

"No dice. Acetylcholine is broken down in the bloodstream as fast as you can pump it in. It has to be produced within the nerve cell itself to have any effect, which can't happen because of CAT inhibition from Drug X."

"Then the only thing left is to block the effects of epinephrine."

"Exactly. And this is tremendously counterintuitive, because when you've got a patient in cardiac arrest, the last thing you want to do is to block epinephrine, which would normally be maintaining the blood pressure and maximizing the heart's ability to pump blood. Under ordinary circumstances, blocking epinephrine would leave the full, unopposed effect of acetylcholine, which would stop the heart cold with no way to restart it. But this isn't an ordinary circumstance; there is no acetylcholine at all. What you have to do is administer a drug in the beta blocker category, like propranolol, which will totally block out epinephrine and allow the heart to recover."

"Steve, if I give a patient in cardiac arrest propranolol, and they die, I'm laying myself wide open for a malpractice suit and possibly revocation of my license."

"That's exactly what I was thinking when the data came back. I did several dry runs of IV propranolol with rats to make sure it would work the way I predicted, and it returned their heart rhythm to normal every single time. And it was the only thing that would do it. Every other rat died if they were given standard resuscitative measures."

"But you said you weren't sure if you could generalize your findings to humans."

"Right again. I can't promise that this will work in humans the way it works in rats, but it's the best I could do in the time I had. I'm sorry, Pete. I can't help you any further unless you can give me a few more days."

"What about pre-medicating with propranolol before they actually went into cardiac arrest? Would that work?"

"I guess it would, but you'd have to build up gradually or you'd bottom out their pressure, maybe throw them into heart failure if the dosage was too high. Besides, you'd have to individually titrate the dose in any given patient depending on their degree of tachycardia and their response to the propranolol."

Peter was busy calculating the dosages of propranolol he would need for each of his patients. He tapped his pen nervously on the pad of paper, which was covered with scribbled notes from the conversation and calculations in the margins.

"It seems to me that my best hope is to pray that these people survive long enough for me to build up adequate dosages of propranolol in their systems, because once they arrest, it will either cure them or kill them, and you can't promise me which it will be."

"That's it in a nutshell, Peter. If it will help, you can use me as a reference if you get into trouble. I've got the data to back it up, even if the FDA hasn't exactly approved it yet. Sooner or later, I'm going to go public with this anyway."

"Then I guess we can both go to hell in a handbasket together. Listen, I'll be in touch as soon as anything happens, and I'll call pathology and get those brain slices to you as soon as possible."

"Sure thing. Hey, Pete …"

"What?"

"Good luck."

Peter had never heard Steve Bergstraum say anything with such a serious tone in all the years he had known him.

"Thanks. Talk to you later."

Peter immediately turned back to the ICU nursing station and ordered an incrementally progressive regimen of intravenous propranolol for Alan that should get his blood level up to adequate dosage, whatever that meant in this situation, in twelve to eighteen hours with careful monitoring of his vital signs. Then, he called the neurology ward and ordered the same regimen for Megan and Mrs. Ivy. Even though they were probably out of the woods, he couldn't take that chance. After hanging up the phone, he headed straight for the neurology ward.

Reaching Megan's room, Peter hesitated for a minute, his hand on the doorknob. At least she wasn't going to die, but this was going to be the second heavy-duty discussion he would have with Megan in three days, and what was said now could make or break their relationship. He took a deep breath, opened the door, and entered the room.

To Peter's surprise, Megan was sitting up in bed, wide awake and very alert. Rachel was seated in the chair by the bedside, and both women were laughing.

"Glad to see you're feeling better."

Startled, Megan turned as Peter walked over to her bed. They both hesitated for an instant, until Megan stood up and gave Peter a hug.

"I missed you, baby. I can hardly remember anything about the last twenty-four hours. Rachel was filling me in on what I've been like, and I can't believe it."

"Do you remember anything about yesterday morning?"

"Not a thing. I remember going to work two days ago and finding out about Mrs. Ivy. It upset me so much that I ate a piece of chocolate cake she had left for me in the refrigerator. I can remember the rest of that day, our conversation late that evening and," she smiled wickedly, "our indoor athletics. But when can I leave this place? I'm feeling a lot better."

Rachel spoke up. "I'd be glad to take care of her while you're at work, Peter. With Daniel gone, there's really not much for me to do during the day."

"Sorry, honey, but I have some new information on what's been going on, and I'm going to ask Dr. Harden to keep you one more day for observation."

Megan pouted. "Peter Branstead, you're being mean."

Rachel, however, seemed quite interested. "What do you mean 'new information?'"

Peter shut the door and sat down next to Megan.

"I have solid evidence that our dear friend, Dr. Albright, has been behind this whole mess. In addition to killing several homeless vagrants, he's poisoned Frank Halleck," Peter hesitated, "and Alan."

"Alan? Alan is dead?" Megan's face suddenly paled.

"No, he's not dead, but he's very sick. He's here in the Intensive Care Unit being monitored closely. I've been working with a friend of mine at the Neurological Institute, and he thinks there may be a treatment, but Alan may be the first patient I use it on."

Megan glared at Peter. "You're using my brother as a guinea pig, aren't you?"

"I can't help it. This is an unregistered drug. Nobody but Albright has ever heard of it before, and he's certainly not going to tell me the antidote. Steve Bergstraum's been working on it all night, and I just found out about this a few minutes ago. There hasn't been enough time to test it out on anything but rats."

"Is it dangerous?" Megan's tone was now more frightened than angry.

"Possibly. But doing nothing is definitely dangerous." He didn't want to go into any more details.

Rachel reached over to comfort Megan. "Don't worry, baby. Alan will be just fine. Listen, why don't you lie down and let me talk to Peter alone for a few minutes, okay? I'll be right back."

Rachel gave Megan a peck on the forehead and pulled Peter outside the room. "Peter, tell me exactly what is going on here."

"Not until you tell me why you're so interested. Why do you and Daniel keep giving me the third degree?"

"Well, for Christ's sake, I ..."

Both Peter and Rachel became aware of the attention they were getting from nurses. Rachel grabbed Peter by the arm and half led, half dragged him down the hallway to the visitors' lounge.

"Daniel and I do have a legitimate interest in what's going on. I, for one, am not accustomed to having my best friend run in front of a truck in her underwear."

Peter sighed. "All right, from the beginning," and he went over the entire saga of the past week. Rachel grilled him on any details he attempted to gloss over until she was satisfied that she knew the whole story.

"This whole situation sounds like big time trouble. Why don't you let the authorities take care of things?"

"Gladly, but up until now, I couldn't get anyone to believe that this was a serious problem. I've been talking to a homicide detective for days, and I think I finally have enough evidence for them to close down East Side Psych and bust Albright. Right now, my primary concern is to make sure nobody else dies, if that's possible."

The loudspeaker in the visitor's lounge blared out a Code Blue in the Intensive Care Unit, and Peter's beeper simultaneously went off for the ICU phone number.

Peter groaned. "Right on cue." He started to go, but Rachel grabbed his forearm.

"You take care of Alan, and I'll take care of Megan. Don't worry. Everything will turn out fine."

Peter ran out of the lounge and up to the Unit. As he had feared, there was a flurry of activity around Alan Lamplin's bed. He pushed his way into the midst of the crowd of nurses, respiratory techs, and nurse anesthetists. Sure enough, Alan was having a generalized seizure and was already turning a dusky blue. Blood-tinged spittle trickled from the corner of his mouth, his eyes were rolled up, and his pupils dilated. He was already intubated. The cardiac monitor was showing an incredibly fast rate, over two hundred fifty beats per minute, but Alan's heart was young and healthy and was keeping up with the strain. At least so far.

"Has he gotten any propranolol yet?"

"Five milligrams IV about an hour ago," one of the nurses called out.

"What did it do to his heart rate?"

"It dropped from two-ten to one-seventy-five, but as soon as the seizure started, it shot right up."

Greg Johnson and Bruce Rathburn suddenly burst through the crowd.

"Hi, Pete. You running a special on these guys?"

"I don't have time to talk. This is Megan's brother." He turned to the nurse. "Give lorazepam four milligrams, IV stat, and prepare propranolol ten milligrams for IV push."

The seizure began quieting down. *The eye of the hurricane*, Peter thought.

"Dr. Branstead, the QRS is widening. Rhythm is now rapid ventricular tachycardia at a rate of two-seventy-five." This was the deadly change in heart rhythm that Peter feared would happen.

"I'll take over from here," Rathburn said. "Give an amp of bicarb, an amp of calcium carbonate, and one milligram of epinephrine, IV push."

"No!" Peter yelled, loudly enough that all action around the bedside stopped and everyone turned toward him. "Cancel the epinephrine. I repeat, no epinephrine. Give propranolol ten milligrams, IV push stat."

The nurse looked at Peter, then looked at Dr. Rathburn, bewildered, not knowing what to do. Rathburn looked at Peter, equally bewildered.

"Propranolol? Are you nuts? Sure, if you give propranolol you'll slow down his heart. You'll stop it cold. Then we'll really be up shit's creek. Let me handle this, Pete. I've done it before, and you haven't. Get the epi ready."

"No." Sweat was beginning to bead on Peter's forehead. "Do not give the epinephrine. Bruce, I don't have time to explain, but this man has been poisoned with a drug that eliminates all vagus nerve function to the heart. It's the unopposed epinephrine that's been throwing these guys into cardiac arrest. What he needs is a beta-blocker like propranolol, and he needs it now."

"Dr. Branstead, the QRS complex is becoming irregular. I'm afraid the patient is going into ventricular fibrillation. Pulse is thready, heart rate three hundred. What shall I do?"

"Do you have any references, any articles, any proof at all of what you're trying to do?"

"It's a hunch, Bruce. An educated guess. I can't explain it any further."

"So you want to give a beta blocker to someone in V fib and no blood pressure on a hunch? You're crazier than I thought."

"Then if you won't do it, I will. This is my patient, and I accept full responsibility. Give propranolol ten milligrams, IV push stat."

"All right, all right, but if you're going to dig us all a grave, let's try to make it a shallow one. Use esmolol. It's got a shorter half-life, and it'll be out of the system faster if we have to shut it off. And nurse, get a dopamine drip ready and order glucagon up from the pharmacy. Just in case."

Peter smiled at Rathbun. "Thanks. I'll explain it all later. Esmolol drip at thirty milligrams."

"Done, Dr. Branstead."

The entire bedside fell into a hush as every eye focused on the monitor and the nurse called out the rhythm and rate.

"Mixed V tach and V fib, rate indeterminate, pulse not palpable."

"Let me at least try carotid sinus massage."

"Don't bother, Bruce. I told you he has no vagus nerve function. It won't help."

"Mixed V tach and V fib, rate two-ninety. It's dropping, Dr. Branstead."

"What's his blood pressure?"

"Not audible, Dr. Branstead."

"Then use the Doppler."

There was an agonizing minute while the nurse struggled to find a blood pressure. "Blood pressure forty over zero."

"Continue the infusion at three milligrams per minute for five minutes."

"Done. Rhythm now V tach, rate two-seventy-five … V tach, rate two-sixty … V tach, rate two-fifty. It's still dropping."

"Blood pressure?"

"Forty-five over twenty by Doppler."

Peter felt his heartbeat pounding through his chest wall. His mouth felt like a wad of cotton, and his eyes burned from staring, unblinking, at the monitor.

"Rhythm is narrow complex supraventricular tach at two-fifty. Looks like atrial flutter at two-to-one block if those are really P-waves. Blood pressure now audible at seventy over forty. Rate is now two-twenty-five … two hundred … one-eighty. Rhythm is now back to sinus tach at one-seventy and holding steady. Blood pressure one hundred over fifty. Dr. Branstead, I think we've got a save."

A communal exhalation of breath was audible from around the bedside.

"You sure got big ones, man," Bruce laughed, slapping Peter on the back. "You are one goddamn crazy son of a bitch, but you did it."

Peter smiled weakly, held onto the bedrail for support, and concentrated on slowing his breathing.

Rachel had taken care of Megan, all right. She had asked the nurse for the "as needed" sedation Jay Harden had ordered and had her knocked out completely. Irked that Megan was asleep, Peter explained to Rachel what had happened with

Alan, telling her to reassure Megan as soon as she woke up that everything would be okay, and then he headed for Amanda Ivy's room.

Walter Ivy had spent the night sleeping in a chair by her bedside. He looked exhausted but far less anxious than two days ago when Mrs. Ivy had been admitted. Amanda was sitting up in her bed, eating lunch. She looked up briefly when Peter entered the room but turned back to her lunch immediately without greeting him.

"Good morning, Walter. Sorry about the accommodations."

Walter Ivy managed a smile through his fatigue. "In thirty years of marriage, Amanda and I have never spent the night apart, and I wasn't about to make this the first."

"How's Mrs. Ivy doing?"

"Much better. Her memory is still off a bit. She might not recognize you yet. But she's been able to keep in her mind that she's in St. Mark's Hospital and not at home. Our son and daughter came by this morning to visit, and she recognized them for the first time since she came in, and she asked about our grandchildren by name. Even better, she hasn't had any hallucinations since she was started on that new medicine yesterday." Walter walked over to Mrs. Ivy and rubbed her back affectionately. "You said you were feeling better, too, didn't you, Sweetpea?"

"Walter, I am doing just fine. Now stop fussing over me and get yourself home. You need the rest. You're looking terrible."

Peter and Walter smiled at each other. The patient was clearly improving. Another few days and she'd be reorganizing the nursing staff.

"The nurses tell me that the heart medicine you put her on is slowing her heart rate down. Isn't that dangerous?"

Peter glanced through her chart. Her heart rate had been around one-seventy-five when she first came in and was now down to one-fifty.

"Not at all, Walter. She's actually still faster than we want her to be, certainly not too slow. She'll probably be off the medication in another day or two anyway."

Walter hesitated for a moment before he asked the next question. "Will Amanda ever get back to her old self?"

"I'm sure she will. I think she'll be home by the weekend."

Walter smiled broadly and rubbed his wife's back again. "You hear that, Sweetpea. We might be home in a few days."

Amanda pushed her lunch tray away and wiped her mouth off with a napkin. "Walter, I can hear everything the doctor is saying, and I do not need an interpreter, thank you."

Peter's beeper went off as he turned and left the room, paging him to the admissions office. As he walked down the stairs, he figured that if he didn't get Mrs. Ivy out of the hospital soon, he might have to admit Walter.

At the admissions office, Peter found Frank Halleck slowly shuffling around the room. Harriet wearily followed after him, gently extricating from his hand telephone receivers and pencils that he aimlessly picked up and trying to guide him back toward the desk of the admissions clerk. Dr. Albright had apparently cut back on Frank's sedation in anticipation of his transfer to St. Mark's, and Frank was restlessly pacing and mumbling to himself, his speech a jumble of grunts and incomprehensible sounds, periodically punctuated by the utterance of a single, clearly distinguishable word: "CAT."

"Dr. Branstead," Harriet sobbed, "I think we've lost Frank. He's getting worse and worse."

Peter put his fingers on Frank's wrist and checked his pulse. It was regular, but it was going at one-fifty. Even if he didn't convulse, this heart rate was a dangerously rapid pulse to sustain for very long in a man of Frank's age.

"Don't give up hope quite yet. If my suspicions are correct, this is all reversible, but Frank's not out of the woods. The next twenty-four hours are critical. I'm going to have him monitored in the ICU. I'll be able to tell you a lot more tomorrow afternoon."

"This all has something to do with Dr. Albright, doesn't it?" Harriet asked. He didn't have to respond; she already knew the answer. "If it takes my last breath, I'll see that man pay for what he did to my Frankie."

"Don't worry, Harriet, we'll get him. In the meantime, we have to think of Frank first. Let's get him up to the ICU quickly."

Peter wrote orders for physostigmine and donepezil, a slowly incremental course of intravenous propranolol, specific orders for IV esmolol, and, clearly written in bold capital letters, NO EPINEPHRINE FOR VENTRICULAR ARRHYTHMIAS. Just to make certain that there were no screwups, he left a message on Bruce Rathburn's voicemail telling him to expect trouble. Satisfied that all bases were covered, Peter left to go to his office.

The rain had stopped, and the storm clouds that had drenched the city earlier that morning were scattering northeastward over New England by the time Peter left St. Mark's Hospital and rode his bike to his office for the first time in five days. Although his office was closed for new patients and routine office visits, there had been piles of phone calls, insurance forms, and prescription renewals that had been allowed to accumulate, in addition to a few emergencies that had to be worked in. By the time his office work was finished, it was already late afternoon, and he still had one more crucial phone call to make. Peter dismissed his office staff early, closed the door to his office, and dialed the phone. It was picked up on the tenth ring.

"Meinerhoff, homicide." It was the same weary voice Peter heard all the other times that he had called. It could almost have been a recorded announcement.

"Detective Meinerhoff, this is Dr. Peter Branstead. I spoke to you yesterday about some winos that ..."

"Yeah, I remember. Anything new, Dr. Branstead?" To Peter's surprise, Meinerhoff seemed almost pleased to hear his voice.

"Plenty, Detective." And, for the third time, Peter outlined the events of the past several days. As before, Meinerhoff would periodically interrupt to clarify certain points, particularly when Peter tried to explain the complexities of the interactions between the unknown drug and permixitine and the physiology of epinephrine and acetylcholine. Meinerhoff picked it up surprisingly quickly.

"You seem to be pretty well versed in medicine, Detective. I'm impressed."

"In homicide we have to deal with the forensics boys all the time. I spend as much time in the morgue and in toxicology as I do on the streets. I probably know enough medicine by now to hang up my own shingle."

"Do you think we have a case?"

"We've got enough for a search warrant. It's kind of late now, Dr. Branstead, but I should be able to call a judge and get a search warrant by tomorrow morning. Do you think Dr. Bergstraum would mind filling me in some more?"

"As long as you promise not to publish it before he does. Tell him you talked to me about it, and you'll give him full credit in the newspapers when the story comes out. He loves the publicity."

"Sure thing. Thanks a lot, Doc. It's been a pleasure doing business with you."

"Same here. I'd like to be there when you bust this guy. Would that be okay?"

"No problem, Doc. I'll call you tomorrow morning just before the bust. We want to keep things as quiet as we can."

Peter hung up the phone and breathed a sigh of relief. He was finally going to get this whole mess wrapped up and get on with his life.

With the approach of the summer solstice, the warm June sun took its own sweet time lazily dropping below the level of the West Village rooftops. Its deepening orange light painted the buildings gold and ochre before the shadows of the late evening dusk settled over the streets of downtown Manhattan. Peter wearily pedaled his bike down Broadway and turned onto Mercer Street, cursing himself with every push of his legs for not having left his bike at his office and taken an easy cab ride home. Arriving at Mercer Street, he wheeled his bike into the ancient freight elevator and leaned against the elevator wall for support while the aged pulleys and cables creaked and groaned noisily as the elevator made its way to the second floor. Peter stumbled through the living room and into the bedroom and sat down on the bed, trying to find the energy to bend over and pull off his shoes. The ringing of the phone startled him so much he almost jumped.

"Dr. Branstead speaking."

"How's it going, Pete? This is Daniel."

"I didn't expect to hear from you for a while. I thought you were in Ukraine."

"I am. This is long-distance."

"I hope you didn't call collect."

"Don't worry, this is the government's dime. Could you to do me a big favor?"

"Sure. Name it."

"Could you fly to Kiev for a few days?"

Peter was silent for a long moment. "Could you repeat that, please?"

"I said I would really appreciate it if you could meet me here in Kiev for a few days."

"Are you nuts? In case Rachel hasn't told you, Megan's in the hospital and …"

"Save your breath. I've heard the whole story."

"Then why are you asking me to leave Megan, a hopelessly screwed up office practice, and an entire service of critically ill patients to fly out to Ukraine, of all places?"

"Peter, I didn't fly out to Ukraine for some routine consultation. They're in the middle of a constitutional crisis of major proportions, and if it doesn't resolve itself quickly this could affect the political stability not only of Ukraine but Eastern Europe and possibly Russia as well."

"I'm sorry to hear that, but what does this have to do with me?"

"The President of Ukraine has come down with a mysterious neurological disease, and I need your help in figuring out what to do."

"Come on, Daniel. There are neurologists in Ukraine. And if you need an expert, there are loads of world-renowned neurologists right here in New York. Why me?"

"Because you're the only one I can trust. And you're the only one with the expertise I need."

Peter thought for a moment before he asked the next question.

"Does this have anything to do with Albright?"

"I can't answer that right now."

This was not good.

"Peter," Daniel continued after a long silence, "in all our years of friendship I've never asked you to do anything for me. I know exactly what you're going through right now, and, believe me, I would be the last one to ask you to drop what you're doing and come out here. But I can't exaggerate the potential ramifications of what is going on here and how critical it is that you get out here as soon as possible."

"Listen, if this is about that drug, I can tell you everything I know. I can even give you Steve Bergstraum's number. He knows more about it than I do."

"It won't work. There's no way this can be handled without you personally being here. Please, you have to do this for me."

Peter ran his fingers nervously through his hair. "I can't just pack up and leave. I'd have to make coverage arrangements for the ward service. God Almighty, what would happen to Megan? I've got to take care of her after she leaves the hospital. She'd be lost without me."

"Don't worry about Megan; she'll be fine. Rachel will stay in your apartment and take care of her while you're away. When Rachel explains how critical this is, I'm sure she'll understand."

"No, she won't. Get real. I can't just ship out now. She'd feel like I was deserting her. Megan can't handle something like that right now. Sorry, but I can't go. You'll have to make do without me."

"Listen to me. I wish I could tell you more about this, but I can't. What is going on in Ukraine at this time will have major international repercussions, probably involving the security interests of the United States. Suffice it to say that when I'm asking you to come here, I'm not just doing it on my own. This is at the direct request of the highest levels of our government. And I mean the *very* highest levels."

For a moment, Peter was stunned into silence. "What do you have to do with the government? You're bullshitting me."

"I'm not, but I can't explain right now. You've got to believe me."

Peter rubbed his eyes. The fatigue of the past few days was catching up with him. "Let me sleep on it; I'm too tired to give you an answer right now. I'll talk to Megan and call some people first thing in the morning. Call me back at 9:00 a.m., and I'll tell you if I can do it."

"No can do. There's not enough time to think about it. You'll just have to trust me on this one."

By now, Peter was pacing the bedroom, his mind racing nervously. He was finally finishing off one mess and had been looking forward to getting his life back in order. Now, Daniel expected him to go seven thousand miles away, leaving Megan here when she needed him. The obvious first impulse was to say "No" and hang up the phone. But Daniel had never asked a favor of him before and wouldn't ask him to do something like this unless it was critically important. Besides, Rachel was Megan's best friend and could stay with her all day, which he couldn't. And if it were only for a few days, Jay Harden could take over the service. It was Greg Johnson's last month of residency, and he was capable of maintaining the service on autopilot anyway. Peter sighed. It all could be arranged, if Megan would understand and not kill him first.

"Are you still there?"

"Yeah, I'm here. I'm going to kick myself for saying this, but I'll go."

"Bless you. I promise you won't regret this."

"I already do. Tell me what I have to do."

"Fine. Follow these instructions precisely. Tomorrow, as soon as possible, go to the Permanent Ukrainian Mission to the United Nations on East Sixty-Seventh Street. Ask to speak to Mr. Maxim Podalsky, the head of the mission, and tell him you came to pick up a sealed diplomatic packet being held for you in the name of Mikhail Pritsak. It contains airplane tickets to Kiev and a visa. Whatever you do, don't give anyone your name for any reason and only speak to Podalsky. Your flight leaves the day after tomorrow, first thing in the morning. Pack only enough to fit into a carry-on bag. You won't need much. At the airport you'll make your connection with a man sent by Pritsak as an escort. And Peter, tell absolutely nobody about these plans. I'm sorry this all has to be so clandestine, but it's more important than you can possibly imagine that you follow these instructions exactly, and absolute secrecy is imperative."

Peter's misgivings were growing by the second. This had all the makings of a spy thriller, but it couldn't be. It was happening to him, Dr. Peter Branstead, to whom living dangerously meant riding his bike up Seventh Avenue during rush hour traffic. And the closest thing to a weapon he had ever handled was a rubber-headed reflex hammer.

"Okay, I've got it," he heard himself say, his mouth almost disconnected from his brain, which was still trying to process everything that had just transpired. "But I'll have to explain to Megan why I'm leaving."

"That's fine. Blame it all on me, if you have to. And this is also important. Whatever you do, stay as far as you can from Dr. Albright and his crowd. Is that clear? As far as you can. Promise me that."

"All right, already. I promise."

"Good. And don't worry. Everything will turn out fine."

Peter hung up the phone with a sense of foreboding and prepared for bed, but all he could think about was Megan and how he would ever explain this to her. He recalled Walter and Amanda Ivy's thirty-year record of uninterrupted togetherness, and now he couldn't make that claim after only three years. Peter swore aloud to the empty apartment and pounded his fists against the bedroom wall. After he calmed down, Peter turned off the bedroom lights, drew the blinds, and tried to get to sleep in preparation for one more in a steady stream of horrendous days.

In a darkened apartment across Mercer Street from Peter's loft, Rachel shut the blinds, set her binoculars down on a small nightstand, lay down on the mattress set on the floor, and stared up at the ceiling.

Sometimes, she hated this job.

It was shortly after 1:00 a.m. before Gennadi Chursin finished his rounds at the East Side Psychiatric Center, stepped out of the front door, and locked it behind him. At the bottom of the steps, he turned and walked toward Astor Place and the IRT line that would take him home to Brooklyn. He hated New York City. At home in Donetsk, he could walk the streets at any time, day or night, without fear. Not only that, because he was in the Mafia he was treated with respect. Men would buy him drinks, girls would smile at him as he walked by, and he got favorable consideration from the bureaucrats when he applied for an apartment or some other privilege. Here, he was a glorified security guard, barely getting enough salary to pay for a lousy one-room apartment with neighbors who made noise all day while he tried to sleep. But the job was almost over, and he had managed to skim enough of the cash that flowed through the center that he would be able to live comfortably back in Donetsk, maybe even afford a mistress.

Astor Place was virtually deserted. In the middle of the square was a single boozer, dressed in a tattered, thin overcoat, leaning precariously against the monumental fifteen-foot-high black cube that stood, balanced impossibly on a single corner, as a landmark in the center of the traffic island. Chursin swore to himself as the bum left the support of the cube and staggered toward him.

"Hey, man, spare change for some 'shine'?" the bum called out as he approached.

"Get lost, buddy. No money. Beat it."

Chursin avoided the panhandler by walking around the opposite side of the cube, but he was surprised to find that the man had already made his way around the cube and was standing directly in front of him, blocking his way to the subway.

"I said I have no money, now get ..."

Chursin didn't have time to finish his sentence before the wino grabbed him by the throat and smashed him violently against one of the projecting points of the cube. He grunted in pain, but before he could cry out, Chursin saw the glint of a six-inch metal blade in the wino's hand as it reflected the yellow tint of the sodium vapor streetlamp above them. An instant later, it was plunged up to the hilt into the soft indentation just above his right collarbone. The knife sliced through the nerves as they coursed through his shoulder, paralyzing his arm and hand instantly.

He screamed in pain and lashed out with his left arm, but the wino effortlessly ducked his punch, grabbed his hand, and yanked his arm upward. Chursin felt the blade slice into his exposed armpit, cutting through the nerves and paralyzing his left arm as well. Now, both arms hung limply by his sides as he felt his own warm blood soaking his shirt.

A gloved hand grabbed him under the chin and roughly shoved him again against the cube. Helpless to defend himself, he felt the tip of the knife pushed into his throat, blocking his airway. Chursin kicked frantically with his legs as he struggled for air, but his assailant easily avoided them.

"Don't lie to me, Gennadi. You've got money. Lots of money. And I know exactly how you got it. The conditions of your employment did not include the right to steal from the corporation, is that understood? Consider your employment terminated without notice. Go to hell, Gennadi."

As Chursin's eyes bulged in terror, his assailant swept the knife blade sideways, cutting through the arteries and veins in his neck. Unconscious and dying on the concrete sidewalk, his blood made an ever-widening, pitch-black pool in the yellow light of the streetlamp.

His attacker carefully wiped the blade off on Chursin's clothes and dropped his own bloodstained overcoat onto the lifeless body. The corporation would appreciate having one less loose end to account for when the project was over. Now, all he had to deal with was Lone Eagle.

CHAPTER 16

▼

Harriet Halleck awoke on her makeshift bed on the couch in the visitors' lounge of the Intensive Care Unit at St. Mark's Hospital and looked at the wall clock in the dimly lit room, showing 3:00 a.m. She wasn't sure what had awakened her. She was the only person in the lounge and there wasn't a sound in the room. But something made her feel uneasy, some sixth sense of premonitory dread. She pressed the intercom button for the ICU desk clerk.

"This is Mrs. Halleck. Is there any way I could go in and see Frank, just for a minute?"

"I'm sorry, Mrs. Halleck, visiting hours aren't until 8:00 a.m. Why don't you go back to sleep. I'll have the nurse wake you up if anything changes."

"Please, Miss, I won't even go into his room. I just want to look at him from the doorway to see if he's all right. I promise I'll be quiet."

"Okay, Mrs. Halleck. I'll see what I can do."

Frank's nurse came to the intercom.

"You can come in for a minute, Mrs. Halleck, but try not to wake Frank up."

Harriet walked silently down the corridor of the ICU to meet Frank's nurse, waiting for her outside Frank's room.

"Thank you so much, Dear. I had this terrible feeling that something was dreadfully wrong with Frank."

The nurse smiled. "Don't worry. He's been sleeping peacefully all night."

Harriet peeked into the room. Frank was, indeed, asleep. But the monitor, which had been registering a heart rate of about two hundred, had jumped to two-fifty. Frank stirred and awoke from his sleep wild-eyed and terrified, as if he had just awakened from a nightmare, and struggled with his restraints.

"Frank, get back to sleep," the nurse said gently as she tried room to calm him down. "You had a bad dream."

"Who are you? Get away from me!" Frank shouted, his voice piercing the late night quiet of the ICU. "Get away from me," he screamed even louder and pulled at his restraints as the nurse slowly approached his bed. "Harriet. Where's Harriet?"

Harriet stepped into the room. "Frankie, this is Harriet. Remember me? You need to lie down and get some sleep. You're getting yourself too excited."

"You!" Frankie shouted, pointing directly at Harriet, "You've been sneaking around behind my back, you dirty whore. Get out of here. Get out."

By now, nurses from all around the ICU had gathered around the room. One threw her arm around Harriet and led her to the visitors' lounge.

"Gina, call a code. He's having a seizure," Frank's nurse called from his room to the desk clerk.

"Frankie!" Harriet screamed and turned to run back to Frank's room. The nurse held her firmly and pulled her back to the lounge.

"Come on, Harriet, there's nothing you can do there. You'll just be in the way. I'll sit with you for a while."

As the door to the lounge closed, the code team burst in. Already dusky blue, Frank was intubated and suctioned. Thick, bloody sputum was suctioned from his trachea, but at least he was breathing.

"Someone tell me about this guy," yelled Dr. Edward Hughes, the cardiologist on call. Dense stubble darkened his face, his black stringy hair was in disarray, and his white coat had been hastily thrown over the hospital scrubs that he had been sleeping in.

"He's a fifty-six-year-old white male with no significant prior medical history transferred from East Side Psych to Dr. Branstead's service this morning for acute confusional state and mental status change. He just woke up, apparently from a nightmare, with rapidly worsening confusion and went into a seizure, stopped breathing, and was intubated. Per protocol, he was given lorazepam and fosphenytoin, but his seizure hasn't stopped yet."

"Cardiac status?"

"No history of heart disease, Dr. Hughes. He was in supraventricular tachycardia before the seizure. His complexes are widening, and I think he may be going into V tach. He's gotten some propranolol according to a gradually increasing dosage protocol, but it hasn't slowed his heart down much."

"Okay, let's start out with adenosine, six milligrams IV and see what that does."

"The seizure's quieting down. Heart rate is two-seventy-five; rhythm is now ventricular tach, blood pressure seventy over thirty. There's an order written by Dr. Branstead for an esmolol drip in case of ventricular arrhythmia. Shall I start it, Dr. Hughes?"

"Esmolol? No way. Where the hell did he learn his cardiology? Let's give lidocaine one hundred milligrams, an amp of sodium bicarb, and run the fluids wide open."

"Complexes are becoming irregular. He looks like he's going into V fib."

"Shit. Epinephrine one milligram, IV stat."

"There is a specific order in the chart that the patient is not to be given epinephrine, Dr. Hughes."

"Why? Is he allergic to it?"

"It doesn't say, Dr. Hughes, only that he is not to be given epinephrine for cardiac arrest."

"No epinephrine? Esmolol drip?" Hughes shook his head. "What the hell does Branstead think he's doing? Why doesn't he just put a pillow over this guy's face and get it over with?"

"Patient is now in V tach, rate indeterminate. Blood pressure is dropping, now sixty over palp. What shall I do, Dr. Hughes?"

"I'm countermanding Dr. Branstead's order. Give the epinephrine now, and start closed chest massage."

"Epinephrine given, Dr. Hughes. Patient still in V tach. Blood pressure seventy over ... No, rhythm is now ventricular fibrillation, blood pressure unobtainable."

"Damn. If only I had given that epinephrine two minutes ago. All right, everybody, let's get the defibrillator ready. Nurse, give another seventy-five milligrams of lidocaine and another milligram of epi. Set the defibrillator at two hundred joules." Dr. Hughes placed the paddles on Frank's chest and turned to the charge nurse.

"Everybody clear? Okay, people, let's rock."

Peter was awakened rudely from one of the deepest sleeps he had had in months by the sharp tones of the telephone, ringing on his nightstand just inches away from his face. His LED alarm clock read 4:09 a.m.

"Dr. Branstead speaking," Peter said in a voice still dry and hoarse from sleep.

"Dr. Branstead, this is the charge nurse in the ICU at St. Mark's Hospital. Mr. Frank Halleck has just expired."

Peter was suddenly jerked out of his sleep and sat bolt upright in bed.

"What happened?" *Oh, God, I've killed Frank,* he thought.

"About 3:00 a.m. Mr. Halleck got very confused and agitated. His heart rate began picking up and then he went into a generalized convulsion. Right in the middle of the convulsion, his heart went into ventricular tachycardia and then ventricular fibrillation. Dr. Hughes did everything he could, but we couldn't get a pressure or pulse back. We tried for almost thirty minutes, Dr. Branstead, but nothing worked."

Peter rubbed his hand over his eyes, his hopes dashed. Steve Bergstraum was wrong after all.

"Then the esmolol drip didn't work, did it?"

"Dr. Hughes countermanded the order for the esmolol drip. He gave epinephrine instead."

"He did what?" Peter screamed into the phone. "Where the hell is Hughes? Put him on the phone right now, goddamn it!"

"I'm sorry, Dr. Branstead," the nurse stammered. "Dr. Hughes left the unit. I think he had an emergency cath to do in the ER."

Peter fought the urge to scream at the nurse. It wasn't her fault. She had to follow the orders of the physician responsible for the code. He took a few deep breaths to calm himself down.

"Has Mrs. Halleck been notified?"

"She was in the waiting room at the time, Dr. Branstead. Dr. Hughes has spoken to her already."

"Is she still there?"

"Yes, Dr. Branstead. I think she was planning to stay until they took the body to the morgue."

"Please tell her I'm coming in right away, and I'd like to speak to her, okay?"

Peter hung up the phone and rubbed his face with both hands. He certainly had been right. This was going to be a lousy day.

Peter stormed into the cardiac cath lab. The clerk at the desk was talking with a patient, directing him to the preparation area.

"Where is Dr. Hughes," Peter was breathless, having just run up three flights of stairs after racing to the hospital full tilt on his bicycle.

"I'll be with you in a minute, Dr. Branstead. Let me just finish with this ..."

"I need to talk to Dr. Hughes right now, not in a minute." Peter's eyes were wide and his mouth and jaw tight. The desk clerk pointed down the hallway.

"I believe he's in the doctor's lounge. He just finished a cath a few minutes ago. I'll tell him you're ..."

Peter bolted down the hallway to the doctor's lounge and slammed the door behind him. Ed Hughes was sitting in a chair, his feet propped up on a table, with a cup of coffee in his hand. His face had the glazed look of someone who had just done two days worth of work on two hours of sleep and was looking forward to another twelve hours of work ahead of him. As Peter burst through the door, Ed Hughes turned his head, drawn out of his stupor by the commotion.

"Sorry about your patient, Pete. We tried everything we could, but he didn't ..."

Peter strode over to the table and slammed the palm of his hand on it, the sharp reverberation of his slap almost causing Ed Hughes to spill his coffee.

"Why the hell didn't you follow my instructions, Ed?"

"What are you talking about?"

"I left specific orders that in case of a cardiac arrest, there was to be an esmolol drip and absolutely no epinephrine. Why did you rescind those orders?"

"Oh, those orders," Hughes said, the details of the night's events just starting to sink in through the fog of his exhaustion. "Because they were nutso, that's why," he said sharply.

"I wrote those orders for a reason, Ed. I know they sounded bizarre, but Frank Halleck had been given a drug that inactivated his vagus nerve. He needed a beta-blocker, not epinephrine. Didn't Rathburn sign him off to you?"

"No, Bruce never told me anything about this guy. Frank Halleck wasn't on the cardiology service, and as far as I'm aware he didn't even have an active cardiac problem until 3:00 a.m., when he arrested. Why should Bruce sign him out to me?"

Peter stopped for a moment. No wonder Hughes thought the orders were odd.

"But then why didn't you call me if the orders were confusing?"

"You want to know why I didn't call you?" Hughes asked, getting out of his chair and walking toward Peter, his voice steadily rising. "I'll tell you why, Branstead. Because at three o'clock in the fucking morning I was yanked out of my bed to try and save a dying patient. And he wasn't just dying, Peter. He was as good as dead. I had to make a snap decision with not much information and even less time, and I did what I thought was the right thing to do. I'm sorry if I was wrong, but *I* was there at 3:00 a.m. and *you* weren't, so get the fuck off of my case!"

The two physicians stood, eye to eye, in the center of the otherwise deserted doctor's lounge. Not a sound was heard except for their breathing. Peter was the one who finally broke the tension.

"I'm sorry. This patient meant a lot to me. I feel personally responsible for him, regardless of who was or wasn't there." Peter started to walk out the door.

"Wait a minute, Pete." Peter turned around to look back at Hughes, who was shaking his head with fatigue. "When the last pitch is thrown, the score is always God one, doctors nothing. If we're lucky, we can make the game go into extra innings. But we never win, we never tie, and the game is never called on account of rain. We can only do our best." Hughes started to extend his hand, but Peter had already turned and stalked out of the lounge.

Peter walked into the family conference room off of the ICU. The chairs were unoccupied, and the room was empty except for Harriet Halleck, who stood by the window, staring out at the traffic on Seventh Avenue. Harriet heard the door open and without turning around knew that Peter had just entered.

"Frank loved to watch the city from our apartment window. He loved the activity of the city. Sometimes, he would rather look out the window than watch TV." She turned around and smiled at Peter. "He used to say that whoever designed life did a better job than Hollywood ever could." Then Harriet broke down. "I'm trying to be strong. That's what Frankie would have wanted me to do. It's just so hard to be strong without him."

"I'm sorry. We tried, but we just didn't try hard enough."

Harriet dried her eyes with a handkerchief that was already damp. "Promise me you'll make sure that Dr. Albright gets what's coming to him."

"I promise, Harriet."

"Do you learn anything from what happened to Frank?"

Peter recalled his epiphany about CAT and how that had led to Steve Bergstraum's uncovering the secrets of the drug and its potential for disclosing the biochemical basis for Alzheimer's disease. But he also thought of Harriet Halleck caring for the demented and abusive Frank at home for as long as she could and overcoming her personal terror of Dr. Albright to fight for what was most important for her.

"I've learned a tremendous amount. But not just from Frank. I've learned from you, too," and he gave her a warm hug and left to finish his rounds.

His brief stop at Mrs. Ivy's room convinced him that she was improving gradually but would still need a few days more of observation. The physostigmine helped, but her confusion worsened when the dose began wearing off. Although he wasn't sure that it would make a difference in the long run, as its effects were only partial and temporary, he preferred that to sedating her. And so did Walter, who still remained by her side.

Even Alan was getting better. His heart rate was down, and his vital signs were stable, but even better than that, his agitation had diminished substantially. Peter had been able to discontinue the use of the leather restraints. He was already feeding himself and was even cooperating in letting the nurses shave him. Peter knew that sooner or later Megan would insist on visiting Alan, and he was glad that she would see him looking like a human being.

"Good morning, Alan. How are you feeling today?"

"Pretty good. And yourself?" Alan asked between mouthfuls of cereal.

"I've been better," Peter reported wryly. "Do you remember who I am?"

"I'm not sure. Have I met you before?"

"I'm Peter Branstead, Megan's boyfriend."

"Megan, Megan, Megan ..." Alan murmured, struggling to remember. "I have a sister named Megan. Haven't seen her for years," Alan shrugged and continued eating.

Peter turned away and strode off to Megan's room, but before he got very far, he was paged to the neurology ward.

"Dr. Branstead, this is Greg Johnson."

"Hi, Greg. Hope you had a better night than I did."

"I doubt it. I was up most of the night. Three new John Does were brought in early this morning, all of them disoriented, same MO as the others. And that doesn't count the one brought in DOA after a convulsion."

"You're kidding!"

"Nope. And that's not the worst of it. I got a call from one of the neurology residents at Beth El Hospital on the East Side. They got three admitted there last night as well."

"Jesus Christ. Albright must be going berserk. He's absolutely out of his mind. Listen, Greg, we have to sit down and write up a management protocol and convince the cardiologists here and at Beth El that we know what the hell we're doing, or every one of these poor guys is going to die. Frank Halleck died last night because Ed Hughes didn't understand why I wrote the orders the way that I did. It was something that shouldn't have happened, and we have to make sure it won't happen again."

"I'll get started on it, Dr. Branstead. Do you want to make rounds soon?"

"To tell you the truth, something personal has come up, and I've got to leave town for a few days. I called Jay Harden early this morning and he's agreed to cover for me until I can get back. I've explained our mysterious Drug X and given him Steve Bergstraum's number in case he needs it, so I think everything is covered."

"Sure thing. Don't worry about us; you just have a good time."

"Compared to what I've been going through in the past week, anything will be a vacation. See you later."

Peter was about to walk into Megan's room, but he stood for just a moment in the doorway. Megan had finished showering and was still in her hospital robe, gazing out the window with her back turned to him as she brushed her luxuriant brown hair, the sleeves of her robe sliding up and baring her arms. As she sat on the bed, her legs crossed nonchalantly, the bottom of her robe slowly parted and exposed her thighs. Peter watched from the doorway, drinking in her casual eroticism.

"May I come in?"

Megan turned and smiled and patted the bed next to her. Peter sat down and gently placed his hand on her knee. Megan sighed and rested her head on his shoulder.

"I missed you, Baby," Peter murmured softly.

"I missed you too. I was so frightened, so lonely. I needed you so much. The last few days seem like a waking nightmare, like I was falling into some deep black hole that was going to swallow me up." Megan squeezed his forearm gently.

"Don't worry, it's all over. After I come back from Kiev, I promise we'll ..."

"What do you mean, 'when I come back from Kiev?'" Megan drew back.

"Didn't Rachel tell you?"

"Tell me what? I haven't seen Rachel since yesterday afternoon. What's going on?"

"Dan called me up last night from Kiev. He said that Albright's experiments are somehow tied to some major governmental crisis in Ukraine and that the entire stability of the region is at stake unless I go to Kiev and somehow help him straighten things out. It all sounds crazy to me, but he absolutely insisted that I go." Peter paused. "He said that I was being asked to do this by the very highest levels of our government. It sounds serious, Megan. I've got to go. I don't think I have a choice."

"Don't tell me you don't have a choice. You do have a choice. We're starting to get close, and the choice you're making is to leave me. Well, you can't go. I won't let you go. Please don't leave me, Peter. Not now."

Peter rushed over and held onto Megan tightly, as tightly as he had wanted to hold onto his dying father, untouchable in that sterile hospital room years ago.

"I'm not going to leave you. From what Daniel told me, it's important that I go. But you promised you wouldn't leave me, and I promise I won't leave you either. And that means forever."

Megan looked up at Peter. "Do you swear?"

"Cross my heart and hope to die."

"No," Megan said as she stroked Peter's cheek, "don't hope to die. Just come back to me."

Peter smiled. "I promise."

And they embraced as if it would be for the last time.

Peter's thoughts were in constant conflict during the cab ride to the Ukrainian Mission, torn between his sense of duty and the woman he loved. After he recounted the details of the previous night's conversation with Daniel, he got grudging acceptance from Megan, but guilt gnawed unrelentingly at his insides. Several times, he came close to telling the cab driver to turn back, but he had given his word to his best friend, and he felt it was his responsibility to carry this out to the end, whatever that was.

The Ukrainian Mission was surprisingly bland. Its unembellished, gray facade was out of place among the ornate dwelling places of the Upper East Side elite. Even the flagpoles standing in front were kept unadorned by their national standards, emphasizing the low profile that its occupants kept. The only indication that the building was the diplomatic mission of the Republic of Ukraine was a tarnished brass wall plaque, hidden in the shadow of the black overhang that shaded the entranceway, and the presence of five widely spaced security cameras carefully positioned to monitor all approaches to the building.

Peter made his way to the reception room of the mission. A counter separated the reception room from a large business area, occupied by almost a dozen desks, only three occupied. A number of men stood, coffee cups in hand, chatting around one of the barred windows overlooking the street. Peter waited a minute for someone to notice that he was standing by the desk and, when no one did, cleared his throat loudly. A stocky woman in her forties rose from her desk where she had been busy typing, but the men by the window didn't interrupt their conversation, let alone turn their heads.

"Yes, sir. May I be of assistance?"

"I need to speak to Mr. Maxim Podalsky, please."

"Mr. Podalsky is busy right now. Do you have an appointment?"

"No. He's holding a package for me. I came to pick it up."

The woman picked up an appointment book and leafed through it. "I'm sorry, but Mr. Podalsky is booked up today. Would you please come back tomorrow afternoon at 3:00. If you would let me have your name ..."

"I can't come back tomorrow. I'm leaving town tomorrow morning, and I have to take the documents in that packet with me. If Mr. Podalsky is busy, could you please get the packet for me?"

"I have no idea what packet you are talking about. But if you wish to leave your name and phone number, when Mr. Podalsky has a moment, I'll ..."

"I do not wish to leave my name and number." Peter's voice was rising in exasperation. "Please interrupt Mr. Podalsky for a minute and let me speak to him."

The secretary stood her ground. "I'm sorry, but Mr. Podalsky is in an important meeting right now and is very tightly scheduled today. You will simply have to come back some other time or let me know where Mr. Podalsky can get in touch with you."

By now, every head in the office had turned to see what was going on, and a previously inconspicuous security guard had left his post in the corner and was walking toward Peter. It was now or never.

Peter spoke up loudly. "If you won't let me speak to Mr. Podalsky right now, I'll have to notify Mr. Mikhail Pritsak that I was unable to pick up his documents because of your interference. Now, if you would just give me *your* name ..."

Suddenly, a stout, ruddy-faced man with a bulbous nose and a rumpled suit waddled in from one of the back rooms, removed a paper napkin that was still tucked into his shirt collar, and wiped his mouth before he jammed it into his suit coat pocket.

"Yes, sir. I am Maxim Podalsky. May I help you?"

Thank God. "I was told to pick up a diplomatic packet being held for me in the name of Mikhail Pritsak."

"Yes, yes. Of course, of course. Please come in, Mister, er ..."

"Smith," Peter answered with a polite smile.

"Smith. Yes, of course, Mister Smith," Podalsky smiled back, just as politely. "Please come this way to my office. I'll be with you in just a moment."

While Podalsky berated the unfortunate secretary, Peter walked into his office and sat down in a faux leather, vinyl-upholstered chair opposite a desk topped by the remains of a half-eaten tuna salad sandwich on white toast, a cup of coffee, and a *Hustler* magazine

Podalsky rushed in, closing the door behind him, and swept the magazine into a drawer. As he extended his hand, his expression quickly changed to that particular sycophantic smile that bureaucrats keep in reserve for those individuals who may have an impact on their careers.

Podalsky pumped Peter's hand vigorously. "How do you do, Mr. Smith? My deepest apologies for the rude manner in which you were treated. May I get you something to drink? Coffee? Perhaps a glass of vodka?"

"No, thank you. I'm in a bit of a hurry today. I have a number of things to do before I leave town, so if you don't mind ..."

"Yes, yes, of course. You must be a very busy man. I'll get it right away."

Podalsky left the room and returned in a minute or two with a diplomatic pouch containing a sealed manila envelope emblazoned with Cyrillic letters.

After the packet had changed hands, Peter stood up and began to thank Podalsky, who quickly came around the table and placed his arm across Peter's shoulder in a clumsy attempt at amiability.

"I do hope you will tell Mr. Pritsak that we are cooperating fully with his instructions and that you will forgive our little ... inconsiderateness." He turned and glared at the tearful receptionist.

"I will be happy to tell Mr. Pritsak of your solicitude on my behalf."

"Thank you so much, sir," Podalsky remarked, the ingratiating smile still plastered on his face. "Have a pleasant trip, Mr. Smith."

Peter was impressed with Daniel's taste in business associates as he rode down the elevator and examined the contents of the packet. The tickets were there, made out in his name, as was the visa. Peter was surprised at the picture on the visa. It was he, all right, and he recognized the photograph as the one on his St. Mark's ID card. How the hell did Daniel get a hold of that?

It was almost 11:00 a.m. before Peter got back to his apartment and called Meinerhoff.

"Homicide, Schwartzman speaking."

"I'm trying to get in touch with Detective Meinerhoff. Is he there?"

"He left earlier. Some emergency downtown. Can I leave a message?"

"Is he at a bust of East Side Psychiatric?"

"Yeah, I think so. The judge just granted the warrant this morning. Meinerhoff made it sound like a pretty big deal. You know something about it?"

Peter hung up without answering the question.

Peter ignored Daniel's warning to stay away from Albright and raced over to the East Village. At East Side Psychiatric, the scene was of complete pandemonium. The entire street was cordoned off, and about a half dozen squad cars and several police vans were parked outside the building, bubble lights flashing. Police were marching up and down the stairs, carrying forensic materials in and boxes of evidence out, and the usual crowds of gawkers strained their necks by the barricades to catch a glimpse of what was going on inside.

Peter introduced himself to a police officer at the barricades. The officer ran off, and within a few minutes, a graying, worn-looking man in an equally worn-looking suit and a cheap tie fitting loosely around an open-collared white shirt appeared. His skin sagged around his eyes and stubble-darkened jowls, and a cigarette hung loosely from his lips, bobbing up and down as he talked. To the rest of New York City it was not quite noon, but Meinerhoff looked like it was 10:00 p.m.

"Winston Meinerhoff. Glad to meet you, Dr. Branstead, but I'm afraid I have some bad news."

Peter paled. "Not more dead bodies?"

"Nope. No dead bodies. No live bodies, either. No doctors, no nurses, no beds, no furniture, no nothing. The whole damn place is deserted, cleaned out. Come on in. I'll show you around."

Peter and the detective walked briskly up the stairs to the main entranceway and into the lobby. As empty as it had seemed previously, it was now totally barren. Not only had the lighting fixtures and mirrors been removed, the reception desk and even the plush carpet were gone. The two men's footsteps echoed hollowly on the bare concrete floor as they walked to the far end of the lobby. Peter opened the door to the stairwell.

"Save your energy, Doc." Meinerhoff summoned the elevator and the motor hummed into action. "They didn't bother to have the electricity turned off. When we got here, all the lights were on."

"You think they had to leave town that quickly?"

"Possibly. But my bet? It was intentional, to fool anyone into thinking they were still here. And if they had the utilities turned off, they'd have to leave some kind of forwarding address. It would've been a phony one, but Con Ed might have caught them at it and alerted the police, so they figured it would be safer to forfeit their deposit and not leave any traces."

The elevator reached the top floor, and Peter and the detective stepped out. The police had propped the door to the locked ward open, and they walked right in.

Although the secured ward had been stripped bare just like the lobby, being divided up into rooms gave it a less cavernous appearance. The ward was a beehive of activity; walls and desktops were being dusted for prints, floors vacuumed, closets inspected.

"They cleaned this place out pretty well, Dr. Branstead, but I'm sure we'll find some clues somewhere."

But Peter wasn't listening. He immediately walked to Frank's room. The walls had been scrubbed clean, probably right after Frank left, but the faint traces of his graffiti were still visible. Peter shook his head sadly, recalling the tragedy of Frank's last days. Unfortunately, the nightstand had been removed, as had all of the other furniture.

Peter walked back to Meinerhoff, who stood by what once was the nursing station.

"Seems awfully strange, doesn't it, Doc. This was no fly-by-night operation. Must've cost millions to build and furnish. And this guy Albright spends decades building up an academic rep and lining up research grants. Then, one night, BOOM! Everybody pulls up stakes, and the circus leaves town. Pretty odd, don't you think?"

Meinerhoff was on a fishing trip. He figured that Peter knew more than he was letting on and was trying to give him an opening to tell what he knew.

Peter knew, all right. Suddenly, the pieces of the puzzle were fitting neatly into place. His research nearing completion, Albright had been preparing for weeks for the pullout, killing off his guinea pigs and gradually 'renovating' different areas of the center so as not to arouse suspicion as the furnishings were gradually packed up and moved out, probably for resale on the black market overseas. Whatever game Albright was playing, the prize must be a whopper to merit an investment of this nature. And he must have been assured of a safe haven to run to when he closed down. Only two outsiders had known anything about this plot. One was lying dead in the St. Mark's Hospital morgue. The other had just picked up airplane tickets to Kiev.

"You're right. Strangest thing I've ever heard of. Listen, I've got a lot to do today, Meinerhoff. Mind if I leave?"

"Sure, Doc, but if you remember anything else about this, you know my number. Give me a call anytime." He eyed Peter, hoping for a last minute change of heart.

"If I think of anything, you'll be the first to know." And Peter walked out of the building.

For the first time since this entire bizarre episode had begun, Peter was frightened for himself. He had indeed stumbled across some very high stakes gamble that had escaped exposure by the narrowest of margins. There was nothing that

Meinerhoff could do at this point except to ruin everything by subpoenaing him for more information and keeping him from flying to Kiev. By now, Albright was winging himself to safety, and Peter was about to follow, flying directly into the lion's den. There was only one last piece of the puzzle that needed to be fit in.

Peter strode down the hallway to the office of the Ukrainian-American Friendship Foundation. His hand trembled as he grasped the doorknob and turned. Unlocked, the door opened easily.

A lone janitor stood in the middle of what once was the shoddy waiting room, sweeping dirt into a small heap in the center of the floor.

"I'm looking for Mr. Kalchenko," Peter inquired. "I believe this is his office."

"This ain't nobody's office now, pal," the janitor replied. "Everybody packed up and moved out two or three days ago, not that there was much to pack. I'm just cleaning the place up. Landlord wants to rent this place out as soon as possible."

"Any idea where Mr. Kalchenko went to?"

"Do I look like a post office, Mister? Ask them for a forwarding address. He didn't leave any with us."

"Thanks anyway." Peter left the office and walked down the stairs, breathing a silent sigh of relief. Whoever this Kalchenko was, he had taken off just like Albright. The fewer who knew his involvement the better. He could leave for Ukraine knowing that Megan was safe.

Peter left the brownstone and turned west toward SoHo, his mind wrapped up in thoughts of preparations for his trip. Had he not been so engrossed, he might have noticed Yuri Kalchenko sitting at the window table in the cafe across the street, his eyes carefully following Peter's progress down the street from behind the lenses of darkly tinted sunglasses. After Peter turned the corner and was out of his line of sight, he cut the tip of a cigar with the blade of a six-inch knife, then set it back in the sheath that was strapped to his chest underneath his silk suit. As the waitress brought him coffee, he puffed on the cigar and watched contemplatively as the streamers of smoke trailed lazily to the ceiling. He had to think very carefully about what needed to be done.

CHAPTER 17

▼

Megan picked aimlessly at her dinner, pushing small lumps of hardened mashed potatoes and chunks of discolored meatloaf around her plate. It wasn't the hospital food that spoiled her appetite. For three long years, she and Peter had been playing their own little subconscious games, each keeping the other at an emotional arm's length for their own reasons. Frightened of hurting and, in turn, being hurt, Peter chose to withdraw, while Megan, fearful of a repeat of the desertion theme that had haunted her since her mother's death, also chose to remain emotionally distant.

And now, the bittersweet irony was inescapable. The two of them, having finally come to grips with their past, were being thrown apart for some unfathomable scheme cooked up by Daniel, which Peter wouldn't divulge in anything but the vaguest terms. Megan had been ruminating all day over her anger and disappointment until her head hurt. At least she was no longer frightened. Now she was just pissed as hell.

Megan fell back onto the bed and stared up at the ceiling. She resolved to avoid her usual graduate school self-analysis. What she needed now was a good swift kick in the butt to get her up on her feet and back into the business of getting on with her life.

The door to Megan's room burst open as if hit by gale-force winds and in flew Rachel, with Megan's dress in her hands.

"Megan, get up already. Peter's coming to pick you up in a few minutes, and you're still lying in bed? Here, put this on. It'll knock his eyes out."

Megan sat up and glowered at Rachel.

"What did Daniel say to Peter that he would agree to fly a quarter of the way around the world right at this particular moment? I want to know what the hell is so important." Megan jumped out of bed, now eye to eye with Rachel. "And you tell me the truth or get the hell out of this room!"

Rachel's effervescence subsided abruptly. She closed the door and sat down in a chair by the bedside, her face suddenly serious.

"I shouldn't be telling you this, but I owe it to you as a friend. Peter didn't realize it, but when he began investigating Albright's research, he was prying into a conspiracy to take over the government of Ukraine. If the Ukrainian government falls, there will be serious international ramifications, including a profound effect on the national interest of the United States, and Peter is the only person with the knowledge and expertise to prevent this from happening. I'm sorry, Megan. I can't tell you any more, other than there is a tremendous amount at stake in Peter going over to Kiev, and it's the only way we can get back at Albright for what he's done to you, Alan, and Frank."

"What kind of danger is Peter in?"

"Peter will be in no more danger in Kiev than he would be if he stayed here. Don't worry, Megan. I promise he'll be well protected. Daniel has very powerful friends in Ukraine, and they'll be looking out for him. And just for the record, Peter got himself involved on his own accord. But now that he's done that, we need him badly."

Megan thought for a second. "Who's 'we?'"

"I can't tell you that, either," Rachel said flatly.

Megan fumed silently and stared. The silence hung heavily in the air. For a long moment, neither woman moved a muscle.

At long last, Megan grabbed her dress and headed for the bathroom.

"In that case, I'm going to give Peter a night that he won't forget for the rest of his life." Entering the bathroom, she slammed the door behind her.

It would be a long wait before Peter arrived, so Megan took off to see Alan before she left the hospital. Besides, she was too furious at Rachel to stay in the room with her.

She stopped by briefly to visit Mrs. Ivy, who was also preparing to go home. Dr. Harden, covering for Peter and faced with a gargantuan service, had set about discharging everybody who wasn't critically ill, Mrs. Ivy included. Walter was helping his wife get dressed and ready for discharge when Megan walked into the room.

"Amanda, you remember Megan Hutchins, don't you?" Walter said, and then quickly whispered, "She's still a little confused. I'm afraid the drug hasn't worked its way completely out of her system yet."

"Megan?" Mrs. Ivy began hesitantly. "Oh, yes, Megan. Why, how are you, my dear? It's so lovely to see you again." After the surprise of hearing Mrs. Ivy referring to her by her first name wore off, Megan smiled and grasped Mrs. Ivy's hand warmly.

"I'm doing just fine, Amanda. I just stopped by to see if you were well."

"I've never felt better. Walter is going to take me home and prepare me a good home-cooked meal. Aren't you, Walter?"

"Of course I am, Sweetpea, and you deserve it after all this hospital food." Walter turned to Megan and again whispered "Sometimes I wish I just could sprinkle a smidgen of that stuff on her corn flakes every day. But she wouldn't be the same old Amanda, would she?"

"I guess not," Megan said with a smile. Then she put her arms around Mrs. Ivy. "Then I'd better give you a hug while I can." Mrs. Ivy smiled and returned the embrace, rocking Megan gently in her arms. The two women embraced for a long, wonderful moment.

"Good-bye, Amanda. I'm glad to see that you're feeling better."

"Good-bye, dear. It's been so nice to meet you. I hope we'll have a chance to see you again some time."

"I'm sure you will."

She made the walk to Alan's room slowly, with some trepidation in her steps. The last time she had seen Alan was the night of her argument with Peter, and she didn't know what to expect. It was a terrifying experience to have just met her brother for the first time in over two decades and to have come so close to losing him again. She was relieved to come to the doorway to Alan's room and see him sitting up watching TV, a soft Posey restraint keeping him from clambering out of bed and wandering about the ward.

"Hello, Alan, how are you?" Megan asked hesitantly.

Alan turned to Megan with a look of surprise. Megan was saddened to see that the deep, penetrating look that had affected her so deeply on their first encounters was gone, replaced by an empty, almost glazed look, not unlike some of her medicated clients. Alan didn't answer, just stared.

"Do you remember me at all?"

"I think so," Alan said tentatively. "Have we met before?"

"A long, long time ago. I'm your sister, Megan. Do you remember me now?"

There was a glimmer of recognition as Alan's twisted smile played across his face. "I remember. I've missed you, Meggie."

Megan sat down on the bed next to Alan and gave him a hug. "And I've missed you, too." And they embraced like they had done twenty-five years ago when they would comfort each other from the terrors outside their bedroom door.

Alan finally broke the silence, but not the embrace. "Meggie, you always used to sing me to sleep when I was little. I used to know the songs by heart, but I can't remember them now. Can you?"

"Of course I remember them, Alan. Do you want me to sing one to you?"

"Sing them all, if you can. I haven't heard them for years."

Megan sighed and smiled at Alan. "I'm not sure if I can sing all of them, but I'll sing as many as I can." Megan held his hand in hers and softly began

> You are my sunshine, my only sunshine,
> You make me happy when skies are gray.
> You'll never know, dear, how much I love you.
> Please don't take my sunshine away.

Peter and Rachel had been talking together about the events that had just transpired in Megan's room as they walked down the hall to Alan's room, but their voices fell into a hush as they approached and heard Megan singing. Peeking into the room, they saw Megan and Alan, sister and brother, oblivious to all around them. Turning silently, Rachel and Peter walked quietly back to Megan's room.

It was a long time before Megan returned to her room, her eyes melancholy.

"We didn't want to interrupt you," Peter said.

Megan put her arms around his neck and searched his eyes. "Thanks. I really needed time with Alan. Are you okay with that?"

"I'm okay. Alan will be good company for you while I'm away," he said, and he kissed her gently on the forehead.

Rachel interrupted after a minute. "Guys, I've got to go. I'll stop by in the morning before you leave."

It was dark when Megan and Peter left the hospital entrance and Peter flagged down a cab. As they got into the back and Peter gave the driver instructions, he placed his hand on Megan's knee, and the two kissed as the cab pulled away from the hospital.

Rachel sighed as she watched them from a window in the emergency room waiting area, then she called the surveillance agent in the apartment on Mercer Street to tell him Peter and Megan were on their way.

Rachel left St. Mark's Hospital and, instead of walking south toward SoHo, walked westward toward her own apartment. For several days, she had known she was being followed, and she thought it best to take a circuitous route to the surveillance apartment rather than risk having her connection to Peter and Megan exposed. Even the hospital visits had been a calculated risk, but nobody had followed her past the front door, where security would check them for weapons.

Rachel walked briskly down Perry Street. Under other circumstances, she had always enjoyed this walk. The well-kept brownstones and magnificent old sycamores and black locusts reminded her of happier days in Georgetown when she and Daniel had just gotten married. It was as if someone had managed to keep this little corner of Manhattan protected against the inroads of the twenty-first century and the noisy chaos of the city.

But tonight the majestic trees were no comfort. They cast dark, eerie shadows along the street and buildings, where the light from the amber streetlamps could not make it through their leafy heads, shadows that could easily hide an assailant as he crouched in the entranceways to basement apartments hidden under townhouse stoops.

It was only after Rachel turned south on Hudson Street that she became aware of the sharp click of footsteps behind her that interrupted the silence of the night. She noticed that whenever she slowed her walking, the footsteps slowed as well, keeping close cadence with hers. She dared not turn around, but from the sound she estimated her pursuer was about a half block behind her.

It would have been easier to continue down Hudson Street to Houston. Both streets were broad, well lit, and well traveled even at this hour. But that would lead him right to Peter and Megan's, and it was imperative that Rachel lose her stalker before she got out of the West Village.

She turned quickly down Grove Street and headed for Grove Court, a small cluster of nineteenth-century townhouses gathered around a central courtyard, separated from the main street by a high stone wall and a wrought-iron gate. It would be easy to hide in the shadows if she could slip into the courtyard.

Rachel picked up her pace, her heart beating heavily in her chest, her breathing coming faster and harder. She turned the handle to the iron gate, but it wouldn't open. It was locked, and the fence was too high to jump. She knew her pursuer. Screaming for help would offer no deterrent and would waste valuable seconds. The footsteps had turned the corner. They were getting closer. And faster.

Rachel turned quickly onto Bedford Street, trying to get to the safety of Seventh Avenue, where crowds of people would make an assault difficult and where she might be able to flag down a cab. But as she made the turn onto the dimly lit side street, she felt a hand grab her roughly by the arm, spin her around, and force her deep into an alley tucked between two townhouses. A leather-gloved hand pressed over her mouth, blocking her screams and pinning her head back against the brick wall. In the feeble light of the alleyway, she could barely make out her attacker's hard, cold eyes staring into hers, a savage grin evidencing his enjoyment of the moment. With his free hand, he pulled a knife out from under his jacket.

"Now, Lone Eagle, feel Scorpion's sting."

Seeing the knife sweep toward her out of the corner of her vision, Rachel swept downward with her left arm, blocking its arc. She curled the fingers of her right hand and, twisting her wrist as she straightened her arm, thrust her knuckles full force into her attacker's throat. As he grunted in pain, Rachel felt his grip on her mouth loosen. Taking advantage of his surprise, she knocked his hand away from her mouth with a quick sweep of her right arm.

Her attacker lunged forward with his knife and, only by quickly slapping his arm and twisting her torso away from the point of the blade, was she able to avoid being stabbed as his knife hand swept by her waist. Grabbing his wrist while he was off balance, Rachel spun around, twisting his arm straight out behind him. She pushed behind his shoulder with her free hand and kicked behind his knee, throwing her attacker face first into the brick wall of the alleyway and then to the ground. Forcing his wrist into flexion until she felt it snap, Rachel grabbed the knife out of his hand, pushed his face into the ground, and buried the knife at the juncture of his neck and the base of his skull. His body went limp instantly.

Rachel stood up and tried to catch her breath. No matter how much she trained and prepared herself psychologically, she still found each killing just as traumatic as her first one. But something was wrong.

It had been too easy.

As she calmed herself down, her brain went back into a preparedness mode. After taking a handkerchief out of her purse and wiping the knife handle thoroughly, she threw it down on the ground and turned her assailant over on his back. His eyes were fixed in the empty stare of death, his jaw slack as his head rolled limply to the side. He was young, no older than his early twenties—too young.

Rachel tore open his shirt. An enormous tattoo of a three-headed, fire-breathing dragon covered his entire chest.

"Scorpion, my ass. You're an impostor," she snapped. No wonder it had been so easy. As she brushed herself off and picked up her purse, Rachel took one last look at her erstwhile assailant lying stone still on the pavement of the alleyway.

"Never send a boy to do a man's work," she muttered and headed off toward Houston Street.

CHAPTER 18

▼

His head rolling sleepily on the back of his seat, Peter was oblivious to the magnificent palette of colors of the ripening dawn as the cab drove southward toward John F. Kennedy International Airport. He was also oblivious to the repeated thumps as the cab rode over the broken roadbed of the Van Wyck Expressway and to the periodic roar of semis passing the cab on their way to deliveries in Queens and Long Island. His only awareness was of his own total exhaustion and the gentle weight of Megan's head resting on this shoulder, her arms entwined around his and her hands resting lightly on his forearm.

Peter's night had been occupied in quenching Megan's seemingly insatiable lust. Megan had always enjoyed sex, but last night desire had seemed to take possession of her, keeping her intensely eroticized all night. In one all-too-brief night, he and Megan had cast aside any lingering doubts he had about the solidity of their relationship. Their energies had left them both physically and emotionally exhausted, with hardly any time for sleep before Peter's alarm roused them in the predawn darkness.

Peter had hoped that he could say good-bye at their loft, but Megan made it very clear that there was no way on earth he was going to the airport without her. Rachel called as the two were getting ready to leave and also tried to dissuade her, especially so soon after her recovery—also to no avail. Instead, Megan grudgingly accepted Rachel's proposal that the two women would stay in the apartment together until the men returned home.

"Exit to airport, sir," intoned the cab driver, a recent arrival from an unspecified Middle Eastern country. At least he wasn't Russian, thought Peter. He was already paranoid enough about his trip without having to worry about who would be driving Megan home.

Peter rubbed Megan's hand, awakening her as gently as he could.

"Almost there, babe. Time to get up."

Megan roused and smiled at Peter through half closed lids, clutching his arm tighter as if she might somehow keep him in the cab and take him back home with her. Then she closed her eyes and rubbed her cheek on his shoulder as she remembered the night's pleasures.

"If you thought last night was something, wait until you get back," she whispered.

"I'll remember to keep myself well hydrated."

Megan gave his arm a playful squeeze and pulled away from him as he got his carry-on bag ready.

Darkness clouded Megan's face as she rubbed Peter's back and then let her hand caress the nape of his neck. "Promise me that you'll be careful."

"You're making it sound like I'm on a mission of no return. I'm just going over to give Daniel some advice. I'll be back before you even miss me."

Megan shifted uneasily in her seat. "Rachel isn't telling us everything. I don't know what she's leaving out, but I think she's doing it to keep me from getting scared out of my wits. I'm frightened for you." Megan kissed him. "Watch yourself, okay?"

"Okay, okay. I'll be careful. And I promise I'll wear warm clothes and change my underwear every day."

"Peter, stop it. I'm serious." But she couldn't hold back a smile.

The cab pulled to a stop by the curb, and the two got out and walked, hand in hand, toward the terminal.

"It's just not fair," Megan began. "It's taken three years to break down the wall, and now you're leaving me just when we can finally start working things out."

"I'm not leaving you. I'll never leave you. I told you that before. Think of this as a business trip, a conference that I have to go to. Better yet, think of it as keeping a promise that I made to Harriet Halleck."

"I don't care about promises to anyone else. I want to be selfish. I want you all to myself, and I'm pissed as hell at Rachel. It's going to be hard sharing the apartment with her until you're back."

"Try to forgive her. You need someone to take care of you for the time being."

"I do not. I'm fine now, and I can take care of myself, too. I'm not as fragile as you make me out to be, Peter. But I'll miss you anyway."

The two held each other in silence for several minutes until the cab driver impatiently honked his horn.

"Go ahead," Megan said, wiping her eyes with the back of her hand. "You'll miss your plane."

After one long, final kiss, they separated, Peter watching from the curb as Megan got into the cab and waved from the rear window as it quickly pulled away.

Peter sighed, missing her even before the cab pulled out of sight, and walked into the terminal.

Rachel leaned forward from the back seat and tapped the shoulder of the driver of the dark blue Chevrolet that had been parked, motor running, just a hundred feet or so behind Megan's cab. "Go, quickly. And make sure she doesn't know we're following her." She settled back in her seat and stared out of the window as the car pulled away from the curb.

"Occupation: physician-neurologist," the security guard noted curiously as he inspected Peter's visa and carry-on bag. Gray-haired and pot-bellied, this man was difficult for Peter to envision as the nation's first line of defense against terrorism; he pushed the morbid thought from his mind. "You anything like a psychiatrist?" the guard added.

"No, not really. Why do you ask?"

"Had a whole slew of shrinks and nurses on the last flight two days ago. Is there an epidemic of lunatics in Ukraine?"

"Not exactly. There's an international conference on, um, neuropsychiatric manifestations of, uh, phosphodiesterase inhibitors in Kiev, and a number of the top researchers in the field are meeting there in a few days. By any chance, one of the doctors on that flight wouldn't have been a Dr. William Albright, would he? I was hoping to hear his lecture at the conference."

The security guard shook his head. "Sorry, Doc, I can never remember names. Guess I'm getting old-timer's disease, if you know what I mean. One of them looked *very* familiar, but I just couldn't place him."

Suddenly, it clicked for Peter why Albright had always looked so familiar. "Did he look like Sherlock Holmes?"

"That's it! It's been bugging me since I saw him, but that's the one. Basil Rathbone, wasn't it? 'Elementary, my dear Watson,'" the guard said theatrically and chuckled to himself as he waved Peter through. "Have a nice trip, Doc."

At least I'm on the right track, Peter mused as he rechecked his ticket and became somewhat disturbed when he realized that it was only one way.

Peter thumbed through the magazine rack in the bulkhead of the plane and frowned: the selection of magazines was sparse, most were several months old, and half were in Ukrainian. He settled on a three-month-old copy of *Newsweek,* walked to his seat, and opened the door to the overhead luggage compartment.

"Allow me, Dr. Branstead."

A thin, dark-haired man in his midthirties with a dark, swarthy face, heavily cratered from the effects of a childhood attack of smallpox, and wearing a shapeless, dark business suit stood up from his aisle seat next to Peter's and helped him lift his carry-on bag into the compartment. Startled, Peter said nothing until he sat down.

"Do I know you?"

"I don't think so. My name is Dmytro, Dr. Branstead. I've been sent by Mr. Pritsak to escort you on your trip."

Interesting.

"Mr. Pritsak didn't happen to tell you what I was supposed to do once I got to Kiev, did he?"

Dmytro's face betrayed no emotion. "No, he didn't."

He unfolded a Ukrainian newspaper and began reading. *That's a conversation stopper,* Peter thought, staring out the window as the plane took off.

Peter awoke as the pilot announced that the plane was beginning its descent into Kiev. With the exception of dinner, eaten in silence, Peter had slept for virtually the entire flight. His flying companion wasn't much of a conversationalist, and there hadn't been more than a dozen words said between them since takeoff.

It was early evening, and the setting sun painted the cloud-strewn sky with brilliant shades of gold, orange, red, and blue, like a Maxfield Parrish print. Below them, Peter saw a small city, composed exclusively of clusters of nondescript apartment buildings stretching on monotonously for miles, the setting sun casting their shadows like gargantuan sundials.

"See anything peculiar?" Dmytro's voice startled Peter.

"Not really. We could be anywhere. For all I know, we could have flown in a great big circle and we're coming into LaGuardia over Co-op City."

"Look again. See any cars? Any streetlights? Any people?"

Peter looked down. "Come to think of it, I don't. Where are we?"

"This is Prypyat, just north of Chernobyl. It's been a ghost town since the reactor blew up, and it probably will be for another few thousand years. Look down there."

Peter followed Dmytro's finger. They were flying over a vast field full of trucks, bulldozers, and helicopters neatly lined up in rows.

"All that was contaminated when Chernobyl exploded. They should be buried, but the government can't afford to do it. So everything just sits around while black marketers steal radioactive spare parts. Now look over there."

There was no doubt about what Dmytro was pointing at. The huge concrete sarcophagus housing the annihilated Reactor Unit Number 4 of the Chernobyl nuclear power plant loomed ominously like a massive mausoleum, sitting at the northern end of its cooling pond. The lights around the adjacent, still-functional reactors were the only signs of life in the barren vista.

"It was a tragedy of monumental incompetence, Dr. Branstead. The engineers who blew up the reactor bypassed every single safety system." Dmytro shook his head. "I have many friends affected by the meltdown. Some were killed in the explosion, some are dying of cancer, and some lost their houses and became refugees within their own country. It was terrible. And they've found out the casing still leaks radioactive waste after hard rains. They're already constructing another concrete structure around the old one just to keep all the leaks inside. It's supposed to last for a thousand years."

Peter stared down, fascinated by the monstrosity below them. If he wasn't anxious enough, he was now filled with a sense of foreboding, an almost superstitious feeling of presentiment, as the plane continued its descent into Boryspil Airport.

Peter checked his watch. The two had split up immediately on leaving the plane. As per Dmytro's instructions, Peter was to stay in the bathroom while Dmytro picked up the car and was to wait exactly five minutes before leaving the terminal and waiting on the sidewalk for a black sedan, license plate number 75946. Peter didn't like this cloak-and-dagger stuff. It made him very nervous.

Within fifteen seconds of Peter's walking out onto the sidewalk, the black sedan pulled up. The windows were heavily tinted, and it wasn't until the window rolled down that Peter could tell it was Dmytro who was driving, sporting sunglasses in spite of the early evening darkness.

"Please get in the back, Dr. Branstead. Quickly." Peter opened the door and got into the back seat of the sedan. As soon as the door was shut, the car accelerated so quickly that Peter was thrown against the car door.

"I'm sorry, Dr. Branstead," Dmytro said as he removed his sunglasses, "but it is best that we be seen together as little as possible."

"Listen," Peter said angrily, "I'd like to know what this is all about. Why is all this secrecy necessary?"

"I was not told the purpose of your trip, Dr. Branstead. I was only given instructions to accompany you from New York City and take you to your hotel. I am not authorized to tell you any other information, even if I knew the answers."

"Well, can you at least tell me what hotel you're taking me to?"

"I am not authorized to give you that information, Dr. Branstead." And with that Dmytro spoke no more.

Peter sighed and grasped his carry-on bag to his chest. He stared forlornly out the window, hoping to at least catch some sight of Kiev, but the best he could do was to see a few lights from passing churches, their spires lit up brilliantly against the darkened sky. After a few minutes, Peter suddenly felt the front of the car drop downward. Looking out the window, it was apparent that they were entering the underground garage of a hotel. Dmytro parked the sedan in a reserved space, jumped out of the front, and held the rear door open for Peter. They walked toward an elevator just a few feet away where Dmytro inserted a card where the call button would normally be. The door opened silently, and Dmytro motioned Peter into the elevator.

In the elevator, Dmytro unlocked a small door on the panel and inserted the card into another slot and pushed the button to the top floor. Dmytro motioned Peter to get out when the doors opened.

Peter was surprised to find that they were not in a hallway but in a short corridor with a single door at the end. Dmytro unlocked the door, which opened into an opulent suite with turn-of-the-century furniture, elegant eighteenth-century oil paintings on the wall, and floor-to-ceiling burgundy satin curtains completely covering the windows.

"Please make yourself comfortable, Dr. Branstead. Feel free to order anything you desire from room service, but I would ask that you not leave the suite as you cannot leave this floor without a key. Also, please do not open the curtains. We would like to keep your visit as undisclosed as possible. The front desk will wake you up at 7:00 a.m., and I will be by to pick you up at 8:30 to take you to Mr. Pritsak. Have a pleasant evening, Dr. Branstead."

And without a change in expression, Dmytro turned and left.

Peter listened carefully by the door. When he heard the whine of the elevator carrying Dmytro back to the parking garage, he grabbed the doorknob and turned it, but it didn't budge. The bastard had locked him in. Peter then walked over to the window to get a peek of the surrounding area of Kiev, but the curtains were stitched shut in the middle and attached to the wall at either end. Surprisingly, they were not affixed to the floor, and Peter slipped his head under it, only to find out that the window had been replaced by translucent bulletproof glass.

Peter sighed and dialed room service. He was starved, having only eaten a tray of airplane food all day, and mediocre airplane food at that. He picked up the menu by the phone and eyed it ravenously.

"Yes, sir, may I help you?" asked a young woman.

"This is Dr. Branstead. I'd like to order dinner. I'll start with salade orloff, a bowl of bisque of morels, and tournedos with sauce béarnaise. And for dessert, I'll have a Grand Marnier soufflé."

If he was going to be kept prisoner, he was damn well going to be a well-fed prisoner.

"As you wish, sir. Will there be anything else?"

"Could I make a long-distance call to New York?"

"I'm sorry, sir. I am not authorized to allow any phone calls from this room. The phone is only connected to the front desk, not the public phone system."

"Could you please tell me the name of this hotel?"

"I'm sorry, sir. I am not authorized to provide that information. Will there be anything else?"

"No, that will be all, thank you."

About an hour later, there was a knock on the door, and a waiter wheeled in a cart with his dinner. A few quick questions and Peter realized that the waiter didn't speak any English. Peter didn't bother checking the door after the waiter left, but resigned himself to enjoying his dinner.

Peter was again being propelled quickly down the hospital corridor toward the room at the far end, irresistibly drawn as if by a powerful magnet. The dream had changed. This time, he was alone. His mother, the doctors and nurses, all were gone. Finally standing at the doorway to the room he saw the bed, which had previously been his father's. This time, a body totally wrapped in bandages occupied it.

Peter walked slowly to the bedside. A network of lacerations and bullet wounds riddled the man's chest, and blood poured out of the wounds onto the floor in a myriad of small rivulets. Horrified at the sight, but his hand inexorably controlled by the same irresistible force, Peter reached up and tore away the bandages from the man's head.

And looked into his own lifeless face.

Peter awoke, gasping for breath in the darkness of the hotel room. He reached out blindly, almost knocking over the lamp before he felt the switch and turned it on. The welcome light of the lamp instantly flooded the room and chased the dream images out of his consciousness. He was alone in the hotel room, seven thousand miles from Megan. He calmed himself down as he had learned to do so many times before, and when his heartbeat had returned to normal, he switched off the light and went back to sleep.

CHAPTER 19

▼

Peter had barely finished his breakfast when he heard a knock on the door, obviously intended as a courtesy as he had no way of opening the door if he wanted to and no way to stop anyone from coming in as long as they had the key.

"Dr. Branstead, may I come in?"

"Do I have a choice?"

The door was unlocked and Dmytro entered, standing stiffly with his hands clasped behind his back as Peter scraped the last bit of scrambled eggs from his plate.

"I hope you have been enjoying our hospitality, Dr. Branstead."

"The bed was very comfortable, and the food has been superb, but to tell you the truth, Dmytro, I do find myself wondering whether I'm a guest or a prisoner."

Dmytro paused briefly. "I apologize for the highly secretive nature of the arrangements that have been made on your behalf, Dr. Branstead. We are following standard procedures for a personage of your importance to ensure your safety. My superior understands that you have been greatly inconvenienced in coming here and takes personal responsibility for your comfort and well-being during your stay. He hopes that you will not take offense."

"Is your superior Mikhail Pritsak, Dmytro?"

"Yes."

"What position does he hold in the government? What's his job?"

"I'll be taking you to see him right now. You may ask him any questions you wish at that time. I am not authorized to give you further information."

"Will you be taking me to Dr. Falconer, too?"

"You may wish to take your visa and passport with you for identification purposes. Everything else will be quite safe here." Dmytro's stony expression didn't change, nor did he move a muscle.

"Can't you at least tell me ... Oh, forget it. Let's go."

After another silent drive through the streets of Kiev, they arrived at an imposing governmental building, and, after passing through a gauntlet of armed security guards, Peter found himself escorted by Dmytro into a suite that occupied most of the top floor.

After wary scrutiny by one last guard, they were ushered into a spacious but simply furnished office. A large oak desk and an old-fashioned high-backed leather chair dominated the center of the room. Standing with his back to Peter and gazing out of a large window at an expansive vista of the city stood a robust grizzly bear of a man. He was well over six feet tall, and his broad physique solidly filled out a well-tailored suit, giving ample evidence to what must have been a youthful preoccupation with athletics. He seemed deeply wrapped in thought as he made no move as Dmytro closed the door and addressed him in Ukrainian.

"Excuse me, Director Pritsak. Allow me to introduce Dr. Peter Branstead."

His musings interrupted, the man turned from the window toward Peter. He was in his early forties, a handsome man in a rough-hewn sort of way. A head of thick wavy brown hair and a bushy mustache framed ruddy cheeks and a craggy visage that appeared quite familiar with adversity. However, his dark brown eyes had intensity and sparkle to them that attested to a deep gusto for life. In addition to his wrinkles, the forties had brought on a slight paunch, the one flaw in a carefully maintained physique. Peter could see where women would find this man very attractive but suspected that the nature of his occupation would allow few, if any, to get close. The man smiled broadly, the crow's feet by the corners of his eyes deepening, and he walked briskly toward Peter, who thankfully noted the absence of a scar on his extended arm.

"Dr. Branstead, it is so good to see you," he greeted Peter, vigorously shaking his hand. "I am Mikhail Pritsak, Director of the Central Sector, Ukrainian Secret Service. I've been awaiting your arrival most eagerly. I hope your travel arrangements were satisfactory."

"Pleasant enough. They certainly were very ... interesting."

"Excellent," he bellowed, fortunately missing Peter's undertone of irony, and waved Peter's escort out of the room.

"Director Pritsak ..." Peter began.

"Please, Dr. Branstead, call me Mikhail."

"Mikhail," Peter began again, "I am very pleased to be here, and I hope I can be of assistance to you. But if you don't mind, I'd like to find out exactly why I'm here."

Pritsak laughed loudly and gave Peter a hearty slap on the back that might have floored a man of lesser stature.

"I like a man who speaks plainly. Come; let's go next door where we can talk privately." Pritsak motioned Peter toward a set of heavy mahogany doors which, when opened, led into a large conference room lined with the same floor-to-ceiling windows that were in the previous office. In the center of the room, surrounded by elegant, if well-used, leather armchairs, was an oblong mahogany conference table, its surface polished to a mirror finish. It was easily capable of seating ten to fifteen people comfortably, but at its head now sat a lone individual—Daniel Falconer.

"How's it going, Pete?" Daniel asked, rising from his chair and advancing toward Peter. "I hope you remembered to bring your racquet."

Daniel was behaving with his usual cool academic reserve. It seemed to make no difference whether they were at a dinner, a racquetball game, or as was the case, in the secret service building of a nation that now stood poised on the brink of a major political crisis. Peter, however, was a potpourri of emotions that all came together at the same instant. He was glad to see Daniel, but he simultaneously held his friend responsible for having him dragged seven thousand miles away from Megan and into the center of a maelstrom. As Daniel extended his hand, Peter hesitated a second before grasping it. The significance of that moment of indecision was not lost on Daniel.

"I can't blame you for being angry," Daniel remarked as the two sat down at the end of the table, Pritsak sitting opposite them. "I think that after Mikhail and I explain the situation, you'll understand that there was really no alternative. Quite honestly, I would have done it even if it required dragging you on the plane myself."

"A friend in need is a friend indeed," muttered Peter.

"Don't make this any more difficult than it already is. Whether you know it or not, you're in big trouble. At least over here, I can try to keep you from getting killed."

Daniel stopped talking as a secretary set down a tray holding a pot of brewed coffee and three cups and exited the room wordlessly.

"And what the hell was that supposed to mean?"

"Will you please give me a minute to explain?"

"Sorry. Go ahead," Peter said.

"Let me start from the beginning. There is currently a political battle going on in this country as to what course the economy will take and who will control it. The Communists are making a bid for resurgence by demanding continued nationalization of industry and agriculture. The Mafia sees an opportunity of buying out an entire nation at wholesale prices if they can keep foreign capital and competition out of the country. The president, Anatoly Labrinska, supports a free market system open to anyone, either here or abroad, that would help in development of the economy. Because of the peculiarities of the political system here, for the past decade there has been a stalemate involving these three forces, each trying to slug it out for control, with nobody getting anywhere. However, in the past few years President Labrinska and his Liberal Party had managed to pull Ukraine legislatively to the brink of a free market economy and were about to finalize his plans. However, the Mafia has become extremely powerful and has propelled one of their sympathizers into a position of power."

"Prime Minister Valentyn Boshevsky, leader of the right-wing Radical Nationalist Party," Pritsak interjected.

"About a week ago," Daniel continued, "we came across a plot to poison President Labrinska, a plot that, unfortunately, is already being carried out."

"Who is 'we?'" Peter asked uneasily.

"*We* are the Central Intelligence Agency."

Peter's face froze in shock and consternation. "You're with the CIA?"

Daniel nodded. "Rachel, too."

Peter flinched, as if Daniel had thrown a punch directly at his face, but after a brief silence his stunned expression dissolved, and he burst into laughter.

"Oh, come on. You don't really expect me to believe that our government has to rely on dear, sweet, ditzy Rachel to keep the world safe for democracy? Jeez, we're in bigger trouble than I thought."

"We work as a team, Peter. We've been doing this for years. That whole business of my having an academic position at Georgetown was a ruse established for the sake of my résumé. I wasn't at Georgetown at all. Rachel and I were in training at Quantico. The Directorate of Intelligence recruited me, and she's working under the Directorate of Operations, in the Reports Group. As far as the CIA was concerned, it was a marriage made in heaven. I gather information on the political systems of what are now the Commonwealth of Independent States and interact with the security branches of the Eastern European governments. Our goal is to assist them in establishing stable and unified governments that can successfully withstand the forces of disintegration within themselves, particularly the development of organized crime and the resurgence of right-wing and fascistic political movements."

Peter, still dumbfounded, leaned back in his chair and stared at Daniel. "You're serious, aren't you? You're really and truly serious." He shook his head in disbelief. "And how does Rachel fit into this?"

"She has two functions. She types up and edits my reports for dissemination throughout the intelligence community and to foreign governments … and she's my bodyguard. Rachel's training was primarily in ballistics and martial arts."

Peter could sit still no more. He jumped up and agitatedly paced, trying to assimilate what Daniel had told him. "This is too crazy. You're asking me to believe that Rachel is a trained killer? And that for the last five years I've been playing racquetball with a spy?"

"I'm not really a spy, Peter. I share all the information I gather with the host government. Do you think I'd be sitting down for coffee with the head of the Ukrainian Secret Service if I were a spy? Mikhail and I have been working together for years. And I assure you that Rachel is as well trained as anybody else in the CIA, or I wouldn't have entrusted her with Megan's life."

"What do you mean? Is Megan in danger?"

"I don't think so, but I couldn't be certain, so I asked Rachel to stay with her while you were gone. Peter, please sit down and let me continue.

"At any rate, we discovered a plot to poison President Labrinska with a combination of drugs that would first make him appear confused and then demented, thereby discrediting all of the policies he had previously put in place, and would eventually kill him. For security reasons, they were conducting the clinical research on these drugs somewhere in the United States. That's all we knew, and we were helpless to do anything about it. Then I found out that you had accidentally stumbled onto the research facility and were investigating it on your own. Rachel and I had already been exposed, so there wasn't much we could do but try to keep as far away from you as we could so that those involved with the plot wouldn't know that we were connected. That would have put your life immediately in danger. Frankly, I would have rather left you back in the United States, but you were doing too much snooping. Sooner or later, the plotters would have suspected that you knew too much and eliminated you, so we had to get you over here for your own protection. In addition, from what Rachel tells me, you know the antidote."

"I think it's the antidote. I've only been able to try it out once, on Megan's brother, and it seemed to work. If you want, I could call up my chief resident and see if the treatment has worked with other patients."

"No. At this point, any communication between you and the United States is too risky. Right now, as far as we know, the plotters think that you're still in New York and have no connection to Rachel, Mikhail, or me. All of those clandestine procedures we had you go through were designed to keep outside knowledge of your involvement to an absolute minimum for your own protection. I'm sorry I had to be so underhanded, but there's too much at stake, including the lives of you and Megan, to let anything slip out."

In a flash of insight, everything became blindingly clear to Peter. Megan had been absolutely right: one of the most ruthless organizations in the world was aiming for "the big prize," and whether they knew it or not, he was the only thing that stood in their way. *Well, here I am, guys. Come and get me.*

Peter felt his stomach knot up. "Do you know who the plotters are?"

Mikhail, who had been sitting quietly and listening intently to the conversation, cut in. "They are members of a secret society, the Brotherhood of the Trident. We think there is a coalition of ultranationalistic politicians, doctors, criminals, and others who have banded together to gain control of our government. We believe the prime minister is in the Brotherhood, as are Dr. Albright and several other doctors who have control over the president. We suspect many members of the Ukrainian Mafia as well, in particular one known only as Scorpion, who is the most dangerous."

"Who's Scorpion?"

"He is a well-known criminal and murderer. He's spent much time in Ukrainian and Russian prisons, but he has always been sprung by the Mafia. We believe he is the coordinator and enforcer for any big projects the Mafia undertakes. He makes sure that things go smoothly, that people do as they're told, and that there are no betrayers in the ranks. He has his spies everywhere, and he keeps discipline in the organization so tight that even the mention of his name strikes terror into any thug we try to interrogate, and they clam up right away. As you can see, we fear spies even here in the Secret Service, which is why I have ordered Dmytro to keep your identity secret, even to our own security guards. In Ukraine, nobody can be trusted."

Peter's palms suddenly felt clammy. "What does he look like?"

"We don't know exactly. He's very crafty. He constantly changes his name, his identity, even his appearance, so that nobody can identify him. At times, he has even been imprisoned without the authorities knowing who he was until after he had broken out. He has only a few identifying marks; most of them tattoos. Tattooing is very important in the criminal subculture here. It identifies your status in the pecking order and tells other criminals what crimes you have committed and how dangerous you are."

"What sort of tattoos does Scorpion have?"

Mikhail looked at Peter curiously. "Why do you ask?"

"In New York, I met two men with tattoos. One was Gennadi Chursin, head of security at Albright's clinic. He had some beetles tattooed on his hands. The other was Yuri Kalchenko. He was the head of the Ukrainian-American Friendship Foundation, which supposedly provided funding through contributions to Albright's clinic, and he had a bunch of skull tattoos."

Mikhail shook his head. "Chursin was probably a minor criminal since beetles indicate a thief. The skulls you saw on the other man each marked a murder that he had committed. How many of them did you see?"

"Eight."

Mikhail and Daniel quickly glanced at each other. Daniel spoke next.

"Think, Peter. Were there any other tattoos? Did this man have anything else tattooed on his fingers? It's very important."

"I ... there were Cyrillic letters on his fingers, but I can't remember what they were."

"Did he clasp his fingers together at all while he was sitting?"

"Yes, he did."

Daniel turned to Mikhail, who took a paper and pen out of his jacket pocket, scrawled some Cyrillic letters, and pushed the paper across the table to Peter. "Did the letters look like this?"

Peter thought for a moment before answering. "I think they did. Yeah, I'm pretty sure that's what they were. He told me they spelled 'I Love You.'"

Mikhail smiled wryly. "Not quite. In Ukrainian, that's *'Ya Smert'* ... 'I am death.' Congratulations, Peter. You've met Scorpion. And lived."

Peter took in a deep breath. This was looking really bad.

"What can we do?"

"Not much now," Mikhail remarked. "We have to wait for him to show himself. He could be here, or he could be in New York. He still might not know you suspect anything. But can you tell me anything about him?"

Peter described him physically in great detail while Mikhail took notes.

Daniel put his hand on Peter's shoulder. "Don't worry about Megan. She and Rachel are staying hidden. I doubt he would connect the two of them, at least not yet. We'll get the description to Rachel so she knows what to look for."

"There's one other thing that might be important," Peter commented. "I'm pretty sure he's a sinistral."

"A what?"

"Left-handed. I think he's left-handed."

"How do you know?" Mikhail asked.

"When he shook hands with me, his watch was on his right wrist. Most people keep their watch on their left wrist so they can wind the stem easily and it doesn't interfere with their ability to write. Some lefties keep it on their right wrist because it interferes with the use of their dominant hand."

"Are you sure it was on his right hand? I don't recall seeing anything in his dossier about being left-handed," Mikhail asked.

"Yeah, I'm sure. It's my business to know people's handedness. It may be important in determining hemispheric dominance. But some dextrals ... righties, keep their watch on their right hand, too, so I can't be positive."

"He uses a knife as his weapon of choice. If he kept his watch on his left hand, it might interfere with his throwing arm," Mikhail observed.

"Interesting point," Daniel added. "Might come in handy. In the meantime, we have to come up with a plan to save the president. He's gotten so bad that he's been hospitalized in the Kiev Neurological Institute under the care of the Institute's director, Dr. Nikolai Mogilev. This is what we need to do. Mikhail has arranged a meeting with you and Dr. Mogilev, but we'll have to keep it strictly on the QT. Hopefully, you can convince him to give the antidote, whatever it is, to the president. Labrinska's sinking fast, and we don't have much time. However, even if we save the president, we still don't have any direct evidence tying the prime minister into the plot, and unless we catch him red-handed, he'll remain a danger, and he may be able to reformulate a takeover again. I'll have to sneak into the Council of Ministers Building tonight and try to break into Boshevsky's files."

"Are you nuts? You'll get yourself killed," Peter broke in. "Mikhail, why don't you get one of your agents to do that?"

"Because that would be even more dangerous. I have no idea who I can really trust, even within my own organization, when it comes to this matter. Many of my own agents have ties either to the Mafia or the Radical Nationalists. Boshevsky's bodyguard came from within my own organization, but now we cannot even approach him. His allegiance is solidly with Boshevsky. I'm afraid we have no choice, Peter. Daniel knows the risks. There are no other alternatives."

"It's what I've been trained to do," Daniel said. "The fewer people we get involved, the better."

Mikhail slammed his palm down on the table. "Then, it's settled." He reached into a cabinet that stood behind his chair and pulled out a liter of vodka and three shot glasses, filling them to the top and distributing them to Daniel and Peter. "I propose a toast to our own little brotherhood."

"Just a minute, guys. Perhaps nobody's noticed, but it's not even lunchtime yet," Peter objected.

"So what? It's just a toast." Mikhail held his arm outstretched, palm down, and placed his brimming shot glass on the top of his hand. He brought his hand slowly toward his mouth until the rim of the glass just touched his lips. With a show of bravado, he tipped his wrist, spilling the contents of the shot glass into his mouth, then dropped his wrist back, keeping the shot glass upright.

Daniel smiled and picked up his shot glass, motioning for Peter to do the same.

"Here's to Ukrainian vodka: deadly as the Mafia, just takes a little longer." And with that he downed the shot glass in one gulp.

Peter winced and downed the shot glass, feeling its warmth making its way down his gullet. He regretfully surmised that, in one way or another, he'd probably be going home in a box.

CHAPTER 20

▼

In contrast to his earlier ride with the reticent Dmytro, the drive through Kiev with Mikhail at the wheel was as close to a personally guided tour as Peter could have asked for. From the moment they got into the sedan, Peter was regaled with an incessant stream of historical and geographical details from Mikhail's encyclopedic knowledge of the city. Every building, church, and statue became a new source of anecdotes. At times, Mikhail would simply stop the car to allow him more time to explain the significance of a particular monument, to the consternation of stalled traffic behind them, which Mikhail would periodically wave by. For all the furtiveness in getting Peter to the Secret Service building, Mikhail now seemed equally devoted to making their drive as public as possible, although he did insist on having Peter stay inside and in the back seat, shielded from view behind the darkened glass.

Peter glanced at his watch apprehensively as Mikhail stopped in front of one more landmark, backing up traffic for the umpteenth time. "Mikhail, shouldn't we be getting on to my meeting with Dr. Mogilev?"

"Don't worry; we have another hour to get there—plenty of time. I want you to enjoy our beautiful city while you're here. Who knows? You may have to find your way around here on your own someday."

"Well, since it appears to be my life at risk here, I wish you wouldn't draw quite so much attention to us. We've got a regular motorcade behind us."

"It makes no difference whether we're conspicuous or not. I can always count on being followed. This just makes it easier for me to keep track of our pursuers."

Alarmed, Peter glanced around anxiously. "Why didn't you tell me we're being followed?"

"I didn't want you to worry. And stop moving around like that. If anyone can see through the window, they'll get suspicious. Now turn around slowly. See the black Mercedes about five cars back? They've been following us since we left the building. In all the times that I've stopped traffic, that's the only car that hasn't passed us."

"Then for God's sake, get us out of here."

Mikhail turned around to look at Peter and flung his arm up in a gesture of impatience. "Peter, stop worrying. Nobody can see who you are back there. Besides, if I roared out of the garage like a bat out of hell, I would guarantee us an entire entourage of black Mercedes. In Ukrainian politics, we live by an agreement: they follow us, we follow them. It keeps the unemployment rate down."

The car horns behind them were honked, and the drivers cursed as they tried to pass. "But won't they find out about my meeting with Mogilev?"

"Nah. That's on the other side of town. They have no idea where we're going. Besides, I want to show you one other thing before we get there." With that, Mikhail turned around and grabbed the wheel. "Now turn around and tell me what you see."

"Nothing but one big traffic jam for a block behind us and at least twenty-five drivers that would like to have us drawn and quartered."

"Wonderful. Hold on tight."

With that, Mikhail floored the accelerator. The tires shrieked as they spun on the asphalt and the car leaped forward, roaring through the intersection just as the light turned red. The black Mercedes, boxed in by the lines of traffic that had been trying to pass Mikhail's sedan, sat helplessly, the blasting of its car horn lost in the cacophony of the others as Mikhail sped on.

After several blocks, convinced that they were out of sight of their pursuers, Mikhail abruptly jerked the wheel to the right, turning the sedan the wrong way down a one-way street, and slammed on the accelerator again. The color drained from Peter's face as their car sped ever faster toward what he knew would be his inevitable demise. But Mikhail was having the time of his life.

"I'll bet those bastards are shitting in their pants back there," Mikhail chortled loudly as he veered onto the sidewalk, narrowly avoiding an oncoming car blasting its horn furiously as it passed.

"I'll bet they are, because I'm shitting in my pants right here. What the hell do you think you're doing? You're going to get us killed!"

"Calm down," Mikhail admonished, turning back onto the road and slowing the car down to within ten miles per hour of the speed limit. "We have more important things to worry about." He yanked the wheel to the left, turning onto another street as the tires screeched in protest, and slowed down further. "There, we're going the right way now. Does that make you feel better?"

"Much," Peter rejoined, loosening his grip on the seat in front of him and swallowing for the first time in several minutes. "Daniel said you were supposed to protect me. Whose side are you on, anyway?"

"What are you complaining about? You wanted me to lose them, so I lost them, didn't I? Besides, this is the shortcut to where I wanted to bring you."

Mikhail stopped the car in front of a beautifully elaborate church. Its bone white and turquoise colonnaded exterior was graced by four tall spires, each topped by a brilliant green cupola, which in turn clustered around an enormous green dome decorated with ornate gold trim. Mikhail opened the door and motioned Peter to get out.

"Come, I want you to see something beautiful. Don't worry, we're safe here."

Peter followed Mikhail as he bounded up a stairway leading to the church entrance. Turning around at the church door, he saw that they were at the top of a steep hill overlooking Kiev, the broad expanse of the Dnieper River running north and south as far as he could see.

"This is St. Andrew's Church, my favorite spot in the whole city," Mikhail commented quietly and sat down on the uppermost step as the warm breeze at the top of the hill whipped his hair about his forehead. "My family lived not far from here, and after dinner my father and I would walk up Vladimir's Hill and sit on these steps while the sun set over the city, watching the gold domes of the churches below us blaze in the sunset. Sometimes we would talk, and sometimes we would be silent, watching the riverboats steam by. Sometimes he would tell me stories."

"Is your father still alive?"

"No. He was killed in an industrial accident when I was a teenager. He was a great man. He taught me to be independent. He taught me to be strong." Mikhail's crow's feet crinkled as he smiled. "He taught me to drink. What about your father?"

"He died when I was six. Acute myelogenous leukemia. Didn't have a chance. When the leukemia struck, I watched him waste away to nothing but a skeleton before he ..." Peter stopped, unable to continue.

The squeals of a busload of schoolchildren on a class trip interrupted them.

"Good Lord," Mikhail exclaimed, looking at his watch, "we're going to be late." As they rushed to the car, Mikhail pointed to a series of upright concrete posts at the entrance to a street just below the church. "Right below us is St. Andrew's Descent. It's a marvelous twisted little street leading down to the river, full of quaint shops and cafes and blocked off to vehicles. It's wonderfully romantic. You'll have to come back here some day to stroll with your girlfriend."

The two jumped back into the car, but thankfully Mikhail was now very mindful of not attracting unwanted attention. Not only did he keep to the speed limit; he even drove the entire way in the correct direction. On the street.

After a short drive, Mikhail let Peter out on a quiet side street.

"It is best that we not be seen together in town. Go two blocks down and then make a right to get to the Café Verkhovyna. There, you'll meet Dr. Nikolai Mogilev, the president's neurologist. He has been told that you are Dr. Avery Smithson, a visiting American expert on Alzheimer's disease but that, for the president's security, nobody must know you're here. I told him that we had reason to believe the president has been poisoned and he was being set up to be the patsy for the president's death and that you would fill him in on the details. That is all he knows. After you talk, have him take you to the Kiev Neurological Institute. It's just a short walk from the cafe. I'll meet you up in President Labrinska's room."

"How will I recognize him?"

Mikhail smiled. "He'll be the one with the half empty bottle of vodka on his table," and he waved as he sped off in the sedan.

Cafe Verkhovyna was a small unpretentious sidewalk cafe, distinguished from the surrounding shops by a few weathered wooden tables clustered under a green and yellow striped awning, around which were seated a number of casually dressed, young couples. Two ancient chestnut trees with thick, leafy canopies burst through the pavement in front of the cafe, their shade rendering the awning superfluous.

The inside of the cafe was dimly lit and cozy, reminiscent of the Cafe Reggio back in Greenwich Village. As his eyes became accustomed to the dark, Peter noticed a table nestled in a corner, at which sat a nervous-looking, middle-aged man with graying hair and wire-rim glasses, his eyes darting furtively in Peter's direction as he poured himself a glass of vodka from an already half empty bottle.

"Dr. Mogilev?"

"*Tahk?*"

"I'm Dr. ... Avery Smithson. Mr. Pritsak indicated you might wish to talk."

"Please have a seat, Dr. Smithson."

Peter surmised from Dr. Mogilev's appearance that things were not going well with his star patient. His eyes were bloodshot, and his face had a dull, leaden demeanor that, coupled with his two-day growth of stubble, gave Dr. Mogilev the look of a man under extreme duress. Peter was certain that Mikhail's revelations had added a layer of paranoia to the pressure he was already under.

"Mr. Pritsak tells me there is some suspicion that the president has been poisoned, and that you would tell me more about this," Mogilev said, his hand shaking slightly as he poured vodka into the shot glass in front of Peter. "These are very serious accusations, Dr. Smithson, particularly coming from the Director of the Secret Service. I hope that you can enlighten me further."

Mogilev downed his glass in one swallow and set it back down on the table.

"I'll be brief, Dr. Mogilev, as time is critical. In my practice in New York City, I became aware of some experimentation that was being done secretly by a Dr. William Albright, probably in association with Dr. Iosyp Zabrovych and others here in Kiev. They were experimenting with an unregistered drug in combination with permixitine, an antidepressant used here but not in the United States, which I believe President Labrinska has been taking for quite some time."

Mogilev nodded but remained silent.

"The combination of these two drugs, when given in dosages that were being worked out in the United States, induces a disorder clinically indistinguishable from a rapidly progressive Alzheimer's disease, but showing none of the neuropathological alterations of the disorder. At a critical blood level, these drugs cause a prolonged generalized seizure followed by supraventricular and then ventricular arrhythmias, inevitably leading to death unless appropriate treatment is given. Mr. Pritsak and I believe that the president has entered this critical stage, and he was transferred to your care so that, when he died, you would be the one held responsible and suspicion would be deflected from Zabrovych."

Mogilev stared down at his glass. "What you are telling me makes some sense, Dr. Smithson. Mr. Labrinska's deterioration has been unusually rapid, more than I would expect with Alzheimer's disease. Up until now I thought this was an atypical case of Creutzfeldt-Jakob, and I was debating whether or not to ask for a brain biopsy. But I keep careful track of the president's medications, and he has been getting nothing, not even the permixitine, since admission to the Neurological Institute. Nonetheless, he continues to deteriorate."

"This drug has a very prolonged duration of action. Its blood levels can take several days to peak. They may very well have overdosed him just prior to transfer. Has he developed a tachycardia?"

"Odd that you should mention that. He had been in a normal rhythm until this morning, when his heart rate jumped to one-fifty. I gave him a mild sedative, but it failed to slow it down. I will have a cardiologist see the president this afternoon."

"This afternoon will be too late, Dr. Mogilev. Tachycardia is the first sign of overdose. The president is in imminent danger. Can you take me to him right away?"

The exhaustion lifted from Dr. Mogilev's face, although his eyes remained bloodshot and glazed from the vodka. But the ray of hope that Peter had given him seemed to energize him.

"Let's go. But first, a toast to the success of our collaboration," he said, picking up his shot glass.

Peter groaned. *When in Rome ...,* he thought, and downed his glass in one swallow.

The effect was electrifying. Unlike the warm feeling he got from Mikhail's vodka, this burned its way down, as if it had been laced with battery acid. His face flushing a deep crimson, Peter broke out into a sweat and coughed uncontrollably.

Mogilev leaned across the table and patted Peter vigorously on the back. "I see you've never tried Ukrainian pepper vodka. Good for keeping warm on cold winter nights. Come, I'll take you to the president now."

Mogilev grabbed Peter by the arm and assisted him up from the table and out of the coffeehouse. His head swimming, Peter squinted his eyes in the strong afternoon sun as the two physicians walked down the street. Although he respected Nikolai Mogilev professionally, Peter was developing an outright admiration for his liver.

CHAPTER 21

▼

The Kiev Neurological Institute was a plain-appearing, six-story building of the utilitarian postwar Soviet architectural style that Peter had become accustomed to seeing in official buildings all over Kiev. The lobby, although not very expansive, was spotlessly clean and free of the intensive security systems that Peter had become sadly accustomed to in hospitals back in the United States.

Making their way across the almost-deserted lobby, Peter and Mogilev waited for the elevator to arrive. As the door began to open, Mogilev abruptly shoved Peter away from the elevator. Momentarily confused, Peter quickly realized what was occurring. Turning his back to Dr. Mogilev, he walked toward the far end of the lobby, strolling as quickly as he could without appearing hurried. Reaching the far wall, he quietly stood in front of the directory, his heart pounding, pretending to be reading it. Behind him, Peter could hear Mogilev in animated conversation with whoever had just exited the elevator. Even in a foreign language, Peter could clearly identify the lofty, arrogant tones of William Albright's voice in the exchange, along with the voice of at least one other colleague.

From the sound of their voices, he conjectured that Mogilev had positioned himself in such a way that the other speakers had their backs to Peter, but he dared not turn around to look. After what seemed like hours but was probably only a few minutes, Peter heard two sets of footsteps echoing on the marble floor, moving toward the front entrance to the lobby. Even after he heard the door open and then close, Peter remained standing with his eyes fixed to the directory, until he heard Mogilev's voice, in a loud stage whisper.

"Dr. Smithson, please come quickly."

Peter turned and dashed to the elevator. Mogilev let the door close the instant Peter got in.

"I am sorry I pushed you, but that was Albright and Zabrovych. I didn't want them to see you."

"I figured that out," Peter said breathlessly, his pulse slowing as the elevator proceeded to the sixth floor. "What did they say?"

"They had just come from my office. They wanted to thank me for taking over the care of the president. They also wanted to assure me that they wouldn't interfere with my management of the case in any way and that Dr. Nikitin was simply an observer to keep them apprised of President Labrinska's progress. They're washing their hands of the whole affair," he added bitterly.

Arriving at the sixth floor, they walked down the hall to the heavily guarded entrance to the president's suite. An argument developed between Mogilev and the armed security guards, who refused to allow Peter in without proper identification in spite of Mogilev's assurances.

A familiar voice thundered out from the president's suite. "Let him in, you idiots. I told you he'd be coming."

They entered a small anteroom containing a few stuffed chairs and a small cot. Slumped back in a chair was Mikhail Pritsak, shaking his head in frustration.

"That's the problem with our country. When you pay peanuts, you hire monkeys; that's all there is to it. I apologize for any embarrassment you have suffered, gentlemen. I'm sure that many years ago those simpletons' commandant told them to check ID under penalty of firing squad, and to this day, even if they forget to put their pants on in the morning, they will remember to check ID, whether they're asked to or not."

"How is the president?" Dr. Mogilev asked.

"Who's the doctor around here? I thought that's your job to tell me. Go ahead in; he's asleep. But be careful. His wife is as protective as a mother bear."

The three men entered what amounted to a single bed intensive care unit. A cardiac telemetry unit beeped rhythmically next to a bank of electronic IV pumps and a ventilator unit, kept ready at the bedside. Stationed ominously in the corner was a well-stocked crash cart, replete with emergency thoracotomy and tracheostomy trays. All of this, in turn, was constantly monitored and recorded by a crisply efficient nurse. Although unexceptional by American standards, it was everything Ukrainian medical science had to offer, except the right answer.

President Labrinska, the focus of all this attention, was snoring gently. His wife sat reading by the bedside, but with one hand cradling that of her husband at all times. With a sense of déjà vu, Peter's mind flashed back four days and seven thousand miles to Harriet Halleck, but he pushed the image out of his mind. Things would be different this time.

Mogilev interpreted after a brief conversation and introduced Peter to Iryna Labrinska.

"Mrs. Labrinska says she is grateful for you to have come all this distance for her husband, but with your reputation as an expert, she was expecting someone older."

"Tell her that in spite of my age, I have had more experience with treating her husband's condition than anyone else in the United States."

Just don't tell her it was only a half dozen patients, and all but one of them died, Peter thought.

After the interpretation, Mrs. Labrinska's round, ruddy face broke into a smile which, Peter guessed by her haggard appearance, was her first in many days. There was another brief interchange between her and Dr. Mogilev. "She wishes to know whether you and I will be consulting with Dr. Iosyp Zabrovych, his psychiatrist."

Peter resisted the urge to tell her that it was Zabrovych who was responsible for her husband's condition in the first place. "Tell Mrs. Labrinska that Dr. Zabrovych is turning over President Labrinska's care to us and that he did not want to interfere at this critical juncture."

Dr. Mogilev nodded and turned to interpret. However, before he could finish his sentence, Labrinska awakened from his sleep with a start and looked about, his eyes wide and frightened.

"Who are these people? Get them out of my bedroom."

Iryna clutched her husband's hand to her breast. "Toly, calm down. These men are doctors. They are here to make you feel better, but you must be calm and lie down."

Peter noticed uneasily that the monitor was now registering a heart rate of two hundred. Peter's mouth felt like cotton. Things were going to start happening very quickly now.

"No. Get them out of my room. Mama, Mama, I must get out, I must get out, I must get out …"

"Toly, Mama has been dead for thirty years. This is Iryna, your wife."

"I must get out … I must get out … I must get out …"

Mogilev ran to the bedside and ordered the nurse to get a sedative. This just drove Labrinska further into his delirium. His heart rate jumped to two hundred thirty.

"I must get out … I must get out … I must get out …"

Peter swallowed hard. It was time to take control of the situation.

"Dr. Mogilev, get Mrs. Labrinska out of here. She'll just be in the way."

Mrs. Labrinska was led from the room, hysterically screaming her husband's name, as his perseverations echoed louder and louder in the hospital room.

Peter looked around him. Mikhail stood at the foot of the bed, befuddled and overwhelmed by what was happening. Mogilev and the nurse were at the bedside, trying unsuccessfully to convince the president to calm down, their ministrations only exciting him further. Above it all, the monitor beeped frantically, ever faster.

"Stop," Peter shouted. "Leave him alone. We've got to move fast. Get one gram of phenytoin and start dripping it in. Immediately."

Dr. Mogilev stared at Peter. "But he hasn't had any convulsions."

Peter looked up at the monitor, now registering two hundred fifty. "He will soon. We need to start an esmolol drip immediately. Get another nurse in here to monitor blood pressure. And call a Code Blue, or whatever you call it here. He'll need intubation soon."

Mogilev shouted orders to the nurse in the room and over the intercom to the nursing station. Within seconds, another nurse burst into the room with an IV bag and began hooking it up. Outside the room, the hospital overhead paging system intoned something in Ukrainian.

Mogilev then turned to Peter. "The phenytoin is dripping in, but what is esmolol?"

"A rapid acting beta-blocker. We need to slow his heart down immediately."

"We don't have esmolol here. The only beta-blocker we have is propranolol."

Peter groaned. Propranolol would stay in the blood stream much longer than esmolol. If he got the dosage wrong, or if it didn't work as planned, it was too bad. Once injected, there was no turning back. "Then get it ready."

Suddenly, Labrinska's screams were silenced by a grunt of air forced from his lungs by a simultaneous contraction of every muscle in his chest, and all heads in the room turned toward him. In agonizing slow motion, his neck arched back and his arms and legs stiffened out, his eyes almost bulging out of their sockets as they rolled up halfway under raised lids. A trickle of bloody spittle escaped his lips as his stiffly extended limbs trembled spasmodically.

As everyone watched, horrified, Peter glanced up at the monitor. Labrinska's heart rate was two hundred seventy-five, and the rhythm no longer supraventricular tachycardia. The QRS complexes were widening. Several abnormal beats, clearly of ventricular origin, were already interrupting the cardiac rhythm. Peter felt as if an iron-gloved fist were clutching his intestines and twisting as hard as it could.

"Give me the blood pressure," Peter yelled, snapping everyone out of their trance. "Get ten milligrams of propranolol ready. Now!"

At that moment, the door flung open and a tall, slender, gray-haired physician in a white lab coat with a stethoscope around his neck burst into the room. Scanning the room quickly, his gaze rested on Peter, puzzled by the presence of an unfamiliar face.

"Who are you? What are you doing here in the president's suite?" the man asked in Ukrainian.

Mogilev answered in Ukrainian for Peter, who looked to him for guidance.

"This is Dr. Avery Smithson, an American expert on Alzheimer's disease. He is here at the behest of the Secret Service to give us assistance on the president's condition. They believe the president may have been poisoned, and so far he has correctly predicted adverse events that would happen to the president."

With that, the doctor leaned over the bed and shook Peter's hand. "Dr. Radulovich, chief of cardiology. Pleased to meet you. I regret that I do not speak any English," he said in Ukrainian but wasted no further time on niceties.

Labrinska was now in the midst of the clonic phase of the seizure, his arms and legs jerking rhythmically and his chest muscles contracting uncontrollably in spasms. A lack of oxygen in the blood had turned his lips and skin a dusky blue. But this was not what worried Peter or the other doctors in the room. Labrinska's heart rhythm had now evolved into ventricular tachycardia. Labrinska was beginning his slide into eternity.

Dr. Radulovich quickly took control of the situation. "Have anesthesia intubate the president. Nurse, give lidocaine seventy-five milligrams, IV. Start magnesium sulfate two grams, IV over two minutes. I will need blood pressure readings every minute, and call them out loud and clear. What is the current blood pressure?"

Peter looked on, bewildered. He picked up the names of the medications, but that was about it. Mogilev translated into English as quickly as he could, but events were clearly proceeding beyond his ability to keep communications adequate.

"Ninety over forty and dropping rapidly, Dr. Radulovich."

"Quickly, draw up one milligram of epinephrine."

Peter needed no interpretation. "Stop! No epinephrine! No epinephrine! You must give propranolol! You must give propranolol immediately!"

There was silence as all eyes in the room turned to Peter, standing at the foot of the bed, waving his arms and shouting, "No epinephrine. Give propranolol," repeatedly. Mogilev and Radulovich conversed rapidly. Radulovich looked at Peter as if he were a baboon.

"Dr. Radulovich wants you to explain what you mean."

"The president has been given a drug that inhibits choline acetyltransferase. It completely inactivates vagus nerve control of the heart rate. He has absolutely no acetylcholine activity. The unopposed stimulation of the epinephrine will throw him into irreversible ventricular fibrillation. He must be given propranolol immediately, or he will die. You have to trust me on this."

In the meantime, the seizure activity was dying down. Peter eyed the monitor anxiously.

"Pulse is over three hundred. The blood pressure is sixty over thirty and dropping."

"This man is mad, absolutely mad. Nurse, draw up the epinephrine quickly."

Peter shook his head. "No. Epinephrine will be lethal. You must give propranolol. If you won't, then give me the syringe, and I'll administer it myself."

Mogilev looked at Peter and then at Dr. Radulovich, who shook his head emphatically, asking again for the nurse to give epinephrine and calling for the defibrillation paddles to be made ready.

Sweat beading up on his forehead, his hands trembling and his knuckles white as he gripped the bedrail, Mogilev turned to Peter. "I'm sorry, Dr. Smithson. You have no authority in this hospital, and I cannot grant you authorization to use that drug."

Suddenly, Peter felt a presence at his side. Mikhail had been quietly standing in the background, as inconspicuous as a man of his size could be, but now he stood alongside Peter at the foot of the bed. Reaching under his jacket with his eyes fixed firmly on Mogilev, he smoothly pulled a nine-millimeter Makarov automatic out of his shoulder holster and, arms extended in firing position and finger on the trigger, aimed the gun directly at Mogilev. The click of the safety catch releasing reverberated in the hospital room, masked only by the frenzied beeping of the cardiac monitor as Labrinska's rhythm continued to deteriorate, edging closer to ventricular fibrillation.

"This is the only authorization he needs. Give the propranolol. Now."

Mogilev stared directly into the barrel of the Makarov. His complexion, already pallid, turned pasty as the sweat dripped down his temples. He looked to Dr. Radulovich for support, but all he saw in Radulovich's face was a mirror of his own terror.

He turned his head toward the nurse, keeping his eyes fixated on the gun, and moistened his lips before he spoke. "I wish it to be recorded in the chart that I have directed the use of propranolol only under extreme duress."

Peter turned to Mikhail and whispered, "What did he say?"

"He's going to let you give the medicine, but he's not very happy about it."

Peter nodded to Mikhail. "I can't blame him. Neither am I."

Hands trembling slightly, the nurse handed Peter a syringe. "Propranolol ten milligrams, in ten cc saline, Doctor."

Peter raced to the side of the bed opposite Mogilev, making certain that Mikhail's line of fire was unobstructed at all times, and slowly began pushing the propranolol. He motioned for the anesthesiologist to intubate the president, whose breathing was becoming increasingly shallow as his blood pressure fell. Peter slowly emptied the propranolol into the IV line, praying that it was the appropriate dose. He looked at Mikhail, whose eyes remained fixed on Mogilev. Amazingly, he looked cool and unperturbed, totally in command of both himself and the situation in the room.

"Fifty over zero. Blood pressure continuing to drop."

The monitor continued to show deterioration in the QRS complexes. At any moment, Labrinska would go into ventricular fibrillation, and it would be all over.

Unexpectedly, the door flew open again. Peter looked up to see a pudgy, balding man enter and agitatedly look about. His eyes locked momentarily with Peter's.

"What's going on? I heard the president was in trouble."

"Get out, Nikitin," Mikhail bellowed. "You're not needed here." He swiveled and pointed the gun directly at the intruder, who squealed and ran. Mikhail immediately trained the gun back on Mogilev, who hadn't budged an inch.

"Damn it," he swore under his breath. "Damn it to hell."

"Blood pressure now forty over zero. I can't get a carotid pulse."

"Prepare to administer closed chest massage if the pulse drops out," Peter ordered.

"Of what use is that," Mogilev screamed. "You've killed him, you idiot. You've killed the president. And you," he said, turning back to Mikhail, "you'll rot in prison for this."

Mikhail didn't flinch, didn't bat an eyelash, and didn't move a muscle. For a full thirty seconds, the whoosh of the ventilator and the frantic, irregular beeping of the monitor were the only sounds to break the deathly silence.

Then, something changed. Concentrating on slowly administering the propranolol and mindful only of the relentless pounding of his heart, Peter was unable to put his finger on exactly what it was. Nobody had spoken; nobody had moved. But then it struck him. The beeping sound was no longer irregular. It was still incredibly fast, but the beeps were now regular, and there was a distinct, audible interval between them. On the monitor, the QRS complexes were still broad, but they were now regular and rhythmic in appearance.

"Blood pressure fifty over twenty."

Peter stopped administering the propranolol, the syringe finally empty.

"Blood pressure sixty over thirty-five."

Peter looked up at the monitor. The heart rate had dropped precipitously to two hundred twenty, and Peter saw minute little bumps interposed between the broad ventricular beats. The normal cardiac pacemaker was struggling to take control.

"Pressure now seventy-five over forty. I think I can feel a pulse. It's thready, but it's there."

The tension was still palpable in the room, and all eyes remain fixated on the monitor. But for Peter, the weight of the world was slowly dropping from his shoulders. *Bergstraum, if I get back to New York alive I'm going to kiss your ugly mug.*

"Pressure is now ninety-five over sixty. Pulse is now one-eighty-five."

A smile broke across Dr. Radulovich's face. "I don't believe it. He's back in sinus rhythm now. This is absolutely preposterous, but he's back in sinus rhythm."

The room burst out into applause, with the exception of Mikhail, who simply smiled and quietly put his gun back in his shoulder holster. Dr. Radulovich ran to Peter and threw his arms around him in the midst of the melee, joyously hugging him. "You are a madman ... an absolute, certifiably insane madman. But you are a gutsy madman, nonetheless."

Peter had no idea what Dr. Radulovich had said, but he smiled weakly in response and thanked him. He then turned to Mogilev. "Dr. Mogilev, please tell the nurse to amend the record to read as follows: 'Propranolol ten milligrams was cautiously administered intravenously by Dr. Mogilev under appropriate cardiac monitoring. The patient regained sinus rhythm without any loss of pulse.'"

Mogilev smiled and turned to the nurse, who had been far too busy to write anything at all, and directed her on what to put in the record.

Peter felt a strong arm around his shoulder and turned to see Mikhail's beaming face. "Congratulations. How does it feel to be a hero?"

"I believe that the next cardiac arrest I attend will end up being my own."

CHAPTER 22

▼

"This is impossible, absolutely impossible! This is all a nightmare! I am surrounded by incompetent imbeciles!"

Dr. William Albright sat rigidly in a chair in the prime minister's office atop the Council of Ministers Building while Valentyn Boshevsky, his face contorted and livid with rage, screamed in a rabid frenzy, periodically pounding angrily on the desk and walls. The floor was already littered with books, lamps, and desk ornaments that Boshevsky had picked up and thrown against the walls in his rage.

"The perfect drug, I was told. Lethal ... indefensible ... undetectable ... untraceable ..." Boshevsky screamed, punctuating each word by grabbing an item from his desk and hurling it against the wall. "Then why is Labrinska still alive? Tell me! Why?"

Albright answered hesitantly, "We have two theories, Excellency. One is that our experimental subjects were all alcoholics, and this may have changed their metabolism of the drug, throwing off our calculations about the dosage. We anticipated that problem, though, and I believe we adequately controlled for that in our study. If anything, we would have erred on the side of caution and given him too much of the drug. The second theory is that the authorities found out about our plans and managed to figure out the antidote."

"Antidote? What antidote? I was told there was no antidote."

"Not exactly. There is a drug that may be given to counteract the cardiac effects of UR-416, but we didn't believe anybody would dare give it because it would be lethal in any other circumstance than UR-416 intoxication. We know the Secret Service managed to obtain some of our clinical files and sent them to a

CIA contact in the United States, but there was nothing in the files to indicate a mechanism of action. When Dr. Nikitin came into the room at the time of the cardiac arrest, Director Pritsak was there, but he was holding a gun to Dr. Mogilev, and an unidentified man appeared to be administering a drug into the intravenous line. It is plausible, Your Excellency, that somehow this man managed to obtain crucial information about the drug, discovered the antidote, alerted the Intelligence community, and then somehow convinced them to let him administer it at the critical moment."

Boshevsky had calmed down marginally, at least to the point that he was no longer throwing things and was capable of rational thought. And in this situation, rational thought meant plotting for revenge.

"Was the man in Labrinska's room the CIA agent?"

"I don't think so, Excellency. It would take a physician to know the intricacies of UR-416 and the counteractant. Dr. Zabrovych and I believe we have a suspect."

Boshevsky raised an eyebrow, now very interested. "Who?"

"There was a neurologist in New York City, a Dr. Peter Branstead, who assumed the care of my lab assistant, Frank Halleck, after we gave him the drug to silence him. The man Dr. Nikitin saw fits his description. It is possible that he may somehow have figured out the mechanism of UR-416 before Halleck died. I admit this is all is highly improbable, and I still cannot explain how he would have connected with the authorities here in Kiev, but it is the only scenario that makes any sense."

Although his face betrayed no emotion, Albright was relieved that Boshevsky was buying his explanation. At least it served to deflect the prime minister's rage.

Boshevsky resumed his pacing, but now he became very pensive.

"I'll call Kalchenko. Before he wraps up our New York operation, we need to find out more about how much this Branstead fellow knows and whether he is in New York or Kiev. I presume that whoever this interloper is, Pritsak will be keeping him heavily secured. I'll make certain that both this doctor and the CIA agent are found ... and properly interrogated. We must be careful to purge anyone who can connect us to the plan. In the meantime, watch yourself, Albright. The Mafia has been heavily invested in this project, very heavily, and they are not happy with the way things have turned out."

Albright's eyes burned with a sudden terror. "I wasn't told the Mafia was involved!"

"Of course they are, you fool. Who do you think bankrolled your beautiful psychiatric clinic? Who do you think has been funding your expensive research?"

"I was told that the Ukrainian-American Friendship Foundation was funded by wealthy patriots, nationalists like ourselves," Albright sputtered.

"Don't be so naïve, Albright," Boshevsky sneered. "To perform great works, you sometimes have to make a deal with the devil. But don't worry. I have taken great pains to ensure that we cannot be connected to the Mafia. And don't forget that I am still the prime minister and will remain so. They'll do what I tell them."

For the first time in his life, Dr. William Albright completely lost his composure.

"You are the fool, Boshevsky. These are not people to be trifled with. They will take out their frustrations on our flesh, whether or not you are prime minister."

"You worry too much, Albright. Go home and sleep. I'll take care of things."

With that, Boshevsky waved Albright out of his office and sat down at his desk to make his calls.

"Your Excellency ..." Albright began earnestly, but Boshevsky cut him off curtly as he began talking on the phone.

Albright turned and walked tensely out of the room. Iosyp Zabrovych and Sergei Nikitin were seated in the waiting room outside the office. They had obviously heard the commotion inside and concern showed on their faces. Albright didn't stop to talk but continued walking briskly, his eyes fixed straight ahead. The other two psychiatrists jumped up and raced after him.

"Well, what did he say?" Nikitin asked anxiously as he trailed after Albright.

Not breaking stride or even turning to look at Nikitin, Albright spoke tersely. "He said we are doomed. Not in so many words, you understand, and he may not even realize it himself, but we are all dead men. We just don't happen to have been buried yet. My advice to both of you is to go home, kiss your families good-bye, and quickly put as many kilometers between you and Ukraine as you possibly can."

With that, he stopped and turned to stare directly at his two associates. "We have just crossed the Mafia."

The two psychiatrists gasped, but neither said a word.

"Our research has been bankrolled by the Mafia, not by patriots as we were told. And that megalomaniac, Boshevsky, fantasizes that he holds all the cards. The idiot doesn't realize that he is holding a tiger by the tail. As for myself, I am a man without a country. I am being hunted by the authorities in the United States and by the criminals in Ukraine. I suggest that you both distance yourself from me as much as possible."

And with that, Dr. William Albright turned and marched stiffly to the elevator to exit the building, leaving Nikitin and Zabrovych to stare after him in horrified silence.

It was early evening by the time Mikhail and Peter had made their way back to Mikhail's office. Immediately after Labrinska had stabilized, Peter had given instructions to Dr. Mogilev on the use of physostigmine and donepezil and a gradually tapering dose of propranolol to partially reverse the effects of UR-416 until it had been completely metabolized. With that, Peter and Mikhail had raced out of the president's room, not even stopping to explain what had happened to the near-hysterical Iryna Labrinska, and ran down a back stairway, exiting into an alleyway behind the institute, where Mikhail's car waited for them. Taking several evasive maneuvers on the way in case they were still being followed, they had driven back to the headquarters of the Ukrainian Secret Service, this time walking up ten flights in a secured staircase that led directly to the conference room in Mikhail's office.

Out of breath, Peter collapsed into an armchair. But Mikhail was too elated to sit down, and he paced the room frenetically.

"Did you see Mogilev's face when I pulled the Makarov on him? I thought his eyes were going to pop out of their sockets. God, I loved it. Come, this certainly calls for a drink." And Mikhail reached into his cabinet, pulling out a bottle of vodka and two shot glasses, one of which he filled and set in front of Peter. However, after looking at his own glass, he tossed it over his shoulder in disgust and took an Old Fashioned glass out of the cabinet and filled it half full of vodka.

Raising his glass, he bellowed out, "A toast to my dear friend, Peter Branstead, Hero First Order of the Republic of Ukraine," gave a whoop, and downed his glass.

"Mikhail, I can't believe how you're handling this," Peter commented after he too had downed his drink. "We could've been arrested and charged with assassinating the president, and you didn't even break a sweat."

Pritsak smiled. "When I took this job, I pledged to defend the Republic of Ukraine and its president, to my own death if necessary. I had no fear of dying myself. I was only afraid for you, dragged into this against your will. But listen, it doesn't pay to talk about what might have happened. What's done is done." And with that he downed his second glass. "What we now have to do is deal with the consequences. I have to get you and Daniel out of Ukraine as quickly as possible. Boshevsky and the Mafia will be looking for both of you. Ach, that reminds me. I have to keep track of Daniel."

Mikhail walked back into his office and took a small electronic device about the size of a cigarette pack from a drawer. Walking back into the conference room, he set it on the table and turned it on. It immediately began making high-pitched beeps at intervals of about three seconds.

"Daniel has a microtransponder in his mouth, about the size of a large vitamin pill. It is pH sensitive, and as long as he keeps it in the basic environment of his mouth, it will send out beeps. However, should he be captured and swallow the device, it will be inactivated in the acidic medium of the stomach."

"But shouldn't we be able to track him? What if they take him somewhere else?"

"Don't worry about that. It would be too dangerous for Boshevsky to move him from the Council of Ministers Building. They would interrogate and kill him right there," Mikhail said flatly, and downed his third drink.

This gave Peter cause for reflection, and the two men sat silently for a few minutes. As they listened to the subdued beeping of Mikhail's receiver, Peter realized that, from now on, he would always have a more visceral response to being paged.

"But what about Nikitin? I'm certain that he can describe me to Albright, Boshevsky, and even the Mafia. What can we do about him?"

"That's why I have to get you out of the country quickly. I'm sure he went right to Albright, and Albright has put two and two together. There's nothing further that we can do about Nikitin. But I wouldn't worry too much about him—or Albright or Zabrovych for that matter. Once the Mafia finds out that their plan failed, I wouldn't give a shot of vodka for the three of them," said Mikhail, smiling mischievously.

The two men suddenly flinched. In place of the gentle beep, the receiver gave a sharp, high-pitched shriek, which continued for about fifteen seconds before it slowly faded into silence. Peter looked anxiously toward Mikhail, who stared blankly at the receiver and slumped back in his chair.

"Now we're in for it. Daniel has been captured."

Across town, Dr. Sergei Nikitin finished packing his suitcase and called for a cab. His wife was perplexed as to why he had to suddenly run off to a conference in the middle of the night, particularly since the radio news had just declared that the life of his most important patient, President Anatoly Labrinska, had just been saved and that he was expected to make a gradual but complete recovery. To her, this would be the ideal time to stay in Kiev and catch some of the glory for having been part of the team that had saved the president's life.

"I'm sorry, dear, but this conference just came up out of the blue. I've been asked to present a paper tomorrow, and I must leave tonight or I won't get there on time."

They both heard the honk of the cab's horn outside their apartment, and Nikitin grabbed his suitcase, giving his wife a quick kiss on the cheek.

"Give my love to the children when they wake up tomorrow morning."

"Sergei, won't you at least tell me where you are going and when you'll be back?"

Nikitin had already grabbed the doorknob by the time she finished the sentence. "I'll call you as soon as I get there," he called, dashing out the door and leaving his bewildered wife standing in the hallway.

Rushing down the stairs and out the front door, Nikitin threw his bag into the back seat of the cab and jumped in after it.

"To the airport, and hurry, please," he stammered nervously.

The cab driver turned and smiled.

"You may have to rethink your travel plans, Dr. Nikitin."

The driver picked up a gun from the seat next to him and pointed it at Nikitin, whose plaintive whimper was cut short as the nine-millimeter bullet hit him right at the bridge of his nose. Before the cab driver turned around to shift the cab into drive, Nikitin lay dead in his seat.

Dr. Iosyp Zabrovych chose not to fly out. He knew the airports would be closely watched, as would the railroad stations. Zabrovych had managed to save a portion of his meager salary, and, coupled with funds that he had skimmed from what he had thought were financial contributions to his research, had bought a car. It was a short drive to the Belarus border. From there, he could make his way westward.

"Iosyp, this is crazy. You just came back from America; already you're running off to Belarus, and you won't even tell me why."

Zabrovych stopped packing, looked for a long moment into his wife's eyes, and then he gently kissed her forehead.

"I've made a terrible mistake, Renata. I have a debt with some men that I cannot pay back. They will be coming after me shortly, and it would be best for both you and the children if I go far away and you didn't know where I was going."

"These men, are they from the Mafia?"

Zabrovych nodded.

Renata Zabrovych burst into tears. "Iosyp, how could you do something so stupid? Listen, I'll sell my jewelry. Father can lend us money. There must be a way ..."

Zabrovych shook his head. "It is not a debt of money. I can't explain it, but there is nothing that I can do. If they find me, they'll kill me, no matter what."

Zabrovych hugged his wife one last time. "I'll call for you in a few months when I think it's safe. Just tell the children that I had to go to L'vov for an emergency."

He turned and left the apartment, not daring to look back at his sobbing wife.

Throwing his suitcase in the trunk, he sat down in the driver's seat. Looking up to his apartment window, he saw the outline of his wife framed by their bedroom window, waving to him. He waved back as he put the key in the ignition and started the car.

Fortunately, Iosyp Zabrovych never felt the explosion that sent pieces of his body as far as three blocks away and reduced his car to a burning mass of rubber, glass, and twisted steel. And since Renata was leaning out the opened window when it exploded above her, she was spared the agony of having thousands of razor-sharp fragments of glass embedded in her when she finally awoke from her concussion two days later.

Dr. William Albright sat in his bedroom and reflected on his life. His mother, an unwed mother from a small farming village in western Ukraine, had emigrated in shame to the United States right after World War II, when it was briefly possible to get out from behind the Iron Curtain and seek refuge in the West. His citizenship ensured when she married an American, Albright had spent his childhood enthralled by her tales of what he always considered to be his home, and he had pledged to return there some day. Throughout the years of medical and psychiatric training, he'd kept that dream alive. And so he was honored when the Ukrainian-American Friendship Foundation agreed to fund his research, particularly when he was told it would help return control of his native country to his own people and away from foreign domination.

The irony of facing death within a few days of having finally made his journey back home was not lost on him. If he had had any idea that Yuri Kalchenko, whom he had talked to by phone but had never met in person, was the laundering source for Mafia money, things might have been different. But it was too late to dwell on that now.

Albright picked up and examined the gun lying on his kitchen table. If there was one thing he had learned from all of his years of clinical psychiatry, it was how *not* to attempt suicide. Ironically, the scores of patients he had seen throughout his career rendered brain damaged by failed attempts at overdose, drowning, hanging, and botched, self-inflicted gunshot wounds had taught him that there was a correct way of doing things. Death didn't frighten him, but he dreaded the thought of a vegetative existence or, worse yet, being captured and tortured.

He had considered defenestration, but his apartment building was not tall enough to make death a certainty, and he did not want to risk being found only injured. And so he sat by the kitchen table, gun in hand, waiting for the right moment to pull the trigger.

He was alerted by a knock at the door.

"Who is it?" Albright called out. It was a rhetorical question. He knew exactly who was outside the door: it was Death.

"Postal service. I have a special delivery package for Dr. William Albright."

"Leave it at the door. I'll pick it up later."

"I'm sorry, sir. You have to sign for it personally."

Dr. William Albright sighed and stared at the ceiling. It was time.

As soon as he heard the shot ring out, the "mailman" cursed and threw himself full force into the door, smashing it open as he was flung into the apartment. His instructions had been to bring Albright back alive so that he could be questioned about the fiasco of President Labrinska's recovery. His bosses would not be pleased if Albright was dead. As he took in the scene in the kitchen, he knew immediately that there wouldn't be any opportunity for questioning. Grabbing the corpse under its arms, he swore every step of the way at Albright's inconsiderateness as he dragged it down the stairs and threw it into the trunk of his car with the suicide weapon. Hopefully, this would be sufficient evidence for his bosses that he wasn't responsible for yet another screwup in the plans.

What neither the mailman nor anybody else in the Mafia knew was that Daniel Falconer and Mikhail Pritsak were the only people who knew the location and identity of Dr. Peter Branstead and could link him to the miraculous recovery of President Labrinska.

Only Prime Minister Valentyn Boshevsky knew that.

CHAPTER 23

▼

Greg Johnson glanced at his watch for the fifth time in ten minutes. It was going to be tight. Very tight. Time would be his adversary for the next thirty minutes, an enemy he could only thwart by keeping it under constant surveillance.

A sixty-two-year-old Caucasian man with a history of well-controlled hypertension and high cholesterol had just rolled into the emergency room with a fresh stroke. Just two and a half hours ago, he had been eating dinner with his family when he dropped his wine glass. His wife and son initially laughed and asked whether he'd had too much too drink. They'd only realized something was wrong when he hadn't answered, and they'd become alarmed when wine had dripped out the corner of his mouth and his right arm had hung limply by his side. Unfortunately, they had wasted valuable time by trying to get him to lie on the couch and had compounded the delay by phoning a variety of relatives and packing a small suitcase before calling for an ambulance. Finally, the ambulance had run into the usual crosstown traffic logjam trying to get from University Place to St. Mark's. Add on the delay in triaging the patient, and the net effect was that Greg wasn't notified about the patient until over two hours after stroke onset. Two hours and seven minutes, to be precise. And precision was critical because he had precisely three hours, or one hundred and eighty minutes, in which to perform the complex decision-making process leading to the initiation of tPA therapy.

Tissue plasminogen activator, or tPA, was the clot-dissolving drug that reduced the morbidity of stroke, but only if it was given within three hours of stroke onset. So when a tPA candidate arrived at the ER, it was always a race against time. Fortunately, the ER apparatus acted as a well-oiled machine in this circumstance, and the CT scan and all necessary lab work was ready for Greg's review by the time he arrived. What remained to be done was to examine the patient, go through the long checklist of potential risk factors for hemorrhaging, the one major complication of tPA, and discuss the risks with the family. It would be tight, but he had twenty-seven minutes. No problem. He had done it in less time before.

Greg had just set his bag down on the tray table by the patient's stretcher when a doctor wearing a white coat and OR scrubs approached him. He had closely cropped light-blond hair and cold, blue eyes that had a hard, steely quality that made Greg uneasy.

"Excuse me, are you Dr. Greg Johnson?"

"Uh, yes. What can I do for you?"

"Dr. Jules Goldstat. I'm from Yale and joined the Downtown Surgical Group last month. I need to find Dr. Peter Branstead stat, and he's not answering his pages. I was hoping you might know where he is."

"He isn't in the hospital at the moment. I'm a little busy right now, but maybe I can help you." Greg eyed the unfamiliar surgeon warily. His speech had an undertone of a Slavic accent. He knew Peter had been investigating someone from Ukraine, and this made Greg suspicious.

"I'm in the middle of surgery on a patient of his, and anesthesia's having some problems with his vitals. I've got to talk to Branstead right away. I think it may be a neurologic problem."

Greg glanced down at his watch. "If you can wait about twenty-five minutes, I'll run right over to the OR."

Goldstat glared at him. "I can't wait twenty-five minutes. I've got this guy cut wide open, and his BP is way out of whack. I need to talk to Branstead."

"Sorry, but he's not available. He's taken a few days off. Personal reasons."

"Can you at least tell me if he's in town, where I can reach him?"

"No. I have no idea where he is. It's none of my business, so I didn't ask. If you'll give me the patient's name, as soon as I'm finished here I'll call his office, have his nurse pull the chart and ..."

Goldstat pointed a gloved finger menacingly at Greg. "You don't get it, do you? I don't want you, and I don't want the chart. I want Branstead. And I don't want him in twenty-five minutes. Or fifteen minutes. I want him right now. In person or on the phone. Or else."

Greg glared back. "Listen, I'm in the middle of my own emergency here. I now have," and he glanced down quickly, "twenty minutes to get tPA into this guy or it'll be too late. I'm sorry you've got problems, but, next time, try to straighten them out before you put the patient under, not after. Right now, there's nothing I can do for you. Dr. Branstead is out on personal leave, and I have no idea where he is or how to reach him, so I hope you'll excuse me."

"You listen to me. I don't need a short coat to give me any lip. Now, I'm going to find Branstead one way or another, and when I do, I'm going to make sure you get raked over the coals, but good. Get that?" And Goldstat turned, tore his gloves off, and furiously threw them into the trash as he stormed out of the ER.

"Asshole," Greg fumed under his breath.

But there was no time to get upset about it now. The immutable one hundred eighty-minute time limit loomed ahead of him, drawing closer to an end with every tick of the clock. With only seventeen minutes to go, Greg flew through the tPA protocol in record time. Fortunately, the family was amenable to the treatment and didn't take up a lot of time with questions. Even with that, the nurse began hanging the tPA only two minutes shy of the three-hour mark.

Greg sat down in the ER doctor's lounge and began filling out the lengthy documentation needed for a tPA case. He finally had time to mull over his confrontation with Goldstat and his discomfort with the obnoxious physician's Slavic accent.

Surgeon, my ass! he thought, with the realization that something didn't quite fit. The first thing you learn in your surgical rotation in medical school is to take your gloves off *before* leaving the operating room.

CHAPTER 24

▼

The moon was full and brilliant in the midnight sky, shining so brightly that Mikhail and Peter had no need to turn on their own lights as they rode their bicycles through the deserted back streets of Kiev. The only sounds that were heard were the whir of the wheels and the occasional clank of shifting gears. Peter could barely make out the hulking outline of Mikhail, a large knapsack on his back, as he led them silently to the Council of Ministers Building, where Daniel was being held captive.

To Peter, the idea that two men, one of them the director of the Ukrainian Secret Service, would stage a midnight rescue by bicycle for a captured CIA operative seemed absurd, bordering on surrealistic. However, Mikhail's plan had an impeccable logic to it. Dmytro was sent out first in the sedan as a decoy to lead the anticipated pursuers on a circuitous ride through Kiev until he'd lost them, at which point he would park somewhere close by with his cellular phone until he was needed. This would allow plenty of time to get to the Council of Ministers Building without being followed.

Although taking a second car would have seemed logical to an American mind, at this hour the only cars on the street were either Mafia-owned or governmental, and a car would have attracted immediate attention. In addition, a car bombing across town had already put the police force on full alert, and cars were being searched at strategic checkpoints.

Finally, there was the problem of what to do with the car once they arrived. A lone car parked all night near the Council of Ministers would be a dead giveaway, whereas a couple of bicycles locked up in an alleyway would easily be overlooked. However, to ensure that they had a ready escape vehicle, Dmytro was instructed to double back after he had been to the airport and meet them outside the building just before sunrise and to page Mikhail and Peter when he arrived. It all seemed so logical and well planned that Peter didn't think to ask how Mikhail planned to infiltrate a heavily patrolled building to locate and rescue a heavily guarded prisoner.

Peter's sole preparation for the raid had been to memorize a street map of the city, a task made even more difficult by Peter's lack of familiarity with Cyrillic. Fortunately, Mikhail's guided tour of that morning had made Peter familiar enough with the city's major landmarks that he could visualize his way around the city fairly well as they rode through the darkness.

Built in the 1930s with the same massive monumental style common to government buildings throughout Kiev, the Council of Ministers Building loomed ahead of them in the cold, white illumination of the overhanging moon. The columns on its curved exterior created alternating stripes of light and shade in the moonlight, giving the building the appearance of a grotesquely overwrought Roman temple, its darkened windows cloaked in pitch-black shadow.

After pausing under the concealment of nearby trees, Mikhail motioned Peter across the street into a courtyard alongside the building, bounded by a low brick wall, where they hid the bikes in a heavily shadowed corner.

Creeping through the shadows, they slipped inside through a side door, easily unlocked by Mikhail's passkey. Mikhail led Peter through the hallways until they reached a men's bathroom, where Mikhail motioned Peter to enter, first taping a sign in Cyrillic to the door.

"Closed for repairs," Mikhail answered Peter's puzzled expression. "One of the most common signs in Kiev. Nobody will disturb us now."

Mikhail pulled two flashlights and a small tool kit out of the knapsack and shone his flashlight on a small metal panel adjacent to the toilet. After removing the screws, he gently pulled the panel from the wall, exposing an opening just two feet square.

"Go ahead," Mikhail pointed the flashlight beam into the opening, "you first."

"What do you mean, me first? I'm not going in there. Fixing pipes is *not* in my job description."

"We're not fixing pipes. That's a passageway. It's going to lead us to where Daniel is being held."

"What are you talking about?"

"This building was built in the late 1930s during the Stalinist purges. The cabinet ministers at the time were terrified that the Russians might have them arrested while they were gathered at work, so the building was designed with a series of passageways between the walls, going up the full ten stories and down into the basement levels, as a hiding place and escape route. To my knowledge, they were never used for that purpose, but the Secret Service uses them all the time." He smiled wickedly. "Very useful for spying."

"Hold on a minute. You're saying that I'm going to have to crawl through a tunnel just two feet square and God-knows how long until we find Daniel, then somehow rescue him and repeat the whole process all over again? Uh-uh. No damn way. You're nuttier than I thought."

"There's no other way. What would you like us to do? Knock on every door in the building and ask if Daniel Falconer is home? Besides, the tunnel only goes on for about fifty feet, and then you'll be able to stand up."

"So what? After that, we'll still be sandwiched between the walls. I can't do it."

"Why not?"

Peter paused, his mouth dry. "I'm claustrophobic."

"Well, well, Peter, you've really entered purgatory now. How about another sign—'abandon all hope, ye who enter'?" Mikhail remarked with a flourish. "A nice literary touch, don't you think?"

"This isn't funny. I'd freak out in there. I'll louse up the whole plan."

"You *will* go in there, and you *won't* freak out. I need you. Not only that, but your best friend needs you, and he's already risked his life for you. Now, get in there."

Peter looked at the opening, almost exactly the dimensions of the tube of an MRI scanner, but pitch black, dirty, and with no possibility of exit.

Mikhail saw his hesitation. "When I was a teenager, my father got me a job in the Odessa shipbuilding yards. I spent ten to twelve hours a day crawling between hulls and through ventilation ducts. After a while, you get used to it. I used to eat my lunch in torpedo tubes smaller than that." Mikhail's face brightened. "I've got an idea." He pulled a liter of vodka from his knapsack and unscrewed its cap. "I was saving this for the end of our mission, but I think we need it right now."

Chagrined, Peter looked first at the bottle, then at the passageway, then back at the bottle. With a shudder, he lifted the bottle to his lips and took a long draught, then stifled his coughs with his hand.

"Let's go. I'm ready as I'll ever be," Peter gasped.

After Pritsak slapped him on the back, Peter reluctantly grabbed his flashlight and crawled into the tunnel on his elbows. With barely half of his body into the entrance, he felt a hard lump forming in his throat; his lungs started to struggle to move the close, heavy air in and out; and he had the terrifying thought that the weight of the entire building was bearing down on his body. Nevertheless he pushed on until his entire body lay within the confines of the tunnel.

It was worse than he had imagined, if that was possible. The flashlight beam was swallowed up by the gloom after about fifteen feet, making the tunnel appear like an endless black hole. At the first blaze of light, clusters of cockroaches scurried back into the safety of the darkness. A rank, musty breeze emanated from the bowels of the building, blowing decades of accumulated stale air and dust into his face as layers of dusty cobwebs waved gently.

Advancing slowly, he discovered why the roaches had been congregating in small groups; piles of rat droppings lay at irregular intervals down the length of the tunnel as far as the light of Peter's flashlight would allow him to see. Most were desiccated and mummified with age, but a few piles were fresh—very fresh.

The size of the enclosure made it impossible for Peter to get up on his hands. He was able to push his body about eight or nine inches off the floor and crawl on his elbows and knees, but if he tried to lift himself any higher his back impacted harshly against the roof of the tunnel. Edging forward, Peter slowly crept about six inches at a time into the tunnel.

About ten feet into the tunnel, the panic became overwhelming. The lump in his throat felt like it was swelling to monstrous proportions, his blood pounded fiercely in his temples, and his breath came in deeper and harsher gasps as his lungs struggled against the sensation that the oxygen was being sucked out of the tunnel. His hands grew icy cold, and his head swam, as the tiny corridor seemed to close in on him. Peter was losing control of his mind.

"Mikhail, I have to get out. I can't go on. Let me out!" But Mikhail had already crawled feet first into the tunnel and used his strength to push Peter further in. Pulling his knapsack in after him, Mikhail grabbed the heavy metal plate and pulled it into the opening, securing it from the inside by two wing nuts.

Now, they were sealed into the passageway.

Overcome by panic, Peter closed his eyes and lay down on the floor of the tunnel, his arms held tightly to his side so they wouldn't touch the walls, just inches away. If he didn't move a muscle and focused on slowing his breathing, he could imagine himself lying on a beach, the gentle waves of a vast, open ocean lapping just a few feet away. He could imagine the broad, endless vista of a limitless sky extending out to an unbounded horizon. He could imagine himself anywhere but where he actually was; trapped in a sealed crypt, the ponderous weight of the building pressing ... pressing ... pressing....

"Christ, Peter, get moving."

His concentration broken, Peter opened his eyes, seeing the dimly lit wall of the tunnel a scant six inches away. Oddly, he saw it gently receding and advancing in front of him. Surprisingly, he wasn't bothered by this at all, but found himself intrigued by the hallucination of the swaying wall.

The vodka was kicking in.

"Will you get moving? We don't have much time."

"I think I'm going to be sick."

"Then for God's sake get out of the tunnel. I don't want to have to crawl through your vomit."

Peter got back on his elbows and knees and laboriously crawled the thirty feet or so to the end of the tunnel, stopping every few yards to fight his rising gorge. Finally, he burst out of the tunnel into a space that remained only two feet wide, but now extended a full seven feet in height. He stood up, staggered a few feet away from the opening, and retched violently against the wall, filling the air in the passageway with the overpowering stench of vomit.

After a minute, Peter's stomach quieted down. He turned to look back at the opening, curious as to how Mikhail had managed to fit his immense body into the space he had just crawled through. Indeed, seeing Mikhail slowly push himself, feet-first, out of the end of the tunnel reminded Peter of toothpaste being squeezed from a tube.

"Sorry," Peter swallowed hard as Mikhail stood up and pulled the knapsack out of the tunnel. "Couldn't help myself. Was that stuff vodka or paint remover?"

"It's multipurpose. Take your choice," Mikhail shrugged. He pressed Peter into the space between two steel beams, squeezed by him, and leaped over the splash of vomit. "Better you got sick now than later. You would've earned yourself a magazine-full of semiautomatic fire if anyone were in the next room. How are you feeling?"

"Sick enough that I could care less about being claustrophobic."

"Good. At least the vodka accomplished something. Ready to go on?"

Peter nodded numbly and followed Mikhail, steadying himself against the beams as he staggered down the narrow passage.

After several minutes, Mikhail motioned Peter to stop. They had come to a crossing, where another passageway traversed theirs. Mikhail shined his flashlight at the entranceway to the new passage. A small, wooden triangle projected an inch out from a beam, about six inches from the floor and a foot or two into the passageway.

"Never, under any circumstances, enter a passageway marked by a triangle. When the building was constructed, a copy of the plans had to be sent to Moscow for approval. The architects knew the Russians would figure out that the design didn't call for three-foot thick walls simply for the sake of structural integrity, so they made a separate set of plans. That was kept here, and they detailed the locations of a series of marked, booby-trapped corridors in case the Russians tried to pursue into the passageways. We have a copy of the plans in the Secret Service archives."

"It's been over sixty years. Wouldn't the booby traps have deteriorated by now?"

"The traps were designed to last forever unless they're sprung. Most consist of boards thin enough to give way under a man's weight covering a pit twenty or thirty feet deep lined with razor wire and studded with six or eight inch nails along the walls and at the bottom. Very effective and low maintenance."

Peter shuddered at the thought of what it would be like to stumble into such a pit: the sudden unexpected fall into a black void, your body pierced by dozens of spikes, and being left to slowly bleed to death, alone in the darkness.

Alone except for the rats.

Mikhail led warily through the passageways for what seemed like hours, continually checking entranceways for the telltale warning triangle. After several turns, the passageway led down a set of stairs that continued downward, past corridors that led off into blackness, some marked as booby-trapped. But finally the steps ended in an unusually broad hallway, about a meter wide, leading off to the left.

"This is the subbasement level," Mikhail whispered. "It's not accessible by elevator, only by a locked staircase and this passageway. It was used as a bomb shelter for the ministers and for interrogations during the Great Patriotic War and the Stalinist purges. Boshevsky's men would have taken Daniel down here, where they wouldn't be discovered. Now, we just have to find them."

"How?"

Mikhail put his finger to his lips and motioned Peter to follow him. A few steps down the corridor, Mikhail got down on his knees and unscrewed something from the wall, gesturing to Peter, who bent down to see what he was doing. What he saw was a double electric outlet, dangling by its wires to the floor, and two holes in the wall where the outlet had been.

"Almost every office and conference room in the building has at least one of these. Each outlet has its own circuit breaker, so we can disconnect the current, remove the outlet, and look into the room. Unfortunately, people sometimes plug things into the outlet, which limits their utility."

"All this just so you can spy on your own government?"

Pritsak shrugged. "Under the Communists, collecting secrets was the chief government function, even if the secrets were our own. To us, information is power. He who controls the flow of information, controls people, and if you can gain access to secrets, then you have power over those affected by it." Mikhail sighed. "But the rules are changing. After the fall of Communism, we're finding that money dictates power, too. Those who control the secrets and those who control the money are now locked in a battle to the death."

Suddenly, Mikhail stopped and signaled Peter not to move. Peter heard the muffled sound of voices in the room next to them. Mikhail dropped to his knees and gently unscrewed two single wall outlets, spaced about six feet apart, and doused his flashlight before he removed them from the wall. Peeking briefly through one hole, he motioned Peter to look through the other, and then quietly rummaged through his knapsack.

The room that Peter peered into was almost blindingly bright and spacious compared to the dark, cramped corridors that they had been walking through for the past few hours. In reality, it was at most ten feet by twelve feet and illuminated by a single, naked light bulb that hung from the center of the ceiling. It was sparsely furnished, with only a small wooden card table and two plain wooden chairs occupied by two men in the midst of a heated conversation.

The man on the left was powerfully built and coarse-featured with jet-black hair and eyes deeply set beneath thick, bushy eyebrows. The man sitting across from him was slender and wore an elegantly tailored suit, probably of imported fabric, in contrast to the rumpled suit of the heavy-set man. His face was thin and angular, and a deep scar distorted his upper lip. In spite of the dim illumination, he wore a pair of dark sunglasses. Peter noticed that his hands, which he waved about animatedly during the conversation, were decorated with skull tattoos similar to Kalchenko's.

Peter turned to Mikhail for guidance as to who these men were and what they were saying, but Mikhail was looking intently through the peephole with a digital camera the size of a cigarette pack.

Peter returned to his peephole. The two men had taken off their jackets and rolled up their shirtsleeves, exposing forearms marked by several scars. The thin man filled a gold goblet with wine and set it in the middle of the table. He heated a large hunting knife over the flame of a cigarette lighter until the edge glowed a dull red and plunged it, hissing, into the wine. Both men slit their forearms with the knife and let their blood drip into the goblet. As they concertedly recited what sounded like an oath, each in turn drank from the goblet until it had been completely drained, put on their suit coats, and silently exited the room.

Back in total darkness, Peter heard Mikhail stifle an exultant cry.

"I've got you now, you bastard."

"Will you please tell me what happened in there?"

Mikhail had picked up his flashlight, and he quickly replaced the sham outlets.

"The man on the left was Prime Minister Valentyn Boshevsky, and you know about him. On the right was Marko Cherkasy, *pakhan* of the Ukrainian Mafia. For months, we've suspected the Mafia was tied in with the plot, but we've never been able to prove it. In addition, Boshevsky has been crafty enough to distance himself from the perpetrators, so we've never been able to prove that he was actually part of the plot.

"They were talking about you. Boshevsky claims to know your identity. He's offered to trade that information and Daniel to Cherkasy in return for a pledge of his safety and the safety of the plotters, Albright, Nikitin, and Zabrovych, in the name of the Brotherhood of the Trident. What you just saw is an ancient Ukrainian tribal loyalty ritual, which the Brotherhood has adopted." Flaunting the video camera, Mikhail gloated. "And we have it all recorded. Come; the easy part is over. We have to rescue Daniel now."

"Wait a minute. I'm a marked man now. How am I going to get out of here?"

"We'll worry about that later. For now, let's go get Daniel."

The two of them crawled silently to the next set of electrical outlets, which Mikhail silently unscrewed. Peter was sickened by what he saw.

The room was devoid of furniture except for a single wooden chair in the center, directly under another bare light bulb. Daniel was tied to the chair, naked from the waist up, his face a swollen mass of bruises and his chest studded by cigarette burns. Standing on either side were two tall, dark-suited men, each wearing a holstered nine-millimeter pistol. Screaming at Daniel was a third man, who periodically pistol-whipped him.

Peter turned away. He felt physically ill, but, hearing a knock, he turned back to look through the peephole again. There was a series of three knocks, then two, and then another three. The man beating Daniel stopped and opened the door, and Marko Cherkasy entered.

Mikhail gently touched Peter on the shoulder and motioned him away from the peepholes to where they couldn't be heard.

"We have to move quickly. First of all, what kind of underwear do you have on?"

"What?"

"What ... kind ... of ... underwear ... do ... you ... have ... on? Is my English bad?"

"N-n-o-o," Peter stammered. "Your question took me a bit by surprise."

"Well? Are they boxers? Trunks? What?"

"Just plain undershorts. White, I think. Do you need to know the brand?"

"No, I don't need the brand. Here, take this and stuff it in your shorts," and he handed Peter a small memory stick. "It's the video. In case I'm killed and you manage to get out of here alive, make certain that you get it to Dmytro and *only* Dmytro. He'll know what to do with it," and he turned to look through his knapsack.

"Why am I putting this in my shorts?"

"If you're caught, that's the last place anyone would search."

Logical. "But how the hell am I supposed to find my way back?"

"Don't worry about it. If my plan fails, in about twenty minutes, we'll both probably be dead. Ah, here it is." Mikhail pulled a long, thin rod from the bottom of the knapsack. "Now, do you want to listen to the plan or don't you?"

"Sorry for interrupting. Go ahead."

"I'm going to go out this passageway to where I can exit just down the hall. That will take me about ten minutes. In twenty minutes, I'll knock on that door, using the code we just heard. This," Mikhail handed Peter the rod, "is a self-igniting, magnesium-phosphorus flare. As soon as one of those men walks toward the door, you pull the cap off the flare and toss it through the peephole, then get your ass away from this wall. When the shooting stops look through the peephole, and if I'm not the only one left standing, get the hell out of here."

"But ..." Peter began.

But Mikhail had already grabbed his knapsack and was heading down the passageway.

Peter sat down in the dark passageway, resting his back against the wall, and reflected grimly on his situation. He was sitting sandwiched between the walls of a building in the middle of the capital city of a country whose language he didn't speak and whose alphabet he couldn't read. The only two people he knew between the Straits of Gibraltar and the Bering Sea would probably be dead within a few minutes, and nestled against his scrotum was a video of the most vital secret of a nation. If Mikhail's plan went awry, somehow he was supposed to crawl through a labyrinth of passageways, avoiding the death traps scattered in his path, make his way out of the building and past legions of Mafiosi and governmental security guards, find Dmytro, and turn the tape over to him. Then, and only then, could he make his way back to the Secret Service building, get his visa and airplane tickets, and get to Boryspil Airport and onto a plane back home.

Peter groaned and buried his face in his hands, terrified by the enormity of what lay ahead of him. He checked his watch nervously. Only five minutes left. Grabbing the flare, Peter crawled to his post by the peepholes and waited.

There was a knock on the door. Peter listened intently for the pattern. Three-two-three. Looking through the peephole, he saw Cherkasy talk to one of the guards, who turned and walked toward the door. Peter swallowed hard, twisted the cap off the flare, shoved it through the opening, and dove onto the floor of the passageway, his hands on top of his head.

From inside the room came the muffled roar of an explosion, followed by an eruption of noise as the wall he had just been leaning on was perforated by high caliber automatic rifle fire. A bizarre constellation of intense, white supernovas was created in the previously solid wall just over Peter's head, while dust and pulverized plaster was kicked up into a choking, swirling cloud all around him.

It probably only took about fifteen seconds or so until the shooting stopped, but the incredible din, focused and amplified by the narrow walls of the corridor, continued to reverberate inside Peter's head. He lay on the floor, too petrified with fear to move. Then, from one of the peepholes by his head, came a voice.

"Peter, are you okay in there?"

CHAPTER 25

▼

Peter made his way out of the passageway, following Mikhail's instructions explicitly, and walked down the corridor until he found a door hanging limply from a single hinge, having been torn from the others by the force of the C4 explosive that had all but vaporized the lock. On the floor lay the well-perforated bodies of the four Mafiosi, each lying facedown in slowly expanding pools of blood, as well as the sizzling remnants of the flare.

Daniel was unconscious and still tied to the chair while Mikhail, a Kalashnikov slung across his back and blast goggles still covering his eyes, struggled with the ropes.

"Is he all right?" Peter asked.

"I think he was overcome by the beating, but he should be okay in a few minutes. Help me get him loose."

Peter untied the ropes while Mikhail lifted up Daniel's head and let some water from a canteen trickle between his lips. Daniel coughed and shook his head.

"I'm okay. Just get me out of here before Cherkasy's men come down."

"What do you mean?"

"There are more waiting outside." Daniel tried to stand but collapsed back into the chair.

Mikhail scowled. "Wait here. I'll be back in a few minutes."

By the time Mikhail returned Daniel had recovered enough to barely stand and walk.

"Well, the good news is that our bikes are exactly where we put them last night and the building's two security guards have been knocked out by Cherkasy's men. The bad news is that Cherkasy's limousine is parked directly in front of the main entrance with three of his goons waiting. We have to make a plan."

"Can't we shoot our way out?" Peter asked.

"My Kalashnikov's jammed. We'd have to use these guys' guns, and since you and Daniel can't fire a gun with any degree of accuracy, it would be three against one, odds not to my liking. And if Dmytro parked anywhere near the building, it would tip them off that something's going on. He has to pick us up at least a few blocks away."

"I'm going to slow you down, Mikhail," Daniel said. "There's no way I can run. I'm too exhausted. You and Peter make a break for it, and I'll try to get away later."

"Won't work," Mikhail countered. "Even if we make it to the car alive, they'd come in after you when they realized who we were. Besides, we've made it together this far, and we're not leaving without you. I'm afraid the only way out of this is for one of us to lure the limo away and the other two to make a dash for the car. I'll be the bait. Peter, you'll have to support Daniel and get to the meeting point as fast as you can while they're distracted. I'll call Dmytro and tell him where to park."

"Hold on," Peter said. "I've got an idea. It's a long shot, but it's the best chance we've got. Mikhail, get the uniforms off of the security guards. I'll bring Daniel upstairs and the two of you get dressed in them. Is there any vodka left?"

"About half the bottle."

"Good. Call Dmytro and tell him to meet me in Contract Square."

"Contract Square? That's several kilometers away."

"Don't worry, I'll get there. I'll tell you my plan while you're getting dressed."

Fifteen minutes later, Daniel and Mikhail were dressed in the uniforms of the unconscious guards. *The fit's not great*, thought Peter, *but when you're buying off the rack you take what you can get.* Peter liberally doused both of their uniforms with vodka and gave the bottle to Mikhail.

A few minutes later, the three had slipped out the side door and, crouching to stay out of sight behind the low courtyard wall, made their way to the two bicycles. Peter grabbed one bicycle and followed Daniel and Mikhail to the gate. With a last thumb's up, Mikhail hooked his arm under Daniel's armpits as

Daniel rested his arm on Mikhail's shoulders, and the two stood up and walked out of the gate.

Peter peeked cautiously over the wall. As soon as the two left the gate they turned right, staggering toward the limousine. Mikhail held the empty vodka bottle in his hand and sang a Ukrainian folk song at the top of his lungs as he supported the sagging Daniel, his security cap held low over his face.

"Well, well, friend. Drinking already at this hour?"

"They don't pay us enough to work and stay sober at the same time. Besides, we work the night shift and sleep during the day. What other time do we have to drink?"

The three goons laughed, and one threw his cigarette to the ground, crushing it with his shoe as he strolled toward Mikhail and Daniel. "It makes me feel good to know our government is being protected by two such fine men. Someone could get killed in there, and you would never know about it."

"Ach, nothing ever happens in there at night. Last night, it was as quiet as a tomb. If my wife would keep that quiet, I would drink at home instead. What are you gentlemen doing here at this hour?" Mikhail continued to stumble forward, past the parked limousine, drawing the three men's attention so that their backs were now toward the gate.

The one gunman was drawing closer. Peter needed just a few more steps.

"We're waiting for our boss. He's supposed to meet us here, but he's running late."

"Just like all bosses. Hurry, hurry, hurry, then they make you stand and wait. Say, why don't you stay here and have a drink with us, friend?" With that, Mikhail threw his free arm around the gunman and held him to his chest while Daniel also threw his arm around him.

It was time. Peter jumped on the bike and pedaled through the gate and to the left, away from the limousine, as fast as he could. Shouting at Peter to stop, the two gunmen by the limo started firing in Peter's direction, but their vision was faulty in the dim light of the emerging dawn, and they missed him by a wide margin. Within seconds, Peter sped around the corner, out of the gunmen's sight. Frantically, the two men raced to get into the limousine.

"Alexei, get your ass in here," one of the gunmen called to their partner, who was struggling to extricate himself from Mikhail's grasp.

"Let go of me, you drunken idiots," he swore, but Mikhail just held him tighter. In the melee, Daniel managed to slip his hand under the gunman's jacket, gently slide his gun out of the holster, and stick it quickly into his own shirt. Finally loosing his grasp, Mikhail let the gunman slip free.

"You imbeciles. You'll die for that," Alexei screamed.

But reaching for his gun, he found the holster empty. He quickly searched the ground, but he found no gun.

He glared at the two ersatz security guards. "After I kill that bicyclist, I'm coming back here to finish the two of you off."

Mikhail let go of Daniel and stood in an exaggerated boxing position, swaying perilously from side to side. "Okay, Mr. Tough Guy. Why don't you just come over here and try it now. Or are you chicken?"

The gunman turned balled his hands into fists and took a step toward Mikhail.

"Forget that guy. The cyclist is getting away."

Alexei began walking backwards toward the limo, pointing his finger menacingly at Mikhail. "You're a dead man. Remember that … You're a dead man."

"Oh, Big Shot here says I'm a dead man," Mikhail bellowed. "Ha. Go and run away, Mr. Tough Guy. You punks all think you're hot stuff."

The thug jumped into the back seat of the limousine, which executed a clumsy U-turn, riding up over the curb. Mikhail smiled as he saw Alexei gesticulating furiously at him as the limo sped off in pursuit of Peter.

As soon as the limo rounded the corner, Mikhail grabbed Daniel and half led and half carried him to the meeting place a few blocks away. All they could do was wait.

Peter crouched down into racing position as he pedaled the bike to his physical limits. He knew that Mikhail's distraction would give him at most a sixty-second head start. He was counting on his maneuverability in the narrow side streets of Kiev to give him an advantage. As he turned a corner, St. Andrew's Church came into view high atop Vladimir's Hill, perhaps three or four kilometers away. But at the same time, he heard the roar of an engine no more than two blocks behind him and closing rapidly. Racing down the street, he made a quick left turn onto a broad street, recognizing it as the street on which Mikhail had made his first getaway. But at this hour, there was no traffic to slow down the oncoming limo, and Peter heard its wheels screeching as it made the turn at full speed.

Slipping into high gear and pumping his legs furiously, Peter sped through a red light at the intersection that Mikhail had burst through the previous day, now devoid of cars in the predawn. Ignoring the light as well, the limousine continued racing after Peter, intent on running him down. At the last second, Peter made a sharp right turn, heading the wrong way down the familiar one-way street, throwing his right foot off the pedal and scraping the sole of his shoe along the asphalt to maintain balance.

The limousine was unable to slow down in time to negotiate the turn, and it flew past the street. Slamming on the brakes and jerking the steering wheel to the right, the driver threw the car into an ungainly one-hundred-eighty-degree spin. Its back end almost scraped the cars parked on the far side of the street, then fishtailed as the driver pushed the accelerator to the floor and turned down the street after Peter.

The maneuver had enabled Peter to regain a precious two-block lead, but the limo roared up the street after him. Damn. *Doesn't anybody in this town obey street signs?* Peter thought.

At the end of the street, Peter made another abrupt turn and followed yesterday's route, which now took him on an upgrade. The limousine slowed almost to a stop behind him to make the tight turn without crashing into the parked cars lining the street, allowing Peter to pull further ahead, but his legs began aching with the effort of pedaling uphill. St. Andrew's Church loomed ahead of him as the terrain became steeper. Downshifting to negotiate the progressively steepening grade, he lost valuable speed. Again, he heard the limo accelerate, swiftly closing the gap between them. He pushed on even harder, ignoring the burning pain in his legs that screamed at him to stop.

Peter had almost reached the church when he saw his destination coming up on his right: St. Andrew's Descent, the twisted pedestrian walkway that led downhill toward Contract Square. He turned sharply, steering his bike between the short concrete pillars that kept vehicular traffic from driving onto the street. But as he turned, he realized there was one thing that he wasn't prepared for.

Cobblestones.

Peter cursed and pushed both feet against the pedals, lifting his rear off the seat. Racing downhill, his raised center of gravity made him very unstable, but there was no alternative. Behind him, the limousine screeched to a halt, unable to follow him. Three shots rang out behind him, and Peter heard two bullets whistle off to his right and the third ricochet off the cobblestones, but the street wound to the right, and he rode out of his pursuer's line of sight. He heard the tires squeal on the tarmac behind him as the limo made a detour to meet him at the bottom of the hill.

Peter crouched as low as he could yet still keep his rear end off of the erratically bouncing seat. A few blocks off to his left, paralleling his path, he could hear the limousine alternatively accelerating and braking as it attempted to wind its way downhill through the narrow back streets of Old Town Kiev in frenzied pursuit. Picking up speed as he raced down the cobblestone incline, Peter saw the chestnut trees that jutted through the sidewalks whizzing by, their crowns illuminated by the first dazzling rays of the rising sun now visible over the apartment buildings on the left bank of the Dnieper. Speeding by the cafes and shops, Peter could now see the concrete pillars at the bottom of the hill marking the end of St. Andrew's Descent and the western end of Contract Square. Peter burst through the concrete dividers and screeched to a halt in the center of the square.

The square was barren, empty of people or cars. His heart sank. No Dmytro. He heard the limousine reaching the bottom of the hill off to his left. In a few seconds, it would round the corner and come barreling toward the square, and Dmytro would arrive in time to find his corpse.

Suddenly, Peter heard three beeps of a car horn off to his right and turned. There was Dmytro, waving frantically from the black sedan parked inconspicuously just off the Square on a narrow side street. As fast as his exhausted, aching legs could carry him Peter ran to the car, jumped into the back seat, and slammed the car door behind him. Dmytro drove off without saying a word. As the sedan pulled out of sight of the square, Peter heard the limousine screeching to a halt behind him. The last thing that Peter could hear of his pursuers was their screamed curses as they kicked the deserted bicycle in impotent rage.

"I told you to meet me in Contract Square. Why did you park on a side street?" Peter groaned. "You scared the crap out of me."

"I didn't think that being the only car parked in the middle of the square at 5:30 in the morning with its engine running was a good idea, Dr. Branstead. My apologies."

"Apologies accepted. Let's get to the meeting place."

Boshevsky left his meeting with Marko Cherkasy in a somber mood. It had not been a good day. Today was to have been the formalization of his accession to power, but now he was reduced to watching his plans crumble into dust, his prize slipping away when it had been almost within his grasp. Labrinska had not only survived but was apparently on his way to a full recovery, and there was nothing that he could do about it.

And if anything could be worse, the Mafia was furious at the plan's failure. Fortunately, the capture of the CIA agent had provided Boshevsky with a bargaining chip. Under blood oath, Cherkasy had ensured his safety and that of the other members of the Brotherhood. Nonetheless, as insurance Boshevsky still held Peter Branstead's name and identity as his own personal secret.

Ivan Turgenev awaited him as he walked up the steps to the entrance of his official residence. "Your Excellency, there is a gentleman parked in a limousine who wishes to talk with you."

Boshevsky was puzzled. A limousine generally meant Mafia, but the arrangement had been that the only Mafioso he would deal with was Cherkasy. No one else was supposed to be aware of his involvement.

As the two men approached the limousine, the back door opened. Boshevsky's instincts told him to get away, and he turned to run. But Turgenev stood blocking his path, his gun pointed directly at him.

"Forgive me, Your Excellency, but it would be best if you got into the limousine."

Boshevsky scowled. "This will mean the documents will be released to your father-in-law."

"I will have to take that chance. I can accept my own death, but they threatened not only me but Katerina as well. I had no other alternative but to cooperate."

He had been trumped. Boshevsky sighed, and stepped into the limousine. In the back seat was a well-dressed but massively corpulent man, his fat neck extruding from his collar like a soufflé. The whites of his eyes were hidden behind swollen, puffy lids, leaving two black holes set deeply in his face under an overly coifed, oily toupee. Sitting quietly in folded-down seats across from him were two well-armed bodyguards.

Closing the door behind Boshevsky, Turgenev stood by the open window.

"I've fulfilled my end of the bargain. I have your pledge that you'll keep yours?"

"Have no fear, Turgenev," The Fat Man replied in a slow, rumbling voice. "The prime minister's evidence has been destroyed, and your wife will come to no harm."

"And what about me?"

"You have outlived your usefulness."

One of the bodyguards drew his gun and fired point blank, hitting the astonished Turgenev with a single bullet to his chest before he could even lift his weapon, and the limousine drove off.

"You didn't have to kill him. He would have told no one," Boshevsky snarled.

The Fat Man shrugged. "Now, his silence is unquestionable."

"Who are you, anyway? My arrangement was that I deal only with Cherkasy, not his subordinates."

The Fat Man laughed convulsively, the rolls of fat under his chin oscillating with the effort. "Your Excellency, my name is not important. But I promise that you are not dealing with one of Cherkasy's lackeys. Marko is one of *my* lieutenants."

The prime minister flushed. "Impossible! Cherkasy is the head of the entire crime organization in the Ukraine. I had this personally investigated."

"In the Ukraine, yes. But he is, nonetheless, my subordinate. You see, Your Excellency, I am in charge of all syndicates south of Moscow and west of the Urals, including Ukraine and the Caucasus."

Boshevsky could not have been more shocked. "Cherkasy would never ally himself with the Russians. He was a nationalist, a patriot. We repeatedly pledged loyalty to the Fatherland to make sure that our industries would stay in Ukrainian hands."

"Ah, yes. The Brotherhood ritual. Marko told me about it. Very quaint." The Fat Man leaned over and patted Boshevsky gently on the cheek. "My dear Valentyn, you still don't understand, do you. Our organization is not divided along national boundaries. We are like any other multinational corporation, with subsidiaries all over the world, each responsible for feeding profits back to corporate headquarters where they are reinvested for the benefit of our stockholders by a board of directors. You see, we view nationalism as a very powerful motivating force for organizing people to a cause so that their energies can be channeled and properly manipulated. But once the flag waving stops, it all boils down to money and power, doesn't it?

"Which brings me to the reason for your abduction. Like any other corporation, on the one hand we have assets," and The Fat Man turned his left palm facing up, "and on the other hand we have liabilities," and he turned his right palm up, level with his left. "We are now stuck with the costs of your little venture, a big liability." With that, his right hand dropped. "And in addition we have a prime minister, or should we say an ex-prime minister," he remarked sarcastically, "who once was an asset but is now also a big liability," and his right hand dropped further. "It certainly would make good business sense to dispose of our liabilities as quickly as possible. Unless, of course, we can somehow convert them to assets."

"And how do you propose doing that?" Boshevsky asked warily.

"You could become a valuable asset in two ways. First of all, you must promise to give your full support to our agenda in the Rada. We still maintain a good deal of influence among certain political parties, and we could engineer a favorable position for you. Perhaps not prime minister, but who knows where it might lead if you cooperate."

"And the second way?"

The Fat Man leaned forward until his face was inches away from Boshevsky's. "As an act of faith you must tell me the identity of the man who saved Labrinska."

"This is a serious decision. I need to think about it."

The Fat Man slowly withdrew. "We have a few minutes before we reach our destination. Feel free to consider your options."

Boshevsky reflected on The Fat Man's revelations. Opportunistic, brutal, corrupt—his enemies had called Boshevsky many things during his rise to power, and he deserved all of it. But he kept one moral compass to which he remained true. Throughout his life, he had fought for the independence of Ukraine. By an ironic twist, he had inadvertently come very close to selling his country out to the Russians, a giant step backward prevented only by Peter Branstead's interference. Boshevsky had become that which he most despised, a traitor to his country and a collaborator with the Russians. Prime Minister Valentyn Boshevsky judged himself guilty of high treason. There was no other possible sentence but death.

"No deal. I'll fight your agenda, whatever it may be, to my last breath. As to the identity of the man who saved Labrinska, I have no idea who he is."

The Fat Man's eyes turned into small, black slits. Obviously, they were having difficulty getting information out of the CIA agent or they wouldn't be bothering with him, Boshevsky thought. The psychiatrists had somehow either kept mum or had evaded capture. That left only Scorpion and himself.

"You will regret your decision, Boshevsky. You have nothing to gain and everything to lose by not cooperating. Who is he?"

"What do you need that information from me for?" Boshevsky asked cagily. "Surely, you can get it elsewhere."

"None of the hospital personnel can identify this man. Cherkasy says we have a New York connection that might know him, but he has gone underground and can't be reached. But don't worry, Valentyn, we will find him without your help."

The limousine slowly drew to a halt, and one of the bodyguards opened the door, motioning Boshevsky out with his gun.

Boshevsky knew exactly where they were. He looked up and saw the massive concrete sarcophagus that housed the remains of the ill-fated Reactor Number 4 at Chernobyl. On the eastern wall of the sarcophagus, illuminated in the predawn darkness by floodlights fixed to its top, was an enormous wooden structure, over fifty meters high and running the entire length of the reactor building. This was the mold for a new concrete outer wall that would further seal in the crippled reactor, hopefully for the eternity it would take the reactor's fuel rods to decay into harmless inert isotopes. Except for the limousine's occupants, the construction site was deserted.

One of the bodyguards took a roll of duct tape out of his pocket and tied Boshevsky's hands together in front of him, then waved a flashlight at the control box atop a massive crane nearby. A cable with a large hook at the end was lowered from the boom of the crane and suspended within a few feet of Boshevsky.

"You have one last chance, Excellency. Give me his name."

Boshevsky didn't say a word but stared straight ahead at the hook slowly swinging in a narrow arc in front of him.

At a word from the Fat Man, one of the bodyguards slipped the hook between Boshevsky's bound wrists, and he was hoisted in the air over an enormous concrete bucket. As he was being lowered into the bucket, the hook suddenly released and he dropped abruptly to the bottom.

Boshevsky tried to scramble out of the bucket but the walls were too steep, particularly with his hands tied, and he fell back into something soft at the bottom of the bucket. He stood up again, but the bucket gave a sudden lurch upwards, throwing him back down as it started to rise from the ground.

Boshevsky strained to see what he had fallen on, but the bottom of the bucket was an impenetrable pitch black. However, as the bucket rose, the beam from the floodlight slowly crept downward until it finally illuminated the lowest recesses of the bucket.

Boshevsky recoiled from what he saw. The corpse of Sergei Nikitin lay at the bottom of the concrete bucket, its arms and legs at bizarre, impossible angles and its staring, lifeless eyes separated by a gaping black hole where the bridge of his nose once was. Backing away in disgust, Boshevsky stumbled over yet another body. As the bucket rose closer to the floodlight and swayed beneath it, the beam of light slowly panned back and forth across the second corpse. Boshevsky recognized the suit and body build of William Albright, but there wasn't enough left of his face, or indeed even of his head, to allow accurate identification. Boshevsky felt sick and vomited repeatedly against the wall of the bucket. He assumed that Zabrovych had met a similar fate, and that the Fat Man had disposed of the body elsewhere.

The interior of the bucket became dark again as it rose above the level of the floodlights and jerked to a halt, then moved forward several meters, swaying rapidly on its shortened tether. He was so close to the boom of the crane that he could clearly hear the cables humming against the drive wheels. After the pendular motion of the bucket subsided, Boshevsky felt it being slowly lowered until its sides clanged against the walls of the mold. For a moment all was still, and the only sound Boshevsky could hear was his blood pulsing frantically in his ears. Suddenly, the bottom of the bucket dropped open, and Boshevsky and the two corpses were flung precipitously into the blackness of the fifty-meter abyss.

Death was instantaneous as Boshevsky's body hit the concrete pilings at the bottom of the mold. It was a merciful death, as he didn't have to witness the final terror of a second, even more massive, concrete bucket being lowered into the opening directly above him, blocking out the few stars still visible in the early predawn hours. With a metallic clang that reverberated thunderously in the enclosed space of the concrete form, the bottom of the bucket opened and spewed a torrent of wet concrete over the bottom of the chasm, burying the three bodies to a depth of five meters.

Valentyn Boshevsky, ex-prime minister of Ukraine, had gotten the eternal monument he had always wished for.

CHAPTER 26

▼

"How are you holding out?"

Rachel poured herself a cup of coffee and sat down on at the kitchen table across from Megan. With no plans to leave the apartment, both women had dressed casually in jogging shorts and tee shirts. The main difference in apparel between the two women was Rachel's shoulder holster and gun, which she kept constantly within arm's reach. It had taken Megan a while to adjust to the shock of seeing Rachel wearing a gun, but by now it seemed as natural on Rachel as costume jewelry.

"I guess I'm okay," Megan sighed, lost in the swirls and eddies the cream made as she poured a thin trickle into her coffee. "The hardest part is not knowing how Peter is doing."

"The last time I spoke to Daniel, he was doing just fine. Right now, they're wrapping up some very important business. I'm sure Peter will call as soon as he can."

"How can you cope with the worry when Daniel goes off alone to Europe?"

"I know Daniel's capabilities. He can take care of himself."

"I know Peter's capabilities, too. That's why I'm worried," Megan said harshly. She looked at Rachel directly for the first time that morning. "He's the most trusting man I know, and you sent him off to fight wolves. What do you expect him to do against a bunch of criminals? He doesn't even know to throw the safety catch before he fires a gun. You sent him over there to die."

"I deserve that. But the truth is that Peter's just as safe in Kiev as he would be here." Rachel touched Megan's hand. "Don't worry. He'll be fine. Besides, Alan's coming over today."

It took Megan a while to calm down, but she sipped her coffee and smiled as she thought of Alan. He had recovered more quickly than anyone had anticipated, probably because his years of exposure to multiple psychotropic medications had souped up his capacity to metabolize drugs to superhuman capabilities. He was going to be staying with them after being discharged later today.

"Now that we're both dressed, what do you say I give Carl a call?" Rachel walked into the bedroom and opened the blinds.

She was referring to Carl Molinaro, the other agent who had been assigned to surveillance and had taken up residence in the apartment across the street. He also doubled as a delivery boy, a position he didn't relish but coped with congenially.

The phone was answered on the second ring.

"Molinaro speaking."

"Good morning. Get a good night's sleep?"

"Yeah. Jim Cortland came by at ten o'clock last night and took over until six this morning, so I caught some shut-eye on the cot. This job is boring enough during the day. At night, it's downright pitiful. Could you do me one small favor?"

"Sure."

"Leave the blinds open tonight. Sharpens my powers of concentration."

Molinaro was sitting in the apartment across the street, binoculars to his eyes, looking right at her.

She let the cord go and the blinds dropped abruptly. "Tough luck, letch. Eat your heart out."

"Can't blame a guy for trying," Molinaro retorted.

Rachel laughed and hung up, but before Rachel had a chance to leave the bedroom, the phone rang.

"Is this the Branstead residence?" asked a voice with a thick Brooklyn accent.

"Yes."

"Could I speak to Dr. Branstead, please?"

"I'm sorry, but he's not here right now. May I take a message?"

"Could you please tell me where he is, ma'am? This is Officer Vincent Graziosi, Fifth Precinct. We've been investigating a break-in and vandalism at his office early this morning. I need Dr. Branstead to meet me at his office and answer some questions. The place is messed up pretty bad, but the perpetrators ignored the petty cash and insurance checks. We suspect they may have been looking for records of some sort."

"Did you call his business manager? I'm sure she could help you."

"I tried that. She's out of town for the weekend. Are you Mrs. Branstead?"

"No. Dr. Branstead isn't married. I'm a friend."

"Could you tell me where he is right now? I've got to talk to him while the trail is still warm."

"I'm sorry, Officer, but I really don't know his whereabouts. I'll give him the message when I see him."

"When's that?"

"Can't say. I don't know when he'll be home."

"Listen, lady, this is an official police investigation, and I don't have all day. Perhaps you could meet me at his office and we could go over some things, and you could pass it on to Dr. Branstead later."

Rachel paused. "Can I get back to you on this, Officer? Give me your badge number and a phone number where I can reach you, and I'll call you right back."

"Sure thing, miss. That's Vincent Graziosi … G-r-a-z-i-o-s-i. Badge number 26925." Then he gave Rachel his phone number and hung up.

Rachel dialed the Fifth Precinct. By now, Megan had come into the bedroom holding Charlie in her arms, curious as to what was going on.

"Fifth Precinct, Rodriguez speaking."

"Officer Rodriguez, I just received a phone call from Vincent Graziosi, badge number 26925, regarding a break-in at the office of Dr. Peter Branstead. Can you verify Officer Graziosi's identification?"

"Who am I speaking to?"

"Adrienne Brancowski. I'm a friend of Dr. Branstead's."

"Vinnie Graziosi's been with the force for over ten years, stationed at this precinct for the last seven years. Good cop, not a mark on his record. We got a call at about five this morning regarding a break-in, and we sent him and his partner, Richard Scanlon, to investigate about two hours ago. Is everything okay?"

"No problem, Sergeant. Just checking things out."

"Don't worry about Vinnie. He's straight as an arrow."

Rachel dialed back.

"Officer Graziosi, this is Dr. Branstead's friend. I'll meet you at Dr. Branstead's office in twenty minutes."

"Thank you very much, Miss. Uh, could you tell me your name?'

"Brancowski. Adrienne Brancowski."

"Thanks again, Miss Brancowski. Just one thing. We've got a lot of leads to run down, and I'll be in and out of the crime scene for a while. If I'm not there when you arrive, have a seat, and don't touch anything. I'll be back within an hour. See you there."

Rachel hung the phone up slowly and stared at it as her mind focused on the details of the conversation.

"Shouldn't I be going? I am Peter's significant other."

Rachel opened up the blinds, picked up the phone and dialed. "Not on your life. It could be a trap. You sit tight, and don't let anybody in."

"Molinaro speaking."

"We just got a call from an Officer Vincent Graziosi with the Fifth Precinct that Peter's office has been broken into. I'm going over there to check things out, but something doesn't smell right. Everybody in the building works during the day, so there shouldn't be anybody going in or out. You plant your butt by the window, keep your eyes peeled, and don't budge. If you've got to pee, do it in your cup, but don't move from that window. And if you see anything suspicious, get your ass over here. Got it?"

"Got it. Have no fear, Molinaro's here."

"Thanks. And if I'm not back in three hours, call for backup."

Rachel threw on a light jacket to hide her gun and gave Megan a hug.

"I'll be back in a couple of hours. Think you can stick it out alone until then?"

"I'm not exactly alone. Carl is right across the street, and I've got Charlie here to keep me company. I'll survive. Now get going."

As the elevator clanked its way down to the first floor, Megan sat back down at the kitchen table and looked around the apartment in dismay. She didn't believe that two homebound women could make such a mess in only two days, but somehow they had managed.

They were both getting cabin fever. Rachel had become edgy and preoccupied. It was obvious with the care she took in having her gun accessible at all times, but she had also become subdued, cautious and evasive, possessed by an alter ego to the bubbly, energetic Rachel that Megan had known for years.

Megan had finished her coffee and was cleaning up the apartment when the doorbell rang. Dropping the clothes on the couch, she peered cautiously out of the peephole.

Standing in the hallway was a tall, handsome police officer in his late thirties with buzz-cut blond hair and eyes sequestered behind designer sunglasses.

"Who is it?"

"Officer Richard Scanlon. I think my partner, Vinnie Graziosi, called a few minutes ago. Didn't he speak with you?"

Megan opened the door slightly, wishing for once that she and Peter had had the foresight to install a door chain. "No, that was our friend Adrienne. She's been staying with us while her husband has been out of town. She should be on her way over to Dr. Branstead's office right now."

"Thanks. I'll run over there in a minute, but I happened to be passing by your apartment, and I was hoping you might answer some questions for me. May I come in?"

"May I see your badge and identification, please?"

Scanlon smiled and opened his wallet for her. Scanlon, Richard H., Badge number 52439. The face matched. Everything seemed kosher to her.

Megan held the door open as Scanlon slowly walked in. Spooked by the intruder, Charlie hissed and disappeared into the bedroom.

Locking the door behind her, Megan became aware that even behind the dark sunglasses, Scanlon appeared to be eyeing her approvingly, and she wished that she had changed into something less revealing.

"Why don't we sit down in the kitchen," Megan offered, positioning herself so her bare legs were hidden from view under the table. Scanlon sat down opposite her and removed his sunglasses. His eyes were a brilliant blue and darted obser-vantly about the room. He didn't focus at all on her breasts, hidden under her tee shirt only by a lightweight brassiere. Instead, he focused intently on her face, par-ticularly her eyes.

"Would you mind telling me your name, Miss."

"Megan Hutchins. I'm Dr. Branstead's girlfriend."

"Pleased to meet you, Miss Hutchins. About the break-in, we don't think any money was stolen, but whoever broke in tore the place up pretty bad. I'm trying to establish a motive here. Do you know whether Dr. Branstead has any ene-mies?"

"Not that I'm aware of," Megan lied, thinking of Dr. Albright.

"Did he have any information that someone might have been trying to get to?"

"I doubt it. He has a pretty standard medical practice. I don't think any of his patients were particularly wealthy or famous, but we never discussed names. Con-fidentiality."

Megan glanced down to the table at Scanlon's hands, gloved in spite of the June heat. It was odd. They were clasped casually, but with one thumb resting awkwardly on the inner wrist of the other.

"Sure, sure. Perhaps you can tell me if Dr. Branstead is somewhere in town where I can get in touch with him?" His eyes continued to dart about, focusing chiefly on her hands and face.

Megan felt uneasy under Scanlon's questioning. Her hands suddenly clammy, she brought them under the table and wiped her palms on her thighs. Scanlon's eyes glanced down briefly but quickly returned to her face. He was staring far too intently, almost indecently, at her face and neck. She almost felt violated.

"I'm afraid not. He's out of town at a conference," she said, stirring her coffee nervously.

Scanlon leaned forward. "Where is this conference, Miss Hutchins?" His voice had changed. No longer gentle and reassuring, it had a prosecutorial edge to it.

"Chicago, I believe. Yes, I'm pretty sure he said he was going to Chicago."

"Do you have any idea what type of conference it was?" Scanlon drew his hands apart and stared intently at her eyes. She felt sweat moistening her forehead. Scanlon looked up briefly then returned to her eyes. With a shock, she had the sudden realization of what he had been doing: Checking her for signs of perspiration, timing her respirations and heartbeat to his own pulse, he had been subjecting her to a visual polygraph.

"I ... I ... don't recall. I'm not certain if we ever really discussed it. It's usually some technical neurology stuff, and it bores me to talk about it."

"It doesn't sound like you have a very close relationship with Dr. Branstead. Your boyfriend leaves town for some vague 'conference' and doesn't even tell you why he was going? You're very trusting, Miss Hutchins. Are you sure he isn't meeting with another woman?"

Megan flushed. "I know he would never do that, and I resent the implication, Officer Scanlon."

Scanlon drew back and changed his approach.

"Then perhaps you can tell me when he'll be back. Maybe a number where he might be reached or the name of a hotel?" His eyes were hard and intense.

"We really didn't talk about it much. He's a very private person."

"He must have told you something, Megan." Megan noted how effortlessly his voice, now tinged with anger, shifted to the informal address. She had enough of this inquisition. She was going to call Molinaro.

"Just a minute, Officer. I do know his travel agent's number. Let me give him a call and see if he has any information." She walked to the living room phone and dialed Carl's number, mentally preparing herself for what she would say.

R-r-r-i-n-g ...

In a voice trained professionally to sound calming in the presence of a potentially dangerous individual, she would ask if this was the Village Travel Agency, and could she please speak with Mr. Molinaro.

R-r-r-i-n-g ...

Then, she would say that there was a police officer in her apartment inquiring about Dr. Branstead and she needed to have him to look up what flight to Chicago Peter was booked on and the date and time he would be back in New York.

R-r-r-i-n-g …

This would give her an excuse to stay on the line and act as if she was on hold. Carl would figure out what was going on, run over and straighten out this creep.

R-r-r-i-n-g …

Megan glanced out of the window to the apartment across the street, wondering what was taking so long for Carl to answer the phone. With a shock, she realized that Carl's face was no longer in the window. Where the hell was he?

R-r-r-i …

Megan turned and saw Scanlon with his finger on the cutoff button.

"He's not there, so I guess you won't be needing this phone," and he yanked the cord out of the wall.

Megan looked into Scanlon's eyes again. They were beyond being coldly inquisitive. His eyebrows and forehead furrowed as his eyelids drew together into cold blue slits, and a snarl pulled at his lips. In an instant, his demeanor had changed to one of arrant savagery.

Megan shivered, not only because of his appearance, but also because of the ease with which Scanlon had shifted his emotions, typically psychopathic. In a flash Megan understood why Rachel had been so edgy, why their apartment had been so closely guarded, and why Rachel had said that Peter would be as safe in Kiev as he would be in New York. This man was hunting for Peter, and now she was alone with him, locked in her apartment.

"Who are you?"

Scorpion, for that's who Officer Richard Scanlon really was, twisted his snarl into a grin.

"*Ya Smert.*"

Megan stepped back and kicked upwards. The tip of her sneaker caught Scorpion in his groin, and he winced with pain. Megan raced to the door, throwing chairs over as she ran. She twisted the locks open and grabbed the knob. But Scorpion caught up with her and pulled her hair back so hard that her hands were wrenched from the doorknob. She felt a wadded handkerchief shoved roughly into her mouth before she could scream. Two powerful hands grabbed her wrists and bound them together behind her with several turns of duct tape, and an additional piece was pressed over her mouth, sealing in the handkerchief. Dragged backward by her hair into the bedroom, she was punched hard in her stomach and thrown roughly onto the bed, fighting for breath. After binding her ankles together with more tape, Scorpion ripped the bedroom phone from the wall.

Scorpion ran his gloved fingers through Megan's hair; then roughly pulled her head back again and pinched her nostrils shut between his thumb and index finger. His face colored with rage, but he spoke slowly and deliberately, savoring her struggles to breathe.

"I gave you a chance, Megan. I was nice. I was polite. I allowed you every opportunity to give me the information I needed without hurting you. But you're too stubborn. You think you love your doctor boyfriend too much to betray him, don't you? Don't play games with me. I've sent more men to their graves than you can count, and each one begged me to hasten his death. I don't plan to let some foolish little girl stand in my way any longer. I've wasted enough time with you."

He released her nostrils and stormed out of the bedroom. Her lungs almost bursting, Megan struggled to get air and fought to quell the panic erupting in her brain.

Scorpion stormed into the kitchen and twisted the dials on the stove to high heat. Rummaging through the kitchen drawers, he took every chef's knife he could find, and lay the blades on top of the heating elements. The smell of heated steel permeated the kitchen air. In a few minutes, the blades would be heated to an incandescent orange.

He grabbed a table lamp, pulled its plug from the outlet and cut the cord. Separating the two wires for a few inches, he stripped off a quarter inch of insulation from each wire and plugged the cord back in. Satisfied with the crackling blue spark that arced between the two ends as he touched them together, he unplugged the electric cord and laid it on the kitchen table. He was ready for the interrogation.

He checked his watch while walking to the bedroom. The Brancowski woman would have arrived at Branstead's office. He had at least forty minutes before she became suspicious at his absence and another twenty to thirty minutes of travel time before her return. There was plenty of time for questioning before he had to stop and set a trap.

Something next to the sofa caught Scorpion's eye. It was an animal carrier, a large plastic box with a handle, a wire cage door and holes along the side for ventilation. But it had a strange air of familiarity to it, and gave him an almost hypnotic sense of déjà vu ...

His feet barely touching the ground, eight-year-old Georgi fairly flew down the pitch-black forest path, lifted into the air by the rough, powerful hand of his father.

"You grimy little bastard, when I say go to bed, you go to bed. No arguments."

"You were hurting Mama. I can't sleep when you're hurting Mama."

"None of your fucking business what I do with Mama, understand?" His voice echoed loudly through the forest. But in this region of the Carpathian Mountains people lived kilometers apart, and no one heard his outburst.

"Please don't put me in the cage, Papa. I promise I'll go to bed."

"You're damn right you'll go to bed. And you'll stay in bed, too, so I won't have to put up with any of your whining shit. And when you learn to keep your mouth shut, you'll sleep in the house."

They arrived in a small clearing where the moonlight was able to penetrate through the trees, and the dim outline of the cage was visible. Made of thick branches tied together with twine, it was high enough for Georgi to crawl into, just wide enough for him to turn around, and long enough to lie down. The makeshift roof of warped boards served to keep light rain showers from drenching its young prisoner but was totally ineffective in a downpour.

"Now get the hell in there, and learn to keep your fucking mouth shut for once." Georgi was pushed roughly into the cage, and a thin, woolen blanket was tossed in after him. His father locked the cage door and staggered drunkenly toward the house.

Georgi set about preparing himself for the night. He made a mattress of leaves that had blown into the cage and set his blanket on top of it. Curling up against the late autumn cold, he tried to get some sleep.

The distant howling of wolves awakened him around midnight. During the summer months, when game was plentiful, the wolves generally stayed away from the vicinity of the house. But with approaching winter, they became bolder and frequently wandered close in search of a chicken or duck that might have escaped its coop. And tonight his cage lay directly in their path.

Georgi could make out their hulking shapes in the moonlight as they entered the clearing. The first few times he had been in the cage with the wolves circling around him had almost scared him to death, but by now he had learned to control his breathing and focus his thoughts. He would hear nothing; he would say nothing. The wolves were not to be feared, the night's bitter cold was not to be felt, and the terror of the darkness was of no concern. He had learned to empty his mind of everything—all sensation, all feeling and all emotion.

Everything but hatred.

Usually the wolves passed by with at most a curious sniff at the cage. But tonight, as the rest of the pack made its way quietly past the cage, one wolf stopped about five meters from the cage and growled. Perhaps it was hunger or the dying frenzy of a rabid animal, but suddenly the wolf charged the cage, shoved its muzzle between the tightly spaced bars and gnawed savagely at the thick wood, less than a half meter from Georgi's face.

Scorpion snapped back to the present. His fingers were gripping the wires of the carrier door so tightly that they dug painfully into his flesh. He cursed and threw the animal carrier across the room, watching it careen off the coffee table and roll against the wall. He wiped the sweat off of his face with his shirtsleeve. He could not afford to waste any more time with the past.

Megan had finally managed to catch her breath, and she now focused on calming herself down and formulating a plan. She had worked with psychopaths frequently but always in a tightly controlled environment. There had always been at least one guard present, the patient had been restrained, and an emergency call button had been at hand. Psychopaths were emotional chameleons, changing their affective display to whatever would best manipulate the people around them, including their therapists. Absolute masters at emotional isolation, their empathy level was at rock bottom. None of this helped Megan at all in her predicament as she struggled to think. Somehow, she had to delay him until Rachel got back. But that might not be for well over an hour, and she might be dead by then. Her only hope was to stall her attacker until Rachel got back. But she couldn't do it with her mouth taped shut.

Scorpion reentered the bedroom and removed his gloves, displaying a macabre array of skull tattoos over the tops of his hands and in the webs of his fingers. He sat down on the bed and flaunted his hands directly in front of Megan.

"In the prisons where I come from, we have a system of tattoos that tell stories about the wearer. For example, each one of these skulls represents a murder I have committed. The more decorative ones represent more important victims. I'm particularly proud of this one," and he pointed to a particularly well-executed skull on the web space between the thumb and forefinger of his left hand. "It was for my father. I was fifteen when I killed him."

He unbuttoned his shirtsleeves and rolled them above his elbows. The coils of an adder wound around his left arm, and the scaly head, neck, and body of a fire-breathing dragon on his right. At every coil of the adder and at every twist and turn of the dragon's body was tattooed at least one skull. Megan couldn't count them all, but the total must have been at least twenty-five. Scorpion unbuttoned his shirt and threw it off.

With its head just below his neck and its body covering the entire center of his chest was a hideously ornate tattoo of a monstrous scorpion. Its eight legs spanned the sides of his chest as if embracing him. Its two front arms curved beneath and around his powerful chest muscles, ending in two massive claws clutching the tails of the dragon and the adder as they extended onto his chest and wrapped themselves in turn around the scorpion's claws. The enormous segmented tail of the scorpion stretched downward over his abdomen, plunging obscenely into his pants.

"This is why I choose to be known as Scorpion."

He gently stroked Megan's hair. She fought the urge to shake her head. She could not think of him as her attacker if she was to stay calm and have any control over the situation.

She had to think of him as a patient.

For Scorpion to have killed his father at age fifteen and have been proud of it, he must have been subject to horrific abuse as a child. His need to dominate, to control, and even to kill was a reflection of a deeply felt insecurity and vulnerability. As crazy as it seemed her only hope for survival, at least until Rachel could get back, was to establish some form of therapeutic alliance with him, to dig deeply into his soul to connect with whatever human part of him remained. This could take years of psychotherapy for resistant patients.

She only had minutes.

Megan looked briefly into Scorpion's eyes, softening her gaze as much as she could, then quickly downcast her eyes submissively and slowly curled her body into a fetal posture. She knew that even with Scorpion obviously in command, she had to use the most nonthreatening body language she could, or he would react with anger and violence.

Scorpion's hand left her hair, and he stroked her cheek with the backs of his fingers, the images of the burning skulls passing in front of her eyes. But she didn't move, didn't struggle until his hand started to wander down to her breasts. Then, she twisted her neck and rubbed her taped cheek against her shoulder, casting a pleading look at Scorpion, and then averted her eyes again. *Whatever you do, don't stare*, she thought. *It will challenge him, set him off.*

"So you want the gag off, do you?" His hand shot up and pulled her head back by the hair again. "Do you really think I would take the gag off so you could scream for help?"

Megan shook her head. Not too vigorously. It had to be firm, not frantic.

Scorpion took his knife and touched the point to her throat.

Keep cool, keep cool, keep cool ...

"All right, then. But if I even *think* that you're going to scream, I'll shove this knife right through your vocal cords. Do you understand?"

Megan nodded her head slightly. It was taking every bit of her training to maintain control.

Scorpion removed the tape and handkerchief from her mouth, but kept the knife point at her throat.

"You have nothing to gain by killing me. If I have the information you need, it will die with me."

"I don't wish to kill you. But one way or another I will get that information. Interrogating men is simple. Cut the tendons behind the knees and a few deep slices running the length of the thighs and the muscles are detached from the bone so the thighs can no longer be drawn together. After five or ten minutes of having their testicles kicked, most men can be convinced that it is in their best interest to cooperate. Interrogating a woman requires some resourcefulness, but it shouldn't be too difficult."

Shouldn't be too difficult? This must be something new to him.

"You generally don't have to interrogate women?"

Scorpion shook his head. "It's the men who have the secrets. Women are bystanders, the innocent victims in men's plans."

Killed his father when he was fifteen. Women are innocent victims. It was obvious that he hated men, but he seemed to be ambivalent about what he was going to have to do with her. It was a long shot, but she had a plan.

"Women aren't the only innocent victims. You were an innocent victim, too, weren't you?"

A surprised look shot across Scorpion's face, and Megan got a fleeting glimpse of vulnerability before he sequestered it, deep within his brain. His face hardened again, but he drew the knife back an inch or two, enough that Megan could relax her neck.

"What are you talking about?"

"It was your father, wasn't it? That's why you had to kill him. He victimized you, and he victimized your mother. Who else did he abuse?" Megan took a calculated risk. "What about your sister?" She was treading on very, very dangerous ground.

"Shut up! Don't you dare talk about my sister!" He gripped the knife harder, but he didn't bring it any closer. His eyes had softened ever so slightly and his grip on the knife loosened. His guard was down.

"My brother and I were victims, too. Our stepfather abused us, beat us, especially when he was drunk." She had to lie. Whatever the reality, in Scorpion's mind, women were never perpetrators. "We had nobody to protect us, except ourselves. You develop a special feeling for someone when they depend on you so much, don't you?"

Scorpion said nothing. Megan glanced up, surprised at what she saw. His eyes were unfocused and distant. Slowly, the knife slid from his hand and dropped to the floor.

"You fat, ugly cow. You're of no use to a man."

Georgi's father's words erupted from his parents' bedroom, followed by the familiar sounds of his father's hands hitting flesh and his mother's cries. Fifteen-year-old Georgi and his thirteen-year-old sister, Anna, sat silently at the dinner table, eyes downcast.

His father burst into the room, naked from the waist up and drunk as usual. He had the wild look on his face that Georgi recognized well, the look he would get before he beat him.

But something was different tonight. For the first time, his father focused on young Anna instead. Now in his self-hypnotized alternate persona, Georgi was deaf to her cries as their father pulled her out of her chair. Nor could he hear the sound of his mother begging for her daughter or the dull thud as her husband pushed her roughly into the wall. And Georgi, still sitting silently and impotently at the table, could only see poor terrified Anna mouthing his name and pleading with her eyes for help as their father forced her into his bedroom.

Scorpion remained silent. Megan could see that he was wrestling with feelings that he hadn't dealt with for decades. She had to press on. Things could go either way, but she had to take a chance.

"You killed your father because he hurt your sister, didn't you?" she asked gently, with as much empathy as she could muster for someone who was about to kill her.

"Stop it," he screamed, and shoved the handkerchief back in her mouth. She had pushed too far, but she had accomplished two things. She had planted the seeds of conflict in his mind about whether or not to kill her. And he had dropped the knife.

There was a sound of movement behind him. Scorpion reflexively reached for the knife, but couldn't find it. Caught unprepared, he was jerked backwards off the bed onto his feet and spun around as a well-aimed fist landed squarely on his jaw, throwing him against a wall.

With the brutal intensity of a street brawler, Alan Lamplin pummeled Scorpion's face and body, cursing with each savage, rapid-fire punch. Stunned, all

Scorpion could do was hold his arms defensively in front of his face and chest to ward off the onslaught of blows. In an attempt to throw him off, Scorpion bent down, grabbed Alan by the waist and bulled him backwards against the wall. But by yanking Scorpion's head up and head-butting him, Alan had Scorpion momentarily dazed. His guard was down just long enough for Alan to punch him full force in the stomach, doubling him over, and with a hard left uppercut knocked him down to the floor by the bed.

Reeling, Scorpion saw the knife on the floor by the bed. He grasped it just as Alan gathered himself for a leap and, as Alan's body flew through the air, Scorpion held the blade rigidly in front of him. The point stuck Alan just below his left breast, and the momentum of his lunge buried the blade up to the hilt in his chest, piercing his heart as he gave an agonizing gasp. Snarling, Scorpion slashed the knife left and right, slicing through Alan's heart before pulling the knife out of his chest and throwing him to the floor. Megan screamed through her gag and watched, horrified and helpless, as her brother died in front of her eyes.

Scorpion sat on the floor for a minute and assessed the damage. Most of the blows had been to his stomach and rib cage, and although he was bruised and sore, nothing was broken. Standing up slowly, he checked his mouth and lips for blood with the back of his hand before wiping the knife blade off on the bedspread and sitting back down next to Megan, her face buried in the pillow. Hooking his fingers under the waistband of her shorts, in one smooth motion he drew both her shorts and panties down to her ankles. His eyes were hard and bitter.

"Therapy session is over, Megan. Back to business," Scorpion said through clenched teeth.

He had barricaded his psyche behind the wall of his anger. He was unreachable again.

"Not locking the door was an oversight on my part," he said, fondling Megan's exposed buttocks. "That was obviously not Dr. Branstead, but whoever he was paid for my mistake. I'm going to lock the door now, and when I return we'll have a little demonstration of how we have sex in Russian prisons."

"Terrific. I've always wanted to watch you go *fuck* yourself, Scorpion."

The sound of a woman's voice behind him took him by surprise again. He looked up to the window, but the blinds were drawn, and there was no reflection. She must have a gun and an intelligence background if she felt free to address him that way. He felt no fear, however. Fear was harmful, even deadly, in his occupation. It was destructive to concentration and coordination. Besides, this woman was weak-willed and unsuspecting or she already would have shot him in the back. The agent across the street had also been weak, and he had died because of it.

For now, he had to concentrate on the plan he had already used several times in precisely this scenario. Most importantly, he needed to focus on her voice.

"I wasn't expecting you back so soon."

"I grew suspicious as soon as I got to the office. No police lines at the crime scene. It only took me a few minutes to find the bodies of Scanlon and Graziosi in the dumpster, and when I saw that you had taken Scanlon's clothes, it was easy to figure out your plan. Give up, Scorpion. Game's over."

Scorpion smiled. He had heard similar words many times before, and all who had said them were dead. Keeping his hands shielded from sight, he slowly picked up the knife and prepared himself mentally for what was to follow.

He had learned a great deal from the woman's brief speech. By the location of her voice, she was about five feet six inches tall and stood about eight feet behind him. The coordinates were critical because he had to precisely aim the knife just two to four inches below her mouth if he was to hit the blood vessels in her neck, and he visualized the spot carefully in his mind. She was clever, more clever than he had given her credit for, and was most likely a law officer herself. As such, she would be holding her gun in the firing stance, both arms stiffly extended. Her arm and shoulder would block the knife if he threw it underhand, and an overhand throw would be too obvious, so he would have to throw sidearm. It was more difficult, but he had practiced that throw thousands of times until he had it perfect.

The woman might very well get a shot in before she died, so Scorpion steeled himself for the expected pain. When the time came, he would gesture with his empty hand, drawing her attention and possibly a bullet. If he were shot, the pain would be sudden and intense; like fear, pain was destructive to his concentration and must be driven from consciousness. But regardless of whether or not he was shot, the knife would lethally pierce her neck. He had never missed before, and he would not miss now. And when she was dead, he would have all afternoon alone with the girl.

"Stand up slowly, and put your hands over your head."

It was time.

From the moment she heard Rachel's voice, Megan stopped crying. There was no time for grief now. She had to regain control. Scorpion had the knife in front of him, hidden from Rachel's view. Unable to force the handkerchief out of her mouth with her tongue, she struggled to get out a warning that he had a knife, but her voice was muffled beyond recognition, even if Rachel could hear her from across the room. When Scorpion stood up, still holding the knife in front of him, she knew what had to be done. Her only hope was to throw Scorpion off balance and give Rachel a chance to shoot.

With all of her remaining strength, Megan twisted her body, shifting her center of gravity as much as she could toward the edge of the bed before she rolled back into the depression in the mattress made by the weight of her body. She tried again, her momentum carrying her just a little further before she rolled back. Out of the corner of her eye, she saw Scorpion take a deep breath. It was now or never. Megan threw her body over as hard as she could, and rolled off the side of the bed.

Scorpion stood up straight, still keeping his hands hidden in front of him, his mind intensely focused, all distractions eliminated. The knife would come at her from an unexpected direction. She wouldn't know he was left-handed. Born left-handed, he had been switched as a child. He wrote, threw balls, and did everything with his right hand except for throwing knives, which he did left-handed.

Nobody alive knew that.

He braced his shoulders back, slowly took a deep breath, then suddenly took a step backward with his right foot and whirled his body to the right. As he turned, he threw his right hand over his head in a broad semi-circle that continued outward and away from his body, drawing attention away from his left arm. At the instant when his turning body would no longer hide his left arm he swung it up, out, and forward at shoulder level, the blade pinched between his thumb and forefinger. When released, it would fly straight to its target, just eight feet away.

Megan landed on the floor right on her unprotected stomach, knocking the wind out of her again. But her momentum was spent when she hit the floor, and she stopped rolling.

Even though she was still struggling to breathe enough air in through her nose, Megan quickly turned her head to the side, and her heart sank. Scorpion had turned his body away from the bed and he was a good two feet away from her as he threw the knife.

She had failed miserably.

At the instant that Scorpion's body was turning away from the falling figure of Megan, a triumphant grin spread over his face. The woman was exactly where he thought she would be. His left hand, still holding the knife, swept outward while his right arm swept high over his head to draw her fire.

Before his left arm had completed its pre-determined arc, Rachel gave a single squeeze of the trigger and fired off a three-round burst. The first two bullets were fired too soon; they whistled past Scorpion's hand before his arm had fully extended and buried themselves in the wall. The third bullet, however, found its mark. Spinning as it raced through the air, the nine-millimeter projectile penetrated the skin and ligaments on the underside of his left wrist and sliced through the taut tendon holding his index finger in its pinch, releasing its tension instantly. It smashed against the wrist bones and exploded in a shower of metal and bone fragments, severing the other tendons and the nerve as they coursed through the wrist. The train of nerve impulses to the thumb muscles ceased abruptly, and his thumb became immediately paralyzed. Finally, the momentum of the nine-millimeter bullet burst Scorpion's wrist and hand backward, reversing their smoothly circular forward course.

Released just milliseconds too soon, the knife flew straight forward rather than continuing in an arc, whizzing by less than a yard to Rachel's right and perfectly level with her neck. Speeding by too fast for her to take evasive action, too fast for her to even see it, the knife plunged itself four inches deep into the plaster wallboard behind her.

Clutching his shattered wrist, Scorpion let out a scream that would have been heard throughout the building and out on the street had it not been masked by the traffic noise out on Mercer Street. It was not a scream of pain but of rage and frustration as he realized his failure and recognized his adversary.

"Falconer! I thought you were dead."

Rachel smiled, her gun pointed at his chest. "Have your bookkeeper check your employee roster. One of your boys didn't pick up his paycheck on Friday."

"I should've killed you myself," he hissed.

"You're absolutely right, but it's too late now to cry over spilled milk. You screwed up this time, Scorpion, so plan on having lots of prison time to spend adding to your tattoo collection."

Scorpion drew himself up and grinned sardonically. Even though she had a gun and he was without his knife-throwing hand, he felt in control of the situation. As he had suspected she was too accustomed to defensive training to use more than minimum necessary force, or she would have shot him already. He weighed his alternatives.

If he distracted Falconer, he might be able to edge a bit closer to Megan. Another half meter, and he would be close enough to get his foot on the back of her neck and use the threat of snapping it to gain bargaining leverage.

"How did you find out I was left-handed?" he asked, and shifted his weight so that he moved slightly closer to the prostrate body of Megan.

"That's for me to know. And move away from her, asshole, or you're history," Rachel snapped. "Give me one excuse, just one, and you're dead meat." Scorpion, still grinning in spite of his shattered wrist, shrugged and backed off. He had other options.

"Aren't you going to arrest me, Falconer? It shouldn't be too difficult to cuff me. I've only got one hand now." He was taunting her to come closer.

She didn't answer and didn't move a muscle.

She must have memorized his dossier, and she wasn't so stupid to come even close to arm's length of him. Even unarmed and with a useless left hand, he was still more dangerous at close range than most fully able men with a gun, and she apparently knew it. For the same reason, she hadn't ordered him out of the room yet. The room was small, and the bed took up most of it. For him to get out, she would either have to back out of the door first, or he would be able to pass close enough to jump her. But it had been worth a try.

He recognized the gun she was holding as a Beretta 93R. The thumb switch was set to three-round burst, which was how she had gotten three shots off so quickly. However, to stabilize the gun and keep it from kicking up with each successive shot and ruining her accuracy, Falconer had folded down the handgrip attached to the front of the barrel and was gripping it with her left hand. She had a cellular phone clipped to her waistband, but to use it she would have to take her left hand off the handgrip, and take her eyes off of him for just a moment to dial, slowing her reaction time and impairing her accuracy. The 93R had limited stopping power and, as long as she didn't hit him directly in the heart or the head, he could take a single shot and still be able to lunge and knock the gun from her hand. He wasn't afraid of death. If you were afraid of death, you would be afraid to take risks. In his business, if you didn't take risks, you died.

So, for the time being, it was a standoff. But all he had to do was wait. Wait until she made a mistake or lowered her guard.

"You'll like American prisons, Scorpion," Rachel suddenly said sarcastically. "Much cleaner than Russian prisons. Lots of activities, too—punching out license plates in the morning, TV talk shows in the afternoon. You'll love it. They don't have *Wheel of Fortune* or *Jerry Springer* in Ukraine, do they?"

What the hell is Rachel doing? Megan thought. *This guy is a psychopath, and she's trying to get him mad? Is she nuts?*

Scorpion's eyes narrowed. "*If* I ever go to prison, I'll be out sooner than you could imagine. And my entertainment won't be television. I'll be spending my time planning the slowest, most painful way for you to die that I can think of."

Rachel ignored his taunts. "I don't know if you'll even want to get out. Who knows, you might enjoy yourself. With a cute butt like yours, it should be easy to make friends, especially when the word gets around that a woman brought you in. At least you won't have problems getting a date on Saturday nights."

Megan glanced up, but from her angle she could only see Scorpion's hand, white and trembling with the intensity of his grip around his shattered wrist. *Jesus, is she pushing his buttons. Hard.*

"I'll bet you were hot stuff in Russia," Rachel continued. "With the protection of your big shot Mafia friends, of course. King of the Prison Shit Pile, weren't you. I'll bet everybody moved out of your way when you walked through the prison yards. Well, not any more, Sweet Cheeks. Over here, you'll be a nice, tight-assed prison bitch for some fat, greasy *pakhan*," she sneered.

"Shut up!" he spat out through tightly clenched teeth.

He's getting close to the edge, Megan thought. *She's trying to provoke him into an attack. But he's got to be too smart to fall for that.*

"Educate me, Scorpion. What's the tattoo for a prison bitch? A rabbit? A pansy? Maybe," she added scornfully, "a nice big bull's eye tattooed right on your ass."

As his father pushed Anna into the bedroom, and his rage churned deep inside him, a long-suppressed image burst into Georgi's awareness. In his mind's eye, Georgi flashed back to the rabid wolf savagely attacking a flimsy wooden cage that protected the child within. The image took over his consciousness and forced out the deaf-mute persona forever.

With his new persona, the smells in the room suddenly intensified and assaulted Georgi's nostrils—the heady, thick aroma of the dinner meat, the delicate smell of his sister's hair, still lingering like a vapor where she had been sitting.

And the overpowering stench of his father's sweat pouring out of the bedroom.

His eyes glowing orange with the reflected firelight, a deep growl erupted in a slow crescendo from Georgi's throat. Every muscle in his body tensed, and he felt a new-found strength he had never had before. His lips curling back into a snarl, he grabbed the carving knife from the table and stalked toward the bedroom.

The blood rushed to Scorpion's face, turning it a deep crimson as the distended arteries in his temples pulsed and throbbed furiously. His eyes narrowed into fierce slits, and the short blond hairs on the back of his neck rose straight up, erect and bristling. Every sinew in his neck bulged tautly, his shoulders drew up, and his back arched forward. Snarling, his nostrils flared and his lips drew back, exposing his teeth.

Scorpion curled his good right hand into a claw, his left hand fixed forever in the grotesque posture produced by the severing of his tendons. He lifted his head up and howled, the last traces of rationality disappearing. But as he gathered himself for a lunge, Rachel wasted no more time. She fired another burst of three shots, so close together that in the confines of the bedroom it sounded like one long, sustained blast. Three black holes appeared in the center of Scorpion's chest, patterned in a tight equilateral triangle, no more than two inches to a side. Thrown backward by the impact of the bullets, Scorpion collapsed limply to the bedroom floor.

Megan was still in shock when she saw Rachel jump on Scorpion and shoved the barrel of the Beretta into his mouth. Her finger tensed on the trigger, but Megan cried out through her gag. Rachel looked at Megan, then took a deep breath to calm herself, and withdrew the gun.

Rachel paid special attention as she palpated Scorpion's neck for a pulse then put her hand on his chest, searching for a nonexistent heartbeat. He was unquestionably dead. There was no chance he would walk on a legal technicality, no chance of extradition to the safety of his Russian masters, and no chance of identifying her, Megan, or Peter to his cronies as he whiled away his prison time plotting his revenge. The game really was finally, irrevocably over.

Rachel rushed over to Megan and removed the saliva-soaked handkerchief.

"Oh, God. It was horrible, horrible."

"I know, Sweetie. Let me cut you out of the tape, okay?"

"Not a knife! There's a scissors in the nightstand. Please don't use a knife."

As soon as she was freed, Megan grabbed Rachel by the arm. "Rachel, tell me. Is he really dead?"

"Yes. Don't worry. I killed him."

"No, not Scorpion. Is Alan dead?"

Rachel had forgotten all about Alan. Throwing a robe to Megan, she went over to the body, checked for a pulse, then sat down on the bed next to Megan and hugged her.

"I'm so sorry, honey."

Megan broke down and sobbed while Rachel rocked her slowly. There was nothing that could be said. Finally, Megan's sobs quieted down enough that Rachel felt she could leave her alone for a minute.

"I've got to go into the living room and kitchen to get some things done. I'll be right here in the apartment. I won't leave you alone again, I promise. Will you be all right for a few minutes?"

Megan nodded her head, drying off her tears with her sleeve.

Rachel wrapped the hilt of the knife with a handkerchief and wiggled it out of the wall. Closing the door behind her, she ran off to the kitchen to remove all traces of the tortures that Scorpion had planned before Megan could see them. That accomplished, she phoned her section chief to arrange for removal of the bodies before the police were called.

As Rachel cleaned up, Megan crawled to where Alan's body lay. Sitting cross-legged in the corner, she drew his body into her arms, gently cradled his head in her breast, and stroked his face and hair.

Rachel strode into the bedroom. "Let's go, time to …"

She stopped short when she saw Megan, turned, and closed the door quietly behind her.

Holding Alan's body, Megan sang in a sad, broken voice

> You are my sunshine, my only sunshine,
> You make me happy when skies are gray …

CHAPTER 27

▼

Darkness had long fallen as Dmytro piloted the sedan toward Boryspil Airport, Mikhail in the passenger's seat, Peter and Daniel in the back. The mood was somber, the final celebration having taken place privately in Mikhail's office after Daniel passed his medical evaluation at the Secret Service Clinic.

The bittersweet news had come from Rachel at midafternoon. Although relieved by Scorpion's death, Peter sank into a deep melancholy.

Daniel broke the silence. "C'mon, give it a rest. You can't blame yourself for something you couldn't possibly prevent. What could you conceivably have done to protect Megan if you were back in New York?"

"I don't know, but at least I could have been there. I deserted her, plain and simple. I ran off and left her alone to face a homicidal maniac."

"You're an idiot. If you had stayed in New York, you'd be as dead as poor Alan. Real comforting for Megan. Two funerals instead of one."

"Cut the crap. You're not helping. It doesn't matter whether or not I could have done anything. Walter Ivy couldn't do anything, Harriet Halleck couldn't do anything, and Iryna Labrinska couldn't do anything, either. But they were there. They were there when they were needed, and I wasn't. I know I couldn't have stopped him. But how the hell can Megan trust me again? How will she know that I won't pack up and leave the next time there's trouble? I've lost her, Dan."

Daniel sighed and put his hand on Peter's shoulder. "Sometimes being there isn't the right thing to do. They were there because there was nothing else they could do, nowhere else they could be. They stayed as much for their own feelings of helplessness, because they were the ones who needed the comforting. I guarantee that if Walter Ivy were told that the cure to Amanda's illness was in Kiev, he would have left on the next flight out to get it. That's why we had to get you out of New York; not just for your sake, but for Megan's as well, and she knows it. You were sticking your nose into Mafia business, and sooner or later both of you would have been killed."

"Wrap it up, gentlemen. We're at the airport," Mikhail interrupted.

"I hope you're right," Peter sighed. "I'll tell you what happened when you get back to New York."

"Sorry, pal. I won't be back home for quite some time."

"How come?"

"I'm leaving here directly for Paris. Rachel's meeting me there for a vacation."

"Terrific. Why Paris?"

Daniel smiled. "You know what they say. Everyone should see Paris before they die."

Dmytro pulled over to the curb outside the Air Ukraine terminal. Peter and Mikhail talked as Dmytro went to the trunk to get out the flight bags.

"Here are your tickets and passport. Dmytro will be accompanying you to New York. You have been routed to Vienna, then Brussels, and finally Gatwick Airport for the flight to New York. Your schedule is very tight, so you won't be spending much time sitting around the airports. Dmytro has a special diplomatic pass to save time at customs. With the time change you should be back in New York tomorrow morning." Mikhail's tone suddenly became less officious as he shook Peter's hand warmly. "Good-bye, Dr. Peter Branstead. It has been an honor to have worked with you." Unexpectedly, Mikhail gave him a warm hug, got into the driver's seat, and closed the door without looking back.

Dmytro walked up to Peter and handed him his flight bag. As they turned to leave, the rear window of the sedan opened, and Daniel stuck his head out.

"Look for my letter," he yelled.

"Just send me a postcard. The Eiffel Tower or Notre Dame would be nice."

"No. I'll send you a letter. Look for it."

"What's the big deal? Tell me when you get ..."

"Just look for my letter. It's important."

And the window rolled up as the sedan drove off.

"Come, Dr. Branstead. We'll be late for our plane unless we hurry."

Peter shook his head as the sedan disappeared into the darkness. *There are some inscrutable people in this world that are made for academics,* he thought ruefully, and raced into the terminal behind Dmytro.

CHAPTER 28

▼

"Rachel, will you please hurry up. Peter's plane has already landed."

"For Christ's sake, I'm going as fast as I can," Rachel grumbled, stumbling along in her high heels as the two women raced past the newsstands, airport bars, and fast food restaurants lining the International Concourse at JFK International Airport. "What's your rush? It's going to take him at least an hour to get through customs. Shoot, I think I broke my heel. Megan, would you please slow down."

"I can't. I've got to be there when Peter clears customs." Megan craned her neck to look over the throngs pouring through the concourse. "Wait, I think I see him. He's through already."

Rachel sighed, balancing herself against the side of a pretzel stand as she pulled off her shoes. "Calm down. It's just someone that looks like him."

"No, it's really him! Peter, over here! Over here!" she waved frantically, shoving her way upstream through the flood of people.

"Son of a gun, it is him. How did he ever get through customs so fast?" Rachel muttered, walking barefoot through the concourse, shoes in hand.

Eyes positioned resolutely ahead, minds focused on their immediate destinations and on the complexities of their disparate lives, the swarm of humanity gushing out of customs parted and flowed around them as Peter and Megan embraced, creating that singular New York entity—an island of isolation in the midst of a multitude.

Megan spoke first, without breaking their embrace. "Thank God you're safe. It's been frightening not knowing what was happening to you. Now that I've lost poor Alan, I feel so alone without you."

"I won't leave you again, sweetheart. I wish I could have been here to protect you from that bastard ..."

"Are you crazy?" Megan stared at him. "That man was a killing machine. The only thing you would have accomplished by staying home would have been to get yourself killed, too. Rachel was right. You had to go. She was the best protection I could have had."

Responding to his hurt expression, Megan smiled and whispered into Peter's ear, "But she can't cook worth a damn."

The sound of a man's throat being cleared behind Peter startled her. "Excuse me, miss. My name is Dmytro Mindaneyev. I am to turn over responsibility for Dr. Branstead's safety to Rachel Falconer. Are you she?"

Rachel pushed her way through the crowd and extended her hand to Dmytro. "I'm Rachel Falconer. I'll accept the transfer."

Dmytro eyed the pretty, barefoot blonde uneasily, uncertain if he should be relinquishing his charge to her.

Peter broke the uncomfortable silence. "Don't worry, Dmytro. She's the one who killed Scorpion."

Dmytro's demeanor changed abruptly, and he in turn extended his hand in grudging admiration, muttering a mild oath under his breath in Ukrainian.

"In the name of the Director of the Ukrainian Secret Service, allow me to convey my country's deepest appreciation for your actions on our behalf." For the first time since Peter had known him, there was the suggestion of a smile on Dmytro's face. "The effect of this information on our prison population will be intriguing to see, at the very least." He gave a respectful nod and walked briskly back toward the Air Ukraine gate.

"Jim, we're all set. Meet us by the International Terminal entrance in five minutes," Rachel directed into her cellular phone, and then stuffed it back in her purse as she pulled Megan by the arm. "Okay, let's get you guys home, pronto. Now, here's the story. As far as we know, everyone who knows Peter's identity is either on our side or very, very dead."

"How do we know that Scorpion didn't tell anyone else?" Peter asked.

"He generally operated alone. Actually, I was pretty surprised when I found that he had sent one of his flunkeys after me. Must've thought that, as a woman, I wasn't worth his time."

"Or he didn't trust himself to kill you," Megan said pensively.

Rachel looked at Megan quizzically for a moment and then continued.

"At any rate, knowledge is power to these guys. They won't tell anybody anything unless they're forced to or they get something in return, so I think you're safe."

The trio stepped out through the terminal's entrance doors. Even though dulled by haze, the morning sun seemed particularly brilliant to Peter after his artificially extended nighttime. The accumulated effects of lack of sleep, jet lag, and the letdown after the persistent adrenaline rushes of the last three days suddenly hit him. He could hardly wait to get home and crawl into bed.

"Terrific. Jim's right on schedule." Rachel raced over to a cab and opened the back door as the driver got out and opened the cab's trunk. "Okay, you two. Get in."

"Aren't you coming with us?" Megan asked as Peter got into the back seat.

"Nope. I've got a flight leaving for Paris in just a few hours. Jim brought my luggage in the trunk."

"What? Can't you even come back to the apartment for a few hours? Aren't you at all curious as to what's happened to Peter in the past few days?"

"Don't worry. Daniel will fill me in," Rachel said offhandedly as she pulled a suitcase out of the trunk and rummaged through it. "I know I packed an extra pair of shoes in here somewhere."

"I can't believe you can't take a few hours to have lunch with us before you leave, particularly after what we've been through."

Rachel seemed not to hear her friend speaking. "Aha! Here they are. Shoot, they don't match my outfit at all. Might have to do some emergency shopping in Paris," she said with a wink at an incredulous Megan. "Sorry, guys. No time for long good-byes. We'll send you a letter, okay? Gotta go." She blew Peter a kiss and gave Megan a long hug around the neck through the open cab window. "I'll really, really miss you guys. More than you'll ever know."

Rachel grabbed her bags and headed back into the International Terminal.

"Rachel!" Megan called out from the cab window. Rachel set down her bags and turned around.

"What?"

"Au revoir, that's all," Megan said with a smile.

Rachel smiled. "Adieu," she said softly. She picked up her bags and walked through the electronic doors to the terminal as the cab drove off.

"What can you tell me about Scorpion?" Peter asked as they rode home.

Megan shuddered and drew closer to Peter, but she felt compelled to speak as if she had to clear her mind of the evil. "He was the worst psychopath I've ever seen. And to top it all off, he was a dissociative."

"A what?"

"Multiple personality disorder. A particular persona would totally take over his mind for a period of time, enabling him to compartmentalize his different emotions. One persona would come out when he was afraid, another when he was in pain, and so on. This would protect his dominant personality from having to experience and deal with unpleasant memories and emotions. But most multiples aren't violent. They tend to turn their aggression inward. Something really horrifying must have happened to him to make him this twisted. I'm sure his disorder is what kept the Mafia thugs in such fear of him."

"What do you mean?"

"I've treated a lot of multiples, but Rachel and I witnessed the most terrifying transformation I've ever seen. When Rachel prodded him into a rage so intense that his other personalities couldn't handle it, Scorpion's control snapped, and he actually behaved like a cornered wolf. I've never seen an animal personality in a multiple before. It was absolutely horrible."

Megan shuddered at the memory but continued.

"Rachel and I figured it out later. She had read in his dossier that nobody, but nobody, in the Mafia organization would ever squeal on Scorpion, even if they were dying. They were terrified of him. Now, it's obvious why. The lower echelons of the Ukrainian Mafia are descended mainly from peasant stock, and werewolf legends are common among the peasantry in that part of Europe. Within the organization, rumors probably floated around that Scorpion was a lycanthrope, the offspring of the devil himself, and that the devil had imbued him with supernatural powers. I'm sure those rumors were encouraged by the higher-ups to cement their control. The Mafia drones were terrified that if they betrayed Scorpion he would exact his revenge on them even after death."

It was Peter's turn to shudder. "The perfect enforcer. I hope Rachel used silver bullets."

CHAPTER 29

▼

The windshield wipers of the cab slapped back and forth in synchrony, beating time metronomically in the steady downpour as the cab made its way south down West Street from the Lincoln Tunnel. Peter held Megan close, grateful for her sake that the heavy rain had held off until after Alan's funeral service was over and the first few shovelfuls of dirt had been thrown on the casket. The last two days in preparation for the funeral had been incredibly draining on Megan, and they were both glad it was over.

Peter and Megan had been the only mourners, standing together in the gray drizzle by a graveside in a featureless cemetery tucked away in the New Jersey suburbs. A hired minister solemnly preached his precooked, all-purpose, True-Meaning-of-Death-and-Eternal-Life sermon, while Megan silently mourned the loss of the first bright candle that had illuminated her life, now forever snuffed out.

Moments after Peter and Megan entered their apartment, there was a knock on the door. It was the CIA agent assigned to check their mail.

"We got a package for you delivered by diplomatic pouch from Ukraine while you were out. Sorry, but we had to open it for inspection before we let you have it. Can't be too careful. Looks okay."

Peter took the package, opening it as he walked back into the living room and sat down. Megan turned on a news channel while she changed into a robe in the bedroom.

Inside the package was a group of letters. Two were written in Cyrillic on official government letterhead and accompanied by an English translation. They were letters from Iryna Labrinska and the acting president of Ukraine thanking Peter for his assistance in rescuing the president and saving the government from chaos. The third was a long letter from Mikhail Pritsak. As he took Mikhail's letter from the box, Peter noticed a small silver case underneath it. Inside the case, resting on a maroon velvet cushion and suspended from a yellow and blue ribbon, was a glittering gold medallion framing an enamel trident in yellow and robin's egg blue.

"Hey, Megan. You've got to see this ..."

Peter was interrupted by a scream from Megan, and he raced into the bedroom. Megan stood transfixed in front of the television, her hands covering her mouth. The image of an automobile turned into a blazing inferno by flames leaping over thirty feet into the air occupied the entire screen.

"... And as yet, no one has taken credit for the explosion that shook this quiet section of Paris early this morning, although Algerian terrorists are suspected. The force of the blast and the heat of the explosion were so intense that authorities fear they will be unable to identify the remains of the victims. But as I mentioned before, authorities believe that they were Daniel and Rachel Falconer, two tourists from New York City who had rented the car yesterday and checked into a nearby hotel last night."

"Has anyone been able to locate the Falconer couple, Bill?"

"Ed, at this time the Falconers are presumed dead. A hotel clerk reported seeing them leave the hotel together moments before the explosion. It's feared that they probably were the victims of the car bombing, perhaps chosen because they were Americans, but ..."

Peter turned off the TV. For an instant, Megan stood in shocked silence, her face drained of color.

"They can't do this to me, Peter."

"Maybe it's mistaken identity. Maybe it's a different car."

"They can't do this to me, those bastards," she screamed. "Those dirty rotten bastards! They killed my brother, they killed Frank, and they tried to kill us. And now they've killed Rachel and Daniel."

Megan grabbed the medal out of Peter's hand and dashed it against the wall.

Peter broke down as he held onto Megan. He couldn't help but reflect on the terrible irony of Daniel's last words to him: *Everyone should see Paris before they die.*

Everyone should see Paris before they die!

"Jesus Christ, Megan. They're not dead!"

"Stop it, Peter. That's not going to make me feel any better."

"No. I'm serious. Rachel and Daniel are not dead. I'm sure of it."

"What are you talking about? I saw the car burning with my own eyes. You heard what the reporter said. That was their car, and they were seen going out just before the explosion. There's no other explanation."

"Everyone *thinks* there's no other explanation. That's the whole idea. But there *is* another explanation: Rachel and Daniel staged their deaths."

Megan looked up at Peter. "Why would they do that?"

"You said Scorpion knew her. He must've known Daniel, too. And Daniel was a public person in Ukraine. I'll bet that the CIA realized that their covers were blown, and they would always be at risk for a revenge killing, so they staged their deaths."

She wiped her eyes. "What makes you so sure?"

"Because Daniel and Rachel have been dropping clues to us, clues that wouldn't make any sense before the bombing, but they hoped we would understand after it. That way, we wouldn't accidentally blow their cover."

"I still don't understand. What sort of clues are you talking about?"

"When I asked Dan why he and Rachel were going to Paris, he said 'Everyone should see Paris before they die.' At first, I thought it was just coincidence that he should have put it that way, but I think it was more than that. He really *knew* he was going to Paris to 'die.'"

"That's an old expression. I think you're reading too much into it. Was there anything else?"

"I think there is. As Dan drove away, he kept saying he would send me a letter, that I should look for his letter."

Peter raced back to the living room and began reading Mikhail's letter. The first two pages were full of such effusive and maudlin expressions of thanks and friendship that Peter had no difficulty picturing Mikhail downing a liter of vodka before sitting down to write them. But as he turned to the third page the handwriting changed to Daniel's familiar fastidious script.

Dear Peter,

I'm writing this letter on our last night in Ukraine and giving it to Mikhail to have it delivered. By now, you and Megan will have heard the news about our tragic deaths in a car bombing in Paris. I'm sorry to have kept you in the dark about this, but I'm sure that by now you realize that no matter how private you think communications are, in Ukraine you always run the risk of being overheard.

Our trip to Paris was planned before I left for Ukraine. The world is too small a place to hide from the Ukrainian Mafia, even with Scorpion dead. The only chance Rachel and I have is to disappear until the whole situation cools off, and only God knows how long that will take, so I won't be contacting you again for a long time, possibly forever.

I wish I could write you everything that is in our hearts about how precious your friendship was to us, and how much we will always miss both of you. But there just isn't enough time. And there's not enough paper in all of Ukraine.

Peter, do me two last favors. First, burn this letter as soon as you finish reading it. And second, don't let another month go by without proposing to Megan.

For always,

Daniel

"But why didn't Rachel tell us?" Megan asked as they watched the ashes of the letter smolder and held each other close.

"We had to have deniability. She didn't know who might be listening. They couldn't tell us anything until they made their escape into hiding. Besides, she did let us know, in her own way."

"How?"

"Do you remember at the airport you said 'Au revoir'—*until we meet again*? Rachel didn't answer with au revoir. She said 'Adieu'—*good-bye*—instead. She knew that we would never see her again."

Megan smiled. "Well, she was wrong."

978-1-58348-472-2
1-58348-472-8

Printed in the United States
153869LV00002B/46/A